"Are you thinking sweet thoughts of me?" Fitzhugh asked.

He smiled that tender smile and melted her anger.

Eben laughed, heartily and without care. It felt so good to laugh the tension away. So good, in fact, that perhaps it was her best defense against him...to never take him too seriously. No, from that moment, she concluded she must never take one word from his mouth in a serious manner again.

"You are outrageous, Your Grace, and absolutely without manners."

"That's very true. I am shockingly uncouth compared to the rest of your society," he agreed, complacent in the knowledge. "Tell me, Little Cat, do you believe in fate?"

"I believe more so in relying upon one's own abilities."

"I believe in fate...preordained destiny. Credit it to my deplorable Muslim upbringing...and while your aunt would not approve of my familiarity...I believe *you* are my destiny...!"

Dear Reader,

When we ran our first March Madness promotion in 1992, we had no idea that we would be introducing such a successful venture. Our springtime showcase of brand-new authors has been such a hit, that it has become a priority at Harlequin Historicals to seek out talented new writers and introduce them to the field of historical romance.

This month's titles include *All that Matters,* a haunting medieval tale about an imprisoned woman and her unwitting rescuer, by Elizabeth Mayne; *Embrace the Dawn* by Jackie Summers, the story of a woman kidnapped by a highwayman and forced to play his bride; a Western from Linda Castle that features a blinded hero and the woman who helps him recover, *Fearless Hearts;* and *Love's Wild Wager* by Taylor Ryan, a Regency-era story about a penniless heiress and the rogue who wins her heart.

We hope you will enjoy all four of this month's books and keep an eye out for all our titles, wherever Harlequin Historicals are sold.

Sincerely,

Tracy Farrell
Senior Editor

Please address questions and book requests to:
Harlequin Reader Service
U.S.: 3010 Walden Ave., P.O. Box 1325, Buffalo, NY 14269
Canadian: P.O. Box 609, Fort Erie, Ont. L2A 5X3

TAYLOR RYAN

Love's Wild Wager

Harlequin Books

TORONTO • NEW YORK • LONDON
AMSTERDAM • PARIS • SYDNEY • HAMBURG
STOCKHOLM • ATHENS • TOKYO • MILAN
MADRID • WARSAW • BUDAPEST • AUCKLAND

ISBN 0-373-28862-X

LOVE'S WILD WAGER

TAYLOR RYAN

has a passion for solitary mountain trails, restless cloudy skies and daydreams on rainy afternoons, which led her to trade a penthouse condo and hectic corporate life for the rugged Pacific Northwest, where she indulges her love of historical romance. She is supported by Lou and Joe, who give purrs and approval...no matter what.

To Forbes E—
>Who taught me about the world.
>Then loved me enough to let me
>conquer it on my own terms.

Prologue

Early morning lay on the meadow. The first dew still glistened on the spring green of the closely cropped grass, and the warm sun shone a buttercup yellow, coloring everything clean and fresh. Butterflies spread their multicoloured wings, flitting around a three-foot white crossbar hurdle stark with new paint. A bird warbled a song to his mate, who answered a distance away. Far to one side, a pair of spotted goats stood alert. They were there to keep the grass cropped short, and were ever mindful of their responsibility, as their round, low-slung bellies attested. This was their meadow, and they were not altogether pleased at the appearance of the intruders.

"Faster, Jamie! Faster!"

"Wee lasses shouldn't be going any faster. Mind yer hands be sittin' quiet. Don't be bumping the laddie's mouth," the young Irish groom called. The man's merry brown eyes sparkled with pleasure at the excellent seat of his young charge. Never in all his born days had he seen one so young with such a natural flair with a pony. "Mind yer heels! Down, lass... Keep yer heels down and press with yer lower leg. That's a good lass."

"May I gallop, Jamie? May I?" she called, her little girl's voice piping shrill in the clear morning air.

"Nay, lass. Not now," he called with a grin. Her bravado tickled him for she was so dainty.

The dappled gray pony, his dark mane braided and knotted with red ribbons, minced in a circle around the groom. So careful was he, one could well believe he knew what a precious passenger he carried. The child was perhaps three or four, displaying a remarkable seat and control over the pony for one so small. Her ebony hair was braided with gay red ribbons, as well, and her red riding dress lavishly trimmed in ruffles and lace.

"May I jump him, Jamie? May I, pleeease?" she begged.

"Nay, lass. Yer pony is not for jumping. He's not a hunter. You wouldn't ask him to do something he can't do, would you?"

"Joy Boy would do it for me. I know he would, Jamie. Please let me try," she pleaded.

"Nay, lass. You wouldn't want to injure him by asking him to do something he shouldn't."

A horseman aboard a splendid stallion rode into the meadow. The horse was tall and powerful, moving in a series of sideways jumps, as if ready to break free of all restraints. His eyes rolled wildly in his head, and his mouth was held open by the taut pull of the bit. The jet-black hide was white-streaked along his arched neck and across his mighty chest where sweat had foamed into lather.

The youthful rider's copper curls gleamed brightly in the sun, for his protective headgear had disappeared somewhere behind him. As the struggling pair danced closer, the groom could see terror in the wide blue eyes set in the boy's ashen face. Both hands gripped the leathers, so desperately the horse's head was pulled back close to the boy's thin chest. A loud rasp could be heard as the black fought for his wind. The lad could not hold the horse much longer. He would be thrown, and the master's prize racer would be set free with trailing reins, possibly coming to harm, as well. With a quick glance to check the safety of his small charge, Jamie Deal moved to catch the leads and help the young boy control the agitated stallion.

"Sheldon! Watch Joy Boy, Sheldon!" the child shrilled, excited at seeing her beloved brother. Anxious to show off her riding skills, she turned the pony toward the jump and kicked him into a quicker pace. "Watch me, Sheldon!"

"Lassie, no!" the startled groom called. He could do nothing to stop the little girl on the flying gray pony, for his hands were occupied with the straining black stallion. The lassie was in for a fall, but if he turned loose of the leads, the boy would be thrown. "Stop the pony, lass!"

With a high shriek of joy and laughter, the small figure, with red dress billowing ruffles and lace over the pony's fat rump, sat erect in her tiny sidesaddle. Her hands were quiet and her heels down as she set the pony to the very center of the crossbars. The pony's ears came forward, and he measured the jump against the courage of his young rider. Finding the jump not at all formidable and his mistress's courage great, he popped easily over the bars. The child's bottom bumped in the saddle a little, but otherwise her form was excellent. With a whoop of triumph, she turned Joy Boy back toward Jamie and her brother for praise.

The meadow was no longer pretty. The birds did not sing, and the butterflies sat with tightly folded wings. Angry gray clouds overpowered the sun. Both goats slunk away. The magnificent black stallion stood beside a figure inert on the ground at his feet. The child rode up and quickly jumped from the saddle. Her father bent over the figure, and his hand cradled the copper curls, only to come away red...red with blood.

"Sheldon?" she whispered. Her father raised a fierce and terrible face to look at her. His blue eyes burned into hers with an anguish too terrible for a child to see.

"Shoot that horse!" His voice was deadly cold. He didn't look away from her. Her small face distorted, and her sad eyes instantly brimmed with tears.

"No! Don't shoot Joy Boy!" she screamed. "I promise I'll never do it again! I promise, Papa! Pleeease, Papa!"

"Then I'm leaving!" he stated. Quickly mounting the black stallion, he thundered out of the meadow, never looking back at his stricken daughter or his fallen son. Turning to Jamie Deal in panic, she clutched at his pilot coat. Tears streamed from her brilliant blue eyes, matting her black lashes and streaking her pale cheeks.

"Jamie, stop him!" she implored, sobbing. "I promise I'll never do it again! I promise..."

"Nay, lass. I can't do anything."

"Nooo..." she wailed. "Papa, come back!"

Flinging the covers violently back, the girl fought the tangled nightdress trapping her legs and staggered from the bed. Swaying a moment in the total darkness of her bedchamber, she tried to fight her way out of the nightmare and into the present.

"That's not the way it happened," she whispered shakily. "It wasn't my fault."

Turning, she felt her way to the dressing table and lit a candle with trembling hands. Sinking onto the bench, she sought her reflection. Even staring into her own eyes, even with the darkness dispelled by the candlelight, she still felt the horror. The helplessness of a little girl watching her father ride away...her brother bloodied on the ground.

"Oh, Papa," she whispered. Dropping her face into her hands, she allowed tears to come at last...for the father that small child had so loved. Dead now, he would never come home again.

Chapter One

The afternoon's weak winter sun slanted through the window into the library of the once elegant mansion of Victor Mall, falling upon the glossy black head of a young woman poring over a thick stack of accounts, with an elderly man hovering near at hand.

"I have set out the entire amount, miss, just as you requested of me," he said. The solicitor put another sheaf of papers down in front of her. She stiffened, as if she could not believe the figures she read. The silence lengthened uncomfortably before she turned from the papers to spear the man with an astonished blue gaze.

"How was it possible for my father to amass such terrible debts without you stopping him? Could you not have reasoned with him? Brought him to his senses?" she demanded, observing him straighten with indignation and discomfort beneath her accusing eyes and frowning countenance.

"I assure you, miss," he began defensively, "I did speak to His Lordship...many times..."

The dark-headed woman quickly held up her hand to silence him. "I am certain you did. I imagine my father could be very difficult. Very difficult, indeed."

The old man simply sketched a small bow in agreement. A refined, slightly sun-browned hand went to her forehead, to smooth away the frown of worry. She was certain he was speaking the truth. She could well imagine her father would not have listened to anyone who opposed his desires, especially after her brother's death. She scanned the figures again, as if possibly she might have mistaken them.

"Mr. Vandevilt, what am I to do?" she asked, without raising her head. "Or, more to the point, what do I have to sell to settle these debts?"

She had no idea the elderly man had been watching her with an expression of compassion on his kind face. Now he made a helpless gesture before answering. "Such a large sum, miss. I doubt anyone will give you much time to raise funds. You being a young woman and, ahem...without prospects...I greatly fear for most everything. Vicroy House in London, Victor Mall, the farms, the lands, the stables...unless there are prospects of which I am unaware? A marriage, perhaps—?"

The creamy, flawless complexion blanched, causing her brilliant blue eyes to loom large and desperate in her face. She rose from her father's heavy desk and walked the length of the room to jerk the draperies back from the window, admitting the sun, dancing with dust motes. Her knuckles whitened on the dry, dusty velvet, betraying her mental state.

Mr. Vandevilt, senior partner of the firm that had looked after the affairs of the Victor family for more than seventy years, nodded with a heavy heart. He had watched this lovely young girl since her much-celebrated birth seventeen years before and had shaken his head in silent disapproval of the manner in which her father, Viscount Victor, had deserted her after the death of his son, allowing her to grow up as wild as one of the village children.

He could not deny that she was a beauty, but her unorthodox manners and her improper mode of dress greatly discomfited him. Breeches on a woman were just not seemly! It really was unforgivable of His Lordship not to have provided better for his wife and daughter, especially with Her Ladyship ill and exerting little influence over the girl. He could have provided a husband, at least. Now...as things appeared...a decent marriage was practically impossible. The young miss turned from the window, her shapely hands thrust deep in the pockets of the riding breeches confiscated from her brother's wardrobe. Mr. Vandevilt winced and lowered his eyes from the immodest sight, barely refraining from shaking his head.

"We must find some solution. These lands must always belonged to the Victors. The London house I care nothing about, but this estate is my home! And I must retain the land, for without it...and the farms...there is no chance for Victor Mall to survive. There are families here who have lived, worked and died with the Victors...for generations! We are responsible for them. We cannot just turn them out!''

The look of determination on her face was heartrending for the old man. How young she was. How naive. He shook his head. ''Ah, yes, miss...''

''If we sell the London house...'' she began.

''I am sorry, miss. It is entailed, otherwise your father, if you will forgive my impertinence, would have gambled it away a long time ago.''

Sinking into the desk chair again, she asked, ''I suppose that applies also to the contents of both houses? Even the artworks?''

''Almost as if your great-grandfather anticipated that something of this sort would happen, they, too, were entailed by him, and your grandfather arranged everything else in such a manner that it would be almost impossible to liquidate anything...to protect the family history, you understand.'' Mr. Vandevilt hesitated, then added, ''There are the six hundred acres on the west side of the estate, which were your mother's inheritance....''

The blue eyes brightened with expectant hope for a second, then dimmed. ''The village stands there, also a great number of the workers' cottages. I can't take the chance they would be turned out by their new landlord,'' she said.

''The firm and myself stand ready to assist you in any way that we can. I wish I had been the bearer of a brighter forecast. Your future...and that of your poor mother looks grim indeed.''

Briskly gaining her feet with renewed energy, the raven-headed woman extended her hand to the solicitor. He accepted her outstretched hand, hoping his hesitation had not been apparent. The offer of a handshake had baffled him momentarily. How mannish her mannerisms were. However was she to find a husband? Whatever was to be her fate?

''I appreciate your honesty, Mr. Vandevilt. At least I am aware of my exact position. I will look over the papers and accounts you have so kindly brought me. I must, of course, discuss this with my mother before anything is decided. Thank you for traveling to Victor Mall, rather than requiring my presence in London.... I—I so greatly appreciate your thoughtfulness.''

The tone was definitely of dismissal, and Mr. Vandevilt hurriedly bowed himself from the library, relieved to be away from the forceful young woman. Shuffling down the massive granite steps to his waiting conveyance, he allowed himself a sad shake of his head. The astronomical debts, the ailing mother and the hopelessness of her chances for a good marriage were too depressing for the old man. He could see no way out for her but living on the charity of a distant branch of family. Even marriage to a poor village vicar would be out of the question, what with her outlandish behavior. Those breeches . . . dreadful indeed!

Only when she was alone did the girl sink into a chair, exhausted by the interview. She absently rubbed her furrowed brow, trying to ease the ache centered there.

"Oh, Father, why? Surely the drinking and the gambling could not have meant more to you than Victor Mall? More than Mother . . . and me?"

With a sob, the young woman threw herself out of the chair and looked wildly around the room. For the first time, she saw clearly the Oriental carpet her great-grandfather had brought from the Far East, now frayed, and its once bright blues and reds dimmed with dirt and age. She saw the velvet draperies over the towering twenty-foot windows, and the Aubusson tapestry . . . all worn and dusty. She saw striped satin upholstery on graceful sofas and gilt chairs, shabby with torn welting. How could she have been so blind? She wrinkled her nose at the musty smell of the books with decaying leather covers lining the walls of the library.

How could she have not noticed the number of servants dwindling, until the ones remaining could not even keep the place dusted? She ran a finger over a porcelain harlequin of Meissen ware, grinning lasciviously at her through a thick powdering of dust. Shivering, she wiped her hand along her breeches. She had simply not noticed. And her mother hardly noticed anything at all anymore, merely languished in her tawdry suite of rooms. Striding quickly to the desk, she once again looked through the papers. Assets? Priceless paintings, gold and silver candlesticks, jade from the Far East, flawless porcelains, the finest of everything. The list was unending. The gold-rimmed Spode dinnerware itself would bring a king's ransom, but it was entailed like the rest, to ensure it remained intact for future Victors.

"Future *starving* Victors! Fiddle!" Her voice sounded loud in the quiet room. "Meaningless, all of it! Things...just meaningless things collected by long-dead people."

Flipping randomly through papers until she found the sheets she sought, her eyes scanned the ledgers. The racing stable was a failure, for all the money poured into it. The breeding farm was overstocked with mares, most aged, and very few bred to drop foals in the spring. The horses could be sold, of course. But, although they were magnificent animals, they would bring only a fraction of what she needed to cover her father's debts. A deep sigh escaped her.

Born when her brother was twelve, the little girl with the raven hair and creamy skin had quickly stolen her papa's heart, and he had been able to deny her nothing. She had become his shadow, and while she had spent the required hours at the piano and with her needlework, it had soon became apparent her talents lay in more physical activities. Where her brother had been merely adequate, she had excelled. Being long of limb and agile, she had easily mastered the techniques of dancing and fencing, while he had proved clumsy, tiring easily.

Surprisingly, though the little girl had grown up precocious and prone to outrageous behavior, she had been much loved and doted on by the entire household, including her brother, whom she had protected from most of her father's wrath. If there had been any jealousy towards the little imp on the boy's part, it had never been apparent. But her true joy had been the horses, with which her instincts and utter lack of fear had seen her quickly surpass him, for poor Sheldon Henry Victor, try though he might, had been truly terrified of the large beasts.

Sickened by the waste, she shoved the papers into the desk drawer and left the library. Her brother's cracked Wellingtons struck hard on the veined marble of the entry hall. Stooping to swing a gray tabby cat into her arms, the girl buried her face in its dusty, warm fur. A throaty purr indicated its pleasure at the attention. Her scornful eyes swept upward, following the arabesques that ran along the gilded partitions of the walls as if seeing them for the first time.

"Grady, my ancestors were fools. Just look at this place! Foolishness and waste! Nothing of true worth as a thing can only have value if one can sell it."

Absently shifting the purring cat, she confronted a staircase to her right that was breathtaking in its magnificence, rising three full stories above her head. Newel posts, intricately carved with vines and flowers, stood at each turn. Hidden in the designs were delicate unicorns, waiting for discovery by generation after generation of Victor children. The banister was worn mellow, and smooth as satin, from the caresses of countless hands.

Now, as she had done as a child, she dropped her head back, looking straight up three flights to the chandelier suspended from the ceiling. Hanging from an elaborately frescoed dome, the chandelier was thirty branches of blown glass, twined with colorful enameled ornaments and prisms. When that chandelier was ablaze, it was as if a thousand pounds of ice were on fire. She had seen it thus many times, before her brother had died and the house had died with him. Slowly turning her head, she sought the portrait hanging on the first landing, reigning over the massive entry hall. Viscountess Eben Pearl Norview Victor...her great-grandmother, the portrait painted after the much celebrated birth of her first son...commissioned by an adoring husband.

"I have admired her my whole life, Grady," she said to the cat. He promptly dug claws into her shirt, pulling himself higher to rub his cheek against her chin. "But now, I fear, I am seeing her as a very spoiled lady, for sure. So much senseless extravagance and waste!"

Unconsciously the girl drew herself to her full height, as she always did when she contemplated the portrait...for she was the present day Eben Pearl Norview Victor, and must measure up to the past and to the woman. Except for the clothing, the portrait could have been a mirror, for it showed the same creamy complexion, the high, well-defined cheekbones and the same widely spaced azure eyes surrounded by thick, sooty lashes. The same ebony hair, although this Eben's hair was caught back in a tangled braid done by impatient hands, instead of the carefully effected, elaborate style of her ancestor. The only thing that had been missed in the portrait, and that no one could miss in the present-day Eben, was the determination and strong will that coursed through the souls of both Victor Pearls.

Eben thought of her mother, probably still abed, slumbering behind a night shield to shut out the day in the mistress's bedchamber where, as a small child, she had cuddled next to her to share a breakfast tray and hear repeated the story of the

Victor Pearl and her fairytale ceiling of cupids and angels surrounding Venus that dominated the bedchamber of green and gold. Her father's apartments were connected with her mother's through spacious dressing rooms. They were rooms that never lost the smell of that last late-night cigar, and hair creme used on thick black hair. Her beloved father . . . how she had missed him.

"No! I will not think of that!" she said, snuggling her face into the fur again.

Sheldon's rooms had been left just as they were the day he was killed, as if her mother could will him back from the dead, to pick up that silver brush and smooth his chestnut curls. Poor, sensitive, fearful Sheldon . . . hiding in a bottle to escape the fact that he was never going to be the man his father expected him to be. Always gambling the highest, drinking the most, riding the wildest, trying to prove . . . what? That he was as much a man as his sister, a younger sister who would have been the perfect son?

Eben remembered the years when she was small, when the house had been full of guests and laughter. She would sit by the stair rail on the nursery floor, watching the ladies in their jewel-toned ball gowns and the dashing gentlemen in black cutaway coats dancing to magical music, whirling on the veined black marble of the grand hall. And in front of her eyes would be that blazing fire-and-ice chandelier. She could hardly wait to grow up and join that world. But that dashing, exciting world had died with Sheldon. Her father had stayed in London, and she had never seen him again. Her mother said he felt guilty . . . that he had driven Sheldon to do reckless things. But her mother couldn't say what she—Eben—had done so wrong that he would never come home again. And now he was dead. And all this—her eyes swept the hall again—was hers to protect. So many priceless things . . . and the fortune to protect it gambled away. Her anger and helplessness would not allow her to mourn him.

Eben dropped her head and stared at her boot tops. She knew her mother must be told, but she could not face her right now. Sudden anger surged through her body. Dumping Grady unceremoniously into a chair, she squared her shoulders and straightened to her full height. Raising her fist toward the portrait of the first Eben Pearl Norview Victor, with stern conviction in her voice, she proclaimed, "I will not lose my home! I will, I swear, do whatever it takes to protect Victor Mall for my children, my children's children, and their children, as well!''

With that, she tore out of the house, taking the granite steps in a leap, and threw herself upon the back of the black stallion waiting there. She gripped his sides with her strong thighs as he reared, dragging the startled groom skyward before he could loose the lead. Then she was away, losing herself as always in the feel and smell of horseflesh, galloping across the drive, spraying gravel behind the black's flying hooves. With long strides and a mighty leap to clear the five-foot wall bordering the park, she and the black demon-horse disappeared.

Chapter Two

The January wind, heavy with freezing moisture, cast sheet after sheet of sleet against the windows. Howling miserably, it seeped through the cracks in the old sashes, pebbling the panes. A frigid draft whispered through the room from time to time, stirring the faded silk brocade drapes. The fireplace sputtered and flared each time the wind gusted a plume of black smoke down the chimney. Lady Lillian Cromwell Victor, a recent widow of fifty or so years, had long ago become inured to the inconveniences of Victor Mall. Reclining on a low chaise drawn dangerously close to the sputtering sitting room fire, she dozed over a book with well-thumbed pages. She fitfully wakened, pulling her merino shawl closer about her thin shoulders and straightening her lace cap atop chestnut curls liberally sprinkled with gray.

As the second daughter born to the baron Cromwell, an orphan from her first breath, she had been raised with her sister by nannies and strict governesses, receiving the typical education deemed proper for young ladies of the nobility. Lillian had been a shy, naive girl, while her sister had been most outgoing and adventuresome. Though Lillian had been considered the family beauty, and when she became betrothed to the dashing viscount had had numerous offers from which to choose, her older sister had held her own in society through humor and great wit. Now, after losing two daughters in infancy and her precious son at twenty to a riding accident, Lady Lillian slept her life away. She did not mourn overly much the recent passing of her husband. He had long ago deserted her for his own interests, which Lady Lillian had vaguely concluded were mainly horses, spirits and women of questionable virtue, and quite possibly other activities best left undisclosed. She spent long, not discontented days with her romantic poetry and paying close attention to her delicate health.

She roused herself to look over at her one remaining child, Eben Pearl. Lady Lillian loved her daughter dearly, but could not help but feel uneasy when the child insisted on certain improprieties. Such as wearing her brother's clothes, and refusing to even consider a season in London—though the thought of a hectic coming out was more than her health would permit. Besides, her headstrong daughter had proclaimed in no uncertain terms that she did not intend to marry at all. Lady Lillian turned slightly on her chaise and sighed. Whatever did one do with one's life if one did not marry? Travel, as her sister, Adair, did? The thought brought a slight shudder.

"Thirty pounds for mourning candles?" At the sound of her daughter's voice, Lady Lillian started out of her reverie. Carefully she peeked through her lashes at the slender figure seated so tensely at the green lacquer desk.

Eben waved a slip of paper at her that Lady Lillian understood to be some sort of accounting. She shuddered again. She sat up with a resigned sigh, knowing there to be no way of avoiding her daughter once she commenced. Again she wished Eben would marry. The need for a strong male presence during these trying times was apparent. Although she was just turned seventeen, it was never too early to solicit offers. The hated breeches would have to go, and no more tearing around the countryside on that black horse, the very same one that had killed poor Sheldon. A monster, truly, but Eben had refused to hear of the animal being destroyed, saying it wasn't the fault of the horse.

Whoever would have thought a seven-year-old could be so forceful? Oh, poor, dear Sheldon. Brushing away an imaginary tear, Lady Lillian contemplated her daughter. Everything about that face was flawless. Perhaps the mouth was a trifle too generous, and the eyes were much too direct. If only she would learn to tilt her head and look through those dark lashes, she could tempt many a suitor. At present, those eyes looked tired, the tender flesh beneath them smudged with worry and lack of sleep. And the way in which Eben was regarding her reminded her most uncomfortably of her late husband. She plucked at the silk fringe of her shawl and tried to concentrate on the bill for candles.

"Now, Eben, you are aware of the numbers at your father's funeral. We could not appear to slight him or seem shabby. I daresay most of the county was here. It would not have done to make a poor show of it in front of your father's friends," she said in a placating tone.

"But, Mama, we *are* shabby." Eben continued to look at her mother in all seriousness. "And it is all Papa's fault. His debts are shocking! Three hundred pounds for that swaybacked gelding Judge Dittle sold him. And the money just to stock the wine cellar at Vicroy House . . . for his little evenings in!" Rising from the desk, Eben began to pace the floor, her boots ringing out on the dull wood every step she took between the two rugs. "And the people! Great-Aunt Piny's pension is seven hundred and fifty pounds a year, which is all she has to live. She's nearly ninety, and even with one less servant, she can't manage on less. And she's only one of many. And, Mama, there are not funds!"

"I know it seems impossible, dear. But what are we to do with all of them? Without their pensions, they will have to go to the workhouse," Lady Lillian said with a sigh.

"Mama, we pay to keep up the workhouses, so nothing would be served to turn them out. These excesses have gone on for so many years," Eben stated, shuffling noisily through the papers, seeking a particular list. "Here . . . a list of servants the Mall employed only ten years ago. Just look!"

Lady Lillian took the offending list between forefinger and thumb. "Eben, a lady never handles staff! One employs a steward for . . ." Her eyes ran briefly down the list before pushing it back in the general direction of her daughter. "Here . . . I just cannot read all this."

"Mama, one hundred and fifty staff to care for four people and one house! That didn't count the stables or the farms!" Eben resumed her pacing.

Again Lady Lillian sighed and said, "Perhaps I could turn my hand to writing poetry, like Mrs. VanEdge. They say she took up the pen to support her family. . . ."

Since Lady Lillian's handwriting was barely legible, and in kindness one would say her thoughts rambled a mite, Eben turned aside to hide her smile. "I think we could open Victor Mall as a gaming house easier. Rent out the shooting to select guests. I could be a faro dealer in the evenings, and Jamie Deal could be the hunting guide during the day," she countered.

Lady Lillian turned visibly pale. Her hand slowly clutched her sainted mother's treasured cameo brooch, pinned at her throat. Even when she saw Eben was jesting, her color did not return...so horrible was the idea. Eben continued, "Papa once told me he wagered fifty pounds at White's that I would be born a boy. If only I had..." She shrugged and glanced once more at the due notices in her hand, "Mama! Forty yards of black crepe? Three guineas a yard for black silk?"

"It seemed a bargain, and your father always told me to buy quality," Lady Lillian whispered, wishing for more sympathy.

"And see where it has gotten us! Where Papa is, he will never have to worry about it. How like him to be so selfish as to give no thought to what we should do. Better he had wagered he would break his neck in that drunken headfirst tumble down the stairs...."

"Eben!" Lady Lillian admonished her, ignoring the fact that she herself had deplored her husband's selfishness most of their married life. She brought her black-edged handkerchief to her dry eyes and daubed delicately. "If only Sheldon were alive to shoulder this burden."

"Sheldon!" Eben snorted, rounding on her mother. "Sheldon would have rolled down the stairs right behind Papa, to prove he was just as much a man!"

"Eben, please! You know Sheldon was just...too sensitive. I've wished so many times that your father had simply refrained from his criticism of Sheldon's poetry and music. If he hadn't pushed him so hard, he never would have taken to such danger. Never would have been on that horse..." Her voice cracked, and again she touched the handkerchief to her eyes.

"I know, Mama. Sheldon would do anything to prove himself to Papa, and he did find some success in indulging his baser appetites. I imagine he purchased great amounts of admiration...admiration of sorts...from those women of bad character. And heaven knows Papa would applaud that behavior...thus encouraging it."

"Enough!" Lady Lillian warned, but she was not to be heeded by her outraged daughter.

"Papa was addicted to bad behavior, the way some men are addicted to opium. And devoted to those high fliers down on Chelsea Road. I have seen them myself...well, once a long time ago...flaunting their jewels and driving their fancy rigs, bought for them by other women's husbands. I fear Papa's taste in women was no better than his taste in horseflesh. Vulgar creatures...fat, like cows. Very overblown, I'm afraid," she expounded, stomping to the window to stare disagreeably out at the sleet that bound her indoors for the day, a frown creasing her forehead and drawing her brows down.

"Eben Pearl..." Lady Lillian protested faintly. "Ladies do not speak of such things! Wherever do you pick up such information?"

"From Jamie Deal, of course. One can always learn a shocking variety of things from one's groom...or the servants in general, for that matter."

"Oh, my..."

Turning toward her mother, Eben grew silent at the sight of her white, strained face. Stepping quickly to the gilt table beside the chaise, she sprinkled a few drops on a handkerchief from one of the many little bottles gathered there.

"Mama, I am so sorry. Forgive me for being heartless."

"Eben, you really must curb your devastating frankness. It's just not done, dear. It's just not done." Lady Lillian daubed at her nose with the hankie.

"Well, it is time someone was frank around here!" A brusque voice boomed from the doorway, startling both of the women in the chilly gold-and-green sitting room.

"Lady Adair Cromwell, m'lady," Hastings announced, somewhat belatedly, almost muffled behind that lady's considerable bulk.

"Aunt Addie!" Eben leaped to her feet and, rushing toward her best-loved relative, threw her arms around her neck in a giant hug.

"Adair, from what part of the world did you blow in?" Lady Lillian exclaimed, greeting her sister. "We thought you were in Africa."

"Let me extract myself from this...this person...and I shall relate all." Lady Adair looked at her niece from head to toe and back again. "Have I been gone so long that the fashions have come to this? Ghastly, child! Simply ghastly!"

"Dear Aunt Addie. It's just the best thing ever to have you here," Eben said, in turn studying her aunt. The resemblance to her mother was negligible; there was power and energy in this lady's bearing. A grateful sigh escaped Eben.

"I came as soon as I received hint of trouble. In fact, I only docked this week. I have just had a horrid trip out in a hired coach... totally unsprung, I can assure you!" Sailing across the room, she removed wet gloves, trailing the scent of rose-milk and glycerine, and seated herself on the faded sofa, all the time regarding her sister from beneath a large hat, teeming with damp feathers, perched defiantly atop silvery hair. "Lillian, how are you?" she demanded.

"Not well, as usual. I quite suffer from a weak disposition," the lady complained, lying back weakly, as if to demonstrate that fact.

"Utter nonsense! You spend entirely too much time cooped up in this mausoleum. A brisk one-mile walk each day would bring the roses blooming into your cheeks!"

"Good Lord, sister!" Lady Lillian gasped, briskly fanning herself at the very thought. Eben turned aside to hide a smile as her mother obviously decided a hasty retreat was in order. "Adair, the excitement of you is just too much. I feel one of my migraines coming on. Will you forgive me until dinner? I shall just lie down until then," Lady Lillian murmured, pressing her fingers to her head. "Eben, be a dear and ring for Bess? She knows exactly what to do with me when I feel one of these dreadful spells upon me...."

Lady Lillian's venerable dragon of a maid arrived post-haste and without benefit of summons, having undoubtedly been pressing her ear against the door. Casting a baleful glare at Eben for the upset, she tenderly escorted her mistress, along with her shawls, books and nostrums, in the general direction of her bedchamber, murmuring words of comfort all the while. Eben breathed a sigh of relief and turned to find her aunt contemplating her breeches while tapping a forefinger against a pursed mouth.

"Well, what's your verdict? Let's hear it and be done with it!" Eben said, standing with her hands on her slim hips, flaunting the tight breeches.

"You are not so modest, Eben Pearl—" Aunt Adair laughed "—as to not realize you cast an extremely attractive figure in those pants. So handsome, in fact, that I am sure hundreds of men of first breeding will readily offer for your hand, just to see you clad in them."

"Offer? For me? A young woman with no dowry, a mountain of debts, an army of pensioners to support, an estate falling down about my ears ... and, I might add, very little inclination to marry in the first place?" She strode around the room in fresh agitation. Her aunt had struck immediately upon the very subject that had made her nights so sleepless.

"I was afraid, my dear, that was the shine of it all. I received a letter from your great-aunt Piny before I embarked, stating she had not received her pension since your father's passing."

"And I imagine she's in a panic of anxiety." Eben sighed.

Lady Adair nodded while she unpinned her hat and laid it on the sofa beside her. Eben watched her hands smooth her silver hair. Hers were beautiful, well-kept hands, betraying age in the blue tracery of veins, but cared-for nevertheless, and revealing a certain vanity on the part of the formidable lady.

"I liked your father, Eben. He was one of the most fascinating men I have ever met in my life, but he was not one to deny himself anything, and the more elusive it was, the more he wanted it. Lillian was never strong enough for him. Now ... why have I not been offered sherry?"

"I'm sorry! I shall dash down to the library and fetch it straight away," Eben declared.

"What's this? Have we flung all the servants to the winds, and man the house ourselves now?" Lady Adair asked, eyebrows climbing into her fringe.

"They have quite enough to do, for the few of them, without waiting on me hand and foot. Besides, I am fit and able, and shall be no more than a moment."

"Well, since you are going, dear, bring the whole bloody bottle! That way, we'll rest assured one trip made was enough."

Eben raced down the stairs two at a time, in a perfect imitation of anything but a lady. She was so pleased her aunt was here. She could never expect the answers she needed from her mother, but her aunt was just so capable. Dear Aunt Addie! With all the common sense in the family, her history was as eccentric as she was. She had told Eben once that she had been deeply in love with a man of first quality, but he had chosen another. With that settled, she had made a life of her own, but never married. Being somewhat comfortably situated, she had begun to travel, first with a chaperon, and then, as age permitted, with a lady's maid.

Her independence had caused a great deal of talk from those of her peers who thought a woman should marry, raise children and obey a husband. They were not to roam the world and publish books of essays about the heathens with whom they associated. Lady Adair merely laughed and reveled in her fame.

Returning posthaste, as promised, Eben poured a generous amount of the requested sherry. She thought of this wise and experienced lady as the cavalry, just the person to help her straighten out this jumble in which she'd landed through no doing of her own.

"That's the lay of the land, Aunt Addie. The debts are exorbitant, and they are threatening dire things. Then there are the people we support, and Mama cannot even think of it. What am I to do? I must save Victor Mall!" Eben exclaimed.

Lady Adair set her sherry on the gilt table and motioned the girl to the sofa before she replied. For a moment, she studied her beautiful niece seated across from her, sliding her gaze over the perfect features and slim, finely muscled figure in a speculative manner. Self-conscious, Eben slid her roughened hands, with their split nails, beneath her bottom.

"Eben, your father did you a great disservice by allowing you to run wild. To brag on a five-year-old son for such exploits as taking a full-tilt hunter over a six-foot gate is one thing, but to say the same thing of a daughter is quite another. To allow you to tag after the farm workers and studmen . . . even to be in the breeding barns at all . . ."

"But, Aunt Addie . . ." Eben said, interrupting her, "to say this now is fine and good, but those deeds are done. Sheldon is dead, and I do, in fact, manage the stud barns. It has nothing to do with the well-armed firing squad I find facing me at this moment."

"It is all quite simple, my dear. You need funds. And to acquire those funds, you must marry money. Not just someone warm in the pockets, as the current slang has it, but someone with pockets afire!" Lady Adair stated.

Her answer was not to Eben's liking. She had hoped for a solution of a different nature from her self-reliant aunt, but this came as no real surprise—though she would rail at the idea anyway.

"You cannot be serious! It would be degrading...obscene...something I would consider worse than bartering slaves or selling my body in a brothel!" she cried, jumping to her feet and facing her aunt. "You never had to marry, yet you suggest there is no other way for me?"

"Eben, dear. I have a small annuity, plus none of the responsibilities your father so kindly left you. Besides, it is an established British custom to replenish the family coffers at certain times through well-thought-out and intricately arranged...marriage," she said.

"I do not want to hear this!" Eben stated. She trod forcefully to the window and stared out at the wet. The sitting room overlooked the gardens to the side of the mansion. There was little left of the neatly patterned walks, and even from the second floor she could see debris floating in the decorative carp pond.

"Eben, stop stomping about and listen to me. I am telling you, if you want to save Victor Mall and the people who depend on it, you must marry...and marry well. You are far too beautiful to become a governess. Besides, you have never shown the slightest tolerance for children. But if you do wish to apply yourself toward that line, I could let a small house in Bath and install your mother, and, I daresay, faithful Bess there, although I assure you I shall do them both bodily harm the first six months we are together."

"I...I..." Eben turned from the window. The thought of earning her own living had never crossed her mind. And her ideas of how to actually go about it were nonexistent.

"But that sidesteps the fate of Victor Mall, doesn't it?" her aunt continued, her tone softening at the sight of her niece's stricken face. "I consider marriage as your duty, and you shall find, once you reconcile yourself, that it is not totally disagreeable. Your husband will bring you enormous wealth. He will pursue his own interests, whatever they might be, and you can refurbish your beloved Victor Mall. You will find a husband little hindrance if handled properly. More sherry, dear. It is ghastly cold in this place."

"How am I to attract this wealthy, suitable husband, dear aunt, without a decent gown to my name?" Eben asked, refilling the delicate glass held out to her by her aunt.

"Subterfuge, my darling. Subterfuge . . ." Raising her glass to salute Eben, she drained it. "Now, let us see if there is one suite in this monstrosity that does not have mildew creeping beneath the bedcurtains, after which I shall lay out the strategy for you. Then, my dear, let the games begin!"

Chapter Three

The proud set of the Arabian stallion's head proclaimed it of noble blood. The wide-set eyes, in the small dish face, were trusting and intelligently alert, as were the small pointed ears, twitching this way and that, attending to every sound the drumming rain made in the trees. Even though his smoothly muscled body was tense with his new surroundings and the unaccustomed cold wetness, he stood quietly waiting for a signal from the equally motionless man on his back.

Though the rain had found its way beneath the collar of his greatcoat, Fitzhugh Eastmore did not move. He continued to study the estate below him . . . his inheritance. He felt such pleasure viewing the manicured park, the neatly laid-out pastures and fat, sleek cattle. All in all, it appeared the picture of a prosperous English country estate, with its typical English manor. Exactly as it had been described to him by the London solicitors.

The passing of the fifth duke of Eastmore had been of little surprise to anyone in the district. He had been a man well into his nineties, and had suffered ill health for a number of years. The lengthy wait for the sixth duke to put in an appearance had made for an uneasy year. Of course, the estate had not suffered, for it was not luck that the managers and solicitors handling affairs were extremely capable. They had been hired and trained to show great loyalty in the master's absence, for the Eastmores had been, generation after generation, a family of military men, much preferring far-flung, exotic places to farming and attending to petty tenant complaints.

It was for this reason, possibly, that the old duke had never married. Not that the matrons of society with marriageable daughters had not knocked at his door in droves. But he had never cultivated a tolerance for the shy, uninformed English miss, or for the society of the ballroom. This nomadic trait, among other things, contributed to the lack of prolificacy in the Eastmore family. They seemed to have frightful luck marrying, and what sons they produced rarely survived to manhood.

The great wealth of the Eastmores was maintained year after year by well-run farms, with little drain on the fortune from the normal excesses of the ton. With so little of it being spent unwisely, and so much of it being produced, it was no small wonder the matrons stormed the doors of Eastmore Park every season. Although, try as they might, not once had they been able to lure him to London to join the petticoat line, though they had not ceased in their attempts until his eightieth year. It was also no small wonder that every one of the predatory matrons was waiting with eager expectations for the sixth duke of Eastmore to appear and lay claim to his inheritance. All the while praying he had not, in his extensive travels, procured a wife and produced an heir.

Fitzhugh had been born in the hot sands of the Middle East and—this was not unforeseen—he was an only child. His delicate mother had perished at his birth, and his father had kept him, if not with him, at least close at hand. He had grown up in the company of men, and had a clear idea of who and what he was. Proudly he was an Eastmore, and a gentleman who could be depended upon to stand on his word and at the back of his fellow officers. His father had not remarried, and the women who tendered maternal love during his younger years had been enlisted men's wives or hired half-caste women. His rearing, therefore, had been an interesting combination of strictly regimented British tutoring, with an underlying shadow of the indulgent Muslim catering due any firstborn son, producing a young man secure in his very manliness and exacting from the world, and those beings in it, the very things due him because of this manliness. All and all, a young man respected by his peers, but somewhat wild in nature.

At one time, he had been the despair of his father. Entering into the military without benefit of Oxford had afforded him a certain amount of independence at an early age, and he had wasted no time in sampling the delights of such an unshackled existence. He had always known he was heir to the title of

Eastmore, as his father had been before him, but he had never set foot on British soil. Nor had he ever met his great-uncle. His education had been seen to by tutors, in preparation for his future station in English society, but when a man lived as long as his great-uncle, one tended to forget there was an inheritance. His father had been so fulfilled by the nomadic military life, he had never dwelled on succession.

Fitzhugh had matured assuming he would follow in ancestral footsteps, with military service in India or Arabia. But neither had foreseen the cholera outbreak that felled his father. Nor had either of them anticipated the promise extracted from Fitzhugh by his father on his deathbed, to return to England, seek out his great-uncle and make his life as the proper heir; equally, promising to wed, and therefore securing the survival of the title. It hadn't been until he disembarked in London that Fitzhugh learned of the late duke's passing. Hence, he was arriving on the scene as the present, rather than the future, duke of Eastmore. It was not an unpleasant feeling to be titled and wealthy, Fitzhugh had already learned. His treatment had been royal from the moment his identity had been established.

And while he intended to put the nomadic life behind him, the promise to wed did not set well. Though he was thirty years of age, his experience with English womanhood was sadly limited to the young women sent to the military posts in the hopes of catching the eye of a lonely third son, following the failure of more than one season. Obviously these had not been the cream of the crop. Other contact, in the form of bored officers' wives more than willing to engage in an adventure with a handsome officer, was not an accurate gauge, either. He was uncertain, of course, but based upon these examples, he doubted a pale, frightened young miss would spark any interest, as he had grown up and been instructed in the art of love by the dusky, sensual women of Arabia, generous, giving and extremely knowledgable...educated to meet and satisfy a man's every desire.

Thus he intended to lay aside the promise to wed as long as he felt it feasible. But when he did marry, Fitzhugh wished for a partner to complement him. In assuring the continuance of the Eastmore name, considering the Eastmore luck, the typical English miss would not suit. Definitely, sturdier stock was in order. His legacy to Eastmore was to be a nursery filled with strong sons and the start of a new breed of fleet, sensitive race horses. If there was a woman in England to share both these dreams, he would find her when the time was right.

Toward that end, Fitzhugh figured it to his advantage that he was entering society with his past "deplorable tendencies" not too well-known. Although never one to be overly concerned with reputation, he felt he was being presented with a clean slate, and he resolved to contain himself until he had scouted the lay of the land, in view of the fact that notoriety might tarnish his name before he had the opportunity to establish himself. And establish himself he intended to do, as soon as he had things in order. A press of his knee sent the young Arab stallion flying down the hill, scattering white-faced cattle right and left, toward the promise of a weather-tight stable for his mount and a bone-warming toddy for himself.

Fitzhugh lay back in the hot water with a sigh, looking around the dressing room. He had never seen anything like it. It was smallish, of polished wainscoting below and soft leather, the color of ripe wheat, above. The wall lamps were brass, and definitely Arabian. As was the brass dry sink, beside a reclining shaving chair of cane. It was a room for comfort and efficiency in seeing to a gentlemen's personal needs . . . the exact brand of pampering a man who spent time in the East was wont to crave after a long, cold, wet day.

"Well, life has its way of changing," Fitzhugh sighed contentedly and eased his massive body deeper into the hot water. The lamplight played over his heavily muscled chest and shoulders. Big, bold and bronzed, he was a man seemingly larger than life. His face was slightly battle-worn, with eyes that sought the depth in a person, and more likely than not inspired tension if that person had secrets he desired to remain secret.

"Here we are, your grace. Have we soaked enough? If so, just pop over here and we'll scrap our face."

The old duke's valet darted into the room with his customary chatter preceding him. He was perhaps sixty years of age and could have passed for a weasel, so sharp were his features. Fitzhugh, rather than argue with the man, allowed himself to be wrapped in a warmed robe, then seated in the chair, giving himself up to the skillful attentions of the straight razor.

"Strange name, that . . . Beans. Where in hell did you acquire it?" he asked the valet.

"Now that be a tale, your grace. You see, I was cookin' for an outfit in the army. We was pinned down, and our supply teams couldn't get through . . . so all we had to eat was beans. The fellers was right good about it at first, but after a week or so, they commenced to complain, what with sore bellies and it being such close quarters and all." Fitzhugh would have nodded, but the swiftly moving razor advised against it. "Threatened to hang me, they did! Well, the old duke, it being his last campaign and all, was in the regiment. Told 'em to do their own cooking and he took me up to be his man. Saved me life, he did. Here we go, guv . . . a spot of talc and we're all smooth . . . like a baby's butt we are."

Hustled into the bedchamber of gold and rich burgundies, Fitzhugh suffered the dressing and fussing of the little man. Pausing before the bed, he stroked a lamb's wool blanket traced with silken threads thrown over the counterpane, and touched the country of his birth. It gave him a feeling of belonging. "The old gent must have loved Arabia as much as myself. There are many memories . . ."

"He did. He did at that. He loved the heat, and he loved the military life. He was a fine gent, and a fine soldier. We talked of you, we did. Just before he died, he says to me, 'Beans, you take care of the young gent, you hear. I says, don't you worry, you know I will,'" Beans said, brushing imaginary lint from the shoulder of the dressing gown. "It sure will be somethin', dressing a member of the ton. Are we going up to London for the season? Are we going to be looking for a wife? The old duke said . . ."

With a snort of laughter, Fitzhugh threw up a hand in the man's face to stem the constant barrage of questions. "Right now, I am concerned with purchasing more hunters of good lines and blood. A wife will come later. Tell me of the Victors. I understand the best hunters came from their farms." Fitzhugh smoothed his hand over his lapel and thought of the blooded hunter mares he had picked up through an agent at Tattersall's before leaving London. Large, heavy-built animals, with long, smooth muscles; good bone in the leg that could go the distance and then some, with a heavy man on board. Exactly the excellent type of English hunter he planned to breed to the finely boned Arab stallion who could trace his blood straight back to Darley Arabian. It had always been his father's dream, and it had become his dream, as well.

"Not much to tell." Beans snorted. "'Twas the best, but no more. Old guv ruined the lines with racers. His dying left the family in straits.... I hear they be removing to London." He shrugged, as if it were not important, then stepped back to study his new charge. "Yes, sir...browns, tans and golds to suit your tawny good looks. Mayhap reds and..."

Fitzhugh quickly stepped into the hallway and shut the door on the musings of the little man. Shaking his head, he grinned to himself at having acquired a real corker for a personal man. Having instructed a light supper be served before the fire in his great-uncle's library, he started down the stairs. The portraits of the Eastmores watched his progress, too numerous to identify. He felt immediate kinship with the men, rigid in bearing and military dress, but nothing touched him about the sharp-faced, glaring women, except the faint hope that his bride would not resemble any of them. Coming home, at last. He imagined his great-uncle sitting in the library, writing his papers, or reading one of the many books on the bookshelves lining the walls. How nice it would have been to have the old duke still living. The grand times they would have had, re-fighting the great campaigns and reminiscing over after-dinner port.

"Ah, well, some things are just not to be," he admonished himself. "No sense even thinking about what can never be changed."

"I beg your pardon, your grace?" the young footman standing at the end of the hall queried, fully prepared to be solicitous of this large man who was his new master.

"Just thinking aloud. Though I appreciate the interest," Fitzhugh admitted, startled. He would have to become accustomed to his station, with so many of service about. Wouldn't do to be thought of as an absentminded old maid.

Chapter Four

Eben walked slowly through opulent white-and-gold rooms, noting bare places where furnishings and art treasures had been removed. All transported to London...to Vicroy House...to dress the stage for Aunt Addie's performance. The removal had been accomplished with a precision worthy of an army on the move. Everything fathomable of use in entertaining had been sent ahead, then followed a day later by a commanding Lady Adair, a fluttering Lady Lillian and a fractious Grady, in his special basket—all three attended by a disgruntled, grumbling Bess.

Eben, with Jamie Deal, would follow a week behind. She had stoutly refused to spend the time trapped indoors, while the ladies rearranged furniture and attended to yet more shopping. Invitations would not begin to arrive until the family announced themselves in residence. Their friends had too much sensitivity to take note of their arrival until the ladies indicated they were receiving. But once they were ready to face society with assurance, and the announcement had gone out, notes would be flying between the houses. Lady Adair had always been a favorite with the ton, and Lady Lillian, having rusticated in the country so many years, was naturally a great attraction. Plus, this unwelcome arrival, yet another debutante on the scene, must be duly inspected by all to carefully judge the rivalry to their own daughters.

The Mall was closed, for all practical purposes. Holland covers shrouded the rooms. Huge white shapes reflected in dusty mirrors to appear twice as bleak. Only Emma, as housekeeper, and her husband, as steward, would remain, for the entire staff of maids and footmen had been released for the duration. The estate would have to be reclaimed from the mice, the spiders and the weeds once she had her fortune—and, of course, the husband that from necessity went with it. That bare fact brought yet another scowl to Eben's face.

"Blast! Life isn't fair!" she exclaimed. "If only I'd been born a man, I'd not be forced into this distasteful situation."

She'd have had to marry money, either way, she reasoned. But a man did not forfeit his freedom the way a woman did. To be subservient to a man, especially an inferior man, would be devastating. One last binge of freedom was what these last days alone at Victor Mall were all about. Freedom to ride astride and race the wind, taking whatever fences came. Freedom to dress as she pleased, talk as she pleased, and even walk as she pleased. Eben could almost be angry with her unattending mother and her absent father for allowing her these freedoms in her youth, knowing that they could never be hers on a permanent basis.

It was as if everything she was, deep inside herself, must be denied. As a lady, one must be above reproach at all times. One must be demure. One must never speak too loudly. One must be amusing. One must never really laugh, only titter behind one's fan. And one's virtue must never be in question, for one must be innocent in all ways. These lessons had been drummed into her head by her mother and her aunt for the past fortnight. Eben felt as if they were trying to stuff her soul into a box that was far too small. Much like the corsets and bindings that ensured a perfect fit to her new wardrobe, every aspect of her life was becoming far too confining. But she was as polished as a fine Sevres porcelain one wished to auction to the highest bidder. Whoever he might turn out to be!

Striding toward the stables, Eben blinked her eyes rapidly to stem the tears. She was not going to cry...ever again! Crying for what could not be changed was as useless as crying for what should have been. It accomplished nothing except reddened eyes and a runny nose. Blast! She was even beginning to think like Aunt Addie!

"Lass, 'tis clouding up something fierce to the north. Don't be getting yerself caught in the rain," Jamie Deal cautioned as he tossed the light racing saddle on the broad back of the black stallion, soothing the fractious horse with a gentle hand.

"A little wetting will not kill me," she stated. "Besides, sugar melts, but vinegar only dilutes. I'm sure Bess would agree my personality would only improve with the dousing."

Eben wandered down the rows of empty box stalls, mourning the sacrifice of so many beautiful animals. Their sale would finance one season in London. She must snare a husband so that theirs would not be a wasted sacrifice. She stopped to stand before an elegant filly with her glossy coat just turning from baby black to adult dapple gray. Only the black stallion and this filly remained of the bloods, and both would be taken to town to use in promenading before the ton on Rotten Row. Most of the rest were coach teams, servants' utility horses, and a few old hunter mares too old to sell and simply left out on pasture to while away the remainder of their lives in retirement. She slapped her hand on the tarnished brass top of the stall door, in frustration and determination, causing the filly to startle and fling her head up, snorting through flared nostrils at the imagined threat.

"I swear, Jamie Deal, we will rebuild this stable! Once again the Victor Mall hunters will be famous in England. The kennels will be filled with hounds, the hills alive with foxes, and we'll stage grand hunts, with all the nobility invited. Do you remember, Jamie?"

"Now, lass. Don't be worrying yerself over what can't be," he admonished, shaking his gray head at her dreams. "I wouldn't like to see yer heart broken."

"Of course. You're right, Jamie," she said, sadly. She returned to stand beside the black stallion and her dear friend. "Come on, Black Victory. One last run before we head out to London and whatever fate awaits us."

Jamie cupped his hands to boost the girl into the saddle. "'Tis best to remember, a lass must be knowing when to bend, or surely she'll be breaking."

"I am becoming aware of just that, Jamie. Now, dear friend, we must leave early in the morning. Best visit your lassie in the village, if you've a mind to say goodbye," she said, laughing at his pained expression as she tucked her hair securely beneath a brimmed cap. Posting the black across the stable yard, she called over her shoulder. "Take that flashy filly and impress her or she'll be forgetting you for sure!"

* * *

His grace, Lord Fitzhugh Eastmore cast a baleful eye on the seemingly deserted Mall, then to the foreboding clouds to the north, before remounting the mare for the three-hour ride to his agreeable hearth and supper.

"Well, girl. Looks as if no one's home," he said, slapping the mare's fine neck and reining her towards the Park. "I must be finding myself lonely, old thing! Too many years in the company of too many men. And now I find myself reduced to conversations with my horse."

The sleek chestnut mare was a recent purchase at Tattersall's. Having been exceedingly pleased with the Victor Mall line of breeding stock, he had decided it would be to his advantage to visit the Mall personally. Direct acquisition of the mares from Lady Victor herself would bypass the middleman and his time-consuming, condescending role-playing. Having made the three-hour ride to the Mall only to find his repeated pounding on the doors brought no one to assist him, he could only assume the entire place to be deserted. His desire to purchase more stock and establish them in a breeding program in an expedient manner had prompted his calling upon that lady without advance notice having been sent, and he therefore felt he did deserve to be discomfited in some small measure for his unorganized disregard for protocol.

Even with the mare's long stride eating up the distance, the halfway point in his journey caught him still a considerable ride from the warmth of Eastmore Park when the deluge commenced.

"Damn this infernal weather! Nothing but bloody damn wet!" he swore strongly.

Reining in the mare, he scanned the area for shelter to wait out the worst of the downpour. Luck was with him this once, for he spied a weather-beaten barn. A violent crack of thunder sent the mare careening toward it in giant strides. Fitzhugh only hoped the straw wasn't too rat-infested. A mighty gust of wind, combined with the current generated by the mare's speed, conspired against him and tore the beaver topper from his head. Cursing roundly, Fitzhugh was required to circle the mare, dismount and retrieve his hat, further contributing to the deterioration of his mood. Racing straight into the barn, the mare came up short to avoid ramming into the hindquarters of another horse. The black turned and whickered in recognition to the chestnut mare.

"Damn!" Fitzhugh exploded, in a black humor.

He sat in the musty barn, rainwater coursing down his greatcoat, the offending beaver jammed tightly over his eyes, with a steady stream of water flowing from the curved brim. Now, whipping it from his head, he set about beating the water from it, and dragged a hand through his wet hair.

"Would you be willing to share your dry haven with another traveler?" he called out to the unseen rider of the black. Then he paused before dismounting, head tilted for an answer.

There was no verbal response, but sounds of scuffling came from one of the boxes. Dismounting cautiously, he sought to investigate the sounds of an obvious struggle. Moving quietly, he was astonished to find a young lad attempting to aid in the birthing of a foal from an obviously aged mare. It was immediately apparent to his trained eye that the mare was in trouble and exhausted from her efforts. Quickly he shed his greatcoat, as well as his jacket of brown superfine, rolling up the sleeves of his snowy linen shirt.

"Move over, lad. Let us see if we can get this over with, or the old girl will be a goner for sure." Pushing the slim boy out of the way, he knelt beside the mare.

Eben, so rudely tipped off balance, fell on her backside in the straw, with a grunt of pure rage. "Well, the devil! As if I haven't midwifed a mare or two!" she began, but then watched the strong, sun-browned hands run over the mare's bulging belly. It would seem the man knew what he was about. Just maybe he could help the old mare.

"It's a shame to breed a mare this aged," he gritted out. Anger and feelings for the old mare made Fitzhugh's voice raw. "I'm not sure I can save her. This is criminal! She must be at least twenty! Surely the old thing's earned her retirement without this last colt."

"Seventeen...sh-she's seventeen. And the breeding was not intentional," Eben whispered, her throat tight with tears. Spilling over, they ran unheeded down her cheeks.

The old mare was Victory Pearl. She had been foaled the very same day Eben Pearl herself had been born. And in celebration of her birth, her father had presented the filly to his beloved baby daughter and named them both with great cere-

mony at a hunting party of enormous magnitude at Victor
Mall. It was to be the first gift she ever received from her dot-
ing father. Proof that once he had truly loved her. A sob broke
from her tight throat.

"Boy, get out of this box, if you can't quit blubbering! See
if you can find something to dry this foal...if I manage to birth
him alive," Fitzhugh grimly finished under his breath, his
mouth set in a straight line.

Eben fled the angry voice. It would be important to rub the
foal dry, if Victory Pearl couldn't. Striking the tears from her
eyes, she hastened to the back of the barn. Rummaging
through the mouse-riddled straw, she quickly tied twists to rub
the new baby dry and warm his little body. Before she could
gather the great pile of them into her arms, the dark stranger
strode toward her. She gasped to see a wet heap of legs in the
man's arms, which he lowered to the straw in front of her.

"Dry her good. And I'll see to the mare," he ordered, with
little more than a glance at her.

Kneeling by the filly, crooning softly, Eben rubbed vigorously to bring the blood rushing to the surface to warm the
wet, trembling baby, laughing at her immediate attempts to
stand on wobbly legs, then finally helping her with a steadying hand. The filly, as red as her mama, was all legs and joints.
It was hard to imagine her grown and strong, taking fences
under saddle as if she could fly, but she was all Victor Mall
hunter.

"I'll call you...Victory Flame! And you, little girl, will be
the very first of my new stable," she declared, with a gentle
hand on the small red muzzle.

Turning with a wide grin, Eben was startled to see the man
standing before the box, shaking out the wet greatcoat. His
damp breeches, above his Marlborough boots, were molded
most revealingly around muscular thighs, and his once clean
shirt was soiled and open to the waist, displaying a smooth
chest roped with bulky muscles. Her smile slowly faded as she
noted the tired slope to his shoulders, and she knew from his
sad face that the mare had not survived the birth. With a cry
of distress, Eben leaped to her feet, wanting to reach the mare
and somehow make it not true. He stopped her by catching her
against his chest when she would have rushed past him. She
groaned, overcome with a great, consuming sense of pain and
grief.

"Here, now. You can do nothing for her. She gave you her best . . . the filly there. She just wasn't strong enough to bear through this last one."

His kind words murmured in her ear, and his warm, strong arms holding her so tightly, released a dam of misery and hopelessness within her. Great sobs racked Eben's slim frame, and her moans were from genuine pain, for her very soul was splitting apart. Suddenly she wrapped both arms about his waist, and with her head buried against his chest she wept terrible, heartrending sobs that shook her whole body. She needed to be held . . . as no one had held her in so long. Everywhere was death, commencing with Sheldon's death and the abandonment of her loving father . . . then her father's death, the death of Victor Mall, and now . . . Victory Pearl, symbolizing to Eben once more the death of her father's love. It was finally too much. She could be strong no more.

"Here, now, don't take on so," Fitzhugh muttered, taken aback.

"I—I'm s-sorry . . ." Eben wailed. Like a child, she dashed at her tear-streaked face with her hands, unable to stop the sobs and hiccups.

As he roughly patted her back, the awkward gesture dislodged her cap, and a torrent of ebony silk tumbled over his hands. With dawning awareness, he felt full breasts pressing his near-naked chest through her damp groom's sweater.

"Good God, woman!" Fitzhugh erupted. He tossed the coat aside and attempted to push her away far enough to study her face. His hand tangled in the riot of ebony curls that flowed past her waist.

"I'm sorry," she said again. But then, when she would have stepped back from him, he held her firmly. "Wh-what—?" she began, tilting her head back to peer up into his eyes questioningly. "I . . . I'm all right. R-really . . ."

Seeing her face clearly for the first time was like a punch in the stomach for Fitzhugh. Even smudged from the dusty straw and streaked from tears, her beauty was overpowering. His brown-gold eyes darkened to amber as he studied the creamy complexion, the straight black eyebrows, and the startling, tear-filled eyes the color of a deep mountain lake. It was a face to snatch a man's breath from his very lungs. Without even taking a moment to weigh the correctness of it, Fitzhugh bent his head and laid his mouth against her trembling lips, tasting the salt from her tears. A kiss that started out soft and gentle, a kiss meant to be nothing more than comfort, quickly deepened into a hard, demanding question.

Eben had never been kissed before. And in her weakened emotional state, it seemed most comforting, and therefore extremely welcome. She wrapped her arms tightly about his waist again and gave back the kiss, not realizing, in her innocence, that she was answering his question. Fitzhugh swung her into his arms and laid her back on the straw, allowing his weight to bear her down, covering her body with his. His large frame dwarfed hers . . . commanding hers . . . making unspoken demands.

Eben, so hungry for comfort and caring from someone, did not refuse him when his kiss turned into a brutal assault. But then his mouth turned soft again, gentle, yet . . . hungry. Her lips, with a will of their own, eagerly parted and her fingers crept into his wet hair. His mouth moved to her ear, probing there a second before traveling to the side of her neck . . . sucking and nipping. She moaned deep in her throat, arching against him, wanting to get closer, craving his warmth. A heavy molten feeling spread low in her belly. The intense sensation shook her . . . frightened her . . . but she wanted it to never stop.

Fitzhugh had never felt a passion as strong as this young beauty aroused in him. Her kisses sent fire through his blood, and her small cries incited him to an urgency. Tugging her sweater and cotton undershirt up to her chin, he feasted his eyes on her full, quivering breasts topped by berry nipples. She cried out when his head dipped to suck one nipple into his hot mouth. With his passion unleashed and encouraged by her eager responses, he stripped the breeches from her slim hips, only to come to an abrupt halt at her Wellingtons.

"Damn!" he exclaimed at the interfering obstacle.

Fitzhugh tugged at one of the boots, cursing. Finally the tight boot gave, and he jerked it off, slipping one shapely leg out of the breeches. His target bared, he did not bother with the second boot. Sliding his hands up her thighs, one naked and silky, the other bundled in damp buckskin, he stared at the tangle of ebony curls. Using his thumbs, he parted those curls to run a finger over the little nub of pleasure. She gave a spastic cry.

"Wait..." Eben murmured, breathless with sensation. With each unhurried stroke, he explored the hidden recesses of her... until she thought she could not stand one more touch. Her futile attempts to push him back failed. Pushing him was like pushing against a stone wall. "This is wrong.... Oh, this is wrong...." But she could not think clearly enough with him so close... with him touching her... there! Leaning forward, he ran his tongue possessively up the taut flat plane of her belly, dipping into her navel on his way back to suckle her nipples. His hand was trapped against her moisture by her clamped thighs. "Please... wait," she tried again.

"Shhh... my pretty. Don't fight me. Just feel..." he whispered against her breasts. Swiftly Fitzhugh raised her naked leg to his waist. Then, freeing himself, he claimed his moist prize.

"Ahhh... Stop! You're hurting me!" she cried, arching away from him, shoving at his chest with sudden strength.

"Damn!" Fitzhugh muttered to himself. The wench had been a maiden. He lay still, clenching his teeth against the tight pleasure, giving her time to relax, to open to him. Who would have thought it, the way his kisses had been welcomed. It might take a hefty bribe to her father to get past this one. Damn! His first English scandal! "Shhh... relax, and I'll not hurt you again."

Tears seeped from her tightly closed eyes. Her breasts, crushed against his chest, heaved with her agitated breathing. But when he began to move slowly, stroking his full length, she moved with him, as the pain was replaced by the hot spiraling ache of before. Fitzhugh kissed the tears from her cheeks, losing himself in the liquid blue of her eyes as her fear lessened. He tasted blood where she had bitten her lip. He kissed that pain away, also. Being careful with the girl, as he would have from the beginning if he had but known, he felt her once again respond to his kisses. Her breath quickened as he nibbled down her neck and across her nipples, causing her hips to move in unison with his.

Eben's body seemed on fire, flaming where his mouth touched her. She felt a demand... she needed something... to release the pressure building inside her. Her arms eagerly went around his waist, her hands wandering beneath his shirt, over his broad back. Drawing him closer to her, closer... she needed him... needed him so much closer. Suddenly he moaned and grew still. Eben's body trembled with unfulfillment, aching.

With a final kiss on the throbbing pulse in her throat, Fitzhugh raised himself to his feet and handed her the boot he had flung off. To give her a moment of privacy, he turned his back to adjust his clothing.

"Tell me where you live, lass. I'll send a nice present around for you. I would not have been so rough, had I known it was your first time...."

He rambled on and on, not wanting to turn around until the girl had time to recover herself, not willing to cause her embarrassment, and, in truth, not at all sure what to say to her. Suddenly he heard the horses shuffle, and spun just in time to see the girl, with ebony hair flying past her waist, wheel the black beyond the chestnut mare and out the door. Running to the door, Fitzhugh was in time to see the huge black stallion disappear over the rise. An amused grin replaced his frown. He walked back to the abandoned foal.

"So, my fine red filly. Farm girls in England wear breeches and ride astride, do they? Well, she'll not stay away for long. Not while I have you. She'll have to come for you, sooner or later. You'll be my hostage. And I'll trade you for another of those sweet kisses from the fiery lass." Gathering the filly in his arms, he awkwardly mounted the mare. "Come on home with me. We'll find you a new mama, with an udder full of warmth for your empty belly."

Chapter Five

"Eben Pearl Victor! Please attend me when I speak!"

"I am sorry, Auntie. My mind will wander outdoors... How I long for the country and Victor Mall." Eben sighed wistfully.

Lady Adair pushed her exasperation aside and paused in her review of the invitations to study her niece with a knitted brow. She had come to London strangely complaisant and withdrawn.

"Really, Eben, you might show more interest in your presentation. This first appearance in proper society is of the utmost importance, as it could well establish your place in this season. I realize it's very tedious for you, not being allowed any functions until your presentation to Queen Adelaide," her aunt said sympathetically. "But once that's done, and your vouchers for Almack's are obtained, you can relax ever so slightly, and this will become most enjoyable. Now...this stack of invitations is mountainous, and careful selection of functions takes considerable time and skill." Receiving no response, she glanced up at her wool-gathering niece and cleared her throat harshly, with meaning.

"Yes, Aunt Addie?"

"Really, Eben! Are you quite certain you understand what is expected of you during presentation?"

"Yes. I have practiced it so many times, I could perform in my sleep." She sighed, rising to drop into a low, graceful curtsy to please her aunt. Then she restlessly paced to the window to peer out at the gray weather. It was not raining, nor was there any sunlight. It was merely a smoky, even gray...no variations. "How I would love to ride. I am so anxious with all this waiting ... my nerves are quite stretched." She sighed again, deeper this time.

"Patience, dear," her aunt murmured, lost in thought over the invitations.

Eben paced the salon, pausing before the mirror to grimace at her reflection. "Absurd!" she pronounced herself, flapping her arms up and down in a rude judgment of the demigigot sleeves. "You do notice, Aunt Addie, that Bess has been much more tolerant of me since I've taken my rightful place in society? Or do you think she's more approving simply because I've discarded Sheldon's breeches?"

"Humph! Possibly, but your mother is so obviously pleased, and whatever pleases Lillian also pleases Bess. Although she has shown a remarkable talent for taming that wild mane of yours. If you will please just stop tugging at that cap!"

Eben flipped the lace cap insolently before apologizing to her aunt. "I am sorry, Aunt Addie." She sighed again, dropping her hands to twist the ribbon at her waist.

Lady Adair was also on edge with the waiting. She was ready to get the show on the road before Eben unraveled before her eyes. It would serve as a distraction, if she could settle long enough to discuss the mountain of invitations, but they seemed quite beyond her interest. Finally, positive she'd gain no good from one so distracted, she relented.

"Why not take that little mare for a jog in the park? The exercise will do you good. Besides, your pacing is wearing out the only good spot in that carpet."

Eben halted her pacing to stare at the Aubusson carpet, then glance about the salon. In this room, at least, the neglect of his home by the late Viscount Victor was not apparent to the casual eye. It was a masterpiece of white-and-gold French elegance, accented with washes of rose and the drama of deep crimson, fit for King William himself, even if the furniture was arranged just a trifle haphazardly to make the best use of the carpet.

The ladies had dressed several key rooms in which to receive, robbing others to do so. But, as Aunt Addie reasoned, no one should stray from the stage to explore above stairs, anyway. They would not be able to entertain beyond afternoon "at homes," but having just come out of black gloves would make that excuse acceptable. Just as the problem of a stylish wardrobe for Lady Lillian had been sidestepped by deciding that she stay in black, or half-mourning gray and lavender, as befitted a grieving widow. Heaven knew, they had enough black silk of the first quality!

Pausing before the portrait of Lady Eben Pearl Norview Victor, now hanging over the mantel, Eben pondered her ancestor. There had been a ball gown ordered to duplicate the ruby-red gown in the portrait from the dressmakers, although Eben considered it a waste of funds, as debutantes were never allowed jewel colors. But with her in that gown, and with her hair dressed the same, the Victor Pearls merged into one. Of course, the handsome ruby-and-diamond necklace that lay on the bosom of her great-grandmother had been sold or gambled away long ago, and therefore Eben would make do with a garnet necklace of her aunt's.

"Do you think she was forced to marry great-grandfather? Or did she marry for love?"

"Marrying for love would be a marvelous thing, Eben, if one could always be trusted to fall in love with the right person." Lady Adair turned on the crimson-and-white-striped sofa to confront her niece. "As it is, position in society and making the right connections are of utmost importance. When love fades, and it invariably does, it is imperative you have other things in common. If you start out with a correct marriage, you will find great satisfaction in continuing tradition and raising your children to follow suit. It is the best way of ensuring the fortunes and the power of the upper class remain in the proper circles. As to whether she married for love ... I very much doubt it. But they dealt well enough together. You have to admit, at this moment, dear, saving Victor Mall is foremost in your mind, not the pursuit of phantom love."

"There may be truth in what you say. I just wish I knew what he will be like." She knelt next to her aunt, leaning against her knees, and looked to her for kind reassurances. "The uncertainty is hard to bear."

"You have not, my dear, met many young men, which I have always thought has been a mistake, so now it's going to be hard for you to sift the grain from the chaff," Lady Adair said, tilting her niece's chin upward with her fingers. "You are very beautiful, Eben Pearl. You bear an honorable name, and you have a position by birth in this society. All you lack is the fortune. Everyone has their own form of handicap. Your handicap is minor, because you have so much else that is marketable. But you must be very careful to offer it to the right person."

Great tears welled up in Eben's eyes and traced down her porcelain cheeks. But she made no move to swipe them away, nor did her aunt release her chin. "There will be a great many men who will love you, Eben, and doubtless, sooner or later, you will fall in love yourself. But in the world in which you move, for a woman to be free of the restrictions which confine her from the cradle to the grave, she must marry and marry well."

"But she only... changes the jurisdiction of her father and mother for that of a husband," Eben complained, laying her head in her aunt's lap, muffling her voice. Lady Adair stroked her hair with her wonderfully soft, scented hands. Even as she spoke, Eben thought that her parents had never had jurisdiction over her. They had supposedly loved her too much to deny her anything. A husband could possibly be the same. It then flashed through her mind that the ladies of her mother's acquaintance had talked of the love affairs taking place in the ton. Although they had chosen their words carefully in front of her, she had been sharp enough to realize the innuendo in much of what had been said. She had been aware that the men and women concerned were married, but she was also aware their liaisons were secretive ones. And although the ladies had expressed shock, they had not really disapproved.

"Eben, always remember, if you are going to sell yourself, aim for the highest bidder. You are an aristocrat, now act like one. Please regain your feet. You are crushing my gown and my legs have gone quite numb."

Eben rose gracefully to her feet and brushed the tears from her face with a slight laugh at her fears before saying, "I do think I will take your advice and jog Victoire about the park, although I do so hate to take Jamie Deal away from his work. Are you quite sure I cannot ride alone? Never mind! Don't pull a face at me! I know I must take a groom. It's just that Jamie Deal is doing the work of three men. Not only is he my groom, but coachman and stable boy, as well. It's a good thing we only have the four coach horses and the two bloods. Otherwise, even after all these years, he might decamp and desert me."

"Jamie Deal would die for you, and it's entirely possible he would appreciate an escape from the stable for an outing as much as you need to escape this house. Now, off with you, as I must attend to this business." With a wave of her hand, Lady Adair picked up the forgotten invitations. Then, as an after-thought, "And, mind you, ride the mare! It's unseemly for a young lady to race about on that brute!"

After her beloved niece had left the room, Lady Adair laid aside the invitation and mused. A position in British society was a great responsibility for a young girl to accept. While the aristocracy believed in nonstop amusement, they also be-lieved it their duty to look after those who were dependent upon them. This embraced their old-age pensioners and their impoverished relations, their almshouses and their orphan-ages. And since Eben sported all these in plenty, someone must be found to help her shoulder their burden. With a deep sigh, she allowed her mind to wander back to her conversation of the previous afternoon with dear Mary Standiford. A delight-ful chat over sherry, cozied near the fire with the sitting room door tightly closed for privacy.

"Now, dear Mary...I've been away too long. Tell me who's who in town these days. I am on a mission, you know.... Lil-lian is quite unable to cope with this. I need a husband of first quality, and I need him before this season's out."

Lady Mary's eyebrows had risen in mock alarm at her dear friend's confidence. Having her in residence was going to make this a remarkable season. Very entertaining, indeed! "I quite thought you had given up the idea of marriage once you'd been played false, dear."

"Do not gammon with me, Mary. You understand what I am about perfectly well. Come on, tell. Where are the for-tunes!"

With a delighted grin at her old friend, that lady pondered a moment. "Lord Lewis Ottobon, Viscount...probably the best choice...with what you tell me of your Eben. The man's a Corinthian of top drawer. Steeplechase and driving, not much into hunting. Good-looking, heavy-built, goes to Gen-tleman Jim's, so undoubtedly a pugilist. Wonderfully amus-ing with the ladies, no obvious scandals, but a mistress or two, I hear."

"And his fortune? What of heirs? Will he be looking?"

"He doesn't need to marry for an heir—three younger brothers, don't you know—but buckets of money! Simply buckets!"

"He sounds promising. Who else is sitting on the line?"

"More sherry, dear? There's Ellington, but I would steer clear of him. Solid fortune, but seems serious about not letting it lie fallow. Wagers on whether the sun will rise in the morn, and often so deep in his cups that he loses on a regular basis. Beastly temper...chases every lightskirt in town. Barred from most drawing rooms. Should be easy to snare. No one else wants the wastrel."

"Only in an emergency, dear. My niece, as you will soon see, is not a beggar. Who else? Surely the line is not so bare!"

"I mean no disrespect to your niece, Adair." With a wave and a sip of sherry, Lady Adair forgave her, and therefore she continued. "I have always thought Lord Compton a good catch. They say he is to marry this year. Tall, pale, never takes exercise out-of-doors, but a bang-up dancer. Collects...but I'm not sure what."

"You mean Ernestine's boy? I've always thought of them as very...sour people. Figured he'd turn out the same. Pious old lady...widow now, huh? So the boy has come into the title?"

"The fortune is immense, my dear. Though Ernestine will not let go of the purse strings easily. But the fact that she controls the boy so well..." Lady Mary paused for effect, then leaned forward. "Your Eben...if she's as headstrong as you say...could have free rein. If she can get him away from his mama. The earl does have control of the title and fortune, if someone could but convince him of it. What's to say...perhaps your niece..."

"Well, if it does fall in that direction, we would just have to be sure funds are set aside for Victor Mall before the wedding is allowed to move forward." Lady Adair let herself smile for a moment at the thought of the pious, pinch-faced dowager Ernestine Compton coming face-to-face with Eben in her riding breeches. What a comedy that would be!

"Of course, Adair, there's always the marquis," Lady Mary interjected slyly, sliding her eyes to heaven.

"Freddy Portsmythe!" Lady Adair exclaimed. "He's still on the petticoat line? Old smelly Freddy? He must be as old as I am, dear...and so very, very round!"

"Everything you say is true, but he's also so buried in blunt! One of these days someone will snatch him off the line, then he'll be a dear and depart this world...and she'll be most wealthy...and terribly free!'' She laughed as Lady Adair pinched her nostrils together in a rude gesture. ''Well, perhaps the duke of Eastmore might be more to your liking. Wealthy, young and sooo handsome. His estate neighbors Victor Mall.... Building a racing stable...or so rumor has it.''

''He's been dinner-table talk for a year or more. Is he still a pipe dream, or has he actually materialized?'' Lady Adair teased. ''He is more than one debutante's fantasy. Racers... not hunters? A horse is a horse, surely!''

''Oh, he has arrived, though in truth, few have seen him. Met with his solicitors, and left for the Park,'' she said, refilling her wineglass and tilting her eyebrows at her friend in question, only to be waved away. ''Every matron with a marriageable daughter will be flinging at his head. Even debutantes with their own fortunes will be trying for that plum. He'll definitely be the catch of the season. Though the *on dit* has it...he's a bit of a rakehell. So the mamas will watch their daughters closely, but will not let his reputation put them off if there's the merest chance of a buckling being done.''

Lady Adair roused herself from her wool-gathering. Rubbing her tired eyes, she rang for Hastings. A spot of tea would be nice, something warm to revive her mind as she mused. Lord Fitzhugh Eastmore... Eben's chances were slim, but the similarities in their interests were too many to be ignored. And, personally, she'd always thought the rakehells, having sown their wild oats far and wide, knew how to please a woman and, once tamed, made the best and most interesting husbands. And she had no doubt Eben could tame one!

When the tea tray arrived, Grady uncurled himself from the window seat to stretch and yawn, then advanced to perch upon the sofa at Lady Adair's elbow . For lack of a more suitable audience for her plotting, she took him into her confidence.

''If only Eben were more receptive to coaching, I'd set her on the duke's trail. As it is, we'll have to hope circumstance will throw them together long enough for their shared interests to surface. Back off, Grady! No cat feet on the tea tray, you greedy puss!''

Eben wandered the dim, dusty portrait gallery. Contrary to what she had told her aunt, she could not bear to interrupt Jamie Deal's overwhelming work load. She would have not been against lending him a hand, but that would definitely set her aunt's back up if she was found out. Without outdoor activity, she was unable to find a place for herself. The incessant talk of gowns and invitations and prospects had begun to pall the very day she arrived. She was used to exhausting physical exercise, and this sedate life, in which the only approved exercise for a lady was dancing, weighed heavily upon her shoulders. As did the time to think, to recall, to feel...

She aimlessly scanned the portraits of long-dead Victors hanging in untidy rows. She passed one after another, squinting in the poorly lit hall to read the engraved nameplate in the frame of each. Suddenly she found herself staring at the white, drawn face of a young woman, taking a moment to realize that the face surrounded by the modish hair style was her own, reflected in a gilt-framed mirror fairly crusted over with dust. Eben stepped closer to peer intently into the beautiful face. Did she look different...now that she was no longer a maiden? Her aunt's words haunted her. "So much that is marketable, but you must be careful to sell it to the right person..." She shut her eyes and leaned her flushed forehead on the cool, glass surface of a mirror, whispering aloud, "Sell it... I gave a large part of it away, to some dark stranger in a worn-out breeding barn. Fool! What would she say to that?"

Eben shuddered at the thought and sank down upon the tufted bench beneath the mirror. Her mind digressed to that rainy afternoon for the thousandth time.

The barn had been so dim, she doubted she could even recognize the man. She had no face to place on the image...just an impression of immense power and size. A dark-skinned man...possibly even a foreigner...with kind words and strong arms that had held her and let her weep over a long-past-prime mare...Victory Pearl. The mare had been too old and too close to foaling to send to auction with the others at Tattersall's, even if she could have borne that. But to lose her this way had just been too much. A sob broke from her throat. One sorrow too many. Knowing that if she sat still tears would overcome her, she rose again and paced the length of the gallery. The tears turned to anger, displayed in the lengthening of her stride. Why had this all been laid in her lap? She always had to be the strong one, the one to cope, never the one to take to her bed and grieve. Until that afternoon.

Pausing to stare out into the gray day, Eben remembered easiest the gentleness of his brown hands, first on the dying mare's body, then on her own. She felt her face burn. She was not innocent of the breeding process, having never been denied the barns. The ripping certainly had been an expected pain, but the loss of control over her feelings had been a surprise. How could her body take over her resolve so completely, and make demands of its own? That hot, liquid yearning, mounting, until he had stopped. She had wanted more. She had wanted...something for which she still had no name.

Eben touched trembling fingers to her lips, remembering too well her first kisses. She vividly recalled the fire and longing he had evoked inside her, for it came back so readily whenever she thought of him. His strange eyes, golden, like a predator's, so close to her, seeking to peer deep into her darkest soul. A ragged sigh left her parted lips. Turning, she paced again. At least the rash act had not resulted in a child. She had fretted over that until nature had relieved her mind. How humiliated she had been at his offer of a gift. But even the shame could not quiet the longing low in her belly...the desire to experience those wonderful sensations again...to feel his mouth on hers once more.

With a mental shake, she ticked off the things she knew of him. He obviously was a gentleman. But not a very respectable gentleman...to think nothing of taking a servant...against her will, to while away a rainy afternoon...then to offer her a trinket for her maidenhead! But then, would a gentleman be so knowledgeable with the birthing of the foal?

The foal! Another groan of shame escaped Eben. She again resumed her agitated pacing. To think how she had abandoned the red, fuzzy baby...a new start to her stable, indeed! She hung her head in shame. But she hadn't known what else to do but run away. To escape the humiliation of the dark man. If only he had been tender afterward, instead of turning his back on her...making her feel used...as if she had been nothing to him but a passing flight! Victory Flame, her new beginning, abandoned, then disappeared. For Jamie Deal had found nothing upon returning but the dead mare. He had burned the barn over Victory Pearl...piled the dry, dusty straw high over her body and torched it...reducing everything to ashes but the blackened ruins of the wet stone walls.

Eben could never have entered that barn again, but then, neither could she have just left the poor mare there for carrion. Another memory clicked into place. The chestnut mare at the entrance of the barn had been a Victor Mall hunter, one of the mares sent to Tattersall's. Even in her horrified state, she had recognized the hunter. Where had he gotten the mare? And why was he riding on her land? Oh, she was so confused. Her head ached. The shame and pain at abandoning the filly were all mixed up with the feelings of humiliation she felt about the dark stranger. But, never one to feel self-pity for long stretches of time, Eben strode purposefully to the mirror. Rubbing at it vigorously with her hand and squaring her shoulders, she addressed her dusty reflection,

"What's done is done! The most disastrous thing that could have happened has already been avoided . . . a child. If he happens to be a member of the ton, and plays loose with the tale and my reputation, then . . . I'll just handle that if it comes about. No sense worrying about stolen eggs until you see the tracks of the fox!"

The expression brought a smile to her lips. Another of dear, lovable, eccentric Aunt Addie's wisdoms. Oh, well, a body could do worse than to be like her aunt. Eben Pearl held her head high and sailed from the gallery in a fair imitation of that venerable lady.

"Let's just get this façade on mark, marry our fortune, and retire back to the country, where life is real . . . instead of play-acting!"

Chapter Six

Lady Mary Standiford had not planned a large party for Eben's first entertainment following presentation, though her standing was such in select circles that nothing could have prevented her from filling her house on short notice with the cream of the ton, had she so desired. As it was, the list had been designed with a specific goal in mind. Among the elite of the ton whose approval was desired, the three dowagers of Almack's were included to satisfy Eben's need for vouchers, plus a smattering of this year's debutantes, all blond, insipid girls to provide suitable contrast to Eben's dark beauty, and a liberal handful of the wealthiest eligibles.

It was a formidable first outing for a seventeen-year-old girl fresh from the country. All this, Lady Adair had tried to impress upon Eben, was quite a triumph; but to Eben it meant nothing more than that the show was on at last, and except for her desire to commence, endure and complete, she would have reacted with the same stone faced resignation to duty if all had sent regrets instead.

Now, taking her young guest firmly in hand, Lady Standiford drew Eben down the stairs into her salon for introductions. Heads turned to view this girl sprung so unexpectedly upon them from the country. Lady Adair was gratified at seeing her own opinion of her protégée mirrored in the eyes of her friends. Murmurs swept the room as all discussed her . . . but none more than the other debutantes. Elaborate curls and wraps dressed the others' pale hair, but Bess had effected a severe style for Eben, with a tight chignon at the nape of her neck, leaving the planes of her face visible and regal, her straight black eyebrows and thick lashes framing azure eyes clearly defined against the creamy paleness of her skin. Another of her aunt's many stratagems to enhance her niece's many differences. It was this that brought a young man stepping to the bottom of the stairs to be first in line to greet this beauty.

"Miss Victor, may I present Viscount Lewis Ottobon?"

A girl's debutante year could be the most important in her entire life, for her success determined her placement in society. A truly successful year netted a husband, with title and fortune in tow, securing her future and the future of her children. Each girl was paraded, judged and graded as to her beauty, perfection of form—whatever the style of the current season dictated—her family background, her fortune or lack thereof, and any outstanding accomplishments in the feminine arts of conversation and flirting. All this Eben found disturbingly similar to the sales at Tattersall's, and she deplored being subjected to such inspection. Thus she did not greet the viscount's frank appraisal with a great deal of charity in her heart. In fact, he looked up at her with such mooning admiration and avid interest that she was hard put to not laugh in his face.

"*Je suis enchantée,* my lord," she murmured, demurely.

"Not enchant*ed* . . . enchant*ing,*" he told her with great aplomb, and would have expounded further had not Lady Jersey approached in a flurry of loud, nasal voice and violent purple draperies.

"Miss Victor, it is about time that mother of yours stopped hiding in the country and rejoined society. Can't allow the both of you to rusticate now, can we?" she stated, in a voice that carried the length of the room. "Don't worry, girl . . . we'll have a husband settled on you by the end of this season. Quite a success at presentation, after all!"

With that parting remark of rudeness, leaving Eben's face quite pink, she sailed off. Probably to humiliate some other poor unfortunate, she reasoned. Viscount Ottobon bowed himself away with a smile she was afraid to trust. Her embarrassment turned to anger that seethed barely beneath the surface at her treatment.

"Well . . ." Lady Lillian said at her elbow, plying her fan briskly. "She certainly has not changed in all these years, but what can one do, after all? Those three, Lady Jersey, Lady Cowper and Countess Lieven, can, with their disapproval, destroy a girl's chances. Not only would you never be allowed to waltz without the vouchers, but it could be a black mark against your name forever," she said, raising her eyebrows with meaning. "Though it is very true, you were a great success. Quite stood out over all the others. Truly a swan among ducklings!"

Eben recalled vividly standing in line with all the others. Each young lady had been dressed in white, with a bodice cut in a round décolleté showing white shoulders.

"Stand out, indeed! One had only to look halfway down the line before losing the identity of the girls in their sameness. Nothing but a gaggle of geese with shrill voices!"

"Eben, mind your manners! And you did stand out. Did you see the queen speak to anyone else? And did you see Princess Victoria smile at anyone else? Oh look! There's Emily Cowper!" Wisely, with a sway of black silk, she was gone before Eben had time to retort.

"I am happy to see Mama enjoying herself. She seems quite a different person . . . here in London," she murmured to her aunt.

"Lillian always was one to enjoy society. I was so against her retiring to the country and allowing Ebenezer to run wild. But grief can become such a difficult habit to break. Now, you! Just relax, dear. Enjoy this time in your life, because it can never be repeated. One's first social . . . one's first season . . . are as special as one's first kiss."

Eben blanched to think that society was going to be that exciting! She quickly ducked her head, as if her thoughts might be read and, God forbid, understood.

"Egad!" Lady Adair declared, tipping her head in the general direction of the door. "Brace yourself! Here comes a good'n!"

A small lady, very plain and rather dowdy, with iron-gray hair scraped severely from her sharp features, advanced determinedly across the room. Eben was surprised to meet a pair of coldly curious black eyes and a thin, disapproving mouth, even though she had yet to be introduced to the lady. Placing herself squarely in front of Eben to sweep her from head to toe in a calculated stare, she addressed Lady Adair.

"Lady Cromwell, you are back in town?"

"I am pleased to see you, also, Lady Compton. May I present my niece, Miss Victor? The dowager Lady Compton, my dear... and her son, Lord Barnaby Compton."

Startled, Eben raised from her curtsy to stare at the top of the young man's head of thinning mouse-brown hair as he bowed deeply. She hadn't even noticed him behind his mother, so colorless was he. Tall and thin, obviously painfully shy, the man could not even raise his eyes from his concentrated examination of the floor to look at her. Dressed all in the same shade of brown, he quite disappeared from view, which probably was his wont.

Regretfully for Eben, Lady Adair allowed herself to be drawn away by her hostess, leaving her niece in the care of the Comptons until her mother's return. Her departure was monitored with a disapproving sniff from Lady Compton, marking her violent disapproval of the lady, as well as most of society, abundantly clear. She truthfully only moved in these sinful circles for the sake of her son's dubious standing in the ton.

"How are you enjoying your visit to London, Miss Victor?" She turned again to Eben and impaled her with a cold stare, which seemed to come down a long, thin nose, regardless of the fact that the dowager was shorter by a full head.

"Quite well, thank you. We have been driving in the park, and visiting the shops on Bond Street..." She began her society chatter.

"So you like the shops, do you? Barnaby, fetch us refreshments!" she interrupted to order her son. "I must admit, I feel vanity in a young girl should be stamped out diligently at the very first sign. Dreadful waste of money!"

"I cannot say that I have been overspending, but one must replenish one's wardrobe at certain times. My mother and I live very simply in the country. Nothing we had would suit...." Eben explained with strained patience at being attacked by a virtual stranger. Wherever had her mother gone? She'd best be rescued, and soon, for the temptation of an unseemly remark to this dire lady was much too great.

"I would not call some of the gowns young girls are encouraged to buy—" Lady Compton's nose pinched as she raked Eben's sea-green gown with haughty eyes "—as merely replenishing a wardrobe. Serviceability should be the key to smart shopping. This dress, now..." She fingered the dull, gray stuff of her own gown. "Above ten years old, and still giving good service."

"Yes, my lady," Eben murmured, contemplating the tired, limp gown, but could not come up with one appropriate remark to further the conversation. Wisely she kept her own counsel, merely uttering another unintelligible murmur. Actually, nothing else seemed required.

"Ah, Barnaby returns. You do realize my son is to take a wife this season?" Again she raked Eben with a calculating stare. "Probably be the catch of the entire season. You would do well to solicit his attentions."

Becoming increasingly incensed, Eben turned her back on the lady to smile at Barnaby, not so glad to see him as pleased to slight his mother, although that lady would interrupt her move as her merely performing as directed. Eben was in better humor with the shy man, as she shared his embarrassment over the remark. He avoided her eyes and provided no assistance at all with her plight. She strove to initiate a conversation nevertheless.

"Are you enjoying the evening, my lord?"

"Y-yes . . ." he stammered.

"The music is quite nice, don't you think?"

Here he merely inclined his head, unable to move words past his lips. Quickly realizing that any sort of mutual exchange was beyond him, Eben searched her mind for a way to loosen his tongue. As she harked back to her lessons, her aunt's advice whispered in her mind. "Eben, there's nothing a man enjoys more than the sound of his own voice expounding on a subject he believes himself the sole expert upon."

"I understand you are quite the expert on this region's butterflies. Being a country girl, I've always had an avid interest but, alas, never had the opportunity to study them . . . especially with such a noted professor."

The ploy worked, and she found herself audience to a stammering lecture that rambled on with no more required of her than a nod or an occasional murmur. She allowed her eyes to wander over the assembly. Her boredom knew no bounds. Knots of people sat or stood conversing, gossip being the main attraction at such a gathering. It was common practice for the lords and ladies to smile to your face and rip your reputation to shreds with cutting words behind your back. A popular game of elevating one's status while lowering someone else's.

Someone not of your own particular clique, of course. Footmen scurried through the rooms bearing trays of refreshments or soiled glassware. Probably a light supper would be served later, to be followed by more of the same. The very idea of living this sort of life on a daily basis was unimaginable to Eben.

As the brown-clad lord continued his discourse in halting sentences, she took the time to study him. He certainly was not offensive, just . . . pathetic. She wasn't sure if he was so tall or if his very thinness made him seem so. His clothing hung loosely on his bony frame, but then, even Weston and Meyer would be hard pressed to fit his awkward frame admirably. No, this man could never be a Bond Street beau.

Her eyes slipped through the company to light on the Viscount Ottobon. Attired entirely in blue, to further enhance his blue eyes, he was every inch a top-drawer tulip of the ton. Rather short, hardly more than her own height, with his clean-cut features, she supposed one would call him handsome. Her eyes moved from his head to a stiff, elaborately tied neckcloth. Whatever the style, it certainly looked extremely restraining, requiring the neck to be held stiffly, with chin high. He looked every bit as uncomfortable as she felt. With a shock, her blue eyes encountered his blue eyes. He had been watching her leisurely appraisal with a slight smile on his face. Eben looked away quickly, feeling the color rising to her face in a rush of heat.

"To be caught looking was bad enough, but then to blush like I'm guilty of immoral thoughts compounds the folly," she muttered, berating herself.

"I do beg your pardon, Miss Victor?" Lord Compton inquired, ceasing his rambling to lean toward her slightly.

"Oh...nothing," she stammered, thoroughly irritated with herself for being caught muttering to herself like a dolt.

A Lady Lawrence was prevailed upon by Lady Standiford to provide suitable music at the piano for the dancing amusement of the younger people. Eben shrewdly realized that to snare Lord Compton, one must pay court to his mama, for she had no doubt he would marry whoever Mama allowed. Having listened to a lengthy discourse on the sins of that very pastime from that lady, she decided to forgo the pleasure for the evening. First impressions were best firmly set with persons of her cut.

Finally rescued by a tardy Lady Lillian, Eben took her to task as the Comptons moved on. "Mama, whatever took you so long? I was about to commit murder! That woman!"

"Miss Victor? May I have this first dance?" Lord Ottobon asked, bowing deeply at her elbow before her mother could give defense for herself.

"I shall not be dancing this evening, my lord." She smiled at him to lessen the chance of any offense being taken from her refusal.

The voices of the nearby debutantes grew shrill with the excitement of the music. Eben glanced at them, easily picking out the ones without fortunes, as they seemed much more desperate than the ones who were not pressed to make a good marriage. Eben wondered if she looked that desperate. Then, fearing she might, she hardened her face somewhat. Misunderstanding her change of expression, Lord Ottobon rushed to reassure her.

"I can assure you I am considered an excellent dancer. I shall not endanger your feet at all. Pray, if you will take pity on me, I shall produce several former partners who are quite uninjured, and walking most readily, as references."

"What utter rot!" she hooted. "Do sit down and speak sense to me. I shall not dance this night!" This the entertaining lord promptly did.

"Then I shall not dance myself this evening, dear Miss Victor, for to not dance with you shall put me into mourning. Instead, I shall endeavor to entertain and astound my lady with stories of life and victories on the steeplechase course until supper is served . . . which I am hoping you will partake upon my arm."

"I should be most delighted to sup with you, my lord, but only if you promise to speak sense with me, instead of inane society prattle."

"Your servant. Though I swear I shall not be able to eat. I shall merely feast upon your beauty, and that shall sustain me," the viscount vowed, with a hand pressed ardently to his heart.

"But only if you promise to shut your eyes and eat something. Just to retain your strength, you understand . . . so that you might capably carry your rather large load of blarney!" she said, laughing.

"Eben, really!" admonished her mother. "Must you always be so forthright?"

"Saved from a scolding by the bell," Eben said with a laugh as the dinner bell rang in the salon doorway. Rising to take his arm, Eben saw a very disappointed Lord Compton turn away. Obviously he had been hesitantly crossing the floor to plead his case for supper. For a second, she was sorry... not for having missed supper with him, but for being the cause of yet another disappointment in what must be a life filled with them.

After the light meal, desiring nothing more than a moment alone, Eben slipped into a small retiring room set aside for the ladies' use. She found, to her vexation, the room duly occupied by debutantes in full, shrill cry, sounding, for all their youthful sophistication, like a pack of hounds baying on the hot scent of a fox. Without hesitation, she slipped into a curtained niche across the hall and sank into a small bergère chair. With a sigh, she kicked off her slippers and proceeded to rub her feet. Her satin slippers provided no support, and several tender spots warned of blisters. How she longed to be home, piled in a chair with Grady and a good book to occupy her evening. As if out of a dream, words slipped into her consciousness.

"Eben Pearl! Have you ever heard of such a horrid name?" a shrill voice exclaimed, followed by a giggle, one echoed by several others. "Actually, it suits her... such a great goose of a girl."

An eavesdropper never hears good of herself! But Eben could not have pulled herself away, or made her presence known, for the sale of half of London. A murmur from an unseen listener was indistinguishable, but the shrill voice spoke again, and this time she placed a name with the voice. Lady Vernill's debutante niece and namesake... Margaret Vernill.

"Well, my dear," Miss Vernill said to her audience, "you may say so, but I for one think her coloring is unfortunate. She's browned as if she... hoes beans or something on that falling-down place of hers. Makes her appear quite... common, don't you think?"

"Common!" Eben muttered, and squirmed in her chair, but could not muster enough courage to confront, or enough character to depart.

"And I overheard her mother saying somèthing about her muttering...in line at presentation, you know. Perhaps her hearing? We must remember to speak slowly and loudly to her, poor ol' thing." Eben finally summoned enough anger to get to her feet, ready to return to the salon, but she did not make her escape soon enough, for Miss Margaret Vernill had one more thing to say, and that proved the worst of all. "Of course, we all know her father was a wastrel of the first rule. Burned blunt like no tomorrow! Poor as church mice, you know. She must marry for money and...such a dark goose of a girl...probably have to settle for a widower with a parcel of brats."

Eben's feet were released from their paralysis on that last word. So everyone knew of her dire straits and was prepared to laugh behind her back. The thought humiliated her.

"Damn you, Father!" she muttered. "If Miss Margaret Vernill has her way, no one will ever forget your disgrace. They'll gossip and titter about it behind their fans at every social, that because of you, your sunburned daughter must come to town like a beggar at the market to find a man to save her!"

Then, for the first time, the unseen listener spoke intelligibly, "I wonder whether I detect a note of jealousy in your words, Maggie? After all, she has proven quite popular, and the queen did speak directly to her at presentation. Perhaps you envy..."

"And why should I envy? She's welcome to my leavings. And I shall tell her so to her face, if you like. I wish the poor thing no ill will. I...I was merely expressing a concern for one less fortunate than myself. And it's uncharitable of you to accuse me of anything else."

"I repeat...you are envious of her attention, and well she deserves it. I am not alone in thinking she is quite splendid." But Eben had fled without hearing the kind words. Fearing discovery if the debutantes emerged and caught sight of her, she fairly flew down the stairs.

The midnight ride to Grosvenor Square was most welcome, for even with the entertainment of Lord Ottobon's near-constant barrage of jest, the evening had been unbearably long and disappointing. With a frown, Eben remembered the pale, fragile Margaret Vernill and her unseen, waspish friends. It had been a painful lesson. Never again would she forget that the smiles were simply cover for the gossip behind the fans. She must not allow them to make a laughingstock of her.

"You were an unqualified success, my dear." Lady Lillian beamed at her daughter. "Everyone was most agreeable to say so."

Her aunt joined in. "Yes. I even overheard Lady Compton speak highly of you. I think? At least she said you didn't seem to be a flutter-headed miss with a loose tongue. I am quite certain that was spoken as a compliment."

"With Ernestine, one can never be sure.... I could not believe she still wears that gray taffeta. Imagine..." Lady Lillian said, preening over her own bosom, covered by artfully adorned black silk.

Eben let her mind wander away from the tedious conversation to the two nobles she'd met this evening. Though both qualified as to availability and fortune, she without conscious thought placed them in the brood barn in a pile of straw. Lord Compton would not lend himself to the picture for one instant, but the thought of laughing blue eyes and a muscular form over hers was not totally unpleasant.

"If only he was taller..." she murmured to herself.

"If only who was taller, dear? Pray speak up, Eben. Must you mutter beneath your breath? Makes me doubt my hearing... really it does. Now, whom were you speaking of?" her mother asked, displaying temper brought on by fatigue and unaccustomed late hours.

"Oh...Ottobon," she stammered, again pinching herself for speaking aloud. Clearly that was a habit of the rankest kind, and she must be diligent in breaking it.

"Taller does not signify, Eben. As long as his pockets are deep. And I assure you his are...very deep, indeed," Lady Adair answered her sternly. "Do not for one moment lose sight of that important fact."

"I hate it when you make it sound like a contest that only one person can win," Eben stated, her anger rising in distaste.

"And do you think different?" Lady Adair asked, wisely not pressing the point. She did not want to spoil her niece's evening with a debate, though "contest" was a very accurate description of the fight they were commencing. A serious fight indeed.

Eben did not answer, but a thought did invade her mind with lightning speed. *And just how important is the physical side of a union to me? As the feelings and sensations so briefly felt in the brood barn never seem to leave my mind.* With a sigh, she worried her lower lip with white, even teeth. *Does that make me a wanton? Is it possible that, without the proper shielding most young girls have, I have become base and immoral? Like the women in those fancy carriages parading in the park?* Thankfully, the arrival of Grosvenor Square ended her upsetting thoughts.

"I'm going on around to the mews with Jamie Deal. Don't worry about me. Jamie will see me safely in the side door," she said as the ladies descended the carriage at the entrance.

"Don't stay out too late, dear. You'll get chilled and you need your sleep," her mother said fretfully. Eben leaned back into the musty seat squabs with a giant sigh of relief as Jamie Deal drove the team through the arch and around to the mews.

"Why should I set every man I meet against the picture of a mysterious dark man in an old barn?" she mused. "I am not even sure he is the standard I wish to achieve. In fact, I can almost guarantee he's not! I don't even know his name, and wouldn't recognize him in the light of day if I fell over him! Bloody rotter!" Taking Jamie's hand, she stepped down into the stable yard, letting the night air clear her head. "I've taken to talking to myself, Jamie. Bodes ill for my sanity!"

"'Tis nothing wrong with it as long as ye always be agreein' with yerself," he replied, laughing at her.

Moving to lean on the box door, Eben watched the black stallion pace restlessly to the back wall, then come back to push at her with his velvet nose.

"I know, old man. I feel just as caged. As though I could jump out of my skin," she said. "What I need is a long gallop to clear the mind and tire the body."

"That wouldn't be hurtin' the old man. He's about to come out of his hide, as well," Jamie agreed, looking up from his task of brushing the dust from the coach team. "Not so bad for these two, they get out most every day, but the bloods can't." An alert expression lit Eben's face. One Jamie Deal was more than familiar with. She had been using it on him since she was three and turned over to his charge in the stable. "Now, lassie, ye'll not be cookin' up something that will land us in trouble," he warned, shaking the dandy-brush at her.

"Jamie? Do the grooms still run the bloods in Hyde Park at dawn?" she asked, with her eyes narrowing speculatively.

"Aye, lass. But don't ye be thinkin'..."

"Jamie, don't you see? I can help you run the bloods down. You know you need help. Besides, if I don't get out soon, I shall just blow my top, and then the rub will be up for all of us."

"Nay, lass..." he said, trying again.

"But, Jamie, you don't know what it's like for me... being paraded on the auction block..." she whispered. Her large eyes pleaded. "'Tis like Tattersall's... judged and weighed, with merits and faults counted and subtracted..."

Jamie's heart saddened at the sight of her forlorn face. Never had he been able to stand up to her. Not once she turned her big blue eyes on him, to melt his heart. Shaking his gray head, he could only mutter, "Gonna be gettin' yerself, and me, in trouble. Into hot water, for sure!"

Watching him weakening, Eben pressed her advantage. "No one will know I'm a girl. If you can get me a heavy groom's sweater, I have my breeches and boots. We'll run in St. James Park... not Hyde. No one of any account will be there." She started toward the door with a bouncy spring to her step. Turning once more, she smiled at her friend's unhappy face. "Thanks, Jamie," she called in a stage whisper. "It'll be fine, you'll see."

Gathering up her skirts, she ran to the house... forgetting her promise to have Jamie see to her safety. No one who knew Eben as Jamie did would have dared accost her in her own yard. And one foolish enough to try would have been in for the surprise of his short life, for she was not the sort to have patience with nonsense.

Chapter Seven

A light frost had fallen overnight, silvering the ground and sparkling the trees. Eben was as good as her word to Jamie Deal. Just before first light, she was clad in her breeches and stamping the frozen ground impatiently as she drew on leather gloves. Her breath misted in the cold air with her eagerness to be off. A charcoal wool cap succeeded in hiding her long jet hair in such a fashion that, unless inspected closely, she could have been any other groom working the vinegar out of His Lordship's blood horses. A chore diligently seen to on a daily basis so that the spirited cattle would not embarrass the lords and ladies of the ton by unseating them with high jinks and plopping them in the dirt before their peers.

Since the strict rules governing the promenade in Rotten Row by the nobles forbade reckless riding, a number of the more noted horsemen exercised their own steeds in the early morning, and impromptu races and hurdle jumping were wagered upon. Among these notables, on this morning, was the duke of Eastmore.

Over the past month, Fitzhugh had ridden, inspected, and approved every section of Eastmore Park, settled his Arab mares and set out a breeding program with his studmen for the new mares purchased at Tattersall's. Only then had he felt it time to approach London and the season, and therefore set about acquiring a bit of town bronze. He was comfortably settled into a flat near Pall Mall, with his man, Beans, a butler, an excellent cook, three footmen and half a score of maids to see to his ease. He had been dismayed to learn that his great-uncle had maintained no residence in town, although, as explained by his man, it did signify quite good sense, as the old duke had disliked the place so heartily. While Fitzhugh had hired an agent to seek such a residence for sale, he was not overly eager to purchase just yet. It seemed such a thing as a new bride would care to busy herself with, and unless shown an exceptional place, he would allow the future duchess to attend to the acquisition . . . when he decided to acquire her, as well, that is. At present, he was not dissatisfied with his apartment of spacious rooms.

Fitzhugh had made the customary rounds to White's, and attended exactly the right number of preseason entertainments, socializing with just the appropriate pillars of the nobility to firmly establish his worthiness to the ton. If frequenting Gentleman Jim's Boxing Academy and the Royal Fencing Academy had earned his merit as a true member of the set, it had also started a fast friendship with Lord Lewis Ottobon. Likewise with Lord Alfred Ellington, although that gentleman was so oft in his cups that only limited exposure was palatable, unless one was also deep into one's cups, of course.

The general opinion of the male members of the beau monde, the only ones in position to judge thus far, was that in spite of his slightly rakish and careless air, the duke of Eastmore possessed an excellent figure, displayed to perfection by Weston and Meyer, held his liquor and his pasteboards in the manner of a gentleman, sported an opinion that pleased the men and boasted a smile that charmed the ladies. In short, despite his title and wealth, there was nothing toplofty about him. His valet tied an awesome neckcloth, his mistress was infinitely desirable, and his horseflesh was the finest most had ever seen, and his skill in the management of all three proved that he deserved the lot . . . and thus assured his entry into the coveted ranks of the Corinthian set.

Though they normally took their early morning ride in Hyde Park, the three gentlemen, Lord Ottobon, Lord Ellington and Lord Eastmore, happened to be taking their exercise in St. James Park this particular morning just past first light. Their gallop had been halted to praise the conformation and spirit of the black stallion acting a rodeo in front of them. He was long of leg and tight of body, and every taut inch of him was afire. Jet black, with not one white hair on him, he was poetry to the three lovers of blooded horseflesh who watched his spirited actions.

Eben was so pleased to be riding free at last, she foolishly paid scant attention to any other rider in St. James Park, and in truth, her complete concentration was required to keep Black Victory from unseating her with his high jinks. So fresh was he that he stood on his hind legs at an awesome height. No sooner did he set his front hooves on the turf than he would rise again, fighting the restraining bit, creating quite a stir for his audience.

"I'll wager fifty pounds the old man has the young chapo rump-in-the-dust before long," Lewis declared, first to Eastmore, then to Ellington.

"And I will gladly relieve you of your fifty pounds," Lord Alfred Ellington accepted, with glee at the sport. "His nabob would never have allowed the boy to bring the brute out if he couldn't cut the mustard. What say you, Eastmore? Will he or won't he?"

"I am quite sure I could not say. But that is a magnificent animal! What's the stable? Do you know the horse?" Fitzhugh demanded. He thought he recognized the animal, even though he had seen the flying hindquarters disappear over a knoll but once in his life. If he could find the stable, he might find the elusive stable wench who, he knew, rode that same stallion in the country. That was one acquaintance he very much wished to renew, for she was one tasty wench! He had assumed that, the brood barn standing on Victor Mall land, the girl must belong to Victor Mall, also. But upon returning to the scene of the seduction, he had found the place strangely fire-gutted.

His many inquiries had turned up no leads, as the Victor Mall villagers and workers all appeared deaf, dumb and blind. Each one meeting his inquiries with a shake of the head or a shrug of the shoulders. Also, there was the matter of the orphaned filly growing fat and strong on the rich milk of an old Percheron baby-sitter mare in Eastmore Park's stable. That red filly was of noble blood, and very valuable. He desired to return her to her rightful owner or, better yet, make her an addition to his own stable. And now...he found he would very much like to purchase this black stallion, for he was exactly the type of English-bred horse he was looking for to cover his Arab mares. He was unsure at this point which breeding would produce the type of racer he was interested in breeding...for it could be either hunter mare and Arab stallion or the re-

verse. Fitzhugh reached down to pat the arched neck of his
chestnut mare with great affection. Only time would tell.

"I haven't see that brute before. One wouldn't forget him!
But that gray filly the other chap's up on has all the marks of
a Victor Mall hunter. She's a real beauty," commented Lewis,
being a top-o'-the-trees Corinthian and an expert on horseflesh if ever there was one . . . even if hunters were too heavy a
body type for his speedy instincts.

Eben at that moment spied a stretch of turf suitable for letting the black have his head. With a gay laugh over her shoulder at Jamie Deal on the dancing Victoire, she spun the stallion
toward the stretch and let him go. In three strides he had flattened out in a burst of speed that would have left her behind
if she hadn't wound both hands tightly in his mane.

"Bloody damn! He's away with the lad!" Alfred exclaimed, pointing after them with his leather crop waving
wildly in the air.

"No! He's not broken away! The lad's just stretching him
out. Come on! Let's give chase!" Fitzhugh ordered, and with
a great shout of joy he put spurs to the mare. The other two
quickly followed, with much whooping and yelling.

With Jamie urging young Victoire to a powerful stride, and
the three members of the Corinthian set hard on his heels, the
race was on. Eben assumed the classic racing crouch, settling
her slight weight over the stallion's withers, her face low in the
flying mane. Black Victory, sensing her total commitment to
the run, lengthened his giant stride and extended his powerful
body, increasing his speed.

The frozen ground became a blur beneath the thundering
hooves, and the cold wind whipped tears into Eben's eyes.
Extending her arms along the sleek black neck and moving her
body with the rhythm of the stallion's long stride, she felt release from the tension and anxiety that had plagued her. The
enormous speed the black possessed freed her from her earthly
bounds, and together they soared high above responsibilities,
pensioners and troublesome creditors. His strength and power
recharged Eben until she felt as strong and as powerful . . .
invincible. Without her taking note of the riders in hot pursuit or realizing there was a race in the making, the handsome
pair quickly outdistanced the others and disappeared from
their sight through the trees and into the shadowed early-
morning depths of the park.

Lewis easily passed the trio on his fleet, long-legged racer, but quickly lost sight of the black and his rider. Alfred, with his flashy but unsound dun gelding, trailed far behind the field. Fitzhugh knew his game mare, being so heavy-bodied, could never overtake the black stallion or Lewis's racer, especially carrying his great weight, but the morning was fine and the gallop exhilarating, and she was drawing up on the fleet gray filly. Coming even with them, the filly began to slow and swerved to bump the chestnut mare.

"Hey, look out there, my man!" Fitzhugh swerved quickly away from the crowding filly. With both riders drawing rein on their mounts, Alfred thundered past. Fitzhugh turned on the huffing groom in anger. "That was a damn bad rub! You could have tumbled the both of us. Bad show, man!"

"Please, my lord . . . 'Tis sorry I am. The wee lassie is green yet, and seeing her old mum come up aside her that way took her off her lead," Jamie explained, tearing off his hat, and trying to control the dancing filly, for she was determined to sidle up to the chestnut mare. "She didn't mean no harm, sir. No harm at all."

"Dam, you say?" Fitzhugh was taken by surprise, but in the confusion of Lewis and Alfred cantering back to join them with great shouts of excitement, it was impossible to further the conversation over their din.

"Hell's teeth! Did you see that black fly? There's nothing that can touch him, I swear. Nothing could catch him when he's full-tilt!" Lewis was so entranced, he was barely coherent. "Where's he out of? What stable? What's his bloodlines? Bloody hell's teeth!"

Alfred pulled up his fagged gelding. "I—I disagree...we just got a late start. I disagree, you hear! I have a bay in my stable that could . . ." he began, but the others granted him no attention. They were quite used to his excuses and bravado whenever he lost a race or a bet, for he was a notoriously bad loser. Just then, Eben came down the track at a controlled hand gallop. The black was snorting and steaming in the morning cold, but by no means spent. As she drew up to the group, her breath came in little ragged puffs of mist. Without thinking, she reached up to remove the cap to free her hair, only to be halted by Jamie Deal's panicked look. With a saucy grin and elevated eyebrows at him, she swept her gaze over the Corinthians. Seeing Viscount Ottobon, she immediately dropped her head to shade her face behind the brim of her wool cap. Tugging her muffler higher about her chin, she gritted her teeth. Drat it all! She was about to be caught out! If her aunt drew wind of this, the devil would be hers to pay for sure. One of the riders edged his mount closer and directed a question to her. In panic, she made a motion toward her throat that Jamie Deal, bless him, immediately interpreted.

"He can't help ye, my lord. He can't speak, poor laddie," Jamie hurriedly filled in, rambling to draw attention from Eben. "The black is from Victor Mall. But I don't think my lady will sell him. Vicroy House is over on Grosvenor Square, white one on the corner, but I don't think she'll sell."

"It would seem Victor Mall makes a habit of hiring the unfortunate. I have had much the same treatment before," the deep voice mused, "at the Mall."

Eben, with her head down, could only see the chestnut mare's heaving side, a well-molded thigh in shrunken buckskin, and a highly polished Marlborough boot. Her mind reeled. *It's him! Oh, my heaven! It's him!* Her shock was so great, her hands jerked and jabbed Black Victory's mouth, causing him to rear.

"Here, lad! Walk out that horse! Don't ye see him steaming?" Jamie yelled, giving her an excuse to quickly pull out of the group.

Thankfully, Eben did that very thing, and jogged down the track. Once she was out of sight, her sanity somewhat returned. So he was a gentleman...and in London! Which meant she would be seeing him at most of the same socials... perhaps even dancing with him. The thought of his hands on her body again nearly panicked her anew. If only she had dared look at his face. Her teeth worried her bottom lip.

"How am I to recognize him, Black? Unless he rides that blasted mare into the ballroom." She snorted in agitation, her thoughts in a turmoil. Would he know her? Would the elegantly gowned debutante be recognized as the wild wench in breeches? Jamie Deal and Victoire posted alongside her.

"'Twas a close one, lassie. I thought for sure ye was pegged for a lass." Jamie was mopping his face, in spite of the chill. Then, with a grin on his impish face, he said, "But we can be sure they can't outrace ye and the old man, huh, lass?"

"I'm not sure of that, Jamie." Eben set the black for home, her mind filled with worry.

* * *

The afternoon was sunny and much warmer, a brief promise of the spring to come. No matter what excuse Eben invented, the ladies demanded she promenade with them in Hyde Park. She obviously could not tell them that she'd had a spanking gallop that very morning and only longed for some peace to sort out her tangled thoughts. Wearing a new pearl-gray riding costume with scarlet epaulets and covered buttons in the military style, her hair swept under a tall crowned hat adorned with a scarlet ostrich plume, she fervently hoped she looked nothing like the groom of that morning's wild race. And most definitely unlike the wench in the pile of dirty straw! There was nothing she could do but be on the lookout for the chestnut mare. If, in truth, the dark stranger was riding her this afternoon . . .

There was such a crush of smart barouches, high-perch phaetons and tilburies that traffic was very slow indeed. Jamie Deal was wearing his coachman's livery, with a very unhappy hunch to his shoulders. Eben resolved to send posthaste for the coachman from Victor Mall. Jamie Deal was a dear friend, and she could not blame him for being miserable, stuck driving the carriage. Besides, without a groom to escort her, she was doomed to amble sedately beside the carriage.

Lord Ottobon, enjoying the fashionable promenade hour in Rotten Row astride a showy bay gelding, was kind enough to stop by Lady Victor's landaulet to speak to the ladies. "The very best of the afternoon to you all, Lady Victor and Lady Cromwell . . . Miss Victor." The handsome viscount, always correct, executed a perfect bow even from the back of his gelding. "The ton should require you ladies to drive with your top raised, otherwise the sun will retire behind a cloud, in shame at his failure to compete."

"My dear viscount, you really should save your flattery for your ladies young enough to believe it. It's totally wasted here, I assure you," Lady Adair admonished him.

Lady Lillian, bundled into a fur-lined cloak, snuggled beneath a warm lap robe, with a heated brick placed at her feet by the diligent Bess, preened for the viscount. Eben could see just how wasted his flattery was when her mother reddened in pleasure and hid a girlish giggle behind her gloved hand. Actually, it seemed a compliment well received to her.

With a laugh, Lewis turned to Eben. Indicating the gray filly, he inquired, "I say, Miss Victor. Did you have your dressmaker design your very fetching riding costume after the color of your mare, or did you buy the mare to match the costume, for truly they are one and the same?"

"Why, how kind of you to notice, my lord." She smiled up into his blue eyes. Lewis was taller only by benefit of his taller mount. She stilled Victoire's prancing with a gentle hand. "Actually, yesterday she was white. I had her tinted only this morning. Time was short, or her tail and mane would match my plume."

"For shame, Miss Victor. I fear you are telling me a fib. We saw your man riding that filly only this morning along with the other chap, on a raking black stallion," Lewis told her, his tone teasing. "My friend is devilishly interested in that black. He was wondering if the horse might be for sale? Viscountess, had you thought to dispose of him? I mean, since your husband's racing stable has broken up..."

"That wild animal! I most assuredly would like to dispose of him...with a bullet through the brain...but I am afraid Eben has complete control over that matter. I just do not, for the life of me, understand why she would want..." Lady Lillian seemed prepared to ramble on, so Lady Adair decided to quickly intervene before she said something she oughtn't.

"You say you saw two grooms this morning? With both horses?" she queried, glaring sideways at Eben with narrowed, speculative eyes. Jamie Deal's back stiffened noticeably. Eben decided to flee and let him fight it for himself. A cowardly track, but she took it anyway.

"My lord Ottobon, my groom was unable to accompany me today. May I please prevail upon you and your groom to escort me on a slight jog through the park? This slow pace is so tedious, and I do not feel I am benefiting from the exercise in the least." When she looked at him with her blue eyes twinkling and one eyebrow cocked toward her hat, he was hell bound to say yes.

"If it pleases your mother and aunt that I do so, I would be ever so happy to be of assistance," Lewis replied, with a quizzing look at Lady Cromwell, sensing she was in charge of the small group. The frowning lady waved her hand, staring disagreeably at poor Jamie's back, and the two set off at a jog.

"Would you care for a gallop the length of Rotten Row, Miss Victor?" the viscount asked in jest, dancing his bay sideways, as if getting the jump on her.

"I dare not care for that, as you must realize," Eben said, throwing him a saucy glance as he rode close to her side. "Because we would have everyone staring, and my mother would never forgive me for making a spectacle of myself."

Lewis watched in entire approval the ease with which she brought the filly, who was much inclined to take exception to the bustle of London traffic, mincing sedately alongside his bay. If he had had to place a wager at that moment, he would have given odds that Miss Victor's virtuous resolution not to make an indecorous stir in the park would not outlive her first glance of a road suitable for letting the filly stretch her legs.

Eben, setting longing eyes upon the stretch of tan that ran beside the carriage road, found the temptation irresistible, and with one guilty, determined, teasing glance at her blond companion, she sent the filly flying off at a controlled hand gallop. Lewis followed, grinning at having his perceptions proven out. His bay keeping pace with the fleet filly, he thoroughly appreciated the way her cheeks tinted rosy with the exercise and excitement. When Eben drew rein and found him beside her, she laughed and flushed prettily.

"Now, do not reprimand, my lord! For you cannot say a thing to me, as you've done the same as I, and the guilt must be equally shared."

"Ah, but only because it is my duty!" he pointed out self-righteously. "What would your mama have said if I had allowed you to go careering off on your own?"

"They would say you were a lout to tell such a fib! You enjoyed it quite as much as I — *Oh!*"

She broke off suddenly on a sharp exclamation. They had turned their horses' heads to proceed back along the track, and as her gaze ranged over the carriage road and footpath, she observed, with some self-consciousness, that her pell-mell gallop had drawn all eyes upon her just as she had predicted. One tall rider aboard a splendid black Arab gelding broke away and trotted toward them. He had been riding, Eben noted, beside a dashing, Titan-haired charmer who was queening it in an elegant barouche lined with pale rose satin. Eben knew by the satin's color that she was seeing one of the lightskirts being whispered of behind every spread fan in the drawing rooms at every event. The same type of loose woman her father had spent badly needed funds to placate with jewels, fancy carriages and fine horses. Eben would have like to lay her crop across the rouged, laughing face. She glanced at the advancing man to sneer at one who would be seen talking to such a woman in a public park. But something about the man caused her breath to catch in her throat. The very carriage of his body reminded her of the seducer. The tilt of his fine head and the breadth of his shoulders... Could it be him? She dropped her eyes to hands that seemed to tremble, no matter how she fought to still them.

"Miss Victor, may I present to you Lord Fitzhugh Eastmore, the sixth duke of Eastmore? I realize you are neighbors, but since he's newly returned from Tehran, perhaps you have not met. Your grace, the Lady Eben Pearl Victor."

Eben took an incredibly deep breath and released it slowly, then raised her eyes to stare straight into his. So the test had come! Fine! Let it be done and over with. Damn him if he played her false—if it in truth was him! She studied his strong, confident features for a moment, then inclined her head ever so slightly in acknowledgment of the introduction.

How very handsome he was, with brown eyes so pale as to seem amber, almost golden, she decided. She noted further that his skin was burned dark by the sun, and his hair, uncovered by the sweep of his topper from his head, shot through with streaks of blond, as if he spent a great deal of time in very hot sun. Of course, the hot sun of the Middle East! His bronze riding coat fitted to an inch, stretched tightly over shoulders that were broad, tapering downward. His cravat was snowy white next to the sun-browned face and tied intricately. His teeth, when he smiled down at her, were just as dazzling.

Eben watched his eyes closely, but saw no recognition. This could not be the man, she thought suddenly, with hair so light, and merely the admiring look of a tulip of the ton meeting a young woman he thought worthy of attention and nothing more? No, this could not be the man. The tension left her body somewhat, and she smiled openly, with great relief.

"Miss Victor, my deepest pleasure. I have desired to compliment your family on your fine horses. I was fortunate recently to purchase ten excellent mares at Tattersall's of Victor Mall bloodlines," Fitzhugh informed her courteously. "Splendid animals, each and every one. Just splendid!" His eyes raked the excellent figure of the young girl and thought to inquire about the black, but then decided this Victor, with her shy, missish airs, would have no opinion on stable matters, though she did sit the filly prettily.

"Oh...I—I am so pleased to hear you have them. I so wanted them to go to someone who would appreciate them. It was extremely difficult to see them leave the farm. They represent so many years of careful breeding...." The pain in her heart was raw, and tears shone for a second in her brilliant azure eyes at his sincere appreciation of her beloved horses before she shuttered them. Fitzhugh's eyes narrowed in thought as the familiar expression flitted over her face.

"Lord Eastmore was very nearly put into the dust this morning by your filly there, in her excitement at seeing her dam. And I, unhappily, am fifty pounds lighter after the excellent riding of your man on that black," Lewis interjected, feeling the loss of this beautiful lady's attention. He turned to scowl at Fitzhugh, but that lord wasn't paying him any mind. The two seemed absorbed in each other, and that he didn't like! It'd be a cool day in hell before he introduced Eastmore to another lovely! A fact he planned to enlighten the lord upon at first chance. Pressing the bay in closer, he tried again, "Ah, about that black..."

Eben, unable to tear her eyes from the amber ones, suddenly felt awkward and very young beneath the man's half smiling appraisal. So, he had been in St. James Park this very morn! That could mean one of two things.... Either he was the seducer and had ridden the chestnut mare this morning. Or he wasn't the seducer and had ridden the mare. Or... Suddenly a third option flashed into her mind. Was it possible that the man who had seduced her in the brood barn was not even the owner of the mare? For a second she lost track of the conversation and became flustered, grasping upon the last thing she remembered being said.

"I d-do apologize for her. She is an infant still, and m-misbehaves," she stammered. As if to prove the point, Victoire pranced sideways, but was easily brought back under control. The duke laughed at the filly's foolishness, but his gaze never left the girl's face.

"I do understand the antics of juveniles. I have an orphan red filly in my barn at Eastmore Park that has them in an uproar most of the time."

Eben's face turned a dull red, then blanched dead white. Her azure eyes darted to his amber ones in alarm, but before she could read them, her vision narrowed and spots danced before them. She was afraid she was going to tumble from Victoire's back. The buzzing in her ears was so loud!

"Miss Victor...I say! Are you all right?" Lewis was leaning toward her in concern. He laid a hand on her arm to steady her. "I had best take you back to your carriage right away."

"Y-yes...please...the excitement..." she stammered as she allowed Lewis to turn Victoire towards the landaulet. Eben was unable to meet the duke's eyes, knowing they would be alight with satisfaction and lewd remembrance of her wanton responses. "Your grace, forgive me. The black...yes...at a more opportune time, perhaps."

A short time later, lying in her rose-and-ivory room at Vicroy House, with the shade drawn and a cool cloth on her brow, Eben allowed herself to think of it for the first time since she had stared with disbelief into those yellow predator's eyes. Predator's, yes! Like a wolf's! And she was the bait in the trap. She had forced her mind to stay blank during the ride home. Ottobon's groom had brought Victoire home, while she had sat quite dazed in the landaulet with her concerned aunt and mother fussing over her. But what could she say to them, other than that she felt unwell. What, indeed?

Jamie Deal would be worried about her. She should go tell him it was all right. But her body didn't move. The red filly was alive! And at Eastmore Park's stables. His stables! A constant reminder to him of that rainy afternoon and her... sacrifice. The duke of Eastmore...a rakehell. Everyone talked of him. A womanizer...obviously, from the way he acted with a servant, or what he thought to be a servant, in a haystack. And the hussy in the park...! Not a gentleman! Not a man of honor. Definitely not the man for her, for all her mooning over him. But why should that thought even be considered? She would never want a man such as him! Such as her father had been! Never! Had he known it was her...when he had first seen her? Had he just baited her and drawn her out, all the time knowing it was her? Had he remembered how she had clung to him, begging him to—

Eben rolled over on her side and curled into a small knot of misery around Grady. With a groan, she buried her face in the purring cat's warm fur. Her thoughts screamed. How could she not have recognized him? How could her memory be so distorted? His hair was quite blond. Even in the dim barn, his hair would have looked golden. She remembered so well, tangling her fingers in his wet— *Wet!* She sat up abruptly in the four-poster. Wet hair...hair made darker by rain! That was why. But there was no mistaking the size of him...the power of him...the raw desirability of him.

Eben jumped out of bed and roamed around the room, feeling confused and trapped. If only she had someone to talk with...to confide in. Someone to ask what to do...what to feel. A frown creased her forehead. She was at Eastmore's mercy. If he decided to make a shred of her reputation, she could do nothing to stop him. Perhaps if she went to see him...to beg him to keep his silence? But then what? Even if he decided to remain quiet, she would still have to face him. See him...have him staring at her...dance with him...and have him touching her, knowing her in a way no other man had ever known her. With an audible moan, she dropped down on the petit-point stool and studied her reflection. Her blue eyes darkened in her pale face, her pink lips trembled. The duke of Eastmore...the catch of the season...Fitzhugh. When she said his name aloud, it came out as a soft sigh.

"Fitzhugh..."

She could imagine saying it in passion, while he kissed her, lips pouty beneath the word as he touched her, inciting those feelings deep inside her belly again. Slowly tugging a ribbon loose, opening the front of her embroidered nightdress, she stared at the reflection of her full breasts, imagining his hot gaze on them. With one finger, she lightly touched the nipple where his mouth had suckled. Abruptly she dropped her face into her hands, cascading her unbound hair in a waterfall of black satin into her lap, whispering, "Heaven help me...."

Chapter Eight

Fitzhugh sat for the longest time, staring after the departing pair. His amber eyes narrowed, and he idly fingered the coarse hair of the gelding's mane, letting his thoughts run unchecked. So it had been her. He had thought her merely to be an extremely beautiful woman when first seeing her galloping with Lewis. She sat the gray filly admirably, with her scarlet plume waving jauntily, laughing merrily with her gallant escort, Ottobon...his good friend. And, of course, as one of the main obligations of a good friend was to provide introductions to extremely beautiful ladies, he had immediately ridden over to allow Ottobon the opportunity to fulfill that obligation.

Even at the threat of incurring the wrath of the Lady Louise Sinclair, pouting pettily in her rose satin barouche, for his inattentiveness in doing so. He had meant to inquire of the gray filly, and to find out more of the black, if possible. But when she raised her head and he saw those incredible azure eyes, he had felt . . . the way she had searched his face, staring straight into his eyes with such intense questioning . . . that it might be her. How could there be two young women who possessed eyes that blue? Eyes so blue one could swim in them. And then once more he had dismissed it as totally absurd, as she was so obviously a chaste daughter of the ton. But when she had spoken of sending the mares to Tattersall's; the pain in her voice, the ache so apparent in her heart, could only have come from the same wench who had wept bitterly in his arms that rainy afternoon, over the death of a long-past-prime mare. To be sure, he had thought to test her when he mentioned the red orphan filly. Her reaction had left no doubt and had been proof enough of her identity. Lady Eben Victor was the same young woman who had clung desperately to him in grief and then responded with such abandon to his lovemaking.

For no apparent reason, the false spring day suddenly turned chilly. Fitzhugh looked up to see if the sun had disappeared behind a cloud. Or, he thought with irony, someone had just walked over his grave. He hadn't escaped censure for scandal yet. And he might find himself with a bride not of his choosing. Gentlemen were, of course, allowed great freedoms and while the beau monde were prepared to close their eyes to innumerable high jinks among themselves, they disliked open scandal, and many a young gentleman had been banished to the Continent to sit out a grace period for deplorable behavior. Even if one was protected by age, wealth and title, it was not considered the best of ton to deflower debutantes, notwithstanding the temptation by the little chit's wanton responses—responses more readily associated with matrons of advanced experience.

"Tallyho! Hullo, old chap!" Lewis, with Alfred in tow, came careering toward him. "Off to White's! My blood needs thinning after this chill."

The three turned their mounts to ride abreast down the tan strip towards the club and a stiff drink...or ten, amended Alfred, apparently to accompany the ten he had already imbibed, Fitzhugh noted with some disgust, for the hour of the day was still young.

"Is Miss Victor quite recovered? She didn't look top of the knob for a moment there," he inquired of Lewis.

"She assured me she was feeling fine once we left you. I say, old chap, do you always elicit that sort of reaction from the lovelies?" Lewis was in rare form with his ragging, and judging from the much-amused expression on his face, Fitzhugh was not to be let off easy. "Confide, man, is that the reason you've managed to snare the fairest of the fairest so quickly...the lovely Louise?"

"What's this?" Alfred quizzed, always ready to pull another's tail, if he thought the tables would not be turned. The diminutive lord was never able to receive jest without a show of temper. "Let me in on the tale. Am I to understand Eastmore has some sort of firecracker way with the sacred daughters of the ton?"

"I declare, Alfred ol' boy, you should have been there. One moment she's laughing and obviously developing a *tendre* for me, and then Fitzhugh rides up. And in the space of three heartbeats he has her swooning and about to topple from her horse at his very feet," Lewis elaborated.

"Who? Who are we talking about?" Alfred demanded.

"I admit, I did warrant the possibility of her being overwhelmed by my mere magnificence," Fitzhugh conceded, cracking a wry grin at his own humor, which merely reflected his disdain for the advance notoriety he had encountered upon his arrival in London for the season. "Now, cut the rub, you two," he demanded in pretended cross humor, determined to unearth more about her. "Tell me her tale, Lewis. I rode to the estate, and it's rack and ruin. Now here she is flitting around society without a care to be seen."

"Wait! Wait! Hold the horses now!" Alfred shouted rudely, drawing rein in front of them to halt their progress. He was becoming most agitated at being ignored. "First of all, which of this year's crop of skirts are we discussing? And why did she fall at your feet, Eastmore? Or your horse's feet, shall we say?" With a snort of laughter at his own humor, he went on to beg, "Come on, you two, give up the tale before I fret myself sober and have to start all over again. Be a terrible waste of good spirits, don't you know."

Rounding on him, Lewis seized the reins of Alfred's mount and thrust his face near to the drunken lord's and spoke in a measured manner. "We speak, my finely foxed friend, of the Lady Eben Pearl of Victor Mall. Now hush, and stop interrupting your betters." Having effectively handled the blinking lord, he turned back to Fitzhugh, only to call back over his shoulder. "And don't get all blue-deviled over it, either!" Flipping back to Fitzhugh again, he said, "Let's see, never had a season till now...can only be seventeen or eighteen at most. Ol' man Victor inherited the title and one of the finest hunter stables, going great guns...until he turned to racers, hard liquor and soft women, bless their sweet hearts...Lost it all! There was a son, killed young in an accident, when the girl was small. Mother went off her nut for a spell and retired to the country. Father never left town...nor his excesses."

"Truly hard up for blunt!" This from Alfred, who was eager to contribute something. "Played deep...deeper than anybody. They say he was so badly dipped...ran through a half million in a year. Can't credit it myself, but that's what they say."

Fitzhugh pondered for a moment. "Eben Pearl... What happened to the father?"

"Viscount... fell through the bottom of his cups and down two flights of stairs, I hear," Alfred continued. "Neck didn't take the roll well, and did him in... just last year. Of course, all this is hearsay, from Freddy Portsymthe... says he's going to dangle after her. But then, he dangles after 'em all. I was abroad... wasn't in on any of this firsthand.

"What's she doing in town—?" Fitzhugh asked, only to have Alfred rush on.

"I hear she needs a husband with warm pockets. I've yet to see her myself, but I hear she's reasonably presentable."

"Presentable! Presentable, he says?" Lewis pulled his horse to a standstill and looked from Alfred to Fitzhugh in mock despair. "That's fair mild for a look at this one. She has my heart in her little hands already, I can tell you that.... If a parson had been there, I'd have been a gone man. Never have I gotten so lost in a pair of bewitching green eyes that deep. And her laugh is like the song of a bird on a fine spring morn..." Lewis put one hand over his heart, as if to keep it from leaving his body straight through his elegantly cut riding coat of robin's-egg superfine.

"Her eyes are blue," Fitzhugh flatly stated, turning the gelding over to his groom. "Now could we please get out of this cold? I could use that toddy." Lewis turned to tilt a querying eyebrow upward at Alfred before following the duke's broad back into the ornate building, and to a table near the back of the prestigious men's club, receiving only a shrug from that small man in return.

"Seriously enough—" Lewis continued as if their jesting conversation hadn't been interrupted by greetings to cronies, refused invitations for card games, and a bet or two settled with knowledge apparently only he contained "—if a gent had the funds to put her estate to rights, it's a fair piece of property, and she comes from a fine old name, though the title dies if she has no son. Her beauty would not be hard to look at over the years. And she is very accomplished...." Lewis was reflecting aloud. Although he had no need to marry for an heir— his brothers were sure to provide those aplenty—it was certain he possessed the funds to right more problems than she possessed . . . and he did admire her greatly.

"You only think her accomplished as it's said she has a deuced way with horses. Although if she proved to ride as well between the sheets, even I might aspire to her hand," Alfred said with a rude sneer, drawing a dark look from Fitzhugh.

"Alfred! Show a bit of decency, old man," Lewis cautioned casually. "Your track record with the ladies is not one to brag of . . ."

"You speak of rumor . . . and 'twas merely a serving girl."

"Rumor, my stepmother's fat foot!"

"True enough, I didn't exactly ask permission once I got her to the bed. . . . Hmmm, died in childbirth nine months later. I was in mourning a very . . . very long month, don't you know?" He giggled into his cup.

"You are a cad, Ellington." Lewis snorted in disgust. "Best you restrain yourself to the learned married matrons with the sense to prevent such scandals. You disgrace the ton."

Alfred raised his glass in a mock toast to Lewis. "Ah, drink to learned women . . . A woman is learned enough for me if she can distinguish her husband's bed from another's. I've never known a woman yet who doesn't cry, 'Oh, wicked fiend' at first, but comes to like it once it's begun. Ah, yes, there's nothing sweeter than a virgin humbled," he bragged drunkenly. "Dear sweet Miss Victor . . . to have her on her knees, begging for my mercy . . ."

Slamming his glass down on the table with enough force to crack the bottom, Fitzhugh drew interested looks from gentlemen the room over eager to wager on the outcome of an argument. Standing, he looked down at Alfred from his great height, every inch the nobleman. A haughty drawl put him far past the dangerous, into the realm of the deadly. "You had best watch the way you speak of a young lady you have yet to meet. Especially in here! I will not hesitate to stand up for her good name in Hyde Park, since she has absence of father or brothers to do so for her."

Fitzhugh had had enough of Lord Ellington for one day, and would not stand for him slurring the girl's name, even if it took a pistol shot to stop him. In fact, his mood at the moment would be greatly improved if he smashed a fist through the smirking man's face. He remembered too well the stricken look on Eben's face when she'd realized . . . recognized him as the man who had claimed her innocence. He would not let this offensive work of humanity defame her. Alfred dropped his eyes with a shrug of his shoulders.

His aggressive stance and dangerous look having effectively silenced Alfred, Fitzhugh started for the door, ignoring the fact that the three of them had planned a very different sort of evening for themselves, including a romp and dozen at Long's with a party of sporting friends, whose tastes were apt to lead them to entertain themselves later with a visit to the back slums of Tothill Fields, where they would join with the roughest elements of society in reeking gin palaces, or to attend a badger-baiting or a cockfight in the pits of London Market. Altogether the sort of rough evening that would guarantee a sore head from blue ruin the following morning and possibly bruised knuckles from some sort of brawl.

Fitzhugh had sported with this sort of entertainment for many years in the military, but experienced surprise to find the same rough activity in the company of titled gentlemen. The society of men who feared meeting the grim reaper the following day at the hands of a foreign enemy, thousands of miles from home and loved ones, tended to generate a desperate brand of fun. And while understandable of these men, it lost some of its tolerance as the sport of bored gentlemen of the upper class. This was a part of town bronze that had put the taste of brass in his mouth in an amazingly short time. Fitzhugh was unsure he could enjoy a more refined society, but as of this moment he resolved to change some of the circles in which he moved.

Ellington's crass remarks had quite put him off, and he was not altogether sorry to quit the evening early. With a somewhat tired sigh, he swung to the back of the gelding. As he turned toward Pall Mall, a second thought occurred to him. It might very well destroy the reputation of Master Beans, to have the tulip of the ton for whom he was responsible spend a quiet evening with his feet propped before the home fires . . . and with his own brandy in hand! The thought rather amused Fitzhugh and brought a wry smile to his lips, easing the black expression on his face.

* * *

A hovering footman stood near the table, under the direction of the butler. Haverty cleared his throat to draw attention from the wool-gathering duke.

"Yes, Haverty?"

"If your grace is quite finished . . ."

"Oh . . . yes, of course," he answered.

Rising from the table, he removed to the far end of the library. Quite satisfied, he settled himself into a wing-backed chair, his slippered feet propped toward the fire, and a brandy decanter near his elbow. The flames reflected on his gleaming hair and cast shadows upward on his pensive face. Under the butler's watchful eye, the footman quickly cleared the light supper of baked quail, whitefish in cream sauce, slices of lamb in aspic, fresh-baked rolls and a compote of fresh fruit, hastily prepared by a surprised cook, and served by a surprised Haverty. Having been divested of his outdoor things and attired in lounging trousers and ruby velvet robe by a surprised Beans, Fitzhugh had felt the obligatory guilt for destroying their illusions, as he had correctly ascertained the situation of an unplanned evening at home. Living up to the standards of one's servants was such a bothersome chore! But now he relaxed and directed his mind to the real dilemma.

Eben Pearl. What a strange name, and how well it suited her. As best he could calculate, the day he had blundered upon her must have been one of her last in the country. Having just lost her father, finding the family fortune nonexistent, bravely shouldering the full burden while bearing up for an unstable mother, must all have been devastating for the young woman. It explained her reaction to the death of a beloved old mare . . . probably the last straw in a very heavy load. He had seen the same helpless overload of emotions in men during campaigns. The fighting day after day, watching friends and brothers fall one after the other, took a toll upon a strong man. What could the circumstances do to a young, gently reared miss?

Fitzhugh leaned his head back against the chair and closed his eyes. He was a man noted for being soft in the heart for animals, little children and helpless women . . . but he had seduced her. How that rubbed him raw! How could he have mistaken that regal set of her head as belonging to a servant girl? Breeches or not? A slight smile broke the sober look on his face. How could he have mistaken her for a lad? Breeches or not?

He sobered again. He, of all men, should have recognized the grasping of a desperate human for anyone to hold them, to take the pain away, for however short the interval. Her reaction to his lovemaking had not been passion, as he had mistakenly thought. She had merely needed something to block the misery, to deaden the pain. He felt like the worst kind of cad. When everything else was being taken from her, he had taken from her, as well. And then offered her a bauble for her maidenhead! It was no small wonder she had bolted like a frightened rabbit. What a heartless bounder he must seem to her.

With a groan, Fitzhugh refilled his own glass, having dismissed the disgruntled Beans. But he admired her spirit. The strength she must possess, to be seduced on top of all the other disappointments she must have endured in a short period, then remove to town and determinedly seek a fortune to put her home back together again. How despondent ... how bleak ... her eyes had turned when she'd realized he recognized her. How searching her look had been at first ... She was probably thinking now her chances of a good marriage were nil.

His thoughts shifted. How that girl could ride! The magic she instilled in an animal, such as he had only seen in the deserts of Arabia, where the horses gave their all for love and trust of a man rather than to escape the pain of a spur. What a magnificent pair she and that brute of a black stallion made, for now it gave him no doubt that it had been Eben this morning in the park. No doubt at all! A grin appeared when he recalled her groom covering for her.... Mute, indeed! To think of it, the way they all had protected her when he questioned whether anyone knew of a wild young maid riding astride in men's breeches. Somehow the loyalty she received from her people pleased him. It made her seem less alone.

Fitzhugh stood unsteadily and paced around the small rosewood library. Idly touching leather-bound books, spinning the ornately carved globe, and fiddling with implements

on his desk, his eyes glazed…thoughts far away. What would
be her fate? To be married, of course. To Ottobon? Or
drunken Ellington, or to some pompous, odious old man?
Hadn't Portsmythe threatened to dangle for her? To be caged
in a drawing room, presiding over afternoon teas, and attending socials to converse with flighty, dull dowagers? Somehow
he could not see Eben in any of these roles. She only fitted in
his mind astride a blooded horse and free. Totally free to express all the emotions that he sensed were there. He had exchanged so few words with her in actuality, but he felt he knew
her. . . .

Fleeting glimpses of her raced through his mind. The Eben
laughing with the red foal, the joy in her face when she had
first glanced up at him. Then the distorted look of pain when
she had realized the old mare was gone. Her deep grief, with
all the misery expressed in racking sobs. Her soft, tear-streaked
face cupped between his hands, those amazing eyes awash with
tears, making each seem a lake of cool water. Her look of surprise at his first taste of her full lips. A groan escaped Fitzhugh as desire flooded his loins. The unfocused look in those
eyes when he had lain with her in the straw and touched her,
extracting tiny sounds. The very feel of her beneath him . . .
cushioning his weight.

Moving abruptly back to the brandy decanter, he poured a
healthy drop and downed it. Damn her! He pictured the Eben
protected by the people on her land with mute silence. The wild
Eben, crouched over the neck of a flying blood, her bottom in
the air, giving him the dust from her heels. The tame Eben, in
a gray dress with saucy red trim, laughing up at Lewis after a
gallop in the park. Eben, eyes huge with shock when she had
realized it was, in truth, him. It was as if he had a picture album of Eben in his head, and the only picture in his album he
did not like was Eben smiling up at another man. . . .

Fitzhugh pulled himself from his wool-gathering to drop into
the chair. First of all, in polite society, he owed her his name
for compromising her, taking advantage of her. . . . 'Twas the
honorable thing. Raising his glass, he toasted himself for being an honorable man. Secondly, he was to take a wife anyway…and damn her, he just could not picture her with anyone
else. The very essence of her was burned deeply into his brain,

so that he would never be without her. That he toasted, also. Tomorrow morning, at the first decent hour, he would knock on her door and beg an interview. He would ask her to accept him, and his fortune, in answer to her dilemma. Pouring another brandy, he congratulated himself on his plan. He smiled, slightly askew, at the thought of her gratitude. The tears that would come into her beautiful eyes at his magnanimity in saving her ... in not betraying her to society. The image of her lying with one slim leg out of her breeches flitted through his mind. There would be no long engagement. No, sir! Definitely no long engagement.

What a fantastic wife she would make ... what strong sons she would give him. In truth, she might already be carrying his child. What a wonderful idea that was.... He drank deeply in a toast to his son. And with their mutual love of blooded horses, her skill and caring mixed with his ... what a breeding stable they would build. Hunters, once again, at Victor Mall, and racers at Eastmore Park. It would be a fulfilling life they would have together. She would be his Eben Pearl and reign over an empire with him. He drank to the empire. What a master plan!

First decent hour tomorrow ... no, first light they'd breakfast together after he told her. Such a long time to wait... Why not now? He'd just saddle a horse and ride over. She'd forgive him once she heard his offer. He could not wait to see her gratitude ... to feel her kisses of happiness. No, sir! He'd not wait! It must be tonight!

"Beans!" He needed help dressing. Must look top-drawer when he proposed. "B-Beansh ... come here!" He was having some trouble with his tongue. Damn brandy! "Beansh!"

"I'm right here, your grace. Looks a pickle we're in, eh?" Beans easily raised the duke to his feet and guided him toward the bedchamber. "We'll just sleep it off and hope our head is sittin' on our shoulders on the morn."

"No, no, no! Not bed, Beansh! Gotta go out. Help dress me. Tie me a cravat to weep for. Call my groom." Fitzhugh attempted to fend off the hands disrobing him, and make his man understand he had to go out. He was going to propose to Lady Eben Victor and he needed a horse.

"That's fine, guv. I'll go order us a horse. Everything will be just as you say. Now, lay down here and rest for a bit, and I'll see to everything."

Beans expertly stripped Fitzhugh and tucked him into bed, with a worried frown on his face. Something sure had the master tucked up. Something mighty heavy on his mind.

"Eben..." Fitzhugh muttered just once before drifting into a drunken sleep. Beans' frown instantly turned into a grin from ear to ear.

"No trouble...just a bit o' fluff!"

Chapter Nine

A hazy sun shone in the sky, and here and there patches of the frozen road were thawing. March was bowing in tempestuously, melting the snow on tree branches, reducing too many of the roads to a sea of mud. The London *Gazette* printed the usual indignant letters of protest from readers who felt that the paving of all roads was a necessity that should be postponed no longer. In the little fenced park that formed the center of Grosvenor Square, a willow tree leaned with the wind, its tracery of branches streaming outward like a woman's long tresses.

The hour was just barely ten, and the duke of Eastmore stood on the granite steps of Vicroy House, having sent an even earlier note requesting an interview at this time. He was premium, from his highly polished Wellingtons and biscuit-coloured pantaloons to his Weston saffron coat, carefully protected by a greatcoat with a fur-lined rolled collar. Everything about him bespoke the gentlemen of fashion, from his snowy neckcloth tied à la coachman to his sun-streaked hair dressed the gleaming Brutus, now hidden beneath a beaver topper, which he held against the thieving wind. His sun-browned brow was furrowed deeply with the raging remnants of the previous brandy evening, and his mood not the best, considering the task he had set for himself this morning.

He was pleased to note that Vicroy House appeared in better repair than Victor Mall. Of sharply defined white limestone block with clean-cut edges, it rose four floors, with majestic granite steps entering on the second floor. Waiting for admittance, he idly watched his groom take the blooded Arab gelding through an arch to the side of the house, obviously to the mews in the back.

An elderly butler, in correct black livery and an appropriately arrogant posture, opened the door and quickly passed Fitzhugh through the chilly hallway into the front salon, where a welcome fire burned behind dull brass andirons. His eyes swept the Aubusson carpet, the white-and-gold stucco work over the rose-patterned wallpaper, the elegant Grecian sofas and Louis XV armchairs, to come to rest on the portrait of Eben Pearl.

Stunned for a moment, he mused, it must be a very recent portrait, to be so like her as he knew her. The ruby gown, with its transparency of black lace created a subtle, sensual outline of her figure. The straight eyebrows set off the direct look in her eyes, though the artist had mistakenly painted them lapis lazuli. Eben's eyes were more brilliant... more alive. What a magnificent woman she was, he thought, stepping closer to view the artist's signature. Gian Antonio! Impossible! Startled, he quickly stepped back to view the regal lady in red once again.

"My great-grandmother, the Viscountess Eben Pearl Norview Victor."

The whispery voice sounded behind him, causing him to spin about. He paused before speaking, to feast his eyes on the girl as if seeing her for the first time... imagining greeting her thus every morning... well, not quite thus... not at this early hour, at least. In the silence, the wind could be heard moaning down the chimneys and whistling at every crack of window or door to which it could put its blustery mouth. On such a day, it would be good to remain inside, snug and warm by the fire with this beauty. Yes, the step he was to take this day was in the right direction, he conceded to himself, relishing her gratitude, for her very stance in the doorway bespoke of wary tension.

"I thought it a recently done portrait of yourself. The resemblance is that striking," Fitzhugh casually announced, watching her cross into the room, gesturing for him to be seated on the sofa opposite the one she selected.

"I have asked Hastings to bring tea, your grace...unless you prefer coffee, of course. I am aware a taste for the brew is growing in popularity."

Eben kept her voice in a controlled, throaty tone, not daring to look fully at his face. She was not ready to meet those eyes just yet. Even though to do so might give her an early indication of her fate at his hands.

"Tea is most acceptable."

Inclining her head slightly, Eben cleared her throat nervously. "My mother begs you excuse her, due to the early hour. My aunt, Lady Compton, shall join us presently." Although the truth of the matter was that her mother knew nothing of the requested interview and Eben had just this moment sent notice of the duke's presence to her aunt, thus buying herself a half hour at best to determine whether disaster or reprieve awaited her.

"Then I will come directly to the point, Miss Victor, and we will save the chitchat for when that lady joins us." Fitzhugh perched suddenly on the edge of the opposing striped sofa, facing Eben with an earnest, aggressive posture. "What I have to say is best said in privacy."

Startled for a moment, although she herself desired nothing less than to dispense with pleasantries, she leaned back slightly and stared wide-eyed into his amber eyes, noting for the first time the sunbursts of fine lines at the corners, as if he had spent a number of years squinting into strong sunlight. What had he to say? A chill crept over her body, leaving gooseflesh on her arms. She was lost for sure.

For a second, Fitzhugh stilled, lost in her eyes. So blue they slaked thirst like a cool drink of water, and framed with sooty lashes so thick and long they shadowed the tender flesh underneath. Her mouth was dry—from nerves, he assessed—for a pink tongue flicked over trembling lips, lips he wanted to taste again and again and again. Now, clearing his throat, he glanced away before such thoughts carried him into areas best reserved for later.

"Let us speak plainly. First of all, I greatly regret the incident at your estate . . . in the country," he said, clearing his throat yet again. "I realize I acted as a bounder and a cad. I took gross advantage of your innocence, and I am prepared to make amends. I am an honorable man, Miss Victor, and will pay the piper for my transgressions . . . having danced grandly and thoroughly to his music, so to speak."

Eben could only stare at this man who would speak thus to her. If only he weren't so incredibly handsome and up close again, if only he didn't seem so very large and overpowering, she might be able to better understand what he was about. Oh, her thoughts would stray, like her eyes, over that sensual mouth. Her mind refused to act normally, and while she was able to follow his words as he spoke, the meaning of those words took longer to affect her.

"Amends? Transgressions?" she said nervously. "I—I do not understand what you im-imply."

Fitzhugh abruptly stood, rubbing his throbbing headache. Damn this pain, just when he needed to be clearheaded! He walked around the sofa and turned to face Eben again. Studying the wide-eyed expression on her lovely face for an infinitesimal moment to discern if she spoke the truth and was truly uncomprehending, or was merely playing the missish debutante—the latter of which would have set his teeth on edge, as he was finding the going thick as hell as it was. Her startled expression settled his direction. Taking a deep, steadying breath, Fitzhugh backtracked and attempted to speak more slowly and patiently—not a thing to do at ease, as the shortness of the time allotted this private interview pressed most urgently.

"As you are aware, Miss Victor, I have recently come in-to the title...and all else...from my great-uncle. I have plans...plans to establish a racing stable at the Park. For which I purchased the hunter mares from Victor Mall...at Tattersall's," he explained, pausing for a comment she did not give. "It is imperative I marry and produce sons, an heir for the title, you see? I understand your circumstances...your father... Damn, girl! I am offering for your hand...your hand in marriage!" Fitzhugh blurted out, harried lest the elder lady arrived and polite conversation intervened. He knew he was bungling it badly, but forged bravely onward. "So, what say you? Quickly, girl, before your aunt gets down here and the teacups begin to rattle!"

Eben rose slowly and walked to the mantel to study the portrait, gathering her thoughts, not sure what she felt, or rather not understanding why she felt only...insult. And that insult quickly turned into anger. The utter and flagrant gall of the man! Drawing herself up to her full height, she turned to face Fitzhugh. Her color heightened, and anyone acquainted with her might have stepped back at least one step, but the duke, taken in by her eyes, held deceptively wide with missish innocence, stood his ground in blissful ignorance.

"Pray, your grace, if I am to understand you properly, you are offering for my hand in marriage to atone for seducing me, an innocent maid, in a pile of dirty straw, while I was prostrate with grief. And I am to understand that you are a bounder and a cad to have behaved as such?" Eben tilted her head and raised one ebony eyebrow in question. Fitzhugh, not completely understanding why he was so discomfited all of a sudden, slowly inclined his head toward her and cleared his throat once again. "Also, if I am truly comprehending, you are going to breed a new type of racer, despoiling the blood of the fine hunter mares you purchased from Victor Mall, at far below their true value, I might add, because I was in dire straits and had to move them quickly. And, since you propose to use Victor Mall mares as your brood stock, you might as well purchase the daughter of the house to brood your nursery. Especially as you have tried her and she is acceptable. Do I understand you correctly, your grace?"

"My dear Miss Victor..." Fitzhugh was taken aback at her interpretation. He had seriously bungled this whole matter. But Eben was to give him no time to defend his position.

"Since we are speaking plainly and in a rush...let me explain myself clearly, Eastmore," she said, deliberately neglecting his title to emphasize her disdain for it. "There must be no misunderstanding my feelings for your purpose here this day." Walking toward him, she stopped close enough to him that he might see the fire in her azure eyes, as anger made them blaze. When she spoke again, her voice was low and threatening. "While it is very true I must marry for money, that does not mean that I am allowed no choice in the matter. When I do marry, it will not be to a man who tumbles stable maids in the straw or parades with well-known lightskirts in a public park. I am well-informed, by my father's deplorable behavior, of such activities carried out in gin palaces and cockfight parlors, as well as secluded little town houses on Chelsea Road for one's most current mistress, and I abhor them all! As to that afternoon in the barn, pray do not flog yourself. What was given to you, was given freely by me. You owe me nothing for it!"

A moment of silence held them, and then a slight, sardonic smile touched Fitzhugh's lips as he reassessed this young girl

braced before him as if preparing for a brawl. Gently he placed
his thumb in the hollow of her throat, over the wildly beating
pulse there. He felt her start but she made no move to step
backward, lest he think her frightened.

"I have done my duty as I see it. If you choose to fling my
offer back into my face and make light with your own reputation, please allow me to be the first to offer my attendance...if you wish to be so free with your favors in the future.
I could be induced, with little encouragement, to settle an establishment on Chelsea Road for you...if you so desire, for
that seems the direction you are heading."

"Y-you..." With an indrawn hiss, Eben struck out at him.
He caught her wrist in midair, in a bone-crushing grip.

"An open palm stings, my dear, but you would do well to
think first...for I might return in kind!" he warned harshly.
"As it would seem we have already established my character
but moments ago."

"Let go of me, Eastmore!"

She did not deign to struggle against his cruel fingers, but
stood looking up at him with contemptuous eyes. Fitzhugh
coolly studied the angry flush in her cheeks. Whatever could
have happened to the tearful, grateful reception he had expected? He was angry with himself for being fool enough to
place himself in this position...on top of a blinding head, no
less.

"I think not quite yet," he drawled.

"Damn you to bloody hell, then!" she gritted, trying to tear
her wrist from his grasp, with little success.

Fitzhugh's jaw tightened. He was no longer amused. "You
little witch..." he said softly, dangerously.

Eben mistakenly did not heed his tight-lipped expression,
but proceeded to provoke further. "I suppose I must take that
as a compliment of sorts, coming as it does from a man like
you, who delights only in insult!"

"And what do you know of men like me, infant?"

"Y-you...not the kind of man I must deal with! Your rattle
warns of a snake of the most despicable..."

Without warning, Fitzhugh jerked her to him. A ruthless
arm pinned her against his chest, and her chin was caught in a
vise. His breath was warm on her shocked face. For a moment, Eben felt real fear.

"And in that you are so wrong." The icy glitter in his eyes was frightening. "Insult only? Nay, I delight in much more where you are concerned."

He lowered his head to take her mouth with brutal lips. Eben struggled wildly, beating at him with her fists. His hard fingers bit deeper into her chin, his body bearing her arching backward. His mouth was scalding, merciless. Her senses reeled. She shuddered even as her lips parted beneath his. Immediately the pressure from his mouth gentled. She felt his arms loosen. His hand shifted to the front of her bodice to explore, tracing fire with his touch on her nipples. Sudden desire leaped to life within her, and she jerked from his grasp. Two quick steps backward took her safely beyond his immediate reach. Her breath came in gasps that were almost sobs.

"You are abominable!"

"I applaud the perfect blend of fear and outrage, infant."

The arrival of tea prevented him from advancing those two steps, as was his intent. Hastings cleared his throat and arranged the tray on the low table with disturbed side glances at Eben's angry face and the duke's defiant stance. Just then, Lady Adair sailed into the room.

"Your grace! It is such a great pleasure to finally make your acquaintance. I must say you've certainly been the talk of the town. Ah, tea ... Eben, please pour for His Grace."

Such inane conversation, after that brutal assault—and that was the only way Eben could think of it—was insane at best. Glancing at the duke, she took note of his cool appraisal. Raising her chin, she refused to allow him the victory of seeing her flee the room in tears, as she so desperately wanted to do at that moment.

"Yes, Aunt Addie," she managed to say. Carefully she seated herself before the massive sterling tea service and attempted to pour with violently trembling hands. Lady Adair seated herself to the right of her niece and, beaming at the duke, waved him to the sofa facing Eben...displaying her niece appropriately to this most eligible lord.

"It is so pleasant to see someone else out and about this early in the day. People are such lie-abeds and truly miss the best part of the day," Lady Adair declared to the company.

Eben glanced at her aunt in astonishment. That lady was usually in bed with her morning paper and tea until noon, at the very least. She did not hazard a look toward Fitzhugh, to see if he was buying such an obvious load of flummery. By means of stern concentration, she managed to hand her aunt a cup of hot, strongly brewed tea, knowing she must be nearly desperate for want of it. Rising this early could only have been a severe shock to her constitution.

"I do apologize, Lady Cromwell. I came early to... I mean to say..." Fitzhugh floundered, clearing his throat, not readily drawing upon a satisfactory excuse for the early call, when he had quite expected champagne and strawberries to toast upcoming nuptials.

"His Grace called so early, dear Aunt—" Eben paused with a narrowing of eyes and a positively wicked smile on her delicious mouth "—to offer his escort for the Golden Ball tonight. He would have called sooner, I'm sure, had he been privy to the announcement that we were in residence. Just to be neighborly, you understand."

"Oh, what a magnificent idea!" exclaimed Lady Adair, beaming anew at the handsome duke. Her thoughts ran rampant. My, the tongues would wag on this night! What a triumph for Eben! To enter the first main event of the season on the arm of the legendary, much-gossiped-about duke of Eastmore! Such a delight... to see the faces!

"I did, of course, explain to him that we had already made arrangements and would not require his attendance," Eben continued, not taking her eyes off his face, ready to enjoy the first hint of discomfort there.

"Oh...I—I understand," Lady Adair stammered, clearly not understanding in the least. She glanced from the duke to her niece, for the first time noting the tense lines of Eben's body, which insinuated there was more to this call than was being told.

Fitzhugh's eyes narrowed slightly, and a tight smile appeared on his lips. Sliding back on the sofa, affecting a much more relaxed pose, he crossed one elegant leg over the other and joined in the game with a certain degree of prank.

"But, dear Lady Cromwell, I refused to hear that any other arrangements could be as comfortable as what I could offer, and therefore have persuaded Miss Victor to allow me the extreme pleasure of your company for the ball." Fitzhugh enjoyed watching the lovely face rapidly change expressions. She was so obviously struggling with a difficult decision...give in to the desire to verbally murder him and have to explain the situation, or remain in her aunt's good graces. "Just to be neighborly, you understand."

"B-but—" Eben began, only to be interrupted.

Fitzhugh's smile widened, and he pushed her further. "Also, your lovely niece has agreed to stand up in the first set with me...but, she insists, only if it contains a waltz." Eben's head snapped up as her aunt exclaimed in delight. His smile threatened to break into a laugh, and he went one step farther yet. "As well as take supper upon my arm." Her eyes narrowed to slits in threat, and Fitzhugh could have sworn her mouth almost snarled. His obvious amusement at her expense did not help the situation. "It plans to be a most entertaining evening. Most entertaining, indeed."

Lady Adair was thoroughly confused by the interplay between these two, but determined to make sense of an opportunity too good to be sidestepped. "Oh...splendid!" She beamed at the duke, and then frowned at Eben, wondering again about the forbidding thundercloud gathering on her niece's face. "Eben, where are your manners? Lord Eastmore has no tea! You really must, your grace, sample some of the rum tea cakes. Eben?"

She obeyed her aunt, her hands shaking as she lifted the heavy teapot to fill a cup for the disgusting man. She fairly flung several of the tea cakes onto a delicate china plate. But before she could hand it to him, he halted her with an upraised hand.

"If you please, Miss Victor," he said in a soft voice, "I really do not care for tea cake. Perhaps I could try that delicious-looking almond torte." His wide grin threatened to burst into full laughter as he watched the delightful play of emotions on the young girl's face.

"This has g-gone far e-enough..." she stammered, her hand trembling visibly. Lady Adair deftly removed the cup and saucer from her hand just as she would have flung it at his head.

"Whatever is amiss with your manners today, Eben Pearl? Pray, give His Lordship whatever it is he wants."

Unnoticed by Lady Adair, Fitzhugh taunted Eben by allowing his bold amber eyes, eyes she would again label as predatory, wander up the length of her figure, pausing to linger on her full breasts. Despite her anger, she felt a strange sinking sensation drop into the pit of her stomach, and her nipples responded by hardening, as they had but a short time before to his touch. She blushed violently.

The duke had no difficulty imagining what murderous thoughts were chasing behind Eben's lovely brow. Her vivid blue eyes shot sparks every time they chanced to glance in his direction. So the little kitten has claws! Apparently he had underestimated her strengths.... No average missish girl here. But this time the little minx had outsmarted herself. She was proving to be a delightful diversion. The temptation was too great to let her off easy.

"And as she desires to please me, she has agreed to drive out with me, not tomorrow, as you will undoubtedly be resting from the ball, but the day after. I have a new team of matched grays that I like to show off..."

Eben's head again snapped up, wide-eyed. "You own that team?" Lewis had told her of those matched grays, and they were generally acknowledged to be one of the best in London. For a second, she lost her black look and became what she really was...an unsophisticated country girl of seventeen years with a love of blooded cattle. "Lord, what I would give for a turn at that, sir!" Then, remembering her anger, she blushed and dropped her head in confusion, biting her lip and blasting herself for a nitwit at the same time.

"My, it does sound as if you have a bevy of delights planned," her aunt exclaimed. "I..."

"I say, Lady Cromwell, if your niece drives as well as she rides, I might let her take the ribbons herself. That is, Miss Victor, if you are so inclined?" As much as Fitzhugh enjoyed baiting her, he did not want to see her dive headfirst into hot water. Time to relieve the anger just a little, before she blew up and disgraced herself. He had unwittingly interrupted Lady Adair's prattle, having been totally unaware she was even speaking. "And with that settled, I shall not take up any more of the morning. I shall call for you promptly at nine o'clock." Rising with the charming grin upon his face that had successfully melted feminine hearts on more than one occasion, Fitzhugh took his leave of the ladies. "Until then, Lady Cromwell...Miss Victor." With a final bow, he disappeared out the door behind Hastings.

Lady Adair stared after him with her mouth open, speechless. Eben knew her aunt was truly frazzled if she could find no ready words. She herself could only shake her own head slightly, surprised at herself, torn between outrage and another, more confusing, emotion she could not define. Could it be anticipation? Her head ached terribly with unbidden thoughts.

The duke of Eastmore had just offered for her hand in marriage, and she had refused in a fit of anger. She was very aware she had to marry for money. Why was she so insulted, when he had offered the very thing she had ventured to town to achieve? It had so angered her when he implied . . . that his only thought was to buy her and salve his conscious at the same time. But wasn't she here to sell herself? Oh . . . she was all sixes and sevens. Nothing seemed to happen right for her lately. Why, oh, why, had she baited him about the ball . . . for now she was not only attending on his arm, but dancing the first set with him, supping with him . . . *and* she was driving out with him in two days' time! All this when she really wished nothing more than to never set eyes on the rotten bounder again in this lifetime!

"Well! Upon my word . . ." Lady Adair, at last, had found her voice. "Just what do you make of that? I didn't even know you had been introduced to His Lordship. Much less had time to develop such an obvious dislike connected with him."

Eben looked for a way out of the room . . . and this conversation. She did not want to discuss . . . him! Nor did she wish to spend the next three hours dissecting the call, word by word, expression by expression, implication by implication, until its true purpose was discovered. "Lord Ottobon introduced us during our jog in the park."

"Eben, that is not a proper introduction! What will people say?" her aunt gasped. "You really must stay above scandal, or all is lost."

"I quite imagine people will say a great deal, dear Aunt Addie, when I enter the Golden Ball on the arm of the duke of Eastmore . . . a man most have yet to even see but most certainly have included in their daily gossip for the past year!"

"I say, Eben Pearl . . . you surprise me. You are taking to this game quite readily. I had not even thought you aware of that aspect. You shall be most sought-after when it becomes very clear at the start of the season that Eastmore is interested." Lady Adair fairly clapped her hands in triumph and added, "I think we can overlook the slight irregularity of the introduction—just this once, you understand.''

"I rather thought we could,'' Eben replied, with a tight smile. "And now . . . I think I shall ride this morning.''

"Eben! No one promenades on the day of a ball. You should be resting and conserving your strength for tonight. What will people think?''

"Dear Aunt Addie, I am not just anyone, and I have strength enough for ten of these lemon-faced misses of the ton . . . *and* I have no intention of promenading! I intend to gallop and gallop and gallop until I am at peace, regardless of what people think!'' With these stern words, Eben marched out of the room, leaving Lady Adair staring after her with a worried frown.

"Whatever could have put that burr under her tail so early in the morning, and after such a triumph as having Lord Eastmore call?''

Getting no satisfactory reply from the empty room, she turned her attention back to the triumph part of the morning and rose to rush upstairs to inform her sister. Then, perhaps, to retire back to her bed to finish her sleep . . . if she could sleep, with the thoughts racing through her head. Oh, my, yes! Tonight's ball was going to be a delight beyond all comprehension!

Chapter Ten

Eben stared around her bedchamber, attempting to see everything with adult eyes instead of childhood memories. The tied back draperies matched the upholstery on the two Sheraton armchairs, which matched the counterpane, which matched the bedcurtains, which matched the canopy of the oversize bed...every piece in the same cabbage-rose print, and each with the inner folds three times as bright as the faded outer folds. The Brussels carpet was badly burned in front of the fireplace, where a careless servant had dropped hot coals, and the white-painted stucco trim around the mantel was chipped and missing its scrollwork in many places. The rosewood dressing table, with its shirred skirt, and the rosewood washstand, with its porcelain bowl sprigged in tiny pink buds, were the only pieces of furniture in the entire room that didn't need attention from the refinishers.

Eben focused on each defect. She must see every worn spot, every stain, every faded flower. She must see...so that she could tolerate this evening. She must place reason for being paraded before the tulips of the ton, for having them judge her merits and place her on a scale along with the other debutantes—comparing her height with that of Miss Petite, her full breasts to those of Miss Flat-chest, and the slimness of her hips with that of Miss Plump. Eben closed her eyes and clenched her teeth, deploring the whole idea.

"I swear I shall lay out the first one of them who questions the soundness of my teeth! I shall set them upon their ear!" she informed Grady, who had attended her toilette with great feline interest. "This can only be compared to Tattersall's, and nothing can make me enjoy it!" She paced to the bed and absently scratched behind the cat's ears, to his immense delight. It was so unfair that men with fortunes had the choice, while she, with her numerous pressing responsibilities, had none. Actually, she was not even to be allowed the time, according to the seriousness of the letters from Mr. Vandevilt, to induce someone to fall in love with her. She must strengthen her resolve to find a husband and get into his pockets as promptly as possible.

"After that show today with the most eligible of the eligibles, it is very apparent that I need more help than Aunt Addie can give me, for I missed the mark there. Not a month into this cursed season, and I've declined the offer of the catch of the year! Oh, Grady, my fine feline friend, I need a friend so badly. Someone to advise me as to the direction I should take, so that my temper doesn't sink my ship before it's set sail. But . . . we'll just have to take the fences as they come, won't we?"

Turning with a new straightening of her spine and a determined look in her eyes, Eben left the room to join the others downstairs. Eastmore had just arrived, and she knew he would not want to keep his team standing.

Even though there were socials and parties before this ball, all were merely a preliminary. The Golden Ball, held each year at Almack's, was considered the official beginning of the season. The decorations, down to the wax of the candles, were golden, and the dress code represented months of nightmares for every dressmaker in London, for every lady in the ton had been bearing down upon their doors, beseeching and demanding a golden gown that would stand out from all the other golden gowns. The rivalry was quite the thing, and the competition was fearsome.

Almack's was ablaze with lights. It was a splendid ballroom paneled in pale gold brocade, with matching draperies swagged from the French windows that marched the length of the walls. Crystal sconces with golden candles burning, set in niches between the windows, battled for brilliance with the three chandeliers. When one entered the arched doorway, the dazzling sight of muslin, silk and satin gowns in all manner of gold, of glittering jewels, of plumed headdresses waving gracefully in the air against the black relief of the gentlemen's eveningwear, all swaying to the music, leaped into one's eyes. Eben caught her breath at the fairy-tale sight before her. Her childlike reaction, when the popular response would have been one of carefully expressed boredom, delighted Fitzhugh, and he smiled indulgently down upon her. A smile that quite took her breath away and caused her to glance away in confusion.

The entrance was a dozen or so red-carpeted steps higher than the polished dance floor, so that the dancers could observe each new arrival. It staged but the first of the many opportunities of the evening for the ton to judge and speculate on their peers. To contemplate the direction of possible scandals, the candidates for marriages, and which members might conceivably be the most entertaining to observe throughout the season.

Descending the stairs on the arm of His Grace, Lord Fitzhugh Eastmore, caused just the stir Eben had earlier predicted. Heads craned, and more than one dancer missed a step, jeopardizing the balance of their partners. Matrons fairly bumped heads in their urgency to whisper in their neighbor's ear. The music surrounded Eben, and suddenly she wished to waltz the night away. How she could enjoy this, if only the underlying purpose did not weigh so heavily upon her slim shoulders.

With a wide smile and nods in all directions, Lady Adair frantically whispered in Eben's ear. "Remember, no more than two dances with any one partner, no matter who, and no waltzing until you have greeted the three patronesses." No sooner had the words left her mouth than . . .

"I believe this first set is promised to me, Miss Victor . . ."

Fitzhugh grasped her waist and spun her out onto the dance floor into a waltz, leaving Lady Adair with her mouth dropped for a heartbeat before she recovered herself to nod approvingly after them. Holding her lightly, he proved to be an excellent dancer, and the couple made an appealing sight as they disappeared into the crowd.

The laughing eyes never left her own as, with her firmly in his grasp, Fitzhugh led her through the steps of the waltz, his hand resting lightly on her waist, yet seeming to burn through her bodice. His smile matched hers as he whirled her gracefully about the floor until she felt as if she was dancing on the air above the parquet. The heady fragrance of eau de cologne, the firmness of his steps in this first dance, the deep vibration in his chest as he hummed the melody, lulled her, and it took great effort not to step close enough to lay her head against that broad, well-formed chest she remembered so well.

"So, my little cat is enjoying herself."

It took all her will to continue in the steps of the dance, so complete was her surprise at his question, though her smile did not slip. Her wish to answer honestly was quelled when she noted his smug expression. Along with a silent resolve to not give in to this man's false charm, her smile stiffened.

"Pet names, after your deplorable behavior, my lord?" she asked, slowly digging her nails into his palm until he winced.

"So, Eben, you are a little cat. Or shall I beg your permission to speak your Christian name on such short notice? For all that I feel I . . . know you so well." The amber eyes shifted to the exposed tops of her breast, which pleased him with a delightful pinkening.

Eben found herself torn between anger and exasperation at this man. Nothing in her upbringing . . . her limited experience with the men in her country life . . . prepared her for the wild variety of emotions he evoked. She seemed thwarted in every attempt to protect herself from him. She knew, from the looks they inspired as a couple, that she should be swelled with pride at being so envied by the ladies who must content themselves with pasty-faced, nondescript suitors and spouses. She also knew, as if they were all whispering in her ear, that they would gladly trade places with her, to be held so closely by this ruggedly handsome lion of a gentleman with the predator eyes.

In truth, she did feel wonderful in his arms. If only he weren't intent on spoiling this dance for her. If only the smile he beamed down upon her were genuine, instead of taunting. She found, suddenly, that she deeply longed for it to be genuine. So much so, she missed a step in surprise at her realization, but found herself quickly swept back into the rhythm of the dance by his powerful arms, which nearly lifted her off her feet as he spun her about.

"Do not falter at the fence now, my beauty. You may have refused my offer, but I am still in the game, though we shall play by your rules at present. I laid down the rules for our first game . . . if you remember clearly, as I do," Fitzhugh reminded her.

Eben said nothing, staring away in an attempt to avoid those mocking eyes. Strange, she thought, that he should use that phrase, when she herself had thought it such a short time ago.

Was she indeed faltering at her fences because of this man? Was he making her just crazy enough to lose sight of her purpose here? She tried to focus her thoughts on the faded and frayed bedchamber, but that brought thoughts that fueled her blush.

"I have discovered the secrets of your family," he continued when she did not speak. "Though, with your father's excesses, it truly was not a secret."

Eben shifted her gaze to his for a moment, then asked flatly, "Do you always insinuate yourself so swiftly into the private affairs of your dancing partners, your grace?"

Fitzhugh shook his head, pleased that she was choosing to spar with him. Whispering so that she must attend him closely to hear, he replied, "Only when I have made up my mind that my dancing partner shall become my bed partner, Eben Pearl . . . with or without the benefit of banns being posted."

"The d-devil you say!" she sputtered. This time she did stop dancing, and the color faded from her face. But Fitzhugh gathered her in his arms with an embrace that took her breath away, spinning her through the other dancers as easily as if she were a rag doll.

"Here now, little cat! If you swoon, I might be tempted to kiss you while you're at my mercy. And mind that you do not call such attention to us! I do not wish you snatched away from me by one of these parlor fops who are merely waiting to rescue some damsel in distress from an ogre such as myself."

Even as she sought to ignore him, the picture his jest conjured brought a smile in spite of herself. If only he were to remain this light in tone and leave off taunting her with his sexuality, perhaps she could explore some of her reactions to him. In truth, she liked being in his arms. There was a certain comfort there . . . no, not comfort, precisely. More accurate to say safety . . . no, definitely not safety. Oh, her thoughts were so scattered! Admittedly, being held so close in his arms brought to mind things of the baser nature, but for heaven's sake, one did not have to repeatedly put voice to them!

"Are you thinking sweet thoughts of me?" Fitzhugh asked, at length. He smiled that tender smile down upon her and melted her anger.

Eben laughed, heartily and without caring. It felt so good to laugh the tension away. So good, in fact, that perhaps it was her best defense against him . . . to never take him too seriously. No, from that moment, she concluded, she must never take one word from his mouth in a serious manner again.

"You are outrageous, your grace, and absolutely without manners."

"That's very true. I am shockingly uncouth, compared to the rest of your society," he agreed, complacent in the knowledge. "Upbringing, don't you know. Tell me, little cat, do you believe in fate?"

"I believe more so in relying upon God's direction and one's own abilities."

"I believe in fate...preordained destiny. Credit it to my deplorable Muslim upbringing...and while your aunt would not approve of my familiarity...I believe you are my destiny."

She barely suppressed another laugh. Never had she known a man who could taunt her to blue rage, then make her laugh...and exasperate her to tears, while managing to excite her to the very summit of tolerance, in ever so short a time. She felt placed upon an emotional carousel up and down and around in circles, all at once. If only they didn't rub against one another so harshly. If only they could just be friends, forgetting their regrettable beginnings.

"You seem to have read my aunt well enough. Do you have a crystal ball on my family, your grace?" she teased.

"I am aware of your father's gambling and his mistresses, and of your situation, if that's what you mean. But then, we are closer than most couples who have just been introduced, won't you admit?"

He lowered one eyelid slowly in a secret wink, indicating a secret shared. Eben felt the blood drain from her cheeks, and despite her resolution of not one second before to never take him seriously, the pleasure of his nearness dissipated.

"You...you are no gentleman. This time you have gone too far! To repeatedly speak ill of a father newly in his grave! As well as to continually refer to that...that other!" she gasped. "My father's insults to me and my mother do not blot out your own faults, which are plenty, you...you villain!"

"Am I truly a villain?"

"Yes. *Yes!*"

"Nay, little cat. Merely a man...a man captivated by the very sweetness of your temperament, and sure to have his way about it."

"That's pure and utter bull, Eastmore!"

Fortunately for her, at that moment, the dance ended. Stiffly Eben curtsied to him, applauded the musicians briefly and turned on her heel. Her head held high, she started to walk toward the couch where her mother was indulging in a comfortable coze with an elderly gentleman. But Fitzhugh's hand was swiftly locked into the crook of her elbow, and she found herself being handed across the floor.

"Easy there, Eben," Fitzhugh said quietly. "I don't give a halfpenny in hell what these old biddies have to say about me, but I do have a care for your reputation. To walk away from your partner on the dance floor would be food for every gossip in this auction house. My arriving with you at all should be sufficient fuel for gossip this one evening."

Lady Lillian looked up and extended her hand to Fitzhugh, congratulating herself on her daughter's triumph with no notice of the thundercloud on Eben's face. "Your grace, how naughty of you to call at Vicroy House and not wait upon me."

While Eben fumed silently, Fitzhugh proceeded to charm her mother and extract an invitation to call at Vicroy House at any time. After bowing dutifully over her hand once again, which left that lady in a cascade of smiles and flutters, Fitzhugh turned once more to Eben. Using the crush of attendance as cover, he grasped her wrist against his firm thigh, foiling her move to turn her back on him. Smiling a tight smile, he spoke for her ears only.

"Careful, Eben. As you repeatedly remind me, I am not a gentleman . . . any more than you are a lady, if you could but be persuaded to see it. You are more than a simpering twit who lives only to display her husband's wealth upon her back and whose sole occupation is cutting the character of her friends to ribbons. . . ." He gestured about the glittering throng, and she was suddenly aware of a certain untamed strength about him that did not coordinate with this polished company. "Your husband . . ."

"I shall marry whom I please, your grace. Now unhand me!"

"Ah, beware, little cat. If you do consent to marriage with another, I shall see you the youngest widow in history. I am serious in what I say to you. I mean to have you, as wife or as mistress, but have you I will."

Eben could only stare at him in angry disbelief. How dare he threaten her! How dare he make decisions concerning her, then taunt her that she would have no say in the matter! The man was a cad and a bounder...by his own admission, after all.

"Unhand me!"

"When I am ready, little cat. And do not look at me that way, if you please. At this moment, I am the plum in the eyes of the assembly, and it would not do to look as if you were not enjoying my company...would cast you beyond the pale, it would!" Then, swiftly, he brought her wrist to his lips to kiss the red marks he had left there.

Eben glared at him, then smiled sweetly at her mother's questioning glance before turning again to address him, her pleasant expression regrettably taking the sting from her angry words.

"Only a cad would pick a crowded public ballroom for his foul tricks, your grace. If I were not forced to maintain the appearance of a lady..."

"Pray...do let us adjourn someplace private. The more private, the better," he parried with a comical, lecherous leer.

"If I were a man, I would call you out! I'd put a shot through your black heart...." she hissed at him through a tight smile. His delighted smile only fanned her anger.

"Gad, I'd love to take you to Hyde Park and see if you could!" he teased, thoroughly enjoying her discomfort.

"I could...and I would!" she stated through clinched teeth. Snatching her hand free, she turned her back on him in a deliberate snub.

"I do not snub as easily as that. I shall return at midnight to claim my promised supper."

He offered a final bow, and then his sun-streaked head disappeared into the crowd. Eben watched him go, thinking of nothing but scratching the eyes from his head. Although, even with her anger, she found herself anticipating the midnight supper. All the young men fawning over her for introductions and eagerly filling out her dance card were pale beside the dashingly handsome, thoroughly irritating, unbelievably exasperating, tremendously exciting duke of Eastmore.

Chapter Eleven

The evening wore on in a blur of dances, with young and old men in great numbers to fawn over her. Eben had a vague impression of lights, perfume and wavering candle flames, and the steadily rising sensation of heat. During one self-imposed breathing spell, provided by an assigned partner thankfully misplaced in the crush, she stood by her mother, watching the moving crowd, quite content to be apart from it for the moment to study her surroundings. It was the absolute arrogance of the three patronesses, and the unquestioned acceptance of that arrogance by the glittering lord and ladies of the ton, that made Almack's. For, if one looked closely, while the entire suite of rooms, from the crowded dance floor to the curtained alcoves for those who were not dancing, was ablaze with the white, gold and black of the haut ton, the trappings were somewhat ordinary.

"A wallflower, Miss Victor?" The grating voice cut into her reverie. "Barnaby, dance with Miss Victor. We cannot have her embarrassed, being seen sitting with the old women." Lady Compton fairly shoved her shy son into Eben's arms, which automatically extended to catch the off-balance lord.

"Yes, M-Mother..." The red faced young man bowed to Eben. "Miss V-Victor?"

For a fleeting moment, it crossed Eben's mind to refuse the lady's command, as her very attitude was an affront and insult, but that would serve no purpose except to embarrass the shy man all the more. With narrowed eyes, Lady Compton seemed to be observing her closely, as if waiting for an unfavorable reaction and readying herself to quell the rebellion. Not willing to give her a satisfying excuse to criticize, and being ever kind, Eben cooed in her best imitation of a flighty miss as she allowed Barnaby Compton to take her hand.

"I should be delighted to dance with Lord Compton. My lord?"

A high-pitched laugh, artificially loud, struck Eben's ears. Glancing to her left, who should she see witnessing this disparaging scene but that wasp, Margaret Vernill! Eben gritted her teeth to see how quickly she bent to stage-whisper in another's ear.

"The great dark goose has attracted a gangly gander," she declared, which brought laughter from those girls who seemed to flock about her in hopes some of the blond debutante's popularity might find its way to their less successful lives.

Barnaby's ears flamed red as he led her to the floor. Regardless of his embarrassment, and to her relief and surprise, he was a highly accomplished dancer, far more so than Eben herself, and she was initially compelled to devote her full concentration to the steps, lest she embarrass herself. When, at last, she was able to follow his lead without effort, she realized that Lord Compton had yet to utter a single word. Obviously it was up to her to initiate a conversation.

"I recollect, my Lord Compton," she said brightly, "that you and your mother live in a rather large castle with a considerable history?"

"Yes," he mumbled.

"Near to London?"

"Yes."

"Do you have one estate there, or several?"

"Yes," he confirmed. It was clear she must pose some question which could not be answered, however incompletely, by one word.

"And how long have you been in London?" she ventured.

"Upward of three weeks."

"Are you enjoying yourself . . . the season, you know?"

"I fancy so."

Eben, in desperation, tried another tack. "I myself have not been to London since I was a child. And, except for one or two trips then, have resided in the country."

"Um . . ." It was apparent that if she related her entire life history, including the incident in the brood barn, she would elicit no more than a murmur.

"What of your education?" she doggedly continued, in a new approach. "Did you attend Oxford? Or perhaps Cambridge?"

"Yes."

Eben conceded defeat. She had no intention of soliciting another lecture on butterflies, and she shifted her attention to the dancers as they circled the dance floor. At one point she glimpsed Lord Eastmore whirling past, chattering and laughing with a smirking Miss Vernill in his arms. Drat! Anyone but her! An instant of jealousy tugged at her heart before she dismissed it. Drat and double drat! She was totally addlebrained! Jealous of Eastmore's flirting and fearful of Vernill's viper tongue? Blast! Was she so downtrodden as that? Her heart sank, and a throb of sadness set a tempo behind her eyes. The dance finally over, Eben was escorted gallantly back to her mother. With a flaming face, Lord Compton bowed low over her hand and quickly made his escape. But Eben was allowed no such luxury.

"Miss Victor? May I introduce Lord Portsmythe?" Lady Jersey addressed her, her face beaming. One would have thought she was bearing a grand prize, indeed, to lay at Eben's feet, much in the way Grady had of presenting her with fat field mice for praise.

"My lord?"

She dropped a deep curtsy before the older man, then stepped back a pace to examine this paragon. He resembled a toad. His complexion might once have been fair, but decades of high living had burst a hundred tiny veins in his face, leaving him with a red bulb of a nose and a permanent flush to his portly cheeks. His small, watery eyes were a pale shade of blue, and his hair was thin and greasy. But if one word had to be assigned to Freddy Portsmythe, it would be *moist*. He was classically dressed in a straining wasp-waisted coat, and Eben could not but wish he had elected to wear pantaloons instead of knee breeches, for he was perhaps three stone too plump, and his heavy calves fairly threatened to burst through his white silk hose.

Encouraged by her very own mother, Eben allowed him to lead her out for the next set, which proved rather harrowing, starting with a boulanger. Before the dance was in its second round, the portly marquis was dripping profusely about the face. By the end of the rousing romp, he was betraying every symptom of an imminent apoplectic attack, and he staggered off the floor, quite leaving Eben to find her own way back to the sidelines. But not three steps toward that goal, she was swept into motion by Fitzhugh.

"May I? I should have returned earlier, but I could not penetrate the throng of your admirers. I do pray I am not risking conflict with someone you've previously promised...now that you've killed off the portly Lord Portsmythe. No? I daresay I can't be, for you've surely danced twice already with every man here."

"It would certainly seem that way. My feet feel bruised, and it's becoming more and more difficult to be nice to anyone." Eben sighed, quite taking him aback with her frankness before visibly catching herself and snapping at his head. "And I daresay it is no concern of yours with whom, or how many times, I stand up with a partner."

"Ah, a sampling of the foul temper you speak of? Though I confess I am surprised to suspect you are one of those young misses who would, I'm convinced, thoroughly enjoy life in a less civilized age, when custom deemed it a common practice for two churlish swains to hack one another to death for the pleasure of your company," he answered.

"Only if the defeated one could be assured of bearing your foul face and infamous name!"

"What? Claws again, little cat? Perhaps not the proper manner to draw husbands."

"The man rash enough to woo me must take me as I am," she answered with a defiant glare. No need to prompt this man to repartee, as one did with Lord Compton!

"I daresay! Come, I believe this supper is to be mine." Fitzhugh led her toward the dining hall, answering the call of the midnight supper bell.

The dining hall had been set up with assorted tables, seating companies of two, four, eight or ten. A lavish repast was spread upon two matching sideboards, where housemen, in white-and-gold livery, stood ready to serve. Seating Eben at a table for four in a quiet corner, if such a thing existed in the crowded room, Fitzhugh strolled to the buffet to fill plates, making selections of succulent fare to tempt his charge's palate.

Eben drew back into the corner to observe the bright crowd and wonder about the people. One middle-aged husband and wife caught her eye. Having been introduced to them, but not able to draw their names to mind immediately, she noticed how happy they seemed, and envied them a little. Standing at opposite ends of the buffet, the lady glanced the length of the table to meet her husband's eyes. A look of such affection and respect flashed between them that there was about it an almost physical touching. It was the way a husband and wife should be able to look at each other across a room, with comfortable recognition and a sense of security. She glanced away quickly, because she felt she was prying in a private moment, but her intrusion on that look made loneliness flood through her heart.

That was the type of sharing and feeling she wished for in a marriage. In spite of herself, she sought Fitzhugh with her eyes. Without hope or desire, but not without a degree of longing. She allowed a sigh to escape. To him, she was merely a supper partner to bait into anger and taunt with desire, nothing more. There came an ache in her throat for something she might never know. Shifting her glance to Lord Compton, then to Lord Portsmythe, she felt that ache deepen and she sighed again.

A droll voice sounded at her elbow. "If the lady had agreed to sup with me and I caught her sighing so sadly, I swear, I would eat my pistol before the night was gone."

"Upon my word, Lord Ottobon! I was concerned when I did not see your shining countenance in the ballroom tonight." Eben quickly recovered herself to rag the elegant young man whose company she enjoyed so very much.

"I have been here, but quite unable to leave my obligations until now to pay court to the belle of the ball," he teased, easing his muscular frame into the seat beside her, taking care not to muss himself. "But I swear to you, I have been despairing by the moment as I watched you being wrangled around the floor by one inept dancer after another. There were times I fairly feared for your life, not only for your feet."

Eben laughed in delight at his eloquent address. He was so absurd with his compliments that her mood brightened immediately. Fitzhugh approached the table with a frown upon his face that deepened when he saw her delight in Ottobon.

"Should I have brought a third plate, my lord?" he quizzed his friend with an elevated eyebrow. "Or will you perhaps take this one?'' He offered his own plate to Lewis after setting Eben's before her.

"Fitz, you are a champ among men, and we could possibly be the best of friends if only your man was a little less adept with the tying of your neckcloth," he said. "Although I shall never . . . never, you must understand . . . forgive you for being so tall."

Lewis, much to Fitzhugh's dismay, accepted the plate, offered with irony, and commenced to sample the fare. Eben erupted with laughter at Lewis' audacity and Fitzhugh's astonishment. Her pleasure was such that both men, as well as several other people in the room, joined in the laughter with her.

"Seat yourself, Fitz, old man. I will fetch you a plate forthwith . . . if you will allow me to share this delightful lady's company with you."

Though he spoke in a jesting manner, Lewis looked pointedly at Fitzhugh. One word and, by polite convention, he would have taken his stolen plate and removed himself, but Fitzhugh was lenient with his good friend and gave reluctant permission. With a giant sigh of comic relief and a mock mopping of his brow, Lewis left to procure another plate for Fitzhugh, who slid into his seat beside Eben.

"It gratifies me to see you enjoying yourself," he said.

"I do so enjoy his company. He is so absurd with his humor, I cannot keep myself from laughing. But I fear the more I laugh at him, the worse he becomes." She giggled.

"You should laugh more often, Eben. It brightens your eyes and makes your delicious mouth ever so appealing," Fitzhugh replied, his sunbursts deepening with his smile.

Comfortable with the knowledge Lewis was returning and safe in the doubt he could taunt her to any disagreeable degree of temper in so short a time, she cocked her eyebrow at him, and ragged him in return, much to his delight.

"Pray, your grace, be done with the syrup, or you shall quite ruin my supper. Which looks wonderful, by the by, though I have never tasted some of this, and much of it I am even uncertain of its source," she declared as he accepted the offered plate from a returning Lewis with a nod.

"Let's talk about the black brute of a stallion you ride," Fitzhugh said, searching out a favorite yet neutral topic, as he, too, wished for this harmonious truce to continue.

Lewis glanced up in surprise. "I say, Miss Victor," he protested. "You don't ride that animal! Way too much horse for a woman! Taking your life in your hands to be up on him, you know."

Eben threw a big-eyed, admonishing look at Fitzhugh for his statement. It would never do for Lord Ottobon to know she raced the black stallion with the grooms in the mornings.

"My mistake, old man. Meant 'own,' when I said 'ride.' Don't froth so," he said soothingly with a wink at Eben. With a smile of thanks, she was pleased to expound on her beloved Black Victory. After all, he was her favorite subject.

"Isn't he wonderful? And he's not a brute at all. Just because he was carrying my poor brother...doesn't mean it was his fault. There isn't a two-year-old in the country that could have made that jump, put to it as he was..." She defended him with diligence and deep love.

Lewis greatly admired her loyalty, and he looked cow-eyed at her to the displeasure of Fitzhugh. "He's the fastest thing I've seen this year," he said, complimenting her. Then, with a grin, he added, "Almost as fast as my bay, Denouncer."

"Not nearly as fast as my Thunderbolt!" Another voice interceded.

Eben and the two Corinthians glanced around in surprise.

"Go away, Alfred," commanded Lewis. "You have not been introduced, and will damage Miss Victor's standing with the patronesses. You know the rules...."

"Oh, bother the bloody rules!" he raged, standing for a moment before storming off when he saw he was to be ignored.

"Lord Ottobon, that was very rude," Eben protested.

"Nevertheless, we do not need him intruding uninvited upon our supper tête-à-tête, nor our conversation. Do you not agree, your grace?"

This to Fitzhugh, whose supper tête-à-tête he had himself interrupted. Eben snorted with laughter again, especially when Fitzhugh curled a lip at the humorous peacock before turning back to Eben with a grin.

"I would really like to speak to your studman about the background on that stallion. He's something I would be interested in adding to my stud barn," Fitzhugh said.

Eben turned to him with a boldness in her brilliant gaze that surprised Lewis and caused him to sit back in his chair a bit, while Fitzhugh was beginning to expect nothing less than passion from her in everything.

"I would never think of selling him, even if I was down to burning the furniture for warmth and eating the stable bedding. He's a friend, if you have any concept of the word," she stated. Accepting the answer as her direct way of dealing with issues, Fitzhugh merely inclined his head to her in concession. "Besides, I have handled the breeding for the farm since I became old enough to read charts. I am the one who selects the mares to present to the stallions, for no one on the farm knows the bloodlines as well as I do," she further declared. Both men raised their eyebrows. A woman, an unmarried chit, involved in breeding?

"I would be careful to whom you hand that information. There are some ears present that would not understand, as do Lord Ottobon and myself, that you are a very special young lady with special circumstances," Fitzhugh admonished, quite offhandly. Eben blanched at her slip of the tongue. She could set her ship in hot water just by opening her mouth. "Now, tell me the bloodlines on the black," he said, again coming to her rescue, assisting her out of a frustrating, potentially embarrassing situation.

"He's not pure hunter, like the mares you bought. He's from Messenger, through Flying Childers to Darley Arabian. Messenger was fast, as he proved at Newmarket before they sent him to America," Eben said, favoring him with a genuine smile of thanks. "But Flying Childers was the fastest animal in England for his time. Black Victory has all of his speed and then some."

Lewis watched the well-informed miss with astonishment. "Remind me later to ask for your hand in marriage, my dear Miss Victor," he said, leaning toward her with mooning eyes.

"Ottobon, kindly pay court on your own time! This is my supper hour, if you please, where you are merely an uninvited interloper, and at this table only upon my blind charity to the unfavored of the world," Fitzhugh cautioned him. "Besides, I'm sure Miss Victor is well aware of your propensity for wooing the ladies."

"Ah, yes . . . but until now all I have known is lust . . . This love is heady stuff." Lewis continued to moon at her. Fitzhugh chose to ignore his friend and turned to Eben in all seriousness.

"Why did your father never race the black? With that great speed . . . it would have been the turning point in the future of his racing stables."

Eben carefully placed her fork across her plate. Taking a deep breath, she held it for a second before exhaling. Perhaps now was the time, at last, to speak of it. To complete the healing of the wound by giving it the air of publicity.

"You're right there. He was to be the savior of father's racing stable. He has all the speed from Flying Childer's side, plus the strength and amazing stamina of the Victor Mall hunters on his dam's side. He was only two and in training when my brother made a drunken bet that the colt could clear a five-foot fence, even though he was a racer . . . betting on the hunter blood to be stronger. Regrettably, nothing could stop him from taking the black out right that minute to win the bet."

Eben's eyes glazed, and she stared into space, remembering that night, ten long and painful years ago. Her voice softened with that pain. "It was pouring rain, and black as pitch outside, except when lightning lit the sky for a moment. The whole rowdy crew gathered down by the drive. There's a wall there, with a clear space on either side. Sheldon took the colt around to the far side and was to take the jump facing the group. No one knows what happened for sure, but I can see it in my mind . . . and in my gut . . . because I know the size of Black Victory's heart."

"Eben, don't . . . There's no need." Fitzhugh tried to stop her. But she was far away, lost in memory . . . seeing that night clearly.

"Sheldon wasn't a steady rider when he was sober. And when he drank, his nerve outgrew his skill by bounds. I can see him turn the black toward the wall and stretch him out full-bore. Black Victory has an amazing speed from the jump. He would have been fighting the bit for his head, because Sheldon always did use the leathers to maintain his balance . . . to stay on board, you see? The black would have been thinking more about the pain in his mouth than what might be in front of him, when suddenly . . . a flash of lightning and the wall . . . right in front of him . . . without him even knowing it was coming. Too late to refuse . . . He would have tried to take the jump in midstride . . . from wet ground. But with his head that restrained . . . no horse could have made that leap. He caught his forelegs on the wall and fell heavily over it. Sheldon was crushed beneath him."

"My God! I am so sorry, Miss Victor." Lewis' face was pale, her tale moving his own imagination.

"They carried his body into the house, waking everyone. My mother swooned . . . so much blood." Eben shrugged apathetically. "My father raged against the colt, and would have shot him on the spot if he could have found him."

"The colt . . . had he bolted?" Lewis asked. Fitzhugh slipped a glass of champagne into her cold hand, hoping to distract her from the story. Eben traced patterns on the tablecloth with the handle of her fork and shook her head from side to side.

"As soon as I heard his threat, I ran to the barn. Black Victory had come there, to Jamie Deal. His mouth was bleeding where Sheldon had savaged it with the bit, his right foreleg was torn open, and he was trembling so he could barely stand. Jamie Deal helped me hide him. We took him to a brood barn, away from the stable," Eben said, raising her bleak eyes to Fitzhugh. "It was a long way . . . in the rain . . . with him crippled and bloodied. It took hours, but when I returned no one had noticed I was missing. I confronted Papa. . . . I was actually quite small, but I made Papa promise not to hurt him. After the funeral, Papa left . . . and never came back."

"I'm sorry I pried. I never meant to bring up unpleasant memories," Fitzhugh whispered, leaning close and covering her small hands with his much larger ones. Eben gazed into his amber eyes and once again saw the kind, caring man who had been so tender with a dying mare. This was the man she wanted in her life for all time.

"My lords? Do you plan to keep my niece at supper for the rest of the night?" Lady Adair loomed over the table. "The music has commenced, and she has a full dance card to attend, you know."

"Pray, my dearest Lady Cromwell—" Lewis immediately jumped to his feet, turning Lady Adair and giving Eben time to recover "—the blame is entirely mine. Your lovely niece has me totally entranced."

"Give me your arm, Lord Ottobon, and while we return to the ballroom, enlighten me as to your enthralling conversation," she commanded.

"Why, we speak of racers, my lady. And the sport of kings!" Lewis did as she bid and led the foursome away from the cleared dining hall.

"Bah! Horses!" Lady Adair scoffed. "A horse is a thousand pounds of nothing going nowhere! Have you read of the new railroads? Now, that is the way of the future. My word! What have we here—?"

Alfred was advancing rapidly across the floor, disrupting a set of country dances in his haste, fairly dragging a protesting Lady Cowper with him. "I will have an introduction to the lady," he stated. Coming to an abrupt halt in front of the group, he looked at the ruffled lady expectantly.

"Miss Victor, allow me to present Lord Ellington. Adair, your niece is disruptive!"

With the hurried introduction and the snapped remark, she turned on her heel and marched away. Lady Adair's eyebrows rose sharply, and she turned to confront Alfred in a frosty tone.

"Lord Ellington, you had better control yourself and see that you never again involve my niece in such as this!" Having said her piece, she marched away, full sail, to soothe the ruffled feathers of her friend.

"Now I am introduced, and I shall claim this dance," Alfred stated, further compounding his error by gripping Eben's wrist and turning toward the dance floor.

Never one to be manhandled, especially by a personage a full head shorter than herself and one displaying so rude a manner, Eben simply set her feet and did not budge, jerking the little lord backward in an alarming way. Quite fearing an ugly scene, Fitzhugh stepped into the fray and drew Alfred aside. Lewis, taking advantage of his lapse in attention, whirled Eben onto the dance floor, extracting a gay laugh from her and a frown of annoyance from Fitzhugh, left to deal with a very angry bantam rooster.

"One of these days, Ellington, someone's going to spill your claret.... Pray that it is not me!" he growled, then turned away to watch his enchantress held closely in the arms of another man.

Chapter Twelve

Buttoning her black-and-white checked spencer snugly against any chill, Eben scooped up Grady and slipped through the French doors and down the terrace steps into the overgrown garden. The sun was shining, and the day was proving to be one of the most perfect of days for that time of year. And she was delirious with eagerness to be out in it. Dropping the cat on the path, she wandered amid the tangled plants. 'Twas early for Eastmore to be arriving, and yet the urge to be out-of-doors was too strong to ignore. Her thoughts turned to the prospects of marriage to the numerous men who filled her list. Most were not even to be considered. Some, like Freddy Portsmythe, were just too odious to waste thought upon.

And others, like Lord Compton, were acceptable with certain terms. That man wasn't too offensive... in fact, he wasn't much of anything. The fly in that soup was his mother. Eben felt somewhat protective toward him, as one would toward a child. Which, in fact, was what he would be to her... an older child. She could imagine him becoming more absentminded and befuddled as the years advanced. She would be the controller in the marriage. Administering her husband's business affairs and raising her children, quite possibly growing as sour and dependent on religion as Lady Compton was now.

That last thought brought a smile to her face. Never! She would love her children, not bully them. She would raise a rowdy brood, free in the country... all tousled in with puppies, kittens, and pony hunts in the fall. Children brought her thoughts to lovemaking. That, with Barnaby, would probably only be as frequent as she allowed, and restricted to quick fumbling under the cover of darkness. Not pleasurable, but bearable.

"Grady, what think you of Lewis?" she queried the inattentive cat. She pulled a slim tree branch down to trace through the weeds to captivate the mighty tabby hunter, exciting him to leaps and contortions that would have been humiliating to a less secure feline. "I confess to a fondness for him. He's a capital fellow, and great fun. Marriage to him would be a romp. And when the children came, he would let me raise them in the country. But I fear he would always have his town life."

Her thoughts were turning sad. With Lewis, there would always be the drinking, the gaming and, Eben was sure, the Cyprian in the small town house on Chelsea Road. Not because he would think little of her or want to hurt her, but because it was merely an accepted way of life for the ton. But she would have funds for Victor Mall, plus the sanction of her husband for her stable. She could even imagine Lewis not minding her oddities, once he resigned himself to them. It would be a separated life with Lewis. A marriage of convenience, after a few years . . . as the children began to come and he tired of her body and left her bed to seek a fresh conquest. But maybe her fondness would grow into love for him eventually. The thought of the contented couple she had observed at the ball flashed through her mind. If only she could have assurance that that kind of happiness could be possible with a contrived marriage, perhaps her heart would not be so heavy.

And Fitzhugh? A deep sigh escaped her. He confused her so much. Overwhelming and overpowering. When quizzed by her aunt as to her reasons for defying convention and standing up thrice with him at the ball, she could only answer honestly . . . he hadn't asked, only swept her into his arms and onto the dance floor. When she should avoid the man like the plague, why did she feel such a connection with him? Why didn't she feel she must maintain the pretense of being an innocent miss with him? Was it possible that he shared so many of her secrets? Or was it because she had refused his offer, thereby lessening the need to impress him.

Eben lifted her face to the sunshine. No, it was because she knew that somewhere in the paradox of the man was tenderness itself. And when he held her in his arms, she never wanted to leave. And yet . . . he was far worse than Ottobon. He was . . . just as her father had been. Warm, charming, enchanting . . . but given to the same weaknesses . . . a rakehell, entirely capable of breaking her heart, for she truly thought, given the chance, she could love him to distraction . . . as she had her father. That she could not bear!

"No! I refuse to live the life Mama has lived, with a husband flaunting his excesses daily. And that's what life would hold with him. But not Barnaby. Barnaby would be safe."

The decision to consider neither Ottobon nor Eastmore as eligible lifted a weight from her shoulders and opened the option of enlisting one or both as confidants and cohorts in this game of hunt and trap. Her brow furrowed in thought as she strolled the length of the sad little garden. Perhaps not Lewis. While she did not doubt his integrity, or fear he would betray her, she was in a sense attacking unfairly the very fabric of the ton and its rules and practices—that which he accepted, as did Aunt Addie, as the very rightness of that way of life.

Fitzhugh was different, and scoffed openly, as did she, at the rigidity of its absurdities. Besides, who knew her more intimately than Eastmore? She wrinkled her nose at the thought. By his own admission, he was no gentleman, and he called her no lady while seemingly facing that fact with acceptance, even though he would tease her unmercifully.

"Threatening to undo my husband should I choose one other than him. Fash! The bounder!" she muttered, jerking her skirt loose from a bramble with careless hands. "Not the man for me! But as a friend? Most certainly! What say you, Grady? Shall I enlist his aid? Grady? What? Am I abandoned?" She glanced over the brambles and called, "Grady . . . come here, Grady. I must be off."

Eben hurried down the steps of Vicroy House to the black phaeton with its yellow-painted wheels, set behind a pair of matched grays that were definitely top-drawer. She smiled at the pleased look on Fitzhugh's face when she appeared so promptly. She tilted her head with a quizzing expression and put both fists on her hips.

"Did your grace honestly think I would not understand the annoyance of allowing a fine pair to lather at a standstill while waiting for a dittle-headed female?"

"The thought did not enter my mind for one second, Miss Victor. You forget, I have judged your excellent manner with a blooded animal and allowed you the grace to appreciate a fine pair." Fitzhugh laughed, indicating the pair, which were inclined to prance.

The warm smile deepened the sunbursts at the corner of his golden eyes and exhibited white, even teeth. Her heart skipped a beat, but she firmly took herself in hand as she resolved to place her plan in action this very day. Friend and no more than friend, she thought, climbing onto the seat with the duke and seeing Jamie Deal up on the perch as groom, friend, chaperon. And then they were off.

Exasperatingly, there seemed more drays and carts and wagons and carriages on the streets than Eben had ever encountered before. Both she and Fitzhugh were eager to be on the road. The grays were fresh and difficult to handle, although Fitzhugh gave them no leeway to misbehave, expertly maneuvering between a loaded wagon and a lumbering coach.

"Since I have not had them out for a run in two days, I dared hope you might not raise objections if we drove out of town, so as to take their spirits down a peg or two," he remarked, sparing a glance sideways at Eben. "I see your ribbons are tied securely, Miss Victor, so we will move more quickly as soon as there is a break in this traffic."

"I should enjoy it immensely, your grace," she teased, using the same formal address he chose to affect this fine morning.

"I thought as much," he replied, with such a look that Eben hurriedly directed her attention to the team to hide her confusion at his open admiration. She must not think of him in that light, for she had made her decision and would see it through. She was sure it was the right one . . . regardless of the reaction of her foolish heart.

Eben knew enough of driving to realize Fitzhugh handled the pair in a delicate yet masterful fashion, and she felt quite safe with him at any speed. As they cantered around a laboring wagon and avoided an advancing cart, involuntarily she cried, "Oh, well done! Well done, indeed!"

"You do drive, Miss Victor?" he asked, tilting an eyebrow, but otherwise not taking his attention from the team.

"Of course." It seemed to her an exceedingly dense question. "Though I have only driven in the country, I assume there is little difference in the park or on the crowded streets.

'Tis naught but a reduction of speed and some maneuvering."

"Absolutely correct. It is quite fashionable among the ladies of the ton to drive your own vehicle in the park. I could produce a tilbury for you, if you would care to indulge yourself."

"How kind of you, your grace. But I fear I outgrew tilburies when my first pony died." Eben regarded him with some sarcasm. "I fear you are pulling a gammon on me!"

Judging that a wide-open space was to come upon them, Fitzhugh turned the reins to Eben. With a daring glance in his eye and a charming smile on his sensuous mouth, he asked, "Would you care to try the ribbons, then? I can assure you this pair is not someone's first pony."

Eben accepted the challenge and the lines to the two grays and, with glee on her face, set them to a spanking pace, causing Jamie Deal to grip his perch for dear life. The grays, given their heads, bowled down the road as if the weight of the phaeton were nil. Eben's ribbons whipped behind her, and Fitzhugh was forced to touch his silk topper to keep the wind from snatching it from his head. Watching her face, noting the focus and concentration on the task at hand, Fitzhugh laughed aloud. She was so young, so alive, and she made him feel the same.

With a less credible whip than his lass, Jamie might have shouted his protest over the tin horn of the mail coach they were approaching on the narrow road. But the day was bright and sunny, and Eben was in an excellent mood. Jamie Deal knew that in these circumstances she could drive to less than an inch, which she proved with a mere touch of the reins, scraping past the London mail with no more than an inch to spare. Glancing over her shoulder, Eben sprung the lead horse against a sharp angle in the road, reining down coming off the curve and allowed the team their wind. With a sigh of utter contentment, Eben relaxed and allowed the leathers to play through her fingers, rubbing against her gloves.

"Oh, wonderful! Thank you for letting me have the run. It was splendid, and the grays are most admirable."

"You are most welcome. I must say, I expected you to be proficient with the leathers, but Eben! You are much more than that! You are an incredible whip of the first—" he began, only to be cut short.

Eben drew in the horses sharply with an unladylike swear. Without waiting for assistance from Jamie or Fitzhugh, she jumped down from her high perch. Advancing to the near horse, she ran her hand down the foreleg to retrieve the right rear hoof. Fitzhugh joined her immediately, as did Jamie, to see the problem.

"Thrown a shoe!" Eben allowed the leg to drop. Patting the steaming flank and turning to Fitzhugh, she shrugged. "Won't do to let them stand here steaming."

Fitzhugh surveyed the lay of the land. "There's a road-house just up the road. Quite respectable."

Eben bit her lip softly. A roadhouse... without a lady's maid? Aunt Addie would not approve, and yet it would be a shame to lame such a game one as the gray. With a glance at Jamie Deal, she worried her bottom lip a moment before nodding in agreement, much to Fitzhugh's amusement.

The Hogshead Tavern was not a small inn, but a respect-able hostelry. The landlord, having located near to London on purpose, had plenty of experience with the gentry, for they would travel about in their fancy carriages and always with blooded cattle that required as expansive accommodations as they themselves. Within a trice, the duke's team was blan-keted and attended by Jamie Deal, while a stable boy sent for the blacksmith. Eben and Fitzhugh allowed themselves to be led into the best parlor by their host's attractive daughter, with tea and toddies ordered to revive them against the chill.

Eben detained the girl as she would return to her duties. "May I ask your name?"

"Nancy, my lady." The girl bobbed, shy at the attention.

"Thank you, Nancy. Would you please attend me, as my groom is elsewhere?"

"Yes, my lady." The girl's eyes lit up at the idea of a con-siderable tip and a moment to sit in the middle of the morn-ing without work.

"Satisfied?" Fitzhugh inquired, with an eyebrow lifted and satyr's leer curving his lips.

"Quite, thank you," she replied haughtily, as Nancy seated herself the length of the room away from them.

Eben sat in an overstuffed chair drawn close before a good fire. Divesting himself of his driving coat, Fitzhugh dropped into the chair opposite. Quite the dashing lord, in his snowy linen and pantaloons tight enough to reveal a pair of hand-

somely molded legs above his gleaming Marlboroughs, Lord
Eastmore seemed most appealing to her eyes. Suddenly very
warm in the heated parlour, she opened the buttons in her
spencer and fanned her slightly flushed face with her hankie.

"How long do you think before the horse is sound?" she
asked, to distract his gaze from her face.

"No more than an hour or two, depending upon the availability of the smithy," he replied. "Are you discomfited by my
presence? I shall retire to the outer room, if you so desire."

"No, this is fine, as long as the landlord's daughter may remain," Eben said, not meeting his eyes, suddenly shy. "I must
protect my reputation, you know."

"Well, little cat, perhaps that thought should have come
before the excursion was undertaken. If you felt your reputation might be placed at risk with me, why did you come driving with me without your maid?" he quizzed, leaning toward
her intently, eyes touring the flushed face. "The run might
have put your mother, or even your dauntless aunt, off their
feed, but . . ."

"Your grace?" Eben interrupted him, then paused to draw
a deep breath in indecision. Fitzhugh glanced up with an eyebrow raised in question.

She studied his attractive face and considered for a moment the move she was about to take. She so desperately
needed a friend. Someone she could be open with and who
would listen with a sympathetic ear when the playacting became too confining and she felt she had to break out or
smother. Since she had had no female confidantes since her
nanny's death when she was eight—a sad event barely noticed
by her distraught mother, the position therefore never refilled—it seemed the most natural thing for a girl raised in the
company of grooms and studmen to turn to a kind man as a
friend and to be able to meet him on his own terms, with the
frankness that it seemed to Eben that only men shared.

She felt compelled to reach out to him. Would he support
her? Was this a risk she shouldn't be taking? But then again,
she was never one to step back from a risk for fear of the outcome. Befriending this man, who had proved to her already
that he was a snake in the grass, was definitely a risk. He could
destroy her credit with but a few words in the right ears. But
this he could have done easily enough before now, for didn't
he hold more than one deadly secret of hers? No, for all his

temper and taunting, he had proved he did not desire to defame her with the ton. He desired much more, or at least he seemed to speak of little else. That thought brought a smile to her lips, and she rashly decided to implement her plan.

"Your grace," she began again, "we have already developed this relationship from a backward start. I feel drawn to you, in spite of...what...happened between us." Eben chose her words carefully, keeping her eyes down and her hands busy smoothing the soft leather of her driving gloves, for she didn't want any expression of his, whether it be sneering or humorous, to forestall her before she could make her purpose clear. "I think we can agree that we were...impulsive, to say the least...and given better circumstances, would have behaved quite...differently."

Fitzhugh's eyebrows lifted higher in astonishment, as once again this strangely wonderful woman-child took him by surprise. For all her protests, she now broached the subject herself? "Perhaps," he responded, but offered no other comment for fear she would halt her confidence.

"I think we also agree that we would not deal well together with daily rubbing, and the idea of our buckling is best forgotten, as we both know your offer was born totally of your sense of duty. So on that note—" she raised her startling eyes with such an expression of vulnerability, seemingly requesting an open and totally honest answer from him, that his heart went out to her "—do you think we could be friends?" She held her breath for a moment, then rushed on with a great exhalation, as if suddenly afraid to hear his answer, for she felt an unexplainable longing, so forceful in her heart that it frightened her and the desire to beg was strong. "Real friends, as Jamie Deal and I are real friends? Friends, no matter what happens or what is said?"

Fitzhugh allowed his eyes to wander over her lovely upturned face, drinking in her beauty and becoming quite lost in her incredible eyes before he answered. A flush rose delicately to her cheeks at his frank appraisal. He very much suspected that he desired much more from her than friendship, but if that was a place whence to begin building their relationship, then he would accommodate her.

"Yes. I would like that very much. Very much, indeed." He spoke softly, and as solemnly as she, delighted when her face lit and she beamed with overjoyed emotions.

"Oh...splendid! Thank you from the bottom of my heart. And we agree that there shall be no more gammoning about marriage between us? We really would not suit, you know."

"How you wound me! To think there is one woman, one as lovely as yourself, who does beg I desist in paying court for her hand." Fitzhugh affected a pained expression. "And what more would you have me do?"

"I would that you do less, your grace, rather than more," Eben replied, refusing to give in to his prank. There were far more serious matters to settle at hand. "At least in that direction. What I desire..."

"Ah, you need only state your desire and it shall be yours. I take friendship most seriously, you know."

"Capital! How kind," she said, choosing to take his words as sincere generosity. "We shall be friends of the first order, then. I shall call you Fitzhugh, and you shall call me Eben, as you seem to want to do anyway...when company allows, of course, and the...o-other...will never be spoken of again. Never again...do you understand? And our confidences will be protected by a code of honor. Contract?" She thrust her hand toward Fitzhugh to seal the bargain.

"Contract made and honored, Miss...Eben." Fitzhugh beamed a delighted smile upon her. Taking her offered hand, he resisted the desire to feel its smoothness against his lips and shook it as he would a man's.

"Splendid...Fitzhugh."

Her use of his Christian name tickled him and deepened his smile. "And now, what is the desire I am to fulfill?"

"I would enlist your advice, which I would follow to further my end to its best solution, as you are more familiar with these matters than I," she said, feeling as if a great weight had been lifted. Her face visibly relaxed. Fitzhugh's eyebrows jerked up in surprise.

"Ahem...tea, Your Lordship." The landlord's wife entered with a tray of steaming tea, a toddy for Fitzhugh, along with shortbread warm from the oven. Eben poured tea for herself, then, contrary to convention, poured a second cup and carried it the length of the room to the speechless Nancy.

"Might as well make good use of the break, Nancy," she said. "Sugar or milk?"

"M-milk, my lady," the girl stuttered in astonishment. She jumped to her feet and followed Eben back to the tray, as if fearing dire consequence if this lady of such obvious breeding waited upon her further. Without noting Fitzhugh's delighted disbelief, Eben drank deeply of her own cup, grateful for the strong brew, after insisting the girl carry a plate of shortbread back to her seat. Greatly refreshed, she launched directly into her tale.

"I came without a maid because I do not have one. Jamie would have been chaperon enough, if we had not thrown that shoe. But in all honesty...Fitzhugh—" a slight smile touched her lips as she tasted his name again aloud...in public "—my mother and I are in dire straits indeed. Going downhill without breaks! We are making a show of it this one season, but if I do not find a husband, and quickly, the bailiff will be at the door. Mr. Vandevilt sends me letters almost daily concerning Papa's notes, and there are no funds. We only have Hastings, and Cook, and mother's Bess, a few others, and of course Jamie Deal. Mainly because they're truly family. Everyone is doing double and triple duty, wagering their very futures on me and what marriage I can make this season."

"Mr. Vandevilt?"

"Papa's solicitor. The pensioners are in straits, also, as all payments stopped when he died," she explained, replenishing her cup.

"I figured it must be stunted when I saw the hunters selling so cheaply at Tattersall's. But I had no idea it was as urgent as all this," Fitzhugh replied over his toddy mug. He leaned back and crossed one leg over the other, contemplating the shine on his boot.

"Ah, yes...the mares," she whispered. Fitzhugh glanced up at her tone. The raw pain Fitzhugh had seen twice before was there again. Only this time she made no move to shutter her eyes from him, but allowed him to see all the misery she felt at losing the very things she loved above all else. "Sold to buy this...finery...to attract a husband, when all I ever wanted was the Victor Mall hunters. Ironic, don't you agree, that they must be sold to buy a husband with deep pockets, so that I might try to protect the very thing that it costs me?"

"Life does appear to be like that at times."

"That sounds like a pious acceptance of life's trials that I can ill afford. There is no solace for me in that," Eben retorted. She leaned forward earnestly, rattling her teacup roughly on the table in her agitation. Desperation read plainly

on her face. "I sorely need your help. I—I need to know...
Please t-tell me... Hell's blood! Would you show me how to
attract a man? How to bring him up to snuff quickly, by driving him wild with passion for me? So that I might get this over
with, begin rebuilding Victor Mall and escape off this...cursed
market!"

"Good God, woman!" Fitzhugh sputtered, choking on his
toddy to the extent that Eben had to pound him on the back.
So great was his distress that Nancy ran to assist and thought
to summon her father if he did not recover soon. Finally he
was able to speak again, begging Eben and the girl to desist
from their pounding, although his face was red and his voice
raspy. Satisfied the crisis was over, both girls resumed their
seats in relief. "D-do you kn-know...what you are asking?"
Fitzhugh sputtered.

"Yes, I do know what I ask! I want to know the secrets of
the beau monde. I want you to help me skip this ridiculously
formal verbal dance that must be done before anyone can give
a straight answer to an honest question. I want you to aid me
in bringing a man to the altar," Eben forcefully told Fitzhugh, her body tense and her eyes hard.

"And just who is this man to be, that we are going to stalk
with so much zeal?" he wanted to know, quelling the urge to
show levity in the face of her seriousness.

"I—I'm not quite sure. Maybe Barnaby Compton..." Eben
paused a moment in surprise when Fitzhugh's eyebrows jerked
up again. "Th-there are several who might suit, but I'm not
sure how to go about tempting them. I just know that if it's
going to take all season, I shall not bear up." She sat back with
a deep sigh. "And if I do not attract anyone at all..." She
looked up at Fitzhugh and shrugged her shoulders, as if to say
she had no answer if that happened. "I don't think I could
bear it at all if I wasn't able to get out for a run with Black
Victory and Jamie Deal in the mornings. I swear I'd be unraveled by now."

"I knew it had to be you that morning in the park. You and
that black together quite take a man's breath away," Fitzhugh said. Eben waved away the compliment.

"Maybe Ottobon's breath, but I fear Compton would be
appalled, as would most of society. Besides, that way to a
man's heart is not open for me to use." Eben sat very straight
and, in a fair imitation of her aunt's voice and manner, said,

"A lady must never be seen riding rambunctiously, and never...never must she appear to ride better than the object of her designs."

Fitzhugh roared with laughter at her portrayal of her formidable aunt. "Well done!"

"I truly do not understand how men are able to exist in this world with such fragile egos as I'm told they possess."

"Only through blind luck and blundering, I assure you."

"You see, Fitzhugh..." Eben again leaned forward and began in earnest. "I swear, I do not know how to proceed. I have yet to get Compton to even speak to me. And I am not at all sure what Ottobon's looking for in a wife."

"I was not aware Ottobon was desirous of a wife at all...and for Compton, look to the way he relates to his mother for your answer. Though I do not understand why you would want that milksop."

"Because he is nothing like my father. He will not gamble away the bread from his children's mouths, nor trade the gown from his wife's back for jewels to hang around the fat neck of his mistress!" she stated. "Please tell me, Fitzhugh, if men like that...sort of woman...a—a Cyprian...why do they not marry them? It would eliminate the disgrace of the demimonde and save their wives much untold humiliation. No one will give me an answer!"

Fitzhugh's answer was forestalled by the landlord's cough, with Jamie Deal pushing his way through the doorway rudely, glancing worriedly at Eben, then turning a scowl on the duke.

"Horse be sound, lass," Jamie announced abruptly.

"Thank you, Jamie. We will be out in a trice." Eben stood and buttoned her spencer in preparation to depart. "So, my lord, do you have an answer?"

"Yes, Eben. I have an answer for you, but too lengthy for this time," Fitzhugh stated with a wide grin. "Now I should get you back to Grosvenor Square before your aunt has the Bow Street Runners after me for elopement, and you are forced to accept my hand in marriage after all, in spite of your obvious distaste for it," he said, looking at her as if he would look through to her very soul.

"You would regret otherwise, your grace," she said, pulling her gloves on. "It's being said that you do not care to confine your attentions to one woman at any one time."

Turning to Nancy, Fitzhugh pushed a coin into her palm and chucked her under the chin, bringing a giggle of pleasure, unwittingly proving Eben's point. She scowled disagreeably. Men! Must they constantly chase everything in skirts? Was there not one that could display an interest in anything but—? Only one name came to mind. Closely followed by the grim picture of his mother . . .

Chapter Thirteen

The following day was one "at home" for the three ladies and found them in the ornate salon, attired suitably to receive callers. Eben paced the floor restlessly, swishing her day dress and plucking at the tiny fabric flowers serving as trim. She chose to ignore the dark looks Bess sent in her direction, as the only other suitable response that came to mind was to throw her hands up in the sign of the cross and hiss at her. But that would undoubtedly make matters worse, if that was possible. The most recent disagreement between the two, as was fast becoming the custom, commenced over the styling of her hair. Only by Eben's sheer will and stubborn insistence was her hair caught simply back from her face, allowing curls to escape charmingly on her temples and forehead.

"Eben, pray light somewhere. You are as nervous as a cat. I am positive we shall have callers of great import today," Lady Lillian stated, watching her daughter pace about. "Lord Portsmythe..."

"Oh, Mama! You didn't! 'Twill do you no good to push that one at me! I will not even consider that horrid man. First of all, he stank!" She shuddered mightily to show her disdain. "He's fat ... and I cannot even describe to you what it's like dancing with him." Another shudder escaped her. "His hands are wet ... horrid! Absolutely horrid!"

"Well, never mind that for now." Her mother knew better than to press her daughter to stubbornness.

"I'm serious!" she cried. "I certainly shall not marry some fat old man ... just because he has blunt. It would just be my misfortune that he'd snore and snort all night, and in the morning he'd belch and scratch!"

"Eben Pearl...honestly!" her mother admonished. "Must you be so crude? A lady..."

"Enough, Lillian. Eben, do settle yourself. I'm certain I heard a carriage," her aunt cautioned her. Her words were immediately followed by Hastings bowing Lady Compton into the room, attended closely by her pallid son.

Quickly scooping Grady from a gilt chair, Eben carried him the length of the room to the window seat. She settled him there on the cushions, effecting a satisfactory nest with one of her mother's merino shawls.

"Grady, you had best stay here, for I am quite certain yon lady eats fat cat tails down to the nub and smacks her lips for more," she warned him. The tabby cat closely attended her instructions with vibrating whiskers and kneading paws before resuming his nap in the purloined shawl.

"Lady Compton, pray sit here by the fire and warm yourself from the chill." Lady Lillian greeted her unwelcome guests as sweetly as possible, languishing back on the sofa. "You simply must be careful of catching a chill, as I am here to tell you, being of weak health myself..." She sighed deeply and pressed her handkerchief to her chest. "I do declare, I had forgotten how exhausting it all can be. I do not...I repeat...I do not see how I am to get through the entire season."

"It's quite simple, Lady Victor. You should merely decline some of your engagements. Everyone knows you're just out of black gloves," Lady Compton stated, with a crafty look on her face. She seated herself in the offered chair and spread her draperies in a proprietary manner. "All this capering about is not entirely appropriate for a woman of your age, anyhow."

"Decline? Stay home? Why, the very thought!" Lady Lillian straightened up abruptly and sought a more neutral subject. "Ah...ah, Lady Compton, you simply must bring us up to date on your most recent meeting. Hastings, bring fresh tea, if you please."

Lady Lillian was to be on her best behavior, no matter how offensive this disagreeable lady was today. Sister Adair had been more than adamant on that fact. She could only assume there was something afoot, since Ernestine Compton rarely bestirred herself to call on those she considered to be her inferiors in rank. Why her sister insisted on encouraging this pair, she would never understand, as the very thought of being related to Ernestine Compton brought about the shudders, as she promptly demonstrated, to Lady Adair's chagrin. Lady Compton, being less observant, was somewhat mollified by Lady Lillian's solicitous inquiry concerning the dowager's well-known prayer gatherings, and seemed prepared to speak at length upon the subject.

Eben seated herself a distance away from the older ladies and turned her attention to the tall, thin man who at present was engaged in a penetrating examination of his shoes. With a sigh, she began the process of drawing from him some sort of conversation.

"Pray, Lord Compton, take this seat by me. It is most comfortable. I trust you have been well?"

"Er . . . very," he stammered. The young man sat on the tip of the chair, as if ready to fly at the first sudden movement.

So alert, in fact, that Eben thought to jump at him and shout, "Boo." But the deep flush of embarrassment staining his face from his plainly tied neckcloth to his thinning sandy hair, making his already prominent ears even more so, brought out her sympathy. Pensive a moment, wishing ever so much to avoid another push-and-pull conversation, she studied him, then allowed her gaze to slide toward his mother. Her eyes narrowed slightly . . . then widened with a dawning revelation.

"Barnaby, sit back and relax! And please . . . look at me when I speak to you," she ordered, in a somewhat stern tone faintly resembling Lady Compton's. Barnaby immediately sat back and unclenched his hands, raising his weak blue eyes to hers. "That's much better," Eben continued in the same tone, gratified by his response. "Barnaby, do you find me attractive?"

"Oh, y-yes, of course," he stammered, going even redder.

"Then please tell me so," she demanded, leaning toward him and refusing to allow his eyes to drop from hers.

"My m-mother says your looks are quite outstanding . . ." he said, unable to maintain eye contact, dropping his eyes to his nervous hands.

"But what do you think, my lord? What do you think?" she asked, insisting he express his own opinion. Lady Compton eyed them darkly from across the room, but Eben was not to be deterred from her purpose.

"I—I do think you are by far the most—" he swallowed compulsively, finding it hard going "—b-beautiful w-woman I have ever l-laid eyes upon."

"Please look at me!" she demanded again. When the pale blue eyes were on her face again, she affected a coy look and smiled sweetly at him. "Thank you, my lord."

Surprisingly, Lord Compton smiled back at her and in a tone that was downright confiding, he leaned towards her. "M-Mother is having a small dinner party this coming week, and we are inviting your family. M-Mother is quite taken with you, a-and...s-so am I," he finished shyly. His hands gripped his bony knees tightly, but he did not drop his smitten eyes from her face, quite giving Eben hope for him.

"Thank you...Barnaby," she said, using his first name, as if shy, as well, which appeared to give him great courage, for his stammering speech became somewhat more forceful.

"I think you are every bit as alluring as a fine piece of porcelain," he added, suddenly finding the way smoother going and making the most of this newly discovered ease.

"Thank you. Your compliments quite overwhelm me, my lord."

Eben was pleased to see the young man responded so well to coaching. If it was always going to be this easy to set him in the direction she wished to go, perhaps her stay on this cursed market would be mercifully short. She wondered what his answer would be if she told him to marry her, pension off his mother and come live with her at Victor Mall? Heart failure, probably, but he definitely was proving manageable, thanks to Fitzhugh's advice.

"Barnaby! I shall demand you attend me!" Lady Compton had risen and was speaking harshly to her inattentive son. "We have other calls to make, and we must be on our way. Miss Victor, I see you are well."

Eben rose to join Barnaby, who had leaped from the chair as if suddenly discovering it a hot seat. Now he was engaged in draping his mother's wrap about her shoulders in a solicitous manner, as if to diminish any bad temper. And, she reasoned, probably to avoid a lengthy reprimand once they were alone. Again her heart went out to the sadly abused young man.

"Yes, my lady. Quite well, thank you," Eben murmured, dropping to a curtsy to the lady to hide the humor on her face.

To everyone's relief but Barnaby's, the Lady Compton believed in regimenting calls to the conventional fifteen minutes. Sighs went around the room at their departure, none louder than Lady Lillian's. The next callers obviously believed the convention was instigated as an easy escape, and only to be adhered to if one wasn't thoroughly enjoying oneself. Which didn't seem to be the case with the two young men, as well as the three ladies they were entertaining to giggles. Lord Ottobon's cheerful attempts to explain the differences between the pinks, the tulips, the dandies, the blades, the high stickers, the bucks, and the Corinthians, with Lord Ellington protesting he was a member in good standing of the Corinthian set while gently waving a small lace handkerchief that he held delicately between thumb and forefinger, marking him as a dandy of the first stare in Eben's eyes, greatly entertained the ladies. Their absurd comments and constant interruptions of each other held them through second call for tea, which also brought Fitzhugh into the gathering.

The figure that advanced was obviously of the highest ton. As he approached, Eben ran an eye up his immaculate person, and was forced to admit that, though rakehell the man might be, he had a way of presenting himself that no other of her acquaintance had managed to master.

"Your grace, how nice of you to join our group this afternoon." Eben rose to greet him, extending her hand, met his and shook it, soliciting Lady Adair's censure.

"Eben, please! It is not done to shake hands with everyone. If you present your hand to a gentleman in such a manner, he will be constrained to kiss it . . . and no lady will know what to do with it at all!"

"How dreadful!" Eben's left hand flew to her cheek, and she pranked in mock horror, "I pray, your grace, please overlook my unforgivably gauche behavior. I am mortified!" Fitzhugh merely smiled into her merry eyes.

"My Lady Cromwell refines too much. It is not totally out of the ordinary to shake hands. But if you expect your hand to be kissed, you must hold it so," he said, turning her right hand so that the palm lay down. "That, you follow, is an irresistible invitation to any gentleman, who will then do thus." He slid his beneath hers and brushed it with his lips, then lowered the hand slowly. To his great surprise and momentary annoyance, Eben burst into laughter.

"How very droll. What trouble to put on such a show! I confess I've never had it happen to me before." Then, catching herself, she added, "And I am sure it will never be done again as gracefully."

Recovering quickly and smiling at her honest, childlike reaction, Fitzhugh said, "But give me the opportunity..."

Lady Adair broke in before he could carry out the deed again. "Lord Eastmore, you take advantage of an unsophisticated young lady."

"Nay, dear Auntie. He is merely cozening a country bumpkin." Eben laughed, then referred to their secret contract. "Lessons are lessons, no matter what their source."

"Advising, rather than teaching," Fitzhugh murmured, enjoying her delight in their shared secret. Turning, he belatedly acknowledged the company with a deep, sweeping bow. "Ladies? Lord Ellington? Lord Ottobon? Your servant."

"Your grace, pray step closer to the fire and accept a restorative," Lady Lillian tittered, fluttering her fan at him in high humor.

Accepting a proffered cup of tea from that lady, he moved to lean his tall frame against the mantel in a blasé posture, crossing one foot over the other. The movement flexed a powerful thigh muscle beneath tight pantaloons, and forestalled any hint of the dandy in the graceful gesture.

"What have I missed? Anything, or nothing?" he asked the company at large.

Alfred, typical of his personality, burst forth to capture the limelight before anyone else could speak. "Miss Victor is being unkind to me," he stated petulantly. "You will not believe it, Lord Eastmore, but she does not appreciate my compliments."

"I am not at all unappreciative, Lord Ellington," she said interrupting him. "It is just that they seem...too exaggerated to be sincere. Sheer flummery, actually!"

"I would say Miss Victor is showing an admirable good sense for an uninformed country miss," Fitzhugh noted in a lazy manner. "One must remember your behavior at the Golden Ball, now mustn't one?"

"Now you are being unkind, Eastmore. And after my apology to Miss Victor has been prettily made and accepted!" Alfred grumbled.

Everyone laughed. But Eben, watching his expression, felt the small lord hid anger beneath the jesting remark, as if he felt the laughter was at his expense. The manner in which his eyes turned hard and his jowl worked made her exceedingly uncomfortable. She quickly glanced at the rest of the party, but no one else seemed to notice the insulted man's reaction. Was there bad blood between the two men, or did the diminutive lord take offense at teasing remarks from anyone?

"Ellington and myself have come to beg the company of you three ladies for a box party at Covent Garden," Lewis interjected. "And you, also, Fitzhugh. We'll make a night of it!"

Lady Lillian fairly clapped her hands at the thought of the entertainment, and Lady Adair accepted in huge spirits for the three of them. Fitzhugh turned to Lewis to decline, then to beg forgiveness of the three ladies.

"I'm terribly sorry, Lewis, old chap. But I am otherwise engaged. Ladies, I am desolate at my loss. A previous engagement, you understand. Some other time, perhaps? Pray allow me a rain check, or I shall never recover."

Lady Adair laughed in the face of his sorrow, while Lady Lillian rushed to reassure him. Eben, though she was quite at a loss as to the reason, thought the fun had somehow gone out of the invitation, although why that should be so was questionable, for hadn't she assigned him his place in her life? Confidant, and never anything more? While it was true that his company was vastly entertaining, it didn't take away from the fact that the other two gentlemen were equally entertaining.

Allowing the conversation to flow around her, she sat back to ponder her reaction to his declining. She really must stop comparing all other swains to him. Her gaze shifted in speculation. It was not to be a distraction that he was ever so tall and so perfectly fit as to please the eye in every way. After all, was there truly that much difference? Her eyes traveled over his soft, much-rubbed boots, rich as only well-cared-for leather could be. They snugged enviably to a pair of finely molded calves. The buff buckskin pantaloons were so tight, Eben was sure he was standing because he could not sit in comfort. She eased her eyes over thighs that rippled with muscles, flexing powerfully under the cured skin with any shift of his weight, along a taut, flat belly, to the massive chest she knew to be hard yet silken to the touch.

Nothing could have been more perfect than the set of his olive-drab tailcoat across shoulders that had no need of padding. A single fob dangled at his waist. How could his hands, improbably surrounded by a hint of lace, be so masculine . . . and so sensual as they fondled the delicate teacup with such ease of caress. The neckcloth was startlingly white against his skin and tied with so many twists and turns it could only be à la sentimentale, but it did not seem to strangle him, as it did with Ottobon. Quite possibly his erect military bearing commanded the neckpiece instead of the neckpiece commanding the stance.

Attracted by her silence, Fitzhugh glanced at Eben. He smiled a bit at his little cat, caught wool-gathering in company. Her lips were parted, soft and inviting. Her eyes, half closed with the dazed pleasure of her absorbing perusal, traveled slowly up, past the firm jaw, lingering over the sensuous mouth, thinking of slow kisses, then passed the classical nose, to the amber eyes with the sunbursts of lines at the corner. Eyes that were looking into hers with a touch of amusement at her lengthy, sensual analysis. For a moment, their eyes held . . . speaking softly murmured promises in mime. So languid was she that she was no longer aware of anyone in the room but him. Her body slackened and sank back ever so slightly, loose-limbed.

Fitzhugh knew, if only they were alone, he could take her there on the sofa, with her full consent, so drugged was she on her own imagination. The thought of slipping the clothes from her perfect form and covering her body with his was so inviting, his body stirred, responding to his thoughts and her compliant gaze. Fitzhugh watched as she came back to herself. Her eyes widened to blue wonder, then blinked rapidly. A dull pink flush rose from the neck of her gown and rushed to her cheeks. Straightening abruptly, she tore her eyes away from his and glanced around the room, then at her hands, clenched in her lap.

Unable to stop herself, Eben raised a trembling hand to touch the light film of moisture on her upper lip. She shuddered at her uncontrolled emotions, but nothing could have tempted her to raise her eyes again from her lap.

Fitzhugh noted, with no little satisfaction, that her hands trembled even as she held them folded tightly together, and his thoughts turned smug. Ask him to aid her in procuring a husband, would she? All the while spurning his suit over some assigned trait of debauchery that she could only imagine in her untutored mind. Well, mark my words, little cat, you shall belong to me, and no one else. For I will give up the darkest of my dark traits for love of you. Run scared and run far, but you shall be mine. And it will be you who does the pursuing, for your body and heart have pledged themselves to me, whether you will admit it or not.

In a motion vastly welcomed by Eben, the other gentlemen rose, taking their leave with great flourishes of flattery and hand-kissing, amid giggles and remarks from her mother and aunt. Fitzhugh, his departure lagging after the others', came up behind her. His breath on her neck stirred her curls, sending gooseflesh down her arms. Then he whispered in her ear.

"My love, you will have to learn some discretion in public, or you shall have me losing control of myself entirely. It would be unseemly for me to ravish you in company, you know."

"I—I cannot say... I mean..." she stammered, twisting the floral trim so harshly between restless fingers that they detached as fallen blooms in her hands. Heaven only knew just what she did mean, but evidently it did not signify, as he did not wait to hear the explanation, but passed on through the door to the others.

Eben made hurried excuses to her aunt and mother, who would insist on rehashing the afternoon's entertainment to death over yet another tray of tea. This was not something Eben could do, and she escaped to the stable as rapidly as good manners allowed. Leaning her face against the warm neck of Black Victory, she allowed tears of frustration to come.

"Oh, Black! I'm becoming the worst kind of watering pot...and I just don't understand anything anymore! He is not a man I should want. He would cause me the most trouble and heartache, for hasn't he already? I will not want him!" She straightened her spine. "I will go to this entertainment tonight, and I will have a good time. Just see if I don't! To bloody hell with Fitzhugh Eastmore!"

Even without the duke, the box party was a great success. The moving tragedy of *King Lear*—somewhat shortened, she noticed—was followed by a bang-up farce, to the satisfaction of all. Ottobon had invited a Lord Leonard Melton, an older man of the ton, though not a top tulip, to join the party, rounding out the numbers to an even count. The comfort and pleasure of the ladies was their first concern, and Lord Melton, to Lady Lillian's utter delight, proved to be most knowledgeable concerning the occupants of the other boxes and expounded on all in a fashion that entertained most pleasantly. The theater, many-tiered and splendidly appointed, was a fascination for Eben. The posturing of the elite and the gossip adrift among the drop-ins would have been entertainment enough, even if the stage had stayed vacant of performers.

"Come, Miss Victor, stroll with me," Alfred requested, bored with any conversation that did not center around him or his pursuits.

It was a popular custom to stroll the halls during intermissions, of which there were plenty. It allowed for a simple night at the theater to become as social as a ball. Refreshments, in the way of champagne ices for the ladies and chilled wine for the gents, were provided for procurement in the lobby, if one cared to partake. It was during this stroll that Eben caught sight of Fitzhugh. She was rather disappointed to notice that he was escorting a strikingly beautiful lady with flaming Titian hair and yards of plum draperies that swayed seductively with her enticing walk.

"Whoever is the lady with Lord Eastmore? I do not believe I have her acquaintance," Eben ventured, in what she hoped was a casual tone. Craning his neck to see over the crowd, all of whom seemed taller than the diminutive lord, Alfred attempted to satisfy her curiosity.

"That is Lady Louise Sinclair. I rather doubt you do have her acquaintance," he informed her with a malicious sneer. "She is, my dear, almost fashionably impure. Fetching piece, don't you think?"

He went on to add something, but Eben's attention had wandered...to note the manner in which Fitzhugh would bend his head to her with a tender lover's smile. When the attractive couple turned in her direction, she quickly lowered her head, as if closely attending to whatever the petite lord was asking her, nodding and smiling, hoping to forestall an introduction to the woman with the exposed bosoms and vampish air who hung so heavily on Lord Eastmore's arm.

Only when they passed in close proximity did Eben swiftly move her own pale blue draperies aside to avoid touching the plum silk, which was a sharp insult...though the flame-haired beauty did not notice. Fitzhugh lifted one eyebrow and inclined his head toward her with a slightly amused smile, making Eben feel very childish indeed. But she could not have stopped the jealousy that coursed through her if her life had depended upon it. Again she turned to Ellington with questions, unwittingly interrupting him.

"I say, is the lady quite, you know...well?" She momentarily amused herself, pretending the lady was an invalid and required such heavy assistance of His Lordship's arm for her withered and twisted legs could not support her weight otherwise. Then, desiring nothing more than a moment alone to regain her good humor, she sent Alfred on an errand, interrupting whatever answer he would have given her.

"Lord Ellington, I would be most appreciative of an ice. All the laughter has quite parched my throat."

"I shall be no more than a moment. If you will be content here, I shall return in a trice," he said, for once pleasantly obliging. No sooner had he disappeared into the crowd than Fitzhugh's droll voice whispered in her ear.

"Are you enjoying your evening, Miss Victor?"

Swinging to face him abruptly, Eben scanned the crowd behind him to see if he actually had the audacity to confront her with that...that woman on his arm. "Quite! And you?"

"Most enjoyable. Yes, most enjoyable indeed," he answered, giving her no satisfaction by deeming to notice her set face. Eben was unable to follow his example.

"And your...companion?"

"Yes, most assuredly."

He smiled widely with enjoyment at her anger...and jealousy. Finally, seeing that he was not going to volunteer anything to her, Eben confronted him, dropping her voice for what privacy could be gained in a lobby of several hundred people.

"Fitzhugh...how could you! You forgo an invitation with...I mean...to be seen in public with...that...that woman?" She was stammering in her attempt to find the appropriate words to express her outrage without disclosing her real, and possibly her unrealized, feelings of jealousy.

"That woman? Could you possibly refer to the Lady Sinclair? And what feasible objection could you have to Louise? Is she of your acquaintance?" Fitzhugh asked, lifting his eyebrow in an expression of innocence. "No? I thought not."

"You know who I mean! And do you know what...they call her?" Eben whispered, suspecting strongly that he was playing the idiot for her. "Pray do not gammon with me on this!"

"Now that we've established the lady of whom we speak... why not enlighten me as to what they call her? If you would be so kind." Fitzhugh smiled a tight smile that did not reach his eyes, a warning best heeded, had Eben but noticed.

"Surely you jest," she gritted, anger and disappointment taking the place of common good sense. "She is called... almost f-fashionably impure."

"I see. And what does that signify, do you suppose?" Fitzhugh quizzed, still in a conspirator's tone, greatly amused at her childish outrage.

"I...I think..." Eben began, suddenly at a loss to explain something she was unsure she even understood herself but fully expected him to. Then she exploded. "Blast these people and their innuendos! The term implies that she is a borderline, almost accepted, whore! Totally beneath the notice of ladies of the ton, and therefore greatly sought by the gentlemen. Hell's teeth! Why can't they just call a whore a whore! No mistaking that meaning!"

"Well, she is the wife of an elderly husband who can no longer attend her needs, but...a whore?" Fitzhugh raised an eyebrow and turned slightly to study Louise, who was preening in conversation with an older gent, exactly where he had left her but moments before. "Yes...yes, I suppose she is. At least a whore of sorts..."

Eben's face registered utter shock, then affront. To think he would so calmly admit the truth! As if there were nothing wrong with parading a whore in society, regardless of the damage done to his reputation...not to say the way it affected her.

"Eastmore, you are a bloody bounder!" she stated, and turned to leave abruptly, only to have her elbow caught in a grip that would have caused a lesser woman to cry out.

"You are a quick one to case stones, little cat. Perhaps you should take a moment to understand a lady's tale and lend some thought to the ashes gossip can leave in a place where no fire existed. Now, if you will excuse me…'' With this, he took his leave of her.

The arrival of Alfred and her requested ice fortunately forestalled any action on her part, for the action she desired more than anything else at that moment was to rush after him and strike him sharply between the shoulder blades with her fist…no less than three times, and quite possible a great many more … although what good such a move would do escaped her.

Problems and dilemmas fairly dogged her footsteps, she thought. In seeming so attentive to Alfred while actually not listening at all, Eben found, she had agreed to attend a supper and entertainment the following evening at a Lady Dover's house. Depressed over her set-down by Fitzhugh, she desired nothing more than to cry off an evening in Alfred's company.

"Now that I consider it, Lord Ellington, I am not familiar with that lady. I am not at all sure it is proper to accept the invitation," she said, attempting to extricate herself gracefully.

"My dear Miss Victor, I assure you it is all aboveboard. The Baroness Wellington and her brother shall attend us, so that you need not concern yourself with a chaperon." Alfred seemed about to indulge in a fit of anger, characteristic of him when crossed. "No way to cry off now. Very bad show."

"Pray, don't fly into the boughs over it, Lord Ellington. Bargain, then … if the outing is approved by my aunt, we will consider it done."

Turning, she threaded her way back to the box, positive her aunt would aid in extricating her from this tangle her pique at seeing Eastmore with that…that late bloomer had landed her. Upon returning to the box, they found Lady Lillian alone, having agreed that Lord Melton and Lady Adair should promenade before the next scene. This only provided additional fuel for the fire at her feet, for Alfred deftly handled the situation to his best advantage.

"Lady Victor, I have invited your charming daughter to accompany me and two very close friends … Baroness Wellington and her brother, I am positive you are acquainted with them, as they move in the same circles as you yourself do … 'Tis merely a light entertainment and supper. But she refuses to commit without your loving permission. May I beseech you to grant a badly smitten young man his heart's wish and allow her permission?" The pleading lord cast his dilemma at her feet in such an eloquent manner, Lady Lillian became quite flustered.

"Oh, of course, my lord. Baroness Wellington... brother? I don't believe..."

"Moves in the highest circles, don't you know," he stated again.

"Oh... well, I'm sure... very well. Permission granted." Eben closed her eyes for a second. Having been unable to catch her mother's eye to warn her off, she found herself doubly committed to spending an entire evening in this little man's disagreeable company.

Eben's concentration was not as it should be for the remainder of the play, so lost in thought of Fitzhugh and that woman was she. Although she could not see them in the darkened theater, she could well imagine the wanton's hot flesh pressed against his side, and it galled her. There was no doubting now. He was a man such as her father had been... admitted from his own lips. Dedicated to high flyers, probably had this one set up in her own house... possibly the same house he had once offered her! It was the best of decisions... proving her good sense... that she had sealed their relationship as friends and nothing more. Though why there was no solace in that thought, she did not know.

Chapter Fourteen

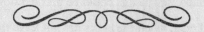

Mrs. Dover's house was a spacious mansion on a dark street a short drive from Picadilly and was filled from top to bottom with frescoed paneling and an abundance of fringed crimson brocades, with massive chandeliers reflecting in numerous gilt mirrors. To some Londoners, it might have seemed overdone, even a trifle gaudy, but Eben, having grown up in the overstated French elegance of Victor Mall, saw nothing amiss and gave her wrap to the maid instead of demanding to return home forthwith. The evening was already threatening to be a disaster, commencing with Ellington's tardy arrival, far after the departure of her mother and aunt.

Then the introductions to the Baroness Wellington and her brother, whose name she still did not retain, had left her with a discomfited feeling, for some reason. She was certain, without a solid concern to state, that her aunt wouldn't approve of these people if she were privy to the company. The baroness's powder and lip rouge were a trifle too noticeable to be quite proper, and her gown was cut so low that she was fearful the lady's abundant charms would not remain so lightly contained all evening. Braving that lady's bored appraisal, Eben felt young and gauche. But Ellington was quite sober, and after all, a new experience was a new experience. She felt capable of extricating herself from any manner of unpleasantness, for she had yet to meet a man she did not feel she could best outright... or outrun, if necessary. The thought of outrunning Ellington, with her elegant green taffeta raked up around her knees, brought a smile to her lips, delighting that gentleman, who mistakenly took it for his own.

The dinner was twelve removes of excellent fare, and while most of the diners seemed to be of acquaintance, Eben did not care to ask to have names repeated after the first introduction. She was more and more certain, from the gowns and liberal use of cosmetics, plus the familiarity of the gentlemen toward the ladies, that she would never see these women in circles in which she moved. But Ellington remained attentive, and while the wine was abundant and his imbibing heavy, he seemed controlled, so the rest could be marked down as life's seasonings.

Even after dinner, when the ladies did not leave the table but remained to enjoy cigarettes and port with the gentlemen and a pretty Miss Marion sang two French ballads accompanied by a coxcomb in a brilliant green coat and most elaborate apricot breeches above high-heeled red shoes, whom Eben found vastly amusing, she still did not feel in danger. After attending his exaggerated movements and flourishes, she had to contend that he was far more feminine than herself. This outrageous thought brought another smile to light her lovely face.

"You find the ballad amusing, Miss Victor?" Alfred whispered.

Drat! she thought. She'd hadn't been attending the songs at all. She turned her smile on him and resolved to pay closer attention, lest he quiz her later. Even with her rustic French, she caught enough of the words to be surprised they were sung by an unmarried girl, even in this dubiously genteel drawing room, and applauded wildly by those of the company who apparently understood all. She held her face in an appreciative smile that she was determined would reveal none of her shock and proclaim her innocence.

Retiring to a crowded ballroom upstairs, Eben was amazed to see all manner of gaming tables set. Whist tables and casino games abound. Here the noise level was high, charged with the winning and losing of great sums of money. The baroness, swaying unsteadily on her feet, insisted the pleasure of showing Eben about the room was to be hers, and Alfred, his eyes gleaming at the stacks of chips to be won on the tables, merely waved her away with a negligent air. With the painted lady leaning rather heavily on her arm and wafting words on wine-tinted breath, Eben became more and more uneasy, and she was very thankful when the tour was cut short by the lady's desire to retire to an alcove for a dubious rest. Quickly Eben retraced her steps back to the roulette wheel, where Ellington was engrossed in the play. Winning at the moment, he was pleased to have her as audience.

"Roulette," he explained, "is just a matter of luck, unlike cards, where you must display some skill. I could try all night to explain the game, but it's best to just watch the play, and you'll soon get the gist."

"You had best let someone else explain it to her, for sure, Ellington!" a rather florid man next to Eben jeered loudly, with a most uncomfortable jab to her ribs with his elbow. "They say no one can predict luck, but I can most certainly predict yours!"

The company within earshot, which, due to the volume of the man's boisterous voice, was large, joined in the laughter. Eben saw the thundercloud gather on the little man's face and was relieved to see the play commence.

Watching the play and the rapidly dwindling stacks in front of the players, with most going to the house, Eben could well imagine the losses. She was amazed at the amounts the women and men wagered, and the lack of concern on their faces when the play went against them. Even Ellington seemed determined to lose his entire fortune in one play, judging by the stack of counters he had placed on one number. A number that, unfortunately, did not choose to come up. This was the town life her father had led. He might have even played at this very house, wagering the fortune Victor Mall had needed to survive. Losing the funds that would have allowed her mother and herself to stay in the only home she had ever known. Eben's thought fused with anger, and she resolved to linger no longer.

"Lord Ellington, the hour is becoming advanced. I feel it is time we retired," Eben advised him, quietly, so as not to disturb the play, although the noise had risen in the room to such a level that a shout would not have been unduly noticed.

"In one moment . . ."

Her suggestion was shrugged off. Alfred, intent on obtaining a full glass of spirits and considering his next play, a play that he was positive would restore his losses, paid her and her request scant attention.

"I shall await you by the door, my lord," she curtly informed him. She turned, sure he would follow in a moment. That was not to be the case, for Eben stood for a full fifteen minutes before deciding she must seek him out again. "Lord Ellington, I must insist you see me home. The hour goes toward midnight," Eben, again advised him quietly, only to have him turn to shout at her.

"Shh...I can't stop now! Have a patience, woman. Can't you see I'm stuck a goodly amount?"

The lord was quite bosky, making no attempt to keep his voice confidential, as Eben had. She stepped back a pace, stunned by his sharp words and his manner in delivering them. Embarrassed by the looks she received from the onlookers, she felt anger and resentment at the ill-mannered little upstart burn her. Eyes narrowed, she again stepped near to him.

"My lord, I am leaving! If you are not at the door by the time I am, I shall proceed home alone, and send your carriage back to you posthaste!" Eben turned on her heel and marched from the room with a dignified air.

Ordering Ellington's carriage brought around, Eben paced the entry. The audacity of the man! Drunken wastrel! His name was to be stricken not only from her eligibles list, but from her memory, as well. Never had she been so slighted, or so cross with herself for allowing herself to be trapped in such a disagreeable situation. Not surprised when the small lord did not appear in a timely manner, she swept down the front steps to mount the barouche. As her foot touched the first step, Ellington caught up with her.

"Now wait a minute! No woman is going to walk out on me! You think to embarrass me? And in front of my friends, too!"

He was in a drunken rage. Not only had he lost heavily this night, but they had laughed at him! When this little twit had stalked from the room, everyone at the table had laughed at him. He would forever be known as the lord whose lady railed at him in public. Ellington jerked her arm to stop her from entering the barouche.

"Unhand me, sir!"

Eben rounded on him, as he pulled her off balance. She was not going to stand for mishandling from a drunken poor excuse of a man, in the driveway of a gaming house...where he never should have brought her in the first place. As she drew herself up to her full height with haughty disdain, Ellington was forced to look up to see her face. That was a galling act, one she should have known to be dangerously inciting to a man as sensitive of his lack of stature as the bosky lord before her, but, like the lord's, her thinking was clouded by blind outrage.

"Why, you teasing little bitch!" he screamed, his voice going high as a young girl's. Ellington was beyond reason now, as he unfortunately displayed by gripping her shoulders and attempting to shake her senseless. Only to find that, with her wide stance, she was far stronger, and he could not move her. Yet another affront to his masculinity. Never one to concede defeat, he shoved her brutally, causing her to slam back against the rigid side of the carriage. The horses started and danced under the dubious control of the gawking coachman.

Quick as the cat Fitzhugh called her, Eben whirled and removed the whip from the stunned coachman's limp hand. "'Tis a brawl you want, my little, ill-mannered lord? Pray, let me oblige you!" With a whirl and a loud crack, she viciously lashed the whip across Ellington's scrawny, silk-clad legs.

"I'll teach— Oooh!" he yelled, swinging his hand for the whip as he danced about in an abortive attempt to avoid the sting of the lash.

"Touch me again, my lord, and I shall whip you to the size of a peahen in a trice!" she grated between clenched teeth, slashing the air.

"You bloody bitch!" he squealed.

Not one to be defamed in such a manner, and no longer content with the spectacle of His Lordship dancing in circles, grabbing at his legs, Eben swiftly inverted the whip and dealt a pitiless jab to his stomach with the butt end. The blow quite put the unruly noble flat on the ground. The crowding audience of grooms and coachmen gave a round cheer at her efficient handling of the nasty little man, for he was known well for savagely abusing cattle and servants alike.

"Brawling in the gravel of gaming halls now, my dear Miss Victor?"

The nonchalant drawl spun her about to face a new adversary. Seeing the elegantly dressed Eastmore leaning carelessly against the barouche behind her with a tight smile on his face, she could not repress the shameless grin.

"Aye, Eastmore. And as my mettle's up still, would you care to go a few rounds? Such a shame to waste a fairly good show of temper on one small lord, do you not agree?"

"Actually, I feel the prudent course of action would be to flee before the guard shows up to impound you for public nuisance. May I see you home? My chaise is just there," he indicated, the smile of dubious humor never leaving his lips.

"I fear you might be quite right about the matter. And I do kindly accept your offer. But what shall we do about yon gentleman in the dust?" Eben turned and deftly tossed the whip, butt first, to the grinning coachman, who saluted her smartly with it.

"His people will see to him. Trust this, when I say he is no stranger to being facedown in the dirt."

Fitzhugh kept up a light banter during the ride to Grosvenor Square, as Eben was riddled with high spirits after the foray. Seeing the house ablaze and having the fact confirmed by Hastings that her aunt and mother had yet to return, Eben requested he join her in the salon for a cordial, to which he readily agreed, having it on his mind to read her the riot act.

"I must admit, dear Miss Victor, I have yet to see a debutante handle a carriage whip as effectively. Not only are you an admirable whip, you should begin frequenting Gentleman Jim's Boxing Academy, as well, for I would not be any more surprised to learn that you spar," Fitzhugh retorted, again with that little tight smile that boded no leniency for her, had she been less animated and more attentive.

"Rest assured, Eastmore, I do not spar. Although I would pay dearly for an hour or two's workout at the Royal Fencing Academy. I am sadly lacking in exercise since this cursed season began." Eben restlessly paced the room, while Fitzhugh lounged on the striped Grecian sofa and watched her through hard eyes.

"You sidestep the question, Eben. Whatever possessed you to appear at that house tonight, unchaperoned?" he quizzed. "Where was your aunt? Surely she did not give you permission to attend that function?"

"Actually...no..." She turned to face her accuser. "My mother gave her consent for Lord Ellington to escort me to Lady Dover's."

"Mrs. Dover is no lady! And a reputedly crooked gaming house is no place for a debutante of the ton to be parading on the arm of a noted bounder such as Alfred Ellington. I wonder at your lack of convention," he said, his tone becoming slightly sharper as his agitation slipped control.

"I did not realize it was that kind of place, until I . . .

although I did wonder when I did not recognize anyone during dinner," she began, defensively. "Besides, as I displayed, I am quite able to take care of myself."

"You, my fine cat, may have just shredded your reputation beyond redemption. You may well never recover your credit...for the possibility of this being bantered around every drawing room by tomorrow is almost certain. I doubt the tale of your laying out a drunken member of the ton in the gravel with a buggy whip, while exiting the notorious establishment of Mrs. Dover's, will amuse the patronesses of Almack's, any more than it will your aunt!" he stormed at her.

"How dare you speak to me thus! What right—?" she stuttered, her banked anger flaring again into flames. "Why didn't you warn—? What of your promise to aid—?" She paused to draw a shaky breath. "And if that place is such a horrible place, what were you doing there?"

"My dear Miss Victor, I am a man of adult years, while you are an infant who, it has just become apparent, must be cared for with uninterrupted mindfulness. There lies the difference." Fitzhugh had risen and advanced on Eben, who stood defiantly before the fireplace and the portrait of the first Eben Pearl. His walk reminded her forcefully of a predator, at once lithe and dangerous. A shiver raced down her spine, but she did not give ground. Raising her chin in defiance, she narrowed her eyes.

"There lies the rub. A man is allowed to do whatever, whenever, to whomever he pleases. While a woman must maintain the silliest notion of innocence. Be it on her head if she gives the slightest hint that she thinks or reasons with any degree of efficiency. The most important thing being whether or not she is fitted with an intact maidenhead."

Fortunately, whenever her anger ran rampant, Eben's voice lowered and became frigid rather than, as with most females, shrill and carrying. Otherwise, the neighbors on Grosvenor Square would have been privy to the most astonishing discussion ever, between two unmarried members of the ton, well after midnight, quite unchaperoned, squared off, in battle stances, before one another. Not one but three indiscretions that would have landed them in the midst of a forced wedding if anyone of consequence had observed them.

"A man prefers to be certain that his heirs are his own blood when he weds a woman," Fitzhugh growled at her, his face close to hers, his eyes shooting sparks.

"Then he had best hope she breeds within the first week of the marriage vows, because it is common practice for a lady to take a lover to while away the lonely afternoons. Afternoons when her loving, devoted husband is showering his mistress with extravagant little establishments in return for his share of the slut's bed." Eben sneered at him, blue eyes snapping fire. "At least a woman gains a lover without undue expense to her family, while a man, at great cost to his heirs, pays dearly for a woman to suffer his attentions. As I am sure you realize, having been in both positions, lover and keeper."

Fitzhugh was shocked into a moment of silence by this tirade. His eyes narrowed to golden slits, and when he spoke again, his voice was deadly. Eben's heart thundered in her ears, but she would never give ground in an argument.

"You, my love, have a guttersnipe's mouth, attractive as it may look. If you have every intention of joining the demimonde, pray let me be allowed to advertise my approval of your charms, having been the first man to sample them." Fitzhugh gripped her shoulders in his strong hands, pulling her warm body hard against his, and glared down at her.

Eben's face flushed a dull red, then blanched a dead white—a hue familiar to Fitzhugh as a display of extreme shock. Fearing she would swoon, he quickly released her, discomfited suddenly to see tears spill down her cheeks.

"Oh, unfair, Eastmore! We agreed never to mention that again! And now you take advantage where no...true f-friend...would. You are no gentleman! You break your word...and take...unfair advantage!" Eben wailed. Running to the door, she turned once more to exhibit a lovely face dissolving into tears of distress, and whispered, just loud enough for the Duke to hear, "I hate you, Fitzhugh Eastmore! I hate you, do you hear?"

Throwing back the door against its frame and rushing out of his sight, Eben fled up the stairs in tears. Fitzhugh spun around to slam his fist down hard on the marble mantel, then raised tormented eyes to the portrait that was so like his Eben Pearl.

"Damn! And I, my fiery darling, am quite hopelessly in love with you!"

Chapter Fifteen

The afternoon was not yet advanced, and the elder ladies had yet to decend the stairs after their late return from Lady Standiford's card party and musical. Eben sat before a delicate secretaire in the salon. Her head rested wearily in her hand as she perused bills and documents forwarded to her via Mr. Vandevilt, and avoided by her for more than a fortnight now, as the creditors were becoming insistent, and he very much wished for good news to tell them, something encouraging concerning her endeavors to buy more time for her pursuits. Her idle hand pleated, smoothed and repleated a portion of her gold muslin skirt.

"Pursuits! I'd just like to hear who was pursuing whom in this madcap season!" she muttered disagreeably.

Not surprising, she felt the more pursued. Much like a harried fox driven from its lair by the hounds baying for its blood. With a sigh, she withdrew a sheet of paper and prepared to write a note explaining that, as the season was young, she could not announce good news, but she and her mother...blah, blah, blah! Her hand stilled just long enough to blot a great stain of ink on the parchment from the poorly feathered quill. She quickly wadded the sheet into a ball and threw it in the general direction of the fireplace.

"Tar and fiddle! Pray tell, what will mollify the man for a while longer? If only I could send him this desk and chair! Both are worth more at auction than my hand at this moment."

"Taken to conversing with ourselves now, are we?" Fitzhugh observed as he strolled forcefully into the room.

Numbed for a moment, Eben turned a pale, haggard face up to him, believing this to be some illusion on her part, but no such luck. And judging from his frowning countenance and forceful tread, she was due yet another lecture. A distressing thought, as she had neither desire nor energy to make war with him this day.

"I thought I had instructed Hastings to tell you I was not at home to you, today or ever again," she declared coldly, clenching the quill tightly to still any trembling of her hand. Fitzhugh strode the length of the room until he was towering above the desk before her.

"I persuaded Hastings otherwise," he answered tersely. "Do you think there is any servant...any door or lock...that could keep me from you, if I desired differently?"

The quill in her hand snapped in two as she jumped to her feet and, with a slightly panicked look on her face, reached for the bellpull. "We shall see about that!"

"I would think a moment, if I were you.... There is no burly footman available to deposit me in the driveway, and I do think you would be doing a grave injustice to Hastings, at his advanced age, to request it of him. For I have no doubt that, out of loyalty to your family, he would attempt your wishes, whereupon I would be forced to ruffle his dignity," Fitzhugh warned, painting such a comical picture of poor, aged, bent-over Hastings attempting to manhandle this powerfully built lord from the doorstep that Eben burst out with an involuntary hoot of laughter. "Now, that's better," he said approvingly, his tone softening. "Quickly, don your riding togs. Ottobon and Ellington are waiting for us to ride in Hyde Park this fine afternoon."

"Ride with Ellington! Not to see him hanged!" she interjected in astonishment. "Eastmore, you are addlebrained to even entertain such a thought that I would ride with either of you."

"What's this? Are we being declined?" Lewis joined the couple. "Get a move on, girl, my sorrel grows restless. You'll be seeing his shine dulled by sweat before he's gone a mile."

"Lewis..." She beamed upon seeing him.

Fitzhugh scowled to see her pleased expression. "Ride you will, miss," he concluded, pulling her around the desk, gently but firmly. "Now, change quickly...or I shall be required to help you dress? I do believe you told me you are quite without adequate servants at present. I do not mind...I assure you. I have a way with froth and ecru lace," he offered as he propelled her into the hallway with a firm grip on her shoulders to encourage her reluctant step.

With an irritated gasp, Eben wrenched from his grasp and trotted partway up the stairs before turning to glare at him, hands defiantly set on her hips.

"Desist with your nonsense, and inform me just why I should attend a notorious woman-beater..."

"Miss Victor...don't you see?" Lewis joined him on the bottom step. "To stop any rumors that are bound to have leaked out. Gotta save your credit, old girl! Fitz here spoke to Ellington's coachman, but the man has little love for his master, and the tale of his set-down at the hands of a fire-breathing debutante with a buggy whip will be too juicy by far to keep to himself. But who would believe such a blarney tale, especially since the young lady in question was seen quite amiably riding with the gentleman in question the very next day!"

"And no claws showing, mind you!" Fitzhugh warned, advancing up the stairs, backing Eben up, step by step, as he told her, "No bloodletting! No barbed remarks to incite a riot! Now hurry, or I swear I will dress you myself...after I undress you! I do not mind, I promise."

"Bloody rotter!" Eben yelled over her shoulder in false bravado as she fled up the stairs.

"I say, Fitz, that's a bit brown, don't you think?" Lewis asked, shocked at his friend's familiarity with the debutante.

"My word! What's this?" Lady Adair asked, narrowly missing being trampled by her niece on the stairs. Startled at seeing not one, but two, sharply attired Corinthians halfway up the stairs and her niece in full flight, she frowned. "I say! Ghastly bad ton, Eastmore. Do you have an explanation as to all this?"

"Just offering to play lady's maid for your niece, Lady Cromwell. Pray do not fret, she has declined," he said, laughing as he strolled down the stairs and out the front door, with a confused, doubtful Lewis hard on his heels.

"My word!" huffed Lady Adair. "I must keep a closer eye on that girl! Something's astir there. Something tasty!" Then, with a secret smile to herself, she admitted, "Oh, my! I do so love a lusty man!"

In just fifteen minutes, Eben casually strolled out the front door, pulling on her riding gloves, sparkling in sapphire blue. Jamie Deal stood tending both the black stallion and an excited Victoire, with the Corinthians appraising the pros and cons of both. A very sour Ellington sat, rather slumped, on the dun gelding that showed more flash than sound, with his back turned moodily on the party.

"Ah, here's Miss Victor now. I am so pleased you are a speedy dresser. It would be a shame to let this beautiful spring day go to waste," Lewis called, sounding falsely cheerful, rotating an uncertain look from Eben to Fitzhugh to Ellington. He was no stranger to disagreements among his cronies, but this was his first experience involving a young, unmarried miss in a fray of this magnitude. Fitzhugh led the dancing Victoire forward.

"I will ride the black this afternoon," Eben announced, passing Fitzhugh to advance on Jamie Deal and the black stallion.

"You will ride the filly and cause no undue talk, miss!" he gritted. Grasping her slim waist in both hands, he deposited her, rather roughly, in the saddle aboard Victoire.

Gasping as her bottom slapped leather, Eben could only glare at Fitzhugh's snort of amusement. Turning toward Ellington, with prepared politeness, she greeted him, for, after all, she could afford to be magnanimous, since it had been her dubious victory.

"Good day, my lord. That's a dashing dun you have under saddle today. Good Lord!" she exclaimed as the slight lord turned toward her with undisguised hatred in his eyes. His left eye was quite purple, and there was a discolored swelling on that cheek and his lip was decidedly split and bruised.

As the foursome moved out of Grosvenor Square at a brisk trot, with Jamie Deal bringing up the rear, she edged Victoire next to Lewis's raking sorrel. "You are quite right, my lord— no one will question a rumor once they see how friendly I and this half-beaten lord are with each other," she mused sweetly. "Lewis, how could you?"

Ottobon turned big, innocent eyes on her, deadpanning. "I thought you did that. The way Fitzhugh told the tale, you gave the poor drunken fool no quarter!"

She swiveled to glare at the duke. He just gave her a cool look with one eyebrow elevated toward his gray silk, which sat jauntily over his sun-lightened hair. His amber eyes were unreadable. Jamie Deal, overhearing this exchange, grinned from ear to ear, barely suppressing an Irish ditty. Leaning over to slam the black on the neck, he whispered to the big fella,

"Our lass has finally met her match, old man. Ye'll soon be serving yon tall gent, mark my words!"

The park was just beginning to come alive with promenaders. The ornate and brightly painted carriages were sparse as yet, and the air was crisp. It promised to be a beautiful afternoon. Victoire was fresh and capering, and Eben's mood began to lighten. The small party rode in comfortable silence for a pace. Taking advantage of the sparse traffic, they wandered off the tracks and through the trees. The air was crisp, but by no means disagreeable. A few hardy birds flitted in the trees overhead. Eben, peacefully lulled into allowing the filly her head to pick her way across the path and down into a shallow streambed, was almost unseated when the filly took it into her mind to act the minx. Lewis watched Eben with a wide grin of admiration spreading across his face as she brought the filly swiftly under control.

"Well done, Miss Victor!" he exclaimed. Alfred snorted in disgust at the display, but all ignored him.

"Thank you, my lord. I see you're up on a spanking new sorrel today," she shot back at him. "What a piece of blood and bone he is, quite up to the nines!"

Lewis gave her a mocking bow and a touch of his silk with his riding crop in acknowledgment. Fitzhugh only smiled and led the crew on a short gallop toward the lake before turning them back to Rotten Row, as it was approaching five o'clock, the most fashionable hour to be seen promenading. Once there, it was not possible to do more than post a trot, and rarely that. The small group was regulated down to a walk, with much nodding and bowing to peers, restricted for Eben's sake, as well as the sake of their plan, to the most well-traveled roadways.

Such a bloody bore, Eben decided. Just when she thought to release herself from the charade, Fitzhugh excused himself to approach a pink tilbury driven by a young lady accompanied by her abigail. Eben's eyes narrowed, and she gave a shiver. Margaret Vernill! How she must preen to have the duke of Eastmore leave the company of the great, dark goose for her own plump, classic beauty. Why men found her pretty, Eben could not fathom. With her very white skin and tight blond ringlets framing a doll's face with a pouty, pink mouth and large china-blue eyes, which she was engaged in blinking rapidly at Fitzhugh just at the moment, she appeared exceedingly false to Eben.

"Well, it would seem Eastmore is quite smitten," Alfred fairly spat out. "I see him more and more in the company of that simpering fool!"

"Alfred, watch your manners in front of Miss Victor," Lewis calmly reminded him with a stern look.

Eben did not give the little man the courtesy of a remark. She could see for herself that the self-centered miss was indeed taken with her own charms, for she would pout and preen for His Lordship. But as Fitzhugh would leave the carriage parade and return to his own party, another stopped him.

"Ah, the Lady Sinclair..." Alfred gloated, casting a sideways look at Eben. Seeing the stiffening of her spine, he rushed to needle her further. "The lovely Louise...Eastmore's *chère amie*..."

"Ellington..." Lewis began, but Alfred chose to ignore the warning and continued to give information that Eben tried not to want to hear.

"...leaves an elderly and ill husband in the country—some say he's on his deathbed as we speak—to retire to town every season. Seems to have snared Eastmore, first as this year's bed warmer, then, possibly, as a replacement, as she's drained ol' Sinclair's coffers dry."

"Ellington, enough!" grated Lewis, glancing first at the offending lord, then at Eben.

Eben stared at the flamboyant lady, because she could not help herself. Eastmore's whore, fashionably impure, a lady of dubious quality who flouted the rules and yet had the title and wealth to withstand the criticism. True, she was no longer young, thirty if she was a day, and the flaming hair could not possibly have achieved that color of its own volition, but as Eastmore was at last seeing fit to rejoin their party, as he had kept them rudely stalemated on the path far too long, she kept her own counsel. Yet she could, and would, glare at him with all the disapproval she felt.

Alfred, brought out of his blue funk by her discomfort, began to express his opinions on people met along the track, as well as his political views. With great effort, Eben found herself listening to the lord's discourse on the merits of sterner discipline for children in the mines, a subject upon which he apparently thought he was qualified, because of the number of them on his land.

"It should be beaten into them, if necessary, that their place is to toil for their masters and earn their keep! After all, these children would otherwise be thrown on the mercy of the local almshouse, which is supported by me. Next thing you know, they will want to read and write."

"Perhaps that is not a conversation we should continue in present company, Ellington," Fitzhugh cautioned, as he noticed color he could not attribute to exercise rising in Eben's cheeks.

Eben gritted her teeth. How like a man to think a subject of substance to be beyond a woman's comprehension. Why did the male of the species insist on believing the female brain deficient in most every way? Or was it that they truly were fearful that the feminine mind, admittedly somewhat devious and far more crafty than theirs, once given the opportunity to express itself fully, would be impossible to ever contain again behind the walls of prejudice and arrogant bigotry? She could control her tongue no longer.

"I, for one, think child labor is despicable! If I were a man..." she began, only to be interrupted rudely.

Alfred turned on her, furious at having his views questioned, especially by a female, and this female in particular. "Yes, Miss Victor? What would you do if you were a man? Your estate is already penniless because of the drag of your almshouses and workhouses... supporting your poor."

"Miss Victor, I think I should take you home, before this boor says something that earns him yet another beating." Fitzhugh moved his horse between the filly and Alfred's dun.

"No, Eastmore, let me answer him!" Eben put her hand out to stop Fitzhugh from turning the filly's head. "Ellington, if I were a man, I would first of all take you to Chalk Walk and fill your backside with buckshot. Then I would proceed to marry the peanut-brained Miss Vernill, take her money to the country and set about teaching my poor almshouse children to read and write, so that they might better themselves in this life. That would make them more productive citizens and less a drain on my pocketbook than working them into an early grave, as you want to do!"

Alfred's bruised face turned dark with rage, the distortion making him ugly and frightful. So much so that Jamie Deal crowded close to the group with the fractious black stallion, in case the need to defend his lass should arise.

"I think you are full of bloody talk! You sound like our softheaded queen, with your talk of reform. If you were a man, indeed! Actually, you should be a man," he spat out. "I'll test the size of your pellets for you. I wager a stakes race! My bay against your black! One thousand pounds, and winner takes papers!"

"That's enough! The two of you are like children!" Fitzhugh demanded. Thinking to separate them before it came to blows, he took charge of the filly's head. "Lewis, turn him away!"

"That's a fair safe bet you make, Ellington. One you know I cannot take up. I have no money to wager!" Her voice steely, she struck a deadly blow. "You are a small man in more ways than one!"

Alfred screamed in rage, jerking at the leathers in an attempt to loose Ottobon's hold. Putting cruel spurs to his gelding, he strove to drive his mount into the side of the filly. People began to gather in interest on the path.

"Enough! You make a spectacle. And you, Ellington, insult a lady!" Fitzhugh tried to put a stop to the fray before it spread through the entire park, spoiling their plan to avoid undue gossip. "And the lady does not act like a lady! Miss Victor, you egg him on. Desist, at once!" he said, rebuking Eben, as well.

Turning a set face with narrowed eyes on Fitzhugh, she politely begged his forgiveness in a tone that belied her furious expression, an attitude that did not surprise him overly much.

"I apologize, your grace, for my unforgivable behavior. I shall leave you to your friend, as I do not find either of you a man who improves upon continued acquaintance. I bid you good-day! Lord Ottobon, my apologies."

With those pretty words, Eben, with as much dignity as her anger would allow her, wheeled Victoire and left the group, with Jamie hard on her heels. Alfred performed the same abrupt departure in the opposite direction. Lewis sat stunned a moment, then slumped in his saddle in mock fatigue.

"Whew. I feel like I've just gone five rounds in the ring and am flung on the ropes. She is magnificent, but what a temper!'' He sighed. Fitzhugh merely smiled his tight smile, confounding Lewis all the more. "All right, Eastmore! Out with the tale! What is the rag between you and our fair Miss Victor?"

"Just neighborly concern for an unprotected spitfire who wants to destroy her credit at each and every turn. Nothing more,'' he answered, turning his mount in the direction of White's. He badly needed a toddy to settle his nerves.

"Taradiddle!'' Lewis ragged, setting a pace beside him. "You lie, old man. The minx has captured your heart, hasn't she?''

Fitzhugh suddenly reined in across the path, blocking Lewis's sorrel, his face was set. "Do not press me too severely, dear friend,'' he grated. "My temper has been sorely tried this afternoon, and I would step lightly if I were you.''

Lewis elevated an eyebrow and studied his friend for a second, then let out with a rolling hoot of laughter.

"But you d-do have it b-bad!'' he sputtered, bending over with his uncontrollable laughter.

"Ottobon, desist!'' Fitzhugh tried to growl, but finally ended with defeat and joined in the laughter with his merry friend.

The promenading haut ton was treated to quite a show on this day. First an argument of sorts between Lord Ellington and Miss Victor. And now the duke of Eastmore and Viscount Ottobon indulging in a fit of uncontrollable laughter. All this following a certain tale of spite between a lord and a debutante. Strange goings-on, for certain. The ton fairly buzzed.

Chapter Sixteen

The speculation concerning an incident no one had seen, but everyone had heard of, died out rapidly; as everyone had heard a different version and any inquiries were met with ignorance or flat denials from the strangely bruised Lord Ellington. Of course, no one had the audacity to approach Eben—except her aunt, and she endorsed, with tongue in cheek, the denial of her niece. But the gossip did bring the dark-haired beauty to the foreground attention of the petticoat line. While it had always been accepted as very bad ton to discuss ladies at White's, it seemed Eben was discussed everywhere else by the young bloods. Several of whom learned, the painful way, that she was not to be spoken of lightly in the hearing of the duke of Eastmore.

Lewis also championed her cause as readily. It was apparent by her dance card and the rapid path to her door of the most tonish tulips to invite her to suppers, theaters and promenades that she was the most sought-after catch of the season, even without a feather to build a nest. Just as it was much noted, and duly discussed, that several dances were always saved for the painfully shy Lord Compton.

But for Eben, the popularity had begun to pall no sooner than it had commenced. The late nights, and the early mornings that made the late nights bearable, plus the pomp and formality, were wearing at her natural vitality. She desperately needed a respite, but as Lady Adair warned, out of sight was out of mind, and to further their purpose, the trail must be followed while it was hot. Blessedly, the letters had ceased from Mr. Vandevilt, as he must have realized additional pressure at the present time would accomplish nothing. And for this, at least, Eben would be eternally thankful, although she was positive they would start again as soon as the season began to wind down without good news from her, or if he heard one breath of scandal that would mar her chances.

She seldom glimpsed Fitzhugh without the vampish Louise Sinclair upon his arm, or lately—and somehow much worse— the triumphantly smug Maggie Vernill. How he could not see through the vacant expression that one affected, how he could abide the habitude of high-pitched, senseless giggling at every word he uttered, she would never know. Men! Their fickleness in preferring vapid beauty that faded over time to brains and wit that only increased and ripened to more enjoyment with age was beyond her.

As for the elegant duke, she supposed he had merely taken her at her word and turned his teasing amber eyes in other directions. Regretfully, she imagined the break between them was permanent. Evidently her behavior had been so deplorable this time, he could not overlook it. More than once she had berated herself for causing a scene in the park after his concerted efforts to set right a very bad show at the gaming hall. But always her chin would rise and she would lay the blame back at his door for he should have warned her off Ellington from the beginning.

Furthermore, it had been entirely his idea to force the deplorable man's company on her the very next day! So he might slight her if he wished! He might avoid her company all he desired, as it was just as well as far as she was concerned. Though she mourned the loss of a much-needed friend, she found him too disturbing to be around. He was not to be trusted as a friend to keep his word. Thus she vacillated in her own mind over the duke of Eastmore.

Thankfully, Lewis was a regular in her party, and while not to be considered seriously as a husband or even a confidant, he was a welcome and amusing escort. What Eben really needed, or thought she needed at this time, was to bring Barnaby up to snuff, as she had decided he was to be the mark. But Barnaby, weak and stumbling, had yet to declare himself as to any advancement on any subject without heavy coaching from Eben.

The proposed dinner at Compton Castle was to be a draining experience. By declining the offer of escort in the Comptons' coach, Eben had sought to relieve herself of the strained embarrassed silence of Barnaby's company, trapped with him in a closed carriage for any length of time, only to find her mother willing and able to make her just as miserable with her repeated harping.

"I just don't know why we have to do this, when Eben has no notion of leading Ernestine's boy on with pretended interest," Lady Lillian complained fretfully. "I wish I had just stayed home. Or Emily Cowper is having a card party tonight. We could have attended there."

"Lillian, you and I have discussed this to death! It would have been a slight of the first kind for you not to attend Ernestine tonight," her sister began to explain in strained patience. "And you know very well, we can not afford to offend Ernestine... because of her strong influence over her son. And Eben is considering this union. We've talked of all this!"

"I just can't bear the thought of Eben marrying into that family! Not when she has suitors by the droves." Lady Lillian was not to be denied her complaint. "There have been four offers already for her hand. Won't any one of them suit?"

"Five, Mama. Not one from a first-run tulip." Eben sat forward, with a direct gaze at her mother. "Not one with enough money to set Victor Mall to rights and settle Papa's debts..."

Her brow furrowed for a moment as she berated herself with inner chastising. Liar! Fitzhugh's offer had been the first, and he had more than enough blunt to right her life. If only he had proved to be the man of honor he proclaimed himself to be. The engagement would have been announced, and she could be at Victor Mall supervising the rebuilding of her home at this very moment, rather than traveling an uncomfortable two hours to spend time in the disagreeable company of Lady Compton. She sighed to herself. What a terrible muddle she had made of this whole thing, starting with the first time she'd laid eyes on him. Her mood began to turn dark, as it seemed to do each time he came to mind lately. And that was too often for comfort.

"Eben, pray finish..." her mother complained petulantly. "You're wool-gathering again. Most irritating habit..."

"Mama, I know it distresses you, but as far as Barnaby Compton goes, I will accept an offer readily enough, if he will promise to leave his mother at Compton Castle and live with me at Victor Mall. Or if I can figure out some way to dispose of Lady Compton without bringing the guards down on my head.''

"Eben! You wouldn't!'' gasped her mother.

"No, Mama, I would not do bodily harm to Lady Compton. I was jesting. To lighten your mood," she reassured her.

"I meant, you would not marry that whey-faced mama's boy!"

Lady Adair sat tapping a forefinger against a pursed mouth, contemplating her niece. She was looking strained and worried of late. Something was amiss here, and she'd bet it had something to do with that rake Eastmore. If only she could get a fix on it, she would throw her weight in the direction of that union, for it was perfect for all purposes. But the duke had been noticeably absent from their salon, and any party that was put together, as of late. Something was definitely amiss!

The Gothic spires of Compton Castle came into view, and Eben had her first glimpse of the ancient pile of gray stones that had housed successive generations of Comptons for countless years. It was not a welcoming sight. Centuries of weather and moisture had darkened the stone to a dismal black, except where the green of mold defaced it. Ivy ran rampant over the narrow façade, further adding to the general appearance of depression and gloom. An occasional glint of afternoon sun reflecting off the diamond-paned windows did nothing to provide relief.

Their arrival at the front entry brought grotesque gargoyles leering down from every cornice and niche, and distressed little shrieks from Lady Lillian when it was suggested she depart the carriage. Led by a nervous Barnaby down stone corridors decorated to the beams with implements of medieval torture and examples of artwork that Eben was convinced were visual nightmares of deranged artists and should be studied by doctors of the mind seeking insight into why people commit unspeakable acts against their own kind. Eventually they were shown into a vast hall dominated by massive tapestries, detailing the exploits of Compton ancestors. A closer inspection would have shown bloody battle scenes of glorious victory over some smaller enemy, but that pleasure was declined by all three ladies. At the far end of the chamber was a small grouping of chairs drawn up to a huge fireplace in which burned a piteously small fire to combat the chill of the cavernous room.

"There's M-Mother!" Barnaby exclaimed, drawing an extremely reluctant Eben forward to Lady Compton, leaving the others to trail closely behind.

Eben uncomfortably found herself being studied by the small woman, dwarfed in a great throne chair carved with ball-and-claw feet that she surmised suited the lady perfectly. Attired in shroudlike black draperies, Lady Compton appraised Eben's sedate gray watered silk from head to toe with her black, beady eyes before greeting her.

"Good afternoon, Miss Victor. We are pleased you were able to come to our home. Barnaby, pull those chairs closer!"

Home? Eben thought, bobbing a knee to the lady and murmuring something she hoped was appropriate. This great, echoing pile of damp, moss-covered stones, a home? Perhaps to the Comptons, but never to her! Just look at the two of them! The only resemblance between mother and son was their total lack of color. Hair, skin, and eyes seemed to blend into one muddy hue. Hers gray and his brown. A rat and a mole! She gratefully stepped back to allow greetings from her aunt and her mother. Lady Compton's reception held the very air of a monarch holding court for her out-of-favor subjects. The company was not one of warmth and welcome, and for once Lady Adair did not still her sister's tongue as she prattled on about inane subjects such as the weather, the ride out from town and the latest gossip, in a nervous manner. All three ladies were thankful that time was limited and dinner was advanced to allow for the two-hour drive back to London.

An excellent dinner was accomplished with the aplomb of numerous servants, all of whom appeared to be as frightened of the sharp-tongued harpy as her son. Barnaby did not utter more than three words the entire meal, no matter what Eben said to draw him out. Actually, most questions directed to his end of the table were answered by his mother, without a shift in his attention from his plate. He seemed to be withdrawing farther and father into himself, disappearing from her sight. Unable to command him at the table with an audience, Eben too fell silent. After the final remove, the ladies—or Lady Compton, rather—deemed it ridiculous to retire the ladies from the gentleman.

"Barnaby is the only male present," she expounded in her irritatingly shrill voice, "and as retirement is mainly to allow the gentlemen freedom to smoke and consume spirits, neither deplorable addiction Barnaby suffers with, the custom shall be overlooked this once . . . as no important guests are present.''

Lady Lillian's mouth popped open and closed twice at this blatant insult, and even Lady Adair sniffed, but she controlled herself as the company rose to remove, hopefully to somewhere warmer, as the lofty dining hall was decidedly drafty. Almost to her wish, tea was served in a smaller, cozier parlor that could have been quite comfortable with a few feminine touches, such as cushions to soften a stone room and rigid chairs.

"Barnaby, show Miss Victor your butterflies," Lady Compton commanded with a flip of her hand, as one dismissing children.

"Y-yes, M-Mother. This way, Miss Victor," he stammered, jumping to his feet and indicating she was to follow him.

For an infinitesimal moment, Eben thought to decline, just to see if Lady Compton could make her go. But the desire to escape the stilted atmosphere in the parlor was stronger than her defiance, and she allowed Barnaby to hand her from the room.

Lady Lillian, knowing her daughter well, saw the instant of defiance and held her breath until Eben rose from the chair and departed the room, practically willing her to make a scene that would necessitate their immediate removal to town and away from the threat of this merger. She sighed a long sigh of resignation as Eben left the room. Fiddle! How inconsistent of her! At another, inappropriate time, her volatile daughter could have been counted upon to make a fuss. Why not now?

"So, Ernestine . . . do you agree with your son that the Victor line would easily combine with that of the Comptons?" Lady Adair asked, helping herself to another creamed muffin from the desert tray, not betraying the mischief she felt.

Lady Lillian choked on her tea, requiring immediate assistance in the form of a slap on the back from her sister. With little concern for Lady Lillian's recovery, the dowager focused her attention on Lady Cromwell. Regarding her through narrowed eyes, she cleared her throat and pursed her thin lips, as if she were considering the question. Lady Adair remained silent. And Lady Lillian could not have uttered a suitable remark had her very life depended upon it.

"The Victors can only trace their lineage back a small number of years, and Ebenezer Victor . . . pardon me, Lillian, but

I must speak the truth...was an absolutely despicable man...."
The dowager smiled a thin smile that did not for a moment
make her appear apologetic. "And while Barnaby does believe lineage important, he feels she is impressionable as yet,
and therefore trainable. Once ensconced at Compton Castle,
we feel, she will be sufficiently awed into making a commend-
able wife for my dear Barnaby. Of course, she has been raised
far too lenient and has almost made a gossip morsel of herself
over this last episode, but we are prepared to overlook that as
ill-mannered high jinks. As long as we post the banns immediately, and remove her from the decadence of London society posthaste, we feel she will come to no harm. Yes ... yes,
with the proper influence at Compton Castle, I am certain she
will make a fitting wife, and in time, an admirable daughter-in-
law."

"What if the two youngsters wish to reside at Victor Mall
instead of in this, er ... castle?" Lady Adair ventured, in a
purely conversational manner.

"That will not be allowed," stated Lady Compton. Just that
statement, no more.

Lady Adair pushed the point. "Even if your son should wish
to maintain the Mall as an alternative residence? The privacy
of newlyweds ... you understand?"

"Not one penny will be spent on that place! Things of value
will be properly stored—selling what isn't entailed, of course—
and later, if his second or third son wishes to make use of the
place and manages to marry into wealth, then we will see. Old
retainers and Ebenezer's debts will be taken care of...after the
marriage is consummated and the girl is with child. We will not
have it said the Comptons do not do their duty." Lady Compton was adamant upon this subject. "The castle is quite spacious...there are two small rooms in the east wing that will do
nicely for Lillian. I do not suppose you—" the dowager dismissed Lady Adair with an abrupt wave of her hand, as if
further discussion were not necessary on that one point
"—intend living off us too. My present companion, of course,
will be sent into Sussex to live with her sister. No sense over-
running the place with unnecessary people. I am sure Eben or
Lillian will not be averse to running the few small errands that
are now her occupation. I am a charitable person, not hard to
please."

"I am quite sure." Lady Adair spoke somewhat loudly, in an attempt to cover Lillian's snort of outrage. "But let's not be too hasty, as Eben has not yet consented to marry Barnaby. She has had many offers."

The dowager's mouth sagged a bit, and her hand tightened on her teacup. "Barnaby is taking care of that right now! She would be foolish, indeed, to delay over such a superb catch as my son. If she does wait too long and he decides on another, she will regret it the whole of her life, especially when the bailiff's at the door. Barnaby could aim much higher than a mere Viscount's daughter, and a penniless one, at that."

"Careful, dear Ernestine, you border a third time on insult," Lady Lillian said quietly. Lady Compton, as well as her sister, turned startled to stare at that usually flighty lady.

Unaware of the conflict in the parlor, Eben was seated on a window seat watching the sun set behind a range of hills and thinking of all the beautiful butterflies that had had their lives snuffed out for this one spoiled man's enjoyment, just because he did not believe in sharing. Although who would he share them with? It was quite obvious, friends for her son were not encouraged, now or possibly ever, by Ernestine Compton. Tentatively Barnaby seated himself beside her, as if afraid to disturb her thoughts. Fumbling in his pocket, he withdrew a small velvet box. Tilting the lid open, he displayed its contents and reached for her hand, only to withdraw his own before touching her. Then, determinedly, he reached again, and this time successfully took her small hand in his. Eben stared at the ring the box held. Enormous, heavily etched gold, with a square-cut ruby, set all around with diamonds, the ring glittered in the waning light.

Barnaby cleared his throat and swallowed several times before stammering, "Miss Victor, I w-want to ask you ... what I mean is ... would you accept this as a t-token of our ... uh, engagement?"

Eben stared at the ruby ring numbly, warring thoughts raced through her brain. Here it was ... the moment she had come for. Finally, the eligible offer that she had only hours ago assured her mother she would accept. Turning back to look out the window so that he could not read her face, Eben fought the urge to make excuses and beg for time. Anything to forestall this decision that was to determine the rest of her life

"You flatter me greatly, my lord. I am pleased you think of me as a fitting wife for you."

"I have come to think of you as one of my priceless possessions, Miss Victor. I—I will put you on a pedestal and worship you the rest of my life. You will be my living masterpiece," he declared passionately, waving his hand about the room.

"Is that the way you see me, Barnaby?" Eben thought of the poor butterflies—worshiped, also. Pinned to look so alive and full of flight, but dead!

"Y-yes, yes...of course...E-Eben." He stumbled over her Christian name.

With a stiffening of her resolve to bring this off to her best advantage, Eben turned and moved closer to him. "Do you want to kiss me, Barnaby?" she asked softly, looking at his poor eyes and weak chin. Perhaps closed eyes were called for in this situation. Without expecting a response, she leaned forward and closed her eyes to be kissed. She so desperately wanted to feel something pleasant for this man who was asking her to be his wife and the mother of his children.

"Oh, m-my! Y-yes!"

Eben felt a butterfly brush on her forehead and opened her eyes to stare at his reddening neck, with its bobbing Adam's apple. She felt nothing. She swallowed her disappointment, searching for some clue that this was the way she was to turn, and begging silent forgiveness of the butterflies she was about to doom to pasteboard.

"Barnaby, if we marry, could we live at Victor Mall, and let your mother live here? We would be alone there. I could ride and rebuild my stable, while you could canvas the countryside . . . to collect your butterflies . . ."

"M-Mother wouldn't like that. She will want us to stay here," he stated, in a voice that rose a trifle in panic at the mere thought of facing his mother with such a suggestion.

Eben gathered his pale, thin hand in hers, wondering if he always stuttered when he mentioned his mother. Suddenly she felt sorry for him. He was so very shy, and without one shred of self-worth. A marriage between them could be a freedom for him, too. But she could see, also, that he was going to do nothing to set about gaining that freedom without serious prompting.

"Barnaby, wouldn't you like to be alone with me?"

Receiving no response, wished-for or otherwise, Eben gently caressed his white, thin hand, then pressed it innocently to her breast, watching his face turn scarlet, then white, then scarlet again. He stared slack-mouthed at the firm mound that lay against her palm, his Adam's apple bobbing spastically, afraid to move a finger, only able to imagine what might lie beneath the cool gray silk.

"Y-yes, I would like that!" he suddenly swore forcefully. Compulsively he shoved the ring box at her again.

"Not yet, Barnaby. It's too soon. Perhaps after the season is finished." Eben rose and walked toward the door, stalling.

"M-Mother wishes us to be married this coming Christmas, and that is not overly long."

"Yes . . . yes, perhaps Christmas. We could have a Christmas ball and announce our engagement . . ."

"No, married . . . married at Christmas," he insisted, rising to approach her, again pushing the ring toward her hand.

Eben clasped her hands tightly together. Acceptance of the ring made things too final, and suddenly she was frightened of that finality. 'Twas too decisive, for the number of things left unsettled. She had yet to get the declaration of independence from him that she needed before making this ultimate decision.

"We had best return. Please, think about all I've said, and speak to your mother. If we can live at Victor Mall, just the two of us, I'll give you my hand . . . and heart . . . in marriage, Barnaby. But not otherwise, understand?" She held out her hand to him, and he came quickly to her, staring into her eyes as a devoted puppy might. "We'll have a Christmas wedding, Barnaby . . . and then we can be alone at Victor Mall. We'll be free . . . really free!"

"Yes . . . I think it would be nice, with j-just the two of us."

This time Barnaby cupped her breast of his own accord, and even dared to move this thumb over the hardening nipple. Leaning into his hand a trifle, she could not help thinking he was like a faulty pump that, when properly primed, worked fast.

"Come along then, dearest."

Gently she snapped the lid shut on the ring box as he held it in his hand, and he reluctantly returned it to his pocket. Walking quickly, Eben followed the dimming labyrinth of hallways back to the parlour. She knew Barnaby would never be strong enough to stand up to his mother on his own. But she had a weapon that was stronger than any hold that lady might possess. Her young body! And she would not hesitate to use it, if it meant saving Victor Mall. Several doors down the hall from the small parlor where the ladies sat over their tea, she stopped and faced Barnaby. He came to her eagerly, his weak eyes adoring as he gazed at her face.

"E-Eben, I w-will speak to her...I p-promise. She w-will be angry, but I will t-try to stand against her for what we want. I w-will t-try to stand against her for what we want. It w-will be a w-wonderful life, I swear to you. I shall worship you..." he earnestly assured her.

Again Eben felt a rush of sympathy for this quiet, brow-beaten young man. There was truly no meanness in him. For a second she regretted using him so harshly, then relented, for if things worked to her favor, she would be a good wife to him and a caring mother to his children.

"Just remember, dearest, you are the lord, not your mother. You have the power. She only wields it because you are kind enough to allow her the privilege."

Quickly she pressed her soft lips to his thin, dry ones. Surprisingly, he gripped her tightly to him and returned her kiss. It was tight-lipped and slightly painful, but none the less ardent for his inexperience. Eben released herself from his arms, carefully but firmly.

"I'll remember, Eben. P-please, may I touch you just once more?" His eyes glistened with eagerness in the candlelight, his face red as he stared at the soft curve of her breasts beneath the gray stuff of her gown.

"Not now, dearest. Come to me at Grosvenor Square, when you have convinced your mother to let us marry and live at Victor Mall. If you can do that, we will marry at Christmas, and then I will be yours to kiss and touch all you desire."

Eben turned abruptly and entered the parlor to confront the ladies and their questioning looks at her left hand. She felt dirty and cheaply used and somehow strangely defeated. She thought of the difference between Fitzhugh's kisses and Barnaby's kisses.... Suddenly she could not wait to return to London.

Chapter Seventeen

The morning was new. Pale streaks attempted valiantly to brighten the East. No sun would penetrate the heavy rain clouds on this day, and first light had a blue feeling about it. A steady rain fell, washing some of the stench from the morning air over St. James Street and making the cobblestones shine as if they, too, had been cleansed. Fitzhugh sat the slow trot of his chestnut mare, returning to his flat still strangely dissatisfied after the memorable, if not pleasant, night spent with the bountiful Lady Sinclair. His plan was to cut straight across St. James Park to his warm, dry hearth on Pall Mall. The wet climate of England was the one thing to which he doubted he would ever become accustomed. On just such days as this, he longed for the scorching dry heat of the desert with a need deep within his bones. Even his slicker, pulled close around him, and the beaver topper set low over his brow did not dispel the weather that slipped wet, cold fingers down his neck. This, plus the botched ending to the affair with Louise, left him in a dull and dark mood indeed.

The first light of dawn finding him still beneath the Lady Sinclair's bed covers had had much the same effect upon him as dirty washwater dashed into his face. The awakening of an intense dissatisfaction, and the yearnings he was becoming more and more painfully aware of lately—that in his life he wanted very much more from a woman than mere physical passion, which satisfied momentarily yet did nothing to quench the deep-seated urge he was feeling for something of more sustenance. Also, he acknowledged that Louise appealed only to what was least admirable in his character. A side of himself he was less and less proud of.

Suddenly a flash of black caught his attention. It had been a horse and rider, moving quickly toward St. James Park. The glimpse Fitzhugh had had as they crossed the intersection ahead of him, plus their coming from the direction of Grosvenor Square, hinted at their identity, and Fitzhugh eagerly kneed the mare into a posting trot. It could have been the groom, he supposed, out to give the stallion a run, but surely he would have chosen Hyde Park and the company of others like himself on similar errands. In view of the inclement weather, and the very contrariness of the idea, Fitzhugh was willing to wager the rider was the horse's unpredictable owner. His fatigue and wet, foul mood vanished with the delight of giving chase. He would cut through the park and intersect her by the ornamental pond.

Forsaking the muddy bridle path, Fitzhugh set a brisk pace through the trees in a diagonal line to what he hoped the black's route had been, trusting the mare to be surefooted in the wet grass. Dipping low over her neck, he thought to keep his topper from being swept from his head by the tree limbs. The rain might have been less under the trees, but the limbs themselves, heavy with the night's washing, showered him every time he struck one, causing curses to ring anew, though this time there was a sense of prank included. Watching the ground for signs of recent passing, he crossed a small clearing, pulling up in the trees facing the pond. A quick glance at the muddy track showed no horse had passed there, at least not since the rain had softened the surface.

"Of course. Foolish of me to think she would use the mud, when the grass is better. She could have gone in any direction, old girl," he said, giving the willing chestnut mare a pat on the neck.

Pausing a second, he turned his head this way and that... listening intently for the sound of hoofbeats. Hearing nothing but the steady drum of raindrops on the leaves overhead, he sighed. Turning the mare's head toward Pall Mall, he felt strangely deflated, and he jerked his hat lower. "Damn it! Guessed wrong. You'll not see the black today, madame," he said to the mare.

If he had moved on just a bit sooner, he would have missed the rider and horse breaking cover from the trees on his right. But perhaps Lady Luck had decided to smile upon him at last. Fitzhugh halted the mare and remained still to await their approach without making his presence known, hoping to ascertain the rider's identity before showing himself. No sense being made a fool if one could help it! Hunching deeper into his slicker and squinting his eyes against the downpour, he watched.

The rider circled the small clearing, slowing the long-legged black and laughing at his high jinks. The black acted a rodeo, showing displeasure at having his run cut short. The horse and rider seemed to be playing for mastery over the ride, neither truly serious, if one knew them well. If one didn't, it would seem the stallion was trying to unseat his rider. With one hump of his back, the stallion bounced his rider and loosened the wet, brimmed cap. Long ebony hair cascaded down the rider's back, ending Fitzhugh's quandary as to the rider's identity.

"Eben..." He started forward, then pulled back, deciding to linger and watch the handsome pair at play a bit longer.

The minx drew the black to a standstill and tilted her head far back. Straightening her spine and dropping the leathers, she spread her arms parallel to the ground, palms up. Fitzhugh smiled to see her open her mouth wide to catch the rain, as a child would do. He could not see, but imagined, her lovely azure eyes, rimmed with wet, sooty lashes, squinted shut in the downpour. Her breeches and sweater were sodden against her lovely body. What a woman-child she was! How he admired her exuberance for living. He longed to share that...to touch the joys of life founded on the simplest of pleasures, the way Eben did.

What other woman did he know, or had he ever known, who would rise at dawn just to taste the morning rain? None, of course. Certainly not the pampered, bored lady he had just left, snuggled in her satin-and-lace bedchamber scented of stale perfume. Fitzhugh compared the diamond bracelet with which he had adorned the wrist of the greedy seductress of last night to the sparkle and freshness of Eben's morning raindrops...

and found the diamonds less brilliant. Her childlike enjoyment of splashing in the rain quite changed his attitude about the wet. Perhaps it was this freshness . . . the very honesty of emotion that Eben seemed to possess that he yearned for, as a man dying under the hot sun of the desert thirsts for cool water.

Again Eben circled the black at the gallop and, sliding low to one side, with one hand tangled in the thick mane, hung by the crook of her knee in a breathtakingly dangerous move to scoop the wool cap from the ground. Without slowing the circling horse, she wound her wet hair and jammed the cap down securely on her head. Fearing she would break her circle and disappear into the wet trees if he didn't show himself, Fitzhugh guided the mare forward. Eben drew rein in surprise and concern until she saw it was only Eastmore.

"It's raining," he said, not sure how to approach this free spirit, with his heart brimming with feelings as it was this morning.

"The rain only improves my disposition," she parried, settling the cap more securely on her wet hair. "Besides . . . you're out early for a drenching yourself."

Choosing to ignore her comment, he casually retorted, "Would have been a pickle for you if I had been someone less discreet."

"Another lecture on my deplorable behavior, your grace?"

"I thought we were going to be less formal when occasion allowed?" he said, his smile going tight at her tone.

"I reserve that right for my friends. And you have shown yourself not a reliable friend." Eben glared at him, her lower lip tending to tremble. This was not the way she had imagined their first conversation in so long. Why must he always rail at her? At present, her life was in too much of a turmoil to include someone who listed her faults on a nonstop basis, no matter how much she wished for him to be in her life.

"I had understood my allowed place in your life was to be one of adviser and teacher," he parried, unhappy at the direction of their conversation. He had no desire to spar with the little spitfire this morning, as such never ended in the fashion he wished.

"A place too quickly forgotten by you, your grace. I have had two samples of your lessons, and I would be a fool to leave you in a position to viciously instruct me further!" The black stamped his hooves and moved restlessly at the angry tone of his mistress.

"You make it very hard to treat you any other way." He felt his anger growing at her unreasonableness. "You are a spoiled child, but someone must help you snare a husband before you ruin yourself altogether with this outlandish behavior."

"Pray let me assure you, Lord Eastmore, that assistance will no longer be required from you," she said with a snort. "I have just recently received an admirable offer, and acceptance is under consideration with my aunt and my mother at this present time."

"Not one of those second sons or grieving widowers that have been tugging your petticoats lately, I trust?" he quizzed her, in anger and disappointment. "They are decidedly too cool in the pockets for your needs, little cat. Too cool, indeed! Or perhaps some elderly peer has a taste for tender young flesh?"

"Of course not! I will accept Lord Barnaby J. Compton," Eben announced triumphantly.

"Compton?" Fitzhugh was startled. "And be under the thumb of that arrogant, controlling mama of his? I daresay she will not allow you to play in the rain with your big black horse. Nor approve of your parading about in men's breeches!"

"You need not doubt that it will be me who will control my husband, not his mother!" she snapped, fighting tears. "Besides, it is no concern of yours. Now, if you will excuse me, I shall leave you. You have quite ruined my morning's ride, thank you."

Spinning the black, Eben put him to a gallop from the jump over the wet grass and disappeared through the trees, causing the mare to dance sideways, willing to give chase.

"Compton!" Fitzhugh gritted. "'Tis criminal to waste such a warm, responsive girl on that dead fish!"

He, too, spun his mare, but stopped from tearing off in the opposite direction. Instead, he set a sedate pace, muttering to himself, miserable again. Remembering Eben, soft and passionate beneath him, he became angrier. Angry at Eben for being such a pigheaded, ill-tempered spitfire and then angry at himself for the bungling of the whole affair.

Fitzhugh had never felt lower than he did as he plodded home in the rain. He could just imagine Eben's fire and vitality drained year after year by an arrogant, demanding mother-in-law and a weak, insipid husband. How could she accept that poor, pale excuse of a man! Blast! He could see no immediate way to stop her, even though he knew she was destroying something very special. He had thought to give her time without his presence before pressing his suit again, but it appeared he had waited too long. If only they didn't spark every time they came near.

He thought back to their confrontation the night she had whipped Ellington. The last time he had railed at her. She had been angry at his betrayal of their oath of friendship, and he remembered his stupidity in throwing his seduction of her in her face yet again. He always seemed to end up flinging at her head the very things he loved the best about her. Her constant flouting of convention. And the spontaneity that was so childlike. He was a fool to think to give her time...when she did not realize she had time to spare. Now he must move fast, before she buckled herself to that mama's boy and was lost to him forever.

"Blast it all!" Fitzhugh gritted again as he set the mare a sharp pace. "I shall have her hear me out, even if I must kidnap her to do so. I will show her what she throws away!"

True to her word, Eben had ridden straight home. Now she sat curled on the deep window seat at the far end of the salon, staring out at the deluge of rain, her book quite forgotten on her lap. Grady curled up beside her in the shawl he had adopted and promptly covered with cat hair to discourage the original owner from reclaiming it as hers. Lady Lillian and Lady Adair sat near the fireplace with tea, continuing their endless argument over dress styles and gossiping over who had worn what and to which function. Eben wondered again how such a meaningless discussion could occupy them day after day.

She was so heartily sick of the whole thing. While, at first, reading had occupied much of her time, this last batch of books the bookseller had provided were worse than useless, consisting mostly of the novels her mother enjoyed. Eben had read two with moderate enjoyment, but on starting a third she had discovered it to contain the same story as the other two, and therefore it lay unattended in her lap. She was thoroughly weary of romance and spineless women weeping over long-lost loves who had died young. Weary of romance at all, for in truth it did not exist in real life. Only duty and obligation existed in real life.

She just wanted to go home. Home to Victor Mall and the acid smell of a warm stable on a rainy morning, with the horses greedily pushing at her for their morning feed, the feel of fuzzy kittens tucked into hideaways in the bales of straw bedding. Instead of being corseted into ribbons and lace and stuck in a stuffy salon by a downpour, she could imagine piling into the straw loft above the stable with a good mystery, sucking a tart green apple snitched from Cook's larder. And when she tired of reading, she could lay her head back into the straw, letting the beating of the rain on the barn roof lull her into a nap, while the horses shuffled in their boxes below. Would that simple pleasure ever be hers again? Would she be allowed to teach her children that joy? Her and Barnaby's children? Maybe . . . and maybe not. The prospects from that quarter looked dismal indeed!

It had been a full month since she had set the conditions for their marriage, and not a word had come from Compton Castle or Barnaby. Some small comment had been made about the absence of Lord Compton and the dowager from the socials these past thirty days, but Lady Compton was entirely too acidic to be missed overly much, and Barnaby was exactly the sort of person one overlooked totally, never sure whether he had been in attendance or not. Eben could imagine his mother having him locked in his room on bread and water for even daring to suggest such a thing as defying her wishes and living apart at Victor Mall with his bride. If Barnaby had dared approach her at all. It was just possible that once Eben and her enticing body were out of tempting range, the old bat had exerted her control firmly once more.

"My lord Ottobon, my ladies?" Hastings announced from the arched doorway.

Lewis strolled boldly into the room, slightly damp about the boots, but immaculate, as ever, in blue. Bowing and fawning over the elder ladies, he quite put them into giggles in a matter of minutes. Eben watched him with a smile, but dreaded joining the group. Her mood was just that dark and foul.

"Lewis, pray go cheer Eben out of the doldrums. I fear the rain has her mood as gray as the sky," Lady Lillian ordered him playfully, tapping him sharply on the wrist with her fan.

"I will certainly do just that," Lewis said, again bowing over her petite hand. Obediently he advanced toward Eben with purpose. "Miss Victor, such a lovely picture of the pensive miss. You really should come away from the window with your lovely beauty . . . so that the sun will have a fighting chance to show beyond the clouds."

"Oh, give way, Lewis. I'm in no mood."

"As you wish." With a bow over her hand, he seated himself in the window seat before her, leaning his back against the opposite wall. Studying her sober face for a moment, he set out to liven her spirits with all his charm. "Quite a storm brewing out there. Ever tell you when I was within a breath of being laid down and out by a lightning bolt? Struck a tree branch over my head, singed my locks, and fair likely fried my brain. Some say it improved my wit but dulled my intelligence, don't you know?" His gray eyes were so merry, and his handsome face was so cheerful, Eben had to laugh with him. Grady sat up, yawning widely to show annoyance at a disturbed nap, but interested in new company nevertheless.

"Dear Lewis . . ." Eben started to say.

"I say, old girl, heard the most distressing thing about you. The word is about that you are thinking of accepting Compton's offer. Really brown to pick him, you know. Not in your league at all. Why, he can't even ride!" Lewis said, leaning forward earnestly. Grady leaned forward, also, staring into his face expectantly. Eben absently put her hand on the cat's head, scratching behind his ears, not looking at Lewis.

"Doesn't seem to be much of a chance of it, anyway, Lewis. It wants to look as if his mother has won without even a scrap between us. She refuses to advance the funds to right Victor Mall. If I must watch it go to rack and ruin anyway, I'd just as soon do it without her on top of the grief."

"That's good news!" the lord exclaimed. "I just can't see you with that . . . well, just too depressing."

"Except that leaves me with Freddy Portsmythe. So you see, Lewis, the choices are not the easiest, are they?"

Lewis looked even more stricken at that gruesome thought. "Miss Victor, there is something I have been desiring to say to you, but there has not been the right moment until now."

He lifted her hand from her lap and brought it to his lips. Eben glanced up into his face, startled. The weak light from the window showed his face clearly . . . bearing an expression of seriousness totally uncharacteristic of him. Eben recognized the circumstances from the unwanted proposals she had been receiving on a regular basis—eleven to date, counting Barnaby's.

"Please, Lewis, don't . . ." She sought to warn him off, but the viscount was not to be denied.

"Commenced by admiring you, best set of hands on the leathers I've ever seen, driving or aboard, and we do deal so well together. Never known a lady whose company I enjoyed as much . . . a lady of your position, I mean, of course."

"As I enjoy yours," she began eagerly, "but . . ."

Paying her no heed whatsoever, Lewis continued determinedly, as if she had not spoken, "Not doing a bang-up job of this. Never did it before, you know." He drew a quick deep breath and let the words spill out as he exhaled. "Miss Victor . . . Eben . . . would you do me the honor of becoming my wife?"

Eben could tell he was watching her most eagerly. The moment was just so depressing for her. She could think of nothing else to say to him, except the plain truth.

"My lord . . . Lewis," she began, stopping to withdraw her hand ever so gently from his to clench it with the other in her lap. "I hold you in the highest esteem. You are a delightful companion, admirable in every manner." She made no attempt to control her tears or to swipe them away. "But, in spite of that, I cannot find my way to accept your offer. Pray forgive me, as my dearest friend."

"Are your affections . . . engaged elsewhere?" he asked. Then, without waiting for an answer, he stated, "I wouldn't be surprised. Deuced popular . . . all the crack, you know. Everyone's copying your style. Though no one can carry it off like you."

"Oh, no..." She rushed to reassure him. "It's just that ... My friend, be honest with both of us. You do not want to marry me. While you may admire me and feel sorry for my situation, you do not really want a wife. Especially a wife who would take such exception, as I am afraid I would, to the little dark-eyed mistress you have set up on South Street."

"Miss Victor! Not right you should mention— How did you—!" Lewis gasped. "My word!"

"You see, I would continue to discomfit you." She smiled at his face. "In no time at all, you would be quite unhappy with me. And that would make me exceedingly unhappy, as well, for you are truly a dear person to me."

"You do realize I have the funds to set you to rights, old girl?" Lewis tried one last time.

"That does not enter into the consideration. I am just too, too fond of you to make your life miserable. Pray, let's just be the best of friends," she begged, leaning forward.

"I guess you're right on the knob," he finally conceded, taking her hand once more to plant a kiss on the palm before laying it back in her lap.

"Just galls me to see such a fine one thrown to the hounds, you understand? Never knew a girl more suited. Probably find I regret not pushing you. Have the advantage, you know. We'll put our heads together and come up with some way out, don't fret." He paused for a moment, then tentatively tried another avenue. "Uh...what of Eastmore?"

"Come, enough of this! Let's see if the ladies will play whist."

"If that will bring the smile back to your lovely face, dear Miss Victor, then it shall be as you desire," he declared, lending a hand to her.

Eben rose to take his hand, feeling somehow better. Although her situation had not changed, her heart was lighter, since she had been honest with dear Lewis. But she would not discuss Eastmore. He was no help to her and did nothing except list her bad traits every time they met. No, she did not want to discuss anything to do with Eastmore.

"I do warn you, though, my aunt is a fair wizard at this game," she said, with a smile. "Do not let her talk you into setting too high a stake!"

"Oh, capital! I thank you for the warning. I must engage her as a partner." He grinned, tucking her arm companionably in his, apparently none the worse for having had his ardent proposal declined, much to Eben's relief. "Smuggle her into White's and increase my fortune. Come, let us put the proposition to the dear lady."

Chapter Eighteen

May spread over the forgotten little garden behind Vicroy House. The most stubborn plants bloomed with sad little flowers, even though they competed for sun and space with weeds and brambles. Forsythia and crocuses vied with yellow-faced dandelions, and the delicate scent of apple blossoms laced the air. The surging of anticipation, of energy, hung about the place. Eben had begun wandering there among the weeds, for privacy, whenever she felt she had to escape. The rules of polite society were so very confining, and for a young girl used to spending a great deal of time alone, the new crowding of her life with people was unbearable. How she longed for the country and the quietness of spring. Now, in a vain attempt to calm some of her violent restlessness, she set herself the task of weeding some of the worst from the sad, neglected little garden.

Lady Adair reposed in the shade of the apple tree, her well-cared-for hands lying idle in her lap for once, her eyes pondering Eben as she knelt to work with trowel and gloves, digging the scourge of dandelions out of the struggling grass with a vengeance. A frown creased her forehead as she watched her niece, and she tapped a forefinger against her pursed lips. She was concerned, but still unable to fathom her concern, for there was something different about Eben of late. Of course, she had lost much of her vim and vigor in the city, but Lady Adair could not in all good conscience put it down to homesickness and lack of country air. No, there was something afoot with her niece, but for the life of her she could not fit a name to it. And pushing Eben for confidences was never rewarding these days.

"You look as if you wished to do dire deeds to those weeds," Lady Adair said, "the way you are frowning and conversing in such a threatening manner with them."

Eben gave a resisting plant an energetic tug and sat back on the grass, dropping her trowel and stripping off her gloves to pull restless hands through the tangle of her unruly curls, left unbound today in a fit of defiance with Bess.

"I didn't realize I was giving myself away," she retorted with a deep sigh.

"I do wish you would come out of the sun. Your face will be getting as browned as a laborer's," her aunt admonished, patting the bench invitingly.

"Yes, I suppose I shall," she agreed, as if it really did not matter if she did or didn't.

"Yes, indeed you shall. I'll thank you to indulge me and come out of the sun. You're not going to do enough good in that garden to account for your time."

"I think the good was not so much for the garden, actually...but for me," she retorted, moving to sit beside her aunt in the shade, her frown returning. She seemed pensive for a moment, then burst out, "This season wears thin! It's all so stiff and formal.... It's unnatural to have such rigid rules and stricture."

"Gracious!" Lady Adair pulled back in shock. "Who wishes to be informal? For that, one may rest in the country. Society is always formal, and I assure you it is much more pleasant than if there were no rules at all, for then one would have nothing to gossip about. Your enjoyment of it all is tempered by the pressure placed upon you this season. I assure you, if you were not on the ropes, it would be much more of a romp."

"I have been meaning to speak to you." Eben looked down at her hand, which was pleating the blue cotton of her skirt. "I fear I have sadly botched . . . I mean to say . . . I haven't been much of a success. With this betrothal business."

"That's not entirely true, dear." Her aunt laid a hand on the dark head, so near. "You have been a great success. With your concerns over Victor Mall and your resolve to marry for money, you have just not been able to disengage your heart, but do not despair yet. I am sure Compton will come through for you. He is quite taken, you know."

"It has been overly long since I pressed him. I doubt if his mama will ever let him out of her sight again. I'm quite sure she has him chained somewhere. Feeding him nothing but bread and water until he agrees to do her bidding and none other's. Do you think she has dungeons in that horrid place?"

"Undoubtedly! Although I think we will be seeing the Comptons soon. I cannot think they will neglect to show for Princess Victoria's birthday ball. You are certain to have your answer then. I do not think we should resort to drizzling just yet?"

"Drizzling?" Eben quizzed with her black eyebrows climbing, suspecting some of her aunt's buffoonery.

"Of course! An ancient French amusement, my love. Pulling the gold and silver thread from discarded tassels and epaulets to sell by the pound. Many a genteel but impoverished lady has earned her keep that way."

"Dear Auntie, it all sounds exceedingly tedious to me!" She laughed as she rose to shake out her skirt. "Of the two, I should think it will be easier to find a husband. I can always go bat my eyes at one of the swains whose offers I have recently refused . . . bring him back up to the mark."

"Let's put that aside for a time. I don't think we're that far gone as of yet," she said, then paused to peer at Eben. "Unless you have developed a *tendre* for someone . . ."

Eben started, then calmed her face. Eastmore had instantly leaped to mind. Yes, a thousand times yes! She had developed a *tendre* for someone. Someone she wanted . . . needed . . . and desired above all else. But even with that, she needed, wanted and desired that he be an entirely different sort of man from the one he apparently was, so how could one admit to a *tendre* for someone who wasn't even the person she wanted him to be? It was all too depressing, too much to contemplate, much less try to explain to someone of her aunt Addie's bent . . . what with her constant spouting about duty to the ton and such. No, best to sidestep it altogether. It was not something she wished to debate on this day, or any other, for that matter.

"No, it's nothing of that sort. I just wish this to be over. I quite feel I'm being forced against my will into the most important decision of my life, a husband, by creditors and starving pensioners. And it's not as if I even want one of the bloody rotters in my life in the first place!"

Lady Adair chuckled at her niece, and for once did not admonish her for strong language. "Husbands, given the proper one, are rarely a hindrance. In fact, I truly think developing a true devotion to one's husband is a detriment to one's mental health. They will tend to take advantage."

"But, given the choice, wouldn't it be desirable to love the man with whom you are sharing the most intimate details of your life?" Eben asked, only to have her aunt catch her hand and draw her back to the bench to gain her full attention.

"Your father married your mother for love. In fact, it was a grand passion, the talk of the ton. And their love endured beautifully until real life infringed. After the death of their second daughter, your sister, Lillian withdrew from all life, refusing to attend her husband in London, and a rift widened until they had little contact for months on end. I swear, dear heart, if your father hadn't suffered a galloping case of gout and retired to the country for respite occasionally, neither Sheldon nor you would have been conceived."

"Aunt Addie!" Eben laughed. "You are outrageous!"

"Even so, Ebenezer was not a man to be left on his own. As you know, he proceeded to career downhill thereafter...gambling, drink, women..."

"Yes..."

"I know you are young, Eben, and it's considered bad ton to speak this frankly to an unmarried daughter, but I am not one who believes a woman should go into marriage totally unaware. You ask how one knows the suitable husband? Just like forming a studbook. By pairing traits, fortunes and personalities...balancing them all. Your mother was a weak woman, frivolous and self-absorbed. I can say this about her, because she is my sister and I do love her, between spells of wanting to wring her neck.

"Lillian needed a strong man to care for her while she frittered her time away on fashion and society. Your father was not that strong man. He, also, was self-absorbed, and to protect all his holdings and to allow him time for his own pursuits, he should have married a strong woman, one who could mind the store, so to speak, and limit his excesses. They were unsuited, but so-called love intervened, with a disastrous end. Love or no love, they never should have married,'' Lady Adair declared, then grew pensive, a faraway look in her eyes, lost in a private memory. Then she gave herself a shake and continued, "Eben, you are very strong, like me. Unless you can find a man with incredible strength of character and a generous capacity for love and devotion, it is best to buckle to someone like Barnaby Compton. He will need a strong woman to manage his estates, preserve his fortune and replace his mother.''

"I have thought, truly, that marriage to Barnaby will be like commencing the union with one child already. I know what I bring to the union, but I cannot help but feel . . . yearn . . . for something more for myself.'' Eben dropped her head, and thought of Fitzhugh's smile, the whiteness of his teeth in his sun-browned face when he was in good humor with her.

"My dear, Barnaby will right Victor Mall. He will give you jewels, and a more-than-generous allowance. And you'll have more independence than you probably should have, given your propensity for embroilments.'' Pulling her niece to her feet, they strolled back toward the house, arm in arm.

"Embroilments?'' Eben teased. "In all honesty, I think it's those words, 'love, honor and obey'. I'm not sure I can even say them, as I doubt my ability to perform them.''

"Oh, fa-la-la! They're just words!''

Eben laughed and gave her aunt a bear hug. "My worries are settled and my mind eases with that knowledge. On with the hunt! If I don't have to love, honor or obey a husband, how bad can it be? Now come, let me show you my bait for the ball. Our gowns arrived today.''

"Only if you desist from ragging about the hoops.''

"Hoops! All I can see they're good for is to clean dusty shoes and keep distance from ardent suitors. Very uncomfortable and cumbersome!''

"But, my dear, oh so fashionable. And fashion is everything.''

"Well, this gown is totally scandalous, according to Mama. She says I'm flinging British society's rules in their very teeth, and that I'm doing it with that very intention in mind. Although Mama is quite in the rafters over having a new gown of color herself. And while I detest the expense of additional finery, it does seem such a shame that she, who loves the excitement of the season so very much, has to remain in mourning colors while I, who care so little, order gown after gown.''

"Well, I am pleased Lillian is pleased. After all, with the mountainous debts already looming over your head, I suppose one more nail in the coffin makes no difference at this stage of the funeral. If you make your marriage, they will all be paid. And if not . . .''

"Yes, indeed. If I do not, what then?'' Eben quizzed, but Lady Adair had no answer for her at this time.

Chapter Nineteen

Kensington Palace was ablaze with lights the night of the Princess Victoria's birthday ball. Hundreds of carriages lined the drive to discharge the elegantly attired lords and ladies. A tedious two hours passed before the Victor carriage drew even with the steps. Eben thought it would have been much simpler if they had but strolled the short distance, but refrained from any comment to that effect, for the ladies would have been horrified at such an idea. So she curbed her impatience as best she could. Per Lady Lillian's request, the amiable Lord Melton was their escort for the evening, lending dignity to their small group. Watching her mother now, tittering behind her fan and batting her eyes at Lord Melton, she gave a wry smile. It would appear that lady was going to have a betrothal to announce before her daughter did.

A suite of reception rooms, the grand salon and the vestibule were opened for dancing. Both ballrooms had orchestras fitted for quadrille bands, and the two drawing rooms, with the connecting doors opened to form one large suite, had thousands upon thousands of candles reflected in huge pier mirrors set in compartments on the walls, giving a brilliance to the entire place. The crowd was immense, and it discomfited Eben greatly when seemingly every face turned toward the entry when their names were announced by the lord chancellor. But of the three ladies, Eben was the only one to feel thus.

Lady Lillian proudly preened in her new gown of bronze taffeta, with its bodice covered in jet beads and finely tatted black lace. Although it was a fetching color for a lady with graying chestnut curls, the full gigot sleeves and the bell skirt on her round little figure gave her the silhouette of a tea cozy. Lady Adair's head rose even a trifle past haughty as she swept grandly down the staircase with her awesome magenta plume waving. Eben followed, glancing down to her own creation of ruffled layer after ruffled layer of filmy tulle, wafting about her as light as champagne bubbles in the barest hint of apricot.

Admirers flocked to Eben as bees to a honey pot the instant her foot touched the bottom step. Viewing them with quick calculations of eligibility, she hastily scribbled names beside dances, yet wisely left all her waltzes open, much to their despair, for all wished to hold this lovely close. She did not see Barnaby, but she wished to have a waltz available for him whenever he did appear. It was impossible to carry on a conversation during the other dances, and talk with him she must. And though she would not have admitted it to a soul, she could not keep her wandering eyes from searching the dizzying crowd for the sight of a particular pair of shoulders upon which she wished to rest her hand during one unclaimed waltz.

As the hours of the ball passed with one charming partner after another, Lady Adair left Eben under the care of her mother and allowed herself to be led into the card room set aside for those who wished to escape the dancing. Lady Lillian was not Eben's favorite chaperon, as she was not quick to catch discreetly sent signals, and Eben found herself standing up with an assortment of men whom she thought a waste of time and energy, as that lady was desperate to turn the hunt in any direction but the Comptons'. Elderly widowers with modest fortunes, young widowers with babies at home in need of mothers, second sons slated for military service, and worst of all . . . Lord Freddy Portsmythe. And, to compound the affront, it was a waltz! It was at this moment Eben was to pinpoint the turn of a delightful evening into a nightmare that led to disaster.

The rotund, perspiring marquis had indeed been regrouping his spirits with rather a large amount of iced champagne, for he had made up his mind to bend a knee to Miss Victor this very evening. His main focus at the present was to dance her into an alcove for a mite of privacy, while Eben was thinking merely of the destruction of a rather fine pair of white kid gloves from the man's moist hand. Near the end of the dance, Freddy had maneuvered her unexpectedly into a velvet-curtained alcove behind a golden pillared Diana and, at once plumping down upon his knees before her, implored her to accept his hand and heart in marriage. Eben looked down at him in astonishment.

"My lord! You are certainly foxed! I thought so before, and now I am certain of it. Get up at once! I say, you look very silly, and someone may come in!"

Freddy Portsmythe, looking as if cold water had been cast in his face, labored to his feet, a process that required Eben to lend a hand, quite causing her to dissolve into giggles, at which the hard-breathing man took considerable offense. Rounding on Eben, he surprised her by stammering quite furiously, "Don't! Don't you laugh at m-me!"

He then laid hands upon her and attempted to plant his wet, pouty mouth on any part of her face that he could touch, which resulted only in a painful crush of noses and foreheads and considerable disarrangement of her apricot ruffled bodice, nearly baring her to her nipples. At much the same moment, the velvet curtains parted, and Lord Ottobon strolled into the alcove.

"What the devil—!" said the astonished lord, with a stern oath that instantly managed to convince the marquis that he had better stop what he was about. "Unhand her, sir!"

"Oh, Lewis!" Eben gasped. "I am so glad it's you! This horrid little beast—!" She broke off with an oath of dismay as the clumsy Lord Portsmythe, backing away from her, bumped against a small gilt table, causing a large Oriental vase standing upon it to topple with a crash to the parquet floor. "Egad! Do look what you are about!" she implored, while Lewis, his face relaxing at the obvious discomfort on the round fellow's face, began to grin, wider and wider. Eben, seeing this, began to giggle again.

Thoroughly humiliated, Freddy inadvisably began stuttering indignant self-justifications, his florid face going darker, toward purple, and the veins rose in his neck, giving further visual evidence of the state of his mortification.

"I w-will not have you laugh at m-me. I was given encouragement from your mother th-that my intentions would be well received."

He thought to protest further but, seeing the stern look return to Eben's face, immediately desisted and attempted very rapidly to depart, only to find his way barred by a tall figure splendidly turned out in full formal attire, and of a size to block any discreet escape with an awesome barricade.

"I hope . . ." said Fitzhugh, with awful politeness, "I very much hope that I don't intrude."

Lewis looked at him quite cheerfully and, with equal politeness, said, "Not at all, your grace. I believe Lord Portsmythe was just leaving. And so, in fact," he added, catching Eben's hand in his, "are we."

Fitzhugh, looking pointedly at the disarray of the multiruffled bodice of apricot tulle, did not move from his position at the alcove's entrance. Eben, noting the direction of his gaze, gasped and quickly tugged the offending bodice into place, blushing furiously with the sudden conviction that Fitzhugh did not understand in the least how she came to be alone in this secluded place with two gentlemen, her clothing in some disarray and a broken vase upon the floor. It seemed to her a very decadent situation, quite out of keeping with the elegant ball going on just beyond the crimson velvet curtains, and she wished the floor would open and swallow her up. Meanwhile, Freddy, with as much grace as he could muster, slipped past the duke and unobtrusively escaped into the ballroom crowd behind the straight back.

Without understanding why, Eben began to explain to Fitzhugh, wishing ever so much that he would look elsewhere, for his very gaze quite caused her reason to cease to function.

"You see, Lord Eastmore," she began breathlessly, "he brought me in here, though I expected to be returned to my mother, and then he asked me to marry him, and tried to kiss me . . ."

Fitzhugh held up his hand to stop her and commented, "You owe me no explanations. I merely act as a messenger for your aunt. She requested I locate you, and perhaps squire you about the dance floor. If you are quite recovered, I shall carry out her request."

"I—I see," stammered Eben.

"Lord Ottobon, if you will excuse us?" Tucking her hand inside her arm, Fitzhugh propelled her out of the alcove without further comment.

"Oh, Miss Victor...pray give my regards to Lord Grady when next you see him," Lewis called after her, with a merry glint in his eye.

"Lord Grady?" Fitzhugh demanded, in a sharp tone that bordered on the possessive. "Yet another of your many suitors, Miss Victor?"

"Have no fear, Fitzhugh, old man. His hair is quite gray," Lewis assured him, with a wink at Eben.

Eben waved at him with a parting smile as Fitzhugh practically dragged her away with a black scowl on his face. Slightly daunted by the dark look, she glanced back toward the alcove, but Lewis had already turned his attention elsewhere. She then turned toward the sofa where she had left her mother.

"Do you think I am abducting you?" Fitzhugh's droll voice sounded in her ear.

"No, of course not." Eben frowned up at the handsome man. "Though there are others, who do not know you as well as I, who would still deem it an honor to be seen with you. I was merely locating my mother to see that she observes this dubious honor."

"I shall endeavor to do my part, then, to be sure you are swung near her seating," he said, somewhat sarcastically.

"I think not, your grace," she said, disengaging her arm from his hand. "While my aunt may think being seen with you bodes well for my marketability, I myself do not wish to burden you. If you will excuse me!"

The crowd was such that with a quick sidestep she was able to put no fewer than three people between them. By walking as rapidly as the crush permitted, she was lost to him in a thrice. Not in a great hurry to encounter the overwhelming enthusiasm of her mother, nor the censure of her aunt for misplacing the duke, she paused beside a tall glass-paneled door leading to a terrace beyond, longing for an instant of solitude. Observing not one but three of her most ardent suitors bearing down in her general direction settled her decision to step outside for a moment. Softly she pulled the doors shut behind her and expelled a deep sigh of relief at having a little time away from the crowd, the noise and the heat.

The sudden cool of the night air cleared her head. She breathed deeply, the chilly air cleansing the warm air, heavy with the scent of beeswax candles and overheated bodies, from her lungs. Hugging her arms across her chest, she moved to a dark corner of the terrace, overlooking the drive, lit with torches and crowded with carriages. Coachmen gathered in groups to chat and await their lords' pleasure. She watched the red glow of cigar tips, and occasional laughter drifted up to her ears. She knew from Jamie Deal that they discussed the masters' blooded cattle as if it were their own. And, as was true of any gathering of men, regardless of station in life, the juiciest bits of fluffs available.

Her head ached, and her thoughts were so muddled. She must come to the realization of her feelings for Fitzhugh Eastmore. What if this yearning for the irritating man was truly love, and she had dismissed his proposal, railed at his head and possibly lost him forever? But, even for love, would she mire herself in a marriage where he would forever fling her love back in her face with liaisons with other women? No, for if he did that, she would surely come to hate him, and to love and hate at the same time would be unbearable.

Behind Eben, the terrace doors opened, startling her. Quickly she stepped into the shadow of a potted tree, not wishing to share the terrace and this moment with anyone. Peeping about, she saw a man advancing toward the end of the terrace. It did not take the light streaming through the glass-paneled door for her to recognize him. The height of him, the breadth of shoulder, the easy walk, were all familiar to her. He walked unerringly to her, as if the terrace were not dim beyond the windows.

"I thought you could use this," he said, handing her a champagne glass, brimming with bubbly amber liquid. She looked up into his face, but could only dimly make out his features in the dark shadows before taking the glass.

"How did you find me?"

"I observed you outmaneuvering the descending army and thought a break might be in order, and as it is not advisable for you to be out here alone . . ." He bowed a shallow bow to indicate his wish to be at her disposal.

"And I am safer with you here, as well, your grace?" Her quip was met with a deep chuckle, as a refusal to be baited into a verbal sparring with her.

"Do you tire of dancing?"

"I am tired of being on display, and of being pawed by men who can do nothing to save my Victor Mall, but I love to waltz," she answered candidly, sipping the champagne. "I am breaking my aunt's rule, you know. I am allowed only one glass of bubbles an evening, and this makes my second."

The wine bubbled against her lip and made her smile. Suddenly champagne seemed a marvelous idea, it made her effervescent, exhilarated. The music swelled through the windows behind them, sweet and beckoning, a waltz.

"You are ever the one to defy convention, as I have noticed," he said. "Shall we waltz?" Taking the delicate fluted glass from her to set it upon the terrace wall, he gently pulled her into his arms, tight against him, without waiting for an answer. His warmth was welcome, and with her nose pressed into the hollow of his throat, the very male smell of him assaulted her senses.

"Oh, no, please! I must go back inside," she protested weakly, attempting to draw away from his disturbing arms.

"How fearful you are," he said, and put his hand firmly at her waist. "See, you are chilled. This will warm you quickly. And we seem to have the floor to ourselves."

"You would assist me in disgracing myself, your grace?" she asked. Then, with one last worried look toward the lit window, she gave herself up to the spell of the music allowing him to swing her into the waltz.

This was a reckless thing to do, Eben knew. Suppose someone should find them here? But the music sang, and the chilled blood tingled to warmth in her veins. He held her closer than he would have on the public dance floor, and Eben thought she could feel his heart beating . . . or was it hers? Just one more time in his arms, and she must let him go forever. Erase him from her thoughts and her heart, for he was not the man for her. A tear traced down her cheek as he spun her around and around. The music ended. He dropped his arms from her, but did not step away. Her hand slid slowly down his broad chest from where it had lain upon his shoulder. He stood so close, her quickened breath brushed her breasts against him each time she inhaled. She was warm now, and the night air was refreshing. As the music started again, she made the merest move toward the door, but his whisper stayed her, his breath fluttering like a moth against her cheek.

"Don't leave me, Eben."

"I must go back inside," she said, although she did not move.

His hand slipped to her back, and he took a step closer, when she thought he could come no closer. Even though she knew it was going to happen, before she could move away or cry out, his other hand lifted her face to his. For one second, her eyes looked into the glitter of his amber ones and then his lips came down on hers. She should have struggled and fought against him, but she was unable to do so. His kiss was sweet, as she remembered his kisses to be. She lost thought of the fear of discovery, of the dancers a breath away. She was only conscious that his arm around her was strong and that his mouth, firm and demanding, was something beyond comprehension, beyond thought. Not willing to give up something so sweet, Eben sagged against his body, surrendering her mouth totally to his probing tongue. Nor did she struggle when his hand left her face and traveled down her throat to slip fingers beneath her neckline to gently pinch the nipple so lightly covered there.

"Eben, my little love, stay with me," he whispered into her mouth, nibbling there to send gooseflesh down her arms. "Say it, my love, say yes to me . . ."

Eben had no mind of her own. Her whole being wanted this man. If this truly was love, then she welcomed it. Just as she welcomed his touch, which stirred her body with so many demanding sensations. She would live each day for itself, and face the problems she knew to be in their future as they arose. For nothing could have taken her from his arms at that moment. Or so she thought.

Fitzhugh slipped the bodice of her gown down to bare both nipples, pushed upward in such an inviting manner by the French corset. Ignoring the murmured protest she made as his lips left hers, he teased first one, then the other, with his hot, circling tongue. Without being aware of it happening, Eben found she was backed into the darkest corner of the terrace, his large body shielding her from any light. With one arm around her waist, he continued to nibble the tortured tips of her full breasts, while gathering up the filmy skirts and petticoats with the other, bunching them at her waist.

The cool air struck her exposed thighs, but was chased away by his hot, searching hand before her senses could clear. Shoving a hard-muscled thigh between her legs, he pulled her tightly to him by cupping her thinly clad derriere. A gasp escaped her as a tight coiling twisted deep in her loins, growing...building ...until the pressure made her tremble violently. Gripping his shoulders desperately with her hands, she fought to stay on her feet, for her legs were weakening. Her entire body was consumed with the building pressure low in her belly, caused from the friction of his thigh. Her head lolled back, baring her throat to his kisses.

"Fitzhugh..." she sighed. "Fitzhugh, I lov—"

"Fitzhugh? Darling, is that you?" a shrill female voice cut into Eben's whisper. "Fitzhugh! I've been looking everywhere...." The tapping of the lady's heels came across the terrace. Fighting her drugged senses, Eben turned her back on the advancing lady, but not quickly enough. The woman's amused voice stabbed her. "I should have known you would be wooing some woman out here in the dark. Really, darling...this one's hardly more than a schoolgirl." The shrill voice tinkled a laugh, then turned sarcastic. "How can she hope to satisfy—"

"Enough!" Fitzhugh shouted. "Go inside, Louise! I shall be there in a moment."

"See that you are no more than a moment. I am ready to leave. Don't you agree, my warm bed beckons?" Her tinkling laugh and her tapping heels faded as she left.

"Eben, I..." Fitzhugh would have gathered her into his arms again, but she jerked away, falling hard against the terrace wall, knocking the champagne glass carelessly placed there over the side to fall down...down...

"Leave me!" Her voice might have sounded cold to anyone else, but to Eben it sounded disappointed, weak, and full of tears, exactly as she felt.

"Nay, love . . . not like this, never like this," he whispered, pulling her violently trembling body back against his chest.

"No! Don't touch me . . ." she protested weakly.

"Fitzhugh! I grow weary of waiting!" Again the shrill voice sounded from the doorway. Eben's back stiffened, and she jerked herself from his arms.

"Damn! I shall call on you in the morning, Eben," he said. With a quick kiss on her bruised mouth, he left her abruptly. Taking Louise's arm, he propelled her back into the ball-room, rather roughly.

Eben's head dropped down to her hands, and tears filled her eyes. What a fool she was! She loved him. She recognized it at last. She had been on the verge of telling him she loved him, when his mistress had interrupted. His mistress! Never had she been so humiliated. Yes! One other time . . . when this same man had offered her a trinket in exchanged for her maiden-head. Why was her body such a slave to the sensations he evoked that she allowed him to humiliate her time and time again?

Her heart felt as if it were splitting in two. Her fingers touched her bruised lips. She felt empty except for the intense ache in her chest. Weakly she swiped the tears from her face. She must find Barnaby and make some commitments before her body landed her deeper into trouble. It would be safer to be married and left with no choices. This man was entirely too dangerous. She must remove herself from his reach, for to stay within it was agony. To continue with Eastmore was to feel this agony again and again.

Squaring her shoulders, she picked up the remaining glass of champagne and tossed it off in one gulp. Throwing it violently to shatter against the wall, she headed toward the terrace doors with renewed determination, and still-wobbly legs.

"All right, my lady the duchess of Kent, I now owe you one Oriental floor vase and two champagne glasses!"

At the moment, Lord Eastmore was striding as quickly as the crush of people would allow toward the entrance. His hand, tightly gripping Louise's elbow, was carrying her along with him.

"Really, Fitzhugh . . ." she began in protest, attempting to disengage herself from his painful grip.

"Be quiet!" he gritted with such a forbidding look that she clamped her rouged mouth shut and resolved to keep it shut. Being a prudent woman, and having the experience behind her to draw upon, Louise wisely heeded the stern warning in his extremely tight voice. He was furious with her.

A full two hours passed before Fitzhugh had Louise dropped at her door with the explicit understanding that their relationship was irreparably over. His mood foul at the mess his life was did nothing for his hopes which had been dashed this night. How like Louise to misconstrue his intent and then to meddle where she had no business. Having truly thought the entire affair settled after their last evening, he had quite put the liaison behind him, only to be summoned by a note delivered by one of her damned blackamoors. Actually, *summoned* was the wrong term. The note had merely specified the time she wished to be collected . . . by him . . . for the princess's birthday ball. An event he had planned to use to his advantage as an all-out assault on the charming but vexing Miss Victor. In this sense, the note in fact *had* been a summons . . . a summons to an argument. Louise had stormed at him, threatening dire things if he destroyed her credit by reneging on the planned outing.

Fitzhugh settled back comfortably in the carriage. Perhaps he had been too vague. Perhaps there was some truth to what she said. While he had thought it more than a "little" talk, perhaps she had seen it differently. And when he had clasped the diamond bracelet around her wrist, he had meant it as a parting gift . . . nothing more . . . while she had taken it as something else. He frowned with irritation. Only this time at himself. What he had considered a farewell fling and a parting gift of fellowship had been sadly misinterpreted, indeed. And, giving in to her tears and demands, as women did put such store in such things, he had promised to escort her to the ball. Escort only! Not to fill every dance on her dance card or take her to supper—escort only. And as simply as that the disastrous event had commenced.

And now, with Louise out of his life, this time with no misunderstandings, Fitzhugh settled back in the dark carriage to allow his mind to address the second emotion plaguing him. It had to do with the raven-haired beauty he had been forced to abandon on the terrace of Kensington Palace. An audible sigh escaped him as he remembered her fresh sweetness. Raking a hand through his hair, he caught scent of her. He groaned as blood flooded his body with unrelieved desire. His senses were alive with the taste and feel of her. She was so innocent, yet so responsive to his touch. How he wanted her...and now! Tonight! How he longed to return to her and finish what they had started.

Damn Louise for interrupting them... The minx had been defenseless against him, there on the terrace...soft, yielding and compliant. The battle lines between them had been down, and a declaration of acceptance had been trembling on her lips when Louise— Damn! One nod from Eben, and he would have swept her inside to her mother and announced the engagement to the whole of the assembly, binding his love to his side forever.

He was truthful in all he had just declared to Louise. He did intend to be faithful to his wife in all ways. For he was quite certain that this was his fate, and that it would never be fulfilled with anyone other than Eben Pearl. And on the morrow he planned to set everything right. She would accept his offer, or she would be carried off, kicking and screaming, over his shoulder to the magistrate for a special license! He had no more patience with misunderstandings and childish bouts of temper. It was time to settle this once and for all. And the only settlement he would tolerate was her complete and total surrender to his wishes.

Chapter Twenty

Eben slipped through the terrace doors and stood for a moment, allowing the music and heat to surround her. She felt dazed and uncertain, as if she had stepped from one time to another. Mentally shaking herself, she began a methodical tour of the glittering rooms. She must find Barnaby. She would settle the matter of the engagement tonight, then return to Victor Mall, where she was safe. She was heartily sick of London, the season, and the turmoil inside herself.

An hour later found her still searching. There were so many guests, and nearly as many rooms, and the worrisome possibility that he could be circulating just ahead of her or just behind her and she might never find him frustrated her. She felt such an overwhelming sense of urgency. The gaiety, the music, the whirling of the dancers, all contributed to the throbbing just behind her eyes. She actually wanted nothing more than to go home, pound her mattress to pieces and dissolve in tears of rage.

Several times she paused in her search, but to hesitate was to bring forward a number of eager hopefuls, flattering and flirting, demanding dances already signed for but ignored by Eben. Her patience wore thin. It would have been imprudent to inquire if anyone had seen him or to send her army of admirers out in search, or she would have done just that. Anything to accomplish her end before this night was done. Twice during her rounds she saw her aunt still at the card tables. And she noted that her mother was thoroughly enjoying herself in Lord Melton's arms. Lewis was dancing with a debutante in a stiff white dress, and as if her eyes could hear, she could tell he was up to his best in blarney, for the young girl was atwitter and blushing prettily. With a fond smile for her friend, she moved on. Fitzhugh was not to be seen. Eben bitterly imagined he had retired to the warm bed of his red-haired tart, probably to work off the head of steam she had left him with. Forcibly she put him out of her mind. To think of him was to think of that wonderful, powerful, bursting feeling, and to think of that was to rekindle desire for more of the same. Allowing herself a small, sad sigh, she strengthened her resolve and searched on.

Finally, just as she was beginning to despair, in a small side drawing room, quite away from the mainstream of the ball, she spotted her quarry. Lady Compton was seated in a tight group of gossiping ladies, and Barnaby, ever the obedient son, stood behind her chair. Eben imagined he had stood thus since their arrival, many hours before. Patient and never allowing himself to wonder if he was bored or if he might wish to be elsewhere, for it undoubtedly did not enter his mind that he should have a thought other than those that matched his mother's.

But now that she had found him . . . what? Eben stood still, in Barnaby's line of vision, pondering. She could not just walk up to him. For once she wished her mother was beside her, for Lady Lillian's stopping to speak to an old friend would be quite acceptable. But for an unescorted female to approach would most definitely not be.

"Miss Victor, it thrills me to find you quite alone. And I shall forever treasure this moment, if you will allow me to fetch you a glass of refreshment."

She turned to face the sallow man beaming at her. He must have been several years her senior, but Eben felt as old as his grandmother. But she smiled, for it was not in her to be cruel. Besides, who was she to deny another human being a moment to treasure.

"That would be excellent. A champagne ice would be the thing I would desire above all else," she cooed, in her best debutante voice.

Sending the man happily on his way, she once again turned to Barnaby. At that same moment, he saw her standing there. Eben was sure of this by the way his face flamed a bright red. Turning ever so slightly, she gave an appearance of being a part of the group beside her, as it would never do to appear to be waiting for him to notice her. From the corner of her eye, she saw Barnaby bend to his mother and nod in her direction. Turning full-face to acknowledge that lady, Eben was stunned to receive a set face and a frozen look from her.

She shuddered, positive that if she had been closer, it would have stricken her with icicles. But Lady Compton did speak to her son for a moment, then release him to cross the room. Eben watched his awkward approach with a sadness in her heart. It seemed to take him forever, as every person he bumped or crossed must be bowed before and apologized to. Never had there been such a humble man! Eben waited impatiently, every muscle tense for what seemed like her last hope. At last he bowed his tall, thin body before her. "Miss Victor, w-would you dance?"

His face, though an alarming shade of red, was bright and eager. Eben decided to take her pleasure at greeting her as a good omen and allowed him to lead her back to the main ballroom. Thank goodness, the quadrille band was just striking up a waltz. It seemed the first bit of luck she'd had this entire evening. And, as heaven was her witness, she needed some luck that was firmly upon her side, and that was the truth, for she must make this man declare himself this night!

"I have missed you, Barnaby... this past fortnight."

She must not let on that she knew it had been more than twice that long. Eben was again thankful that he was a smooth mover on the dance floor, allowing freedom to converse.

"Yes, M-Mother has been ill. Quite taken to her b-bed. I greatly feared she might never leave it again," said Barnaby, looking over her head, leaving Eben to stare at his bobbing Adam's apple.

Eben chewed on her lip. So the old bat was firmly back in charge. Well, she couldn't very well place this weak fool's hand on her breast in the middle of the dance floor. Swing after swing of the dance steps, she pondered the problem, but no revelation came to mind. A sense of panic and helplessness rose in her throat. Once the dance was finished, would he merely take her back to her mother? Was she to have no chance of a private word with him? Drat! And double drat! Things could not possibly be worse! Not possibly!

When the music ended, he led her off the floor toward her waiting aunt, who stood beside a stiff Lady Compton. Dipping a slight curtsy to that lady, she inquired as to her health.

"Lady Compton, I trust you are feeling better?"

The lady's nostrils quivered as in distaste as her gaze raked the young girl's seemingly transparent gown. The nasty-tempered lady had a calculating gleam in her eye. Lady Adair tilted an eyebrow at Eben, in one of the little signals at which the two were becoming so proficient. Eben held her tongue. Finally, as if a decision had been made, Lady Compton rounded on her son.

"Barnaby, have you spoken to Miss Victor?" she grated, without acknowledging Eben's greeting.

"N-no, M-Mother...I thought...th-there wasn't opportunity," the startled man stammered, running his forefinger around his neckcloth. Eben wished to tell him that it wasn't his neckpiece that was strangling him, but his mother.

"Well, do so!" she ordered. With this command, she merely stood observing the couple, as if attending a scene from a play...one she had orchestrated.

Barnaby looked as if he would fall to the floor in a swoon. He tugged at his neckcloth again, almost untying it in his efforts to gain air. His Adam's apple danced spastically, and his mouth gaped, making little popping sounds that Eben could hear even above the music. He greatly resembled a fish out of water, engaged in its final death throes. Since it seemed that Barnaby would quite possibly swallow himself if no one came to his aid, Eben, without further ceremony, tucked her hand inside his arm and tugged him away.

"Come, Lord Compton," she urged sternly. Turning her back on a fuming Lady Compton, she led the despairing lord away, to an approving nod from her smirking aunt.

Leading the disturbed man through room after room, Eben frantically searched for an unattended alcove. Just when it seemed there was no hope, she located her desire. After installing Barnaby with a stern order to stay put, she procured two champagne ices, praying the drink might calm him, as well as loosen his stammering tongue.

"Here we are. Drink this, dear. It will refresh you," she said, handing him a glass and taking a sip of hers. Third glass this evening! Oh, well, this wasn't the worst of polite society's rules she had flouted this night! She settled herself beside him on the settee. "Now, Barnaby...you wish to speak with me?"

"W-well, M-Mother feels... I mean...it would s-seem..." He stuttered and stammered to a halt. Eben's nerves would not allow her to wait for this utter fool to declare himself. If she waited for him to sift through it alone, she might well expire herself.

"Did you speak to her about us marrying and living at Victor Mall?"

Actually relieved to have the young lady taking control, Barnaby calmed a bit and took a huge gulp of the champagne. "Yes. M-Mother feels we should live at Compton Castle. That there we c—"

"I am well aware of what your mother feels ... and wants, Barnaby. But did you tell her what we want?"

"Y-yes. But she says a young female left alone without a man's advice can't possibly know her own mind. And that a female, alone and defenseless in the world, cannot readily assume control of her own affairs without the guidance of s-superior masculine judgment. And that you sh-should leave the m-management of all affairs to m-me." His brow was furrowed with the diligence of his delivery of the rehearsed speech his mother expected him to recite. He nervously took a gulp of champagne without looking at Eben.

Left to *her* management, she means, thought Eben, then stated in an authoritarian tone. "I am not prepared to debate the natural inferiority of the female versus the superiority of the male. What I need to know, Barnaby, is did you press her? Did you tell her we would rebuild Victor Mall and live there?" She asked this, though already in possession of the answer.

"No, I c-could not." Barnaby turned toward her in his urgency to make her understand. "I feared for her life. She became so enraged that she c-collapsed. I c-could not be the cause of my own m-mother's demise."

"No, of course you could not, dear," she told him in a soft, soothing tone.

With a resigned sigh, Eben drained her glass in one gulp. So...desperate times called for desperate measures. Heaven help her, but she must end this thing. Taking his hands in hers, she leaned toward him, rounding her shoulders slightly, giving him a view of her breasts to the very tops of her nipples.

"Do you want to marry me, Barnaby?" she asked, staring beseechingly at him.

"Oh, yes!" he whispered emphatically. His hands, in hers, twitched, and his Adam's apple danced up and down his throat madly. "Oh, yes...more than anything!" he gasped again, unable to stop his eyes from dropping from hers to ogle her creamy flesh.

"I must live at Victor Mall, dear. It means so much to me...for us to be alone. Promise me, Barnaby. Give me your sworn oath that we will live at Victor Mall and your mother will stay at the castle."

Regretfully, the eyes left her breasts, and he shook his head to say, "I cannot g-give you my oath, Eben. She might become ill again. I dare not take the ch-chance. You must see that! Please say that you see that!"

In exasperation, she rose, and in one fluid motion turned her back on him. Leaning her head against the curtain, she gave a tiny sob. When he did not come to her, she turned to face him. Seeing him sitting with his hands clenched tightly in his lap, she understood that he could not rise without embarrassing himself.

"I just don't know where to turn, Barnaby. Father's debts...the pensioners..." she whispered, as if quite overcome by the weight of her responsibilities.

"But M-Mother says she will not rebuild Victor Mall. Nor c-can we live there. Your father's debts will be paid in full, and your pensioners t-taken c-care of until the end. But..."

The man was so eager and so earnest, she knew a sworn oath extracted from him would be upheld, regardless of the consequences. She tried once again.

"Oh, Barnaby, I just know we can settle these little differences so that we can be happy. Say you'll try to persuade your mother again...say you'll really try, even if she threatens illness...and I'll be your wife."

At Barnaby's nod of agreement, she turned to depart. "I must go tell my mama, Barnaby. I am just so happy. Call on me tomorrow," she flung over her shoulder, quickly escaping the alcove, leaving Lord Compton to stare after her.

Stopping a second to catch her breath, she could not help but smile to herself. She was far better at this seduction business than Portsmythe. Maybe she could offer lessons in seduction. After all, she was learning from the master himself, Eastmore. That thought was a bit sobering, as renewed feelings of her own seduction returned. The memory of her helplessness and longing for that which could never be brought a second of compassion for the man she had just left behind.

Skirting the dance floor, she searched for her aunt. Seeing her still with Lady Compton, she altered her course in favor of her mother. That lady she found surrounded by friends, as usual, and she did not wish to become snared in polite conversation, as the last thing she felt at this moment was polite! Nor did she wish to be detained in this place any longer. She abruptly altered course yet again, with full intent to quit this gathering with as much speed as possible.

"Oh, look! It would seem the great dark goose has lost her gaggle. See how her long neck stretches as she searches?" a shrill voice, accompanied by a titter and the snapping of opening fans to hide the smirks of amusement on insulting lips, caught her as she would pass through the doorway,

"Enough of this!" Eben snapped, swinging back to confront the speaker. "Miss Vernill, in the course of this season, a time period of no more than a few months, you have yet to visit my home, nor have you invited me to visit yours. Beyond noting that we attend most of the same functions, we have exchanged no more than three words to each other. And yet you find it imperative to make disparaging remarks concerning my appearance, my manners and my circumstances at every opportunity presented. I can only assume you do this to elevate yourself in your own mind, for to me it would seem that your opinion of yourself must be severely lacking to constantly demonstrate the need to tear someone else down in such a cruel manner. In my kindness to you, I would suggest you work as diligently to develop a sweet nature, in keeping with your looks, before those closest to you discover what I myself have discovered, and you find yourself quite alone. Alone, and bound for the first port in India to seek someone's third son to take you to wife. Now, I bid you good-evening."

"How d-dare you..." the shocked girl began, fighting tears of mortification.

"No, Miss Vernill. How dare *you!*"

Entering the ladies' retiring room with apricot tulle draperies flying and color high, she quickly penned a note to her aunt to the effect that she had gone home with a headache and would return the carriage forthwith. Only then did she sit for a moment with her head in her hand. What an abominable night! And this last part of it would most certainly earn her a scolding of the first order when news of it reached her aunt, for the audience to the set-down had not been small. But surely the news of her engagement would bring congratulations from that quarter . . . if also moans of despair from her mother. And, in truth, when she should be feeling triumph over the scene, she felt numb all over, except for her heart, which hurt abominably.

At this point, the only avenue open to her was to marry Barnaby, pay the creditors and settle her pensioners, then see if she could manipulate him after that. Manipulate him into standing up to his mama . . . to be a man and help her rebuild Victor Mall. If not . . . then the old lady could not live forever. And when the dowager was gone, then she would be the one in charge . . . with a vast fortune and a malleable husband. Until that time, Lady Compton would have no real power to dispose of Victor property, as it legally belonged to Lady Lillian until her death, then went to Eben's sons. She, and her mother, would have to endure as best they could, and she must produce sons galore before her mother's demise. She must keep foremost in her mind that the real power of the Compton fortune belonged to Barnaby, if only he could be persuaded to use it.

The triumph of Barnaby's capitulation seemed so hollow now that she had acknowledged her love for Fitzhugh. A love she had been so willing to announce, until his mistress appeared to return her somewhat to sanity. Why could he not be an honorable man, instead of a rakehell? Oh, how her heart ached for him and her body cried out for his touch. What a dangerous power he had over her. Drawing herself up, Eben hardened her heart. She might not have love in this marriage she was making, but she would have money, and money

brought power. And, as her aunt admitted, love only muddled the entire affair from the beginning. As for her own brief
experience, love only brought great heartache. And now, she
just wanted to take her foul mood home and to bed. Eben
paused in the hall to dispatch one footman with the note to her
aunt and another to have her carriage brought around.

"Miss Victor! Thank heavens we've found you!" Lewis
called from behind her. Startled, Eben spun to face him, then
raised her eyebrow in question at seeing Lord Ellington, plus
several more toplofty Corinthians in tow.

"What gives, Lord Ottobon?" she quizzed, resolutely
drawing on her outdoor wear as a clear indication of her intent to depart, not be drawn back into the ballroom.

"We've a bracing proposition for you. It's a way out of your
fix, old girl," he stated, taking her arm and drawing her into
a corner of the hall, away from the crowd. "Remember the
wager Alfred, Lord Ellington, extended to you? The black,
and a thousand pounds?"

"Vividly," she answered, with a frosty glance at Ellington.
The other bloods gathered around, eager for the tale to be told.

"Well, we have revised the wager just a trifle. Listen to this."
Lewis fairly beamed. "A match race!"

She looked at him expectantly but he seemed to have nothing else to add. "So?" she prompted, as his statement seemed
incomplete, and her temper was short at best.

"Your black against an open field. Two thousand pounds
and horses' papers for entry, and winner takes all!" he cried,
triumphantly. The group of lords all nodded and grinned, as
if the problems of the world had just been solved. Ellington
stood a distance from the others, his smile anything but pleasant.

She could only stare openmouthed at Lewis. "Have you
quite taken leave of your senses? I haven't that kind of blunt
for a wager, and you are well aware of the fact."

"That's the beauty of this wager, Miss Victor," Alfred said,
moving closer to her to explain the stakes. "You will be required to wager something else, something as valuable to
some—though not to all—as two thousand pounds."

Eben shivered at the implications of his remark. For a moment, his sneer frightened her. Had her reputation sunk that

far? But she refused to step back from him and returned his open sneer with a stern look. Lewis turned her from Ellington with the hope of diverting a blazing scene between the two, as he knew their very presence in the same room could spark.

"Listen to me," he begged. "If you win, you will win all the money . . . there's eight in so far . . . and all the cattle to rebuild your stable. But if you lose, you lose the black to the winner, as well as your hand in marriage." The muscular lord beamed with the brilliance of the idea, then added, "That's your wager! Your hand in marriage!"

Her eyes swept over the eager Corinthians grouped there. Most she knew and had declined already, but all had more than enough pocket to cover this wager. She turned again, her gaze settling on Alfred, trying to shake the feeling that he was setting her up for a fall.

"Are you in on this, Ellington?"

"Of course."

"But why?"

"Because I have a racer in my stable that is faster than your black. I have no doubt I can win. And it is well-known I am a wagering man."

"But does a wagering man wager even when he doubts the value of the prize?"

"Oh, have no doubt that I covet that black stallion. He will improve my line admirably."

"And my hand . . ."

Alfred's open sneer at Eben's question would have damaged him beyond repair in the eyes of the other gentlemen, had it not been quickly concealed with a deep bow, before any of the others witnessed the insult.

"I would like nothing better than to have you as my wife. Your constant companionship would make both our lives complete. I would welcome the challenge of breaking you as much as I would your wild horse," he said smoothly. "For you are ravishing. Even in sackcloth you would be ravishing."

The other men stirred uncomfortably at his tone. None had a deep love for the little braggart, and all held Miss Victor in the highest esteem.

"I say, Ellington . . ." one said.

"Just a bit too brown, old man!" another exclaimed.

"You are insulting, Ellington!" a third joined.

Eben felt sudden hatred for this man who had so much...name, family, fortune...and wasted it in insult and abuse. She fairly trembled with the depth of her feelings against everything concerning him.

"My lord, how is it you make every compliment sound like an insult?"

Lewis, fearing another scandalous confrontation between the two, stepped forward with a dark warning look at Alfred, to query, "What say, Miss Victor?"

"How long a race, and what course?"

She did not remove her eyes from Alfred's simpering expression. While heartened by the support of the Corinthians, she wished for some way, once and for all, to best this little man and set him publicly in his place. What better way than to defeat him soundly at a game of his own choosing?

"Glendale Course, outside of London...mile and a half."

"Mile and a half! You forget my black is twelve years old...against two-year-old racers? Unfair, sir!"

"Twelve's not old, Miss Victor. A horse doesn't even have all his teeth until he's five, and isn't full-grown until he's seven! Have you no faith in your horse?" Alfred asked. Then, knowing her situation, he pressed further. "Besides, there's eight entries so far. That's sixteen thousand pounds, and eight of the best blood racers in the country... if you win."

Lewis leaned close and whispered in her ear, "I've seen their horses race, and I've seen the black turned loose. Your man sits him well. You have nothing to fear...except my bay, of course, and I would welcome you both to my stable."

Eben could not rise to his teasing. She pondered a moment. Sixteen thousand pounds! She knew the black was fast and would give his all for love of her. Oh, to be free and have funds to rebuild her home. And Barnaby? Yes, she would still marry Barnaby, but this money would grant her freedom, if she could not wrest it from Lady Compton.

"When?"

"A fortnight. Gives the boys a chance to bring their cattle up to town." Alfred smiled to see her weaken. "Enough time for you to cry off, if you feel that your black is not up to the race. It would be expected of a woman, anyway."

"I will agree to your wager, my lord. There will be no crying off. And as for your racer... any horse from your stable is certain to be underfed and out of condition, as you, my lord, are no horseman!"

"What? How dare you!" Alfred began, his voice as high and shrill as that of a matron with a mouse in her petticoats.

"Let the race determine who has the best cattle, not a brawl on the ballroom floor," Lewis stated, quickly stepping between the two.

"I would ask one thing," Eben said. "The terms shall remain among ourselves."

Eben drew ready agreement from all except Alfred. She felt a trickle of fear rise above her anger. Not of him, personally, but of his hatred of her, shown now clearly in his distorted expression. That, backed by his low morals, might bring him to harm the black in some manner to ensure he won hands down.

Lewis stepped forward. "You have our word, Miss Victor. And I personally will handle the matter of the race, so that all is fair. Ellington?" That lord would only nod his head, and Eben was forced to accept that as affirmation when Lewis turned to reassure her again. "You have our word as gentlemen!"

Suddenly very exhausted, Eben merely nodded and excused herself. Sitting gratefully in the dark coach, she allowed her head to drop back wearily to the leather and closed her eyes. If she lost... No, best to not think of that. The distance of the race was long, but the black was strong. It was a flat race, no hurdles to increase the chances of injury, and her weight was less than most jockeys carried. The black would stand a better-than-average chance, and she would never doubt he would give his best.

Barnaby? Again, yes, she would marry Barnaby. She did not find the shy man totally repulsive, and the idea of taking him away from his mama pleased her, as did a life as Lady Eben Compton, firmly in charge of her own fortune. With Compton's funds paying off Papa's debts and settling the pensioners, the prize money could be utilized to refurbish the farms that supported Victor Mall. At least she would be free, and she would live at Victor Mall, no matter where Barnaby chose to live. She knew his fascination with her body would bring him to her more than enough times for there to be children. And, suddenly, she knew she wanted children very badly. Lots and lots of rowdy, lovable children to tumble about the great rooms of Victor Mall, filling them with love, laughter, and the everyday noise of living.

But the thought of Barnaby touching her gave her no thrill. Not at all the same as Fitzhugh... Oh, how his very name made her heart hurt. Remembering his embraces on the terrace brought an ache to the pit of her belly. A sob broke from her. Fitzhugh...how she loved him. Though she knew with her whole being that his thoughts were merely lust for the conquest. Tears ran unchecked over the porcelain of her cheeks...memories of his throaty voice begging her to say yes to him fresh in her mind. Yes to what? She had been on the verge of expressing her love to him, but that had not been his question. He had been asking for something from her, but then, as always, he had taken what he wanted without waiting for her consent. So what answer was he seeking from her?

Even his mistress had seemed not in the least surprised at finding him on the terrace with another woman in his arms and her skirts rucked up about her waist. She had apparently not cared overly much...and had been perfectly willing to take him into her bed afterward. But Eben would never be able to live with that. She wanted him to herself. She could not...would not...share her love. With Barnaby, other women—apart from his mother—would never be a question. And that was the way her decision must advance. But how was she to stop loving Fitzhugh, when he was such a part of her?

Chapter Twenty-One

First light brought, along with great trepidation, the enormity of what she'd done. The dawning of her actions bred a horror so great that her mind recoiled from it. In an attempt to justify her actions, she first blamed her seduction by Fitzhugh. She'd been driven to desperation by that humiliation! Even the episode with Barnaby could be laid at his door, the bloody rotter! Then she dropped her head and admitted that the sad situation was nothing more than the result of her deplorable temper. Once again, she had simply reacted without considering the outcome, and through her rash actions she had flouted the rules, the very backbone of the society in which she moved. They would affect not only her standing in that society, but her mother's, as well. Probably, because of her eccentric nature, her aunt could weather the storm, but her mother was likely to retire to the country again in seclusion, humiliated and ostracized by her peers. Just when she had come out of her mourning and attracted the attention of an eligible man who was her age and seemingly quite taken with her company.

Eben rolled over and pulled the covers over her head. How was she going to survive this latest jumble in which she'd landed herself? Oh, why must she always create chaos wherever she ventured? If only she could turn back the clock and have it all to do over again. Counting the series of mishaps in her life, just this past year, she was unsure exactly how far back she would have to reverse the clock to make her life as uncomplicated as she would wish it to be. One year? Or ten? Perhaps back far enough to stop Sheldon from mounting that absurd wager on such a dark and stormy night. And here it was again! The Victor future, about to be determined by a wager. History was merely repeating itself . . . hopefully with less disastrous results this time.

Best she be dressed and downstairs before her aunt, in case there were early callers . . . early, irate callers! Barnaby was to call in the afternoon, to settle plans for the marriage. Unless he got wind of her latest scrape, then he might show up this morning to cry off. If he would even show up at all! However had she thought she could keep this from his ears? And the ears of his fierce mama! There was no way he could help but learn of it, for the bets would be high on a match race of this magnitude. Especially with the public speculation on the rumors adrift already concerning herself and Ellington.

Ellington! How could she have placed any trust in him? He would take giant pleasure in destroying her credit, which was teetering on the edge of disgrace already. The tale of the whipping was sure to be dredged up again. With no chance of the coachman keeping quiet this time. 'Twas too good an opportunity for him to gain stature with his peers in the servants' halls of all the great houses.

What a hoyden she had proved herself to be! Her wayward ways had landed her in one scrape after another. It was really unforgivable the way she had strangled her chance of making a good marriage, her only chance of saving Victor Mall. If she had had her wits about her, she would have accepted the first offer and gone home. No! The first offer had been Eastmore. So, perhaps not the first offer. Perhaps the first decent offer? That would have been Lewis. How she longed to turn the clock back just that far. If only she could, she would swallow her pride and accept him with gratitude, and gladly. At least then she would not be faced with this latest scandal!

Eastmore had said he'd call today, also. Why? Did he think she would become his . . . what? He already had a mistress. Whatever she was to him, it was surely not to her liking. Best he kept his distance. He brought out the worst in her. Not once had she been in his company and survived with good standing and good humor. No, he was poison to her, and best to be avoided.

Wrapping her arms around herself, she allowed her thoughts to touch upon the scene on the terrace. Never had she conceived that there could be such an ecstasy of sensation. That bursting, pulsing, that she had felt last night from his skillful hands and mouth. So that was what lovemaking was all about. That was what she had missed from the first encounter, what she had yearned for so, afterward. Would the result have been the same that first time if he had but continued longer inside her? With a dawning realization, it became clear to her why young girls were kept innocent and watched so closely. Such a powerful and mind-stealing sensation could be as potent as a drug, sought again and again.

Eben rolled over onto her back. What truly puzzled her was the fact that she experienced such intensity with Fitzhugh and nothing with Barnaby. Must one be in love before the emotions were so deeply stirred? Not possible! Else forced marriages of convenience would not be so prolific. Although money, name and fame were as potent a drug to some. Perhaps the right marriage, and a lover one was in love with, created the ideal balance. Secret liaisons were certainly tolerated as the mode of the day among the ton. Or marriage to Fitzhugh, procuring most everything desirable with one man? If only fidelity figured into that one, also. Or did a man even feel the same as a woman? Might he require more than one woman, the proper marriage and a mistress, to inspire the same feelings? Or was she in love with a man who only found that feeling in the conquest of all women? For love him she did. So much so that to share him with another would make life unbearable. Better to live without him, than to spend her life in the hell of jealousy. Oh, what a turmoil for such an early morn! What a mess her life was!

"One person should not be forced to endure so much," she declared as she forced herself from beneath the covers and into the day.

The morning passed slowly, and with much time for self-censure, as she alone descended the stairs before noon. But not one hour past lunch, Hastings was announcing Lord Compton and the dowager Lady Compton. Rising from her window seat, Eben attempted to place a smile upon her pale face, praying fervently under her breath that the news was still contained and this was a positive meeting, for if the news had reached the ears of such recluses as these two, it was a far-spread scandal for sure.

"Lady Compton, Lord Compton. How pleased I am to see you are well this afternoon. Please seat yourselves, and I shall tell my mother and aunt you are here. Hastings?"

"Self-righteous little tart, aren't you?" the pious lady stated, her narrow nostrils fairly quivering with distaste.

"I—I beg your pardon," Eben stammered, her heart plummeting. Immediately accepting the news as widely spread, she was, nevertheless, shocked to be thus attacked in her own salon. Turning to Barnaby, she questioned, although actually expecting no assistance from that quarter, "Barnaby?"

"Do not even speak to him! After what you almost did to his good—!" the lady began, then swallowed as if greatly overcome and demanded attention from her son.

Sweeping into the room in a flurry of persimmon silk, Lady Adair paused at seeing such early callers. Especially this lady! Having had no counsel with Eben after she disappeared with Barnaby the night before, Lady Adair was not at all certain how things stood with this company. But from the look on Ernestine's pasty face, plus her last comment, it must not be to her liking. Which could not bode well for the Victor family.

"Adair! Adair, I must say, in all my born days, I have never been more insulted. To just think of the humiliation, if an engagement had been announced. Even though I am certain, several people must expect . . . so I . . . we cannot hope to escape unscathed. Never!" she said, rapidly fanning herself with a gilded chicken-wing fan, fairly beating it to death with a show of outraged agitation.

"Ernestine, what on earth—?" Lady Adair began, fearing to think what terrible thing was amiss. Something far worse than the loss of control over her weak-willed son had Ernestine Compton up in the rafters. Something that boded evil, not well, for the Victors. One look at Eben's frozen face confirmed that the chills running up her spine were justified. What on earth had the girl done this time, to cause all this horrendous upset?

"I see that you have not heard the gossip? The streets fairly run with the filth. Had not my source been impeccable, totally reliable, I would have cried, 'Liar'! For never would I have believed a girl from a good family—your niece, Adair, your niece, and the girl my son had picked for a wife—could have done such a thing!" the woman wailed, playing her indignation to the hilt.

Eben tried to catch Barnaby's eye, to see if she could tell just how he felt about the tale, for gossip could be far worse than the actual event. No telling how blown out of proportion it had gotten in just twelve hours. But that man would only stand behind his mother's chair and hang his head like a whipped puppy. If he had any feelings for her at all, would he not stand up for her, even a little?

"Adair? Eben?"

Lady Lillian's voice wafted down the hall, then was followed into the room by herself. Seeing the dowager Lady Compton, she attempted to back out again, before anyone saw her, but she was not quick enough and was easily trapped by the dowager's call. She slowly advanced and resigned herself to at least fifteen minutes in that hateful lady's presence. It was totally beyond her why Adair and her daughter insisted on encouraging this pair!

"Lillian, you poor, poor dear! How my heart bleeds for you. To think of the agonies you must suffer, with this terrible child as a daughter. And after losing your precious son, to be left with a bad seed!"

"I—I beg your pardon . . ." Lady Lillian stammered, completely taken aback over this speech, accompanied by such crocodile tears. "Adair?"

Deciding attack was better than listening to any more of this ridiculous dribble, Eben strode to jerk the bellpull with deliberate purpose. She returned to position herself in front of the portrait, needing the feeling that at least one Victor, even one long dead, was behind her.

"Hastings," Eben said when the old man would have stepped into the doorway, eyes round with wonder at all the tension in the room. "Please ask Bess to attend us in the salon—oh, and to bring my mother's salts."

Seeing this and hearing the call for restoratives for Lillian, Lady Adair closed her eyes and, with a whispered prayer, braced herself for the worst. "Lord help us!"

Eben then turned to confront her tormentor. "Now, Lady Compton. Do you think you can tell us what it is you are dribbling about? Straight out, and with as few unnecessary embellishments as possible?"

"Eben!" her mother gasped.

Lady Compton's eyes narrowed, and she stared at the beautiful girl with real hatred in her eyes, ready to deliver a set-down that was to be a pleasure for her. "How dare you speak to me, you dreadful girl! After the disgraceful stunt you have pulled! I've always had my doubts about you, but allowed your popularity and my son's misguided feelings for you to cloud my naturally excellent judgment of people. Never did I think you were good enough for my son."

"Ernestine, pray stop the name-calling and the dramatics and tell us what has your back up," Lady Adair demanded, seating herself on the sofa and spreading her skirts with a nonchalant air. She motioned for Lillian to do the same and pulled the tea caddy closer to the sofa. Lady Lillian remained on her feet for the advantage of a fast exit given the first opportunity. Seeing her impact being diluted somewhat, Lady Compton launched into the tale.

"Your niece, last night..." she began. Seemingly overcome with emotion and unable to go on, Lady Compton lay back in the chair and placed a hand over her heart, whether in earnest or as part of her ploy, Eben was unable to tell. But it was enough to trigger Barnaby into concerned action as he left his strained post behind her chair.

"M-Mama, come. I'll take you home immediately. Too, too much excitement, never sh-should have come," he said, in a decisive manner utterly uncharacteristic of the shy man. He pulled her to her feet and, in a hurried pace, sought to remove the lady from the salon.

Terrified of missing the pleasure of spilling the gossip, Ernestine Compton called over her shoulder in a wheezing voice. "Wagered her virtue, that's what she's done! Wagered her virtue on the outcome of a horse race! Harlot! Harlot!"

"What!" Lady Adair shot to her feet, spilling her tea and rolling the china cup under the fringed drape of the sofa.

"Oh, my..." Lady Lillian sank into a chair, making whimpering sounds that should have alarmed Bess no end. But the elderly maid had plopped into the adjacent chair and was uncapping the salts to wave beneath her own nose.

Eben followed the departing Comptons through the front door to stand in the open doorway of Vicroy House. Lady Adair advanced to stand slightly behind her in a gesture of support she was unsure she felt, for she had a terrible premonition that it was in some way true, and they were lost. Totally sunk from sight, never to recover.

There were children in the small park in the center of the square, playing with a puppy that raced around, nipping at their heels, causing shrieks of joy. They acted as if nowhere in the world was there turmoil and unhappiness. Oh, just for one hour to be that carefree and innocent again! As if in tune with her niece, Lady Adair moved close to put her arm around her slumped shoulders, presenting a united front to anyone who might happen to observe the hasty departure of the Comptons.

"Er...Miss Victor?" Barnaby had come back to stand below her, his weak eyes scanning her face beseechingly.

"Yes, Lord Compton?"

"Not your fault, weak heart, always had it. Can't say I approve of all this, but just wanted you to know, not your fault."

"Thank you, Barnaby. You are a very special man, and there will always be a place in my heart for you," Eben said, earnestly.

Blushing furiously, but not looking away from her, he gave a small bow. "There may yet be a day that I shall claim that place for myself. Good day, Eben. Lady Cromwell, your servant." With that, he climbed into the carriage with his mother. Chapter closed, Eben thought, but not entirely locked away.

"Did you notice, Auntie? He didn't stutter once."

"Come inside, my girl. I sadly fear we have some things to discuss."

Lady Adair drew her niece inside to the salon, where the restored Bess worked diligently to revive her mistress from the depths of a swoon. Fully prepared to listen with an open mind to these latest developments concerning her wayward charge, the lady could only hope it would not prove as difficult as she suspected. Her hope was not to be realized.

Having explained as best she could, without relating the incident with Fitzhugh on the terrace or her behavior in bringing Lord Compton up to the mark, Eben fell silent. She had to admit, without the telling of the true circumstances or an attempt to explain her emotional state, the wager sounded most horrible and unprovoked, even to her own ears.

"Eben, I shall never forgive you! How could you have done such a horrid thing?" her mother wailed. "We shall never be able to show our faces in society again! Never!"

Bess scowled at her and fanned her dear charge, snorting in disgust at the young girl, even though 'twas no less than she had expected. She had always known the girl would come to no good, and had told Mr. Hastings so on more occasion than one.

"I am very disappointed in you, Eben. I expected better. Really I did," Lady Adair said angrily. "You once told me you would rather sell yourself in a brothel than marry for money. Well, I fear you have done one better."

"He can win, Aunt Addie! I know he can win!"

"And what does that signify? You may well be able to pay off a few debts, but you have totally destroyed your credit. Never will you be accepted into society again. Never will you be allowed to make a decent marriage. Winning this race doesn't solve the problems of the world! Eben! Eben! How could you have been so foolish?"

Throwing her hands into the air in exasperation, her aunt swept from the room. Bess, tugging Lady Lillian to her feet to lean heavily on her arm, followed more slowly.

"Mama . . ."

"Do not speak to me, Eben Pearl!"

Eben stood in the center of the salon. Tears ran down her face, but there was nowhere to turn for comfort. Jamie Deal . . . No, she was embarrassed to face him just yet. It was also his future that she had played so loose with.

"His Grace, Lord Eastmore. Well, I never—" Hastings stammered, rudely shoved aside to admit a very angry Fitzhugh. Hastings turned his back and, pulling the door closed, muttered his way down the hall.

"Fitzhugh . . ."

Eagerly turning to face the man she loved, she paled at the sight of his set face. He stood with his feet apart, his hands clenched into fists at his sides, as if he wanted to punch someone to expend a heavy load of anger. His jaw tensely worked beneath his smoothly shaven cheeks. Eben could expect no solace from this quarter either. She was totally alone in this one.

"Good God, woman! Whatever possessed you to do something so totally addlebrained as to wager your virtue, in a match race? A twelve-year-old has-been stallion against some of the fastest two-year-old bloods in the area . . ."

"Don't! Don't you call him a has-been! He may never have had a chance to prove his speed, but he is not a washed-up has-been," she cried challengingly. "Just don't!"

Sobs threatened to break free and overwhelm her if she gave an inch. So he would rail at her head, too! Well, she'd give as good as she took.

"They've set up a board at White's taking bets on the outcome! Placing odds on who will take your maidenhead! What a hoot that is!" he railed, pacing back and forth. "Bloody fools, wagering their best bloods, plus two thousand pounds, for something that I took nearly a year ago. By damn! What a rag it would be for me to tell them!"

Eben's face had turned a dull red, then a dead white, but this time Fitzhugh's anger outweighed his concern, and he made no move to touch her. She blindly put out her hand, searching for the mantel, to steady herself.

"Ellington . . ."

"No, Eben, not Ellington! You! Not Ellington! He did not do this to you. You did this to yourself, with your childishness and your—" Turning from her in helpless anger, he raked his hand through his hair. "You are ruined. I can do nothing, nothing, to save you this time."

Eben felt struck to her very depths. No one would stand up for her?. No one? Numb with shock and feeling more alone than she had in her entire life, she drew herself up to her full height and forced metal into her backbone.

"Your grace, I require nothing from you. Not your help, nor your incessant reprimands. Do not bother yourself with my affairs, for I believe I have told you at least once before, my business really is none of your affair."

"Someone must take you in hand, for you are truly a menace to yourself and anyone who is involved with you."

"For your information, just so we understand one another once and for always, I despise you and your high-handed manners. I wish you to go to your plump, pudding-faced Miss Vernill with your censures. I am quite positive she will never disgrace you. Or take yourself off to the warm bed of your Lady Sinclair... or... or just go to the very bloody devil for all I care!" she said, her voice dropping in tone until it was deadly and quiet.

The duke stood for a moment and looked into the girl's face. His expression was still, and totally unreadable. Then, slowly, he advanced upon her. "So you despise me?" he gritted between clenched teeth.

"Y-yes! And don't you touch me!" she warned, backing up as far as the mantel would allow. Her anger was rapidly replaced by apprehension, for he did look sorely pressed.

"We've already proven that you do not mean those words, even as you utter them. Tell me, Eben, do you despise me when I caress your cheek, like so?" The back of his fingers slid over the smooth surface of her cheek. She flinched away from his fingers, and his angry voice, deceptively wrapped in silk, continued, "And do you despise me when I take you in my arms?"

"Don't touch me!" She attempted to struggle as he pulled her into his hard embrace.

"And is your hatred of me all you think of when your heart beats against mine? Is that the truth, then? Tell me?"

Eben planted both hands against his chest in an attempt to gain some distance between them, as she was fearful of giving in to the promise of comfort in his arms, when she knew there was truly no comfort to be found there.

"Let go of me!"

Gripping her suddenly, Fitzhugh swung her about and shoved her backward to sprawl on the sofa, quickly covering her body with the length of his before she could rise. She gasped as the breath left her body...then again at the intimate feel of the length of him through her lightweight dress.

"And my kisses...do you spurn my kisses, too, little cat?"

He covered her mouth with his hot one, shutting off any protest she would make. Trapped beneath him, she could do nothing to escape his hot, searching mouth as it explored hers. Trusting his weight to keep her confined, he slid his hands up to knead her breasts, rubbing the nipples to urgent attention through her bodice.

Eben gasped as something akin to molten lava spread over her belly and made her want to arch upward to increase the contact. She fought to contain her uncontrollable reactions to the very nearness of him. When she gripped a handful of his hair, the act that was to have pulled his mouth from hers seemed, as if of its own volition, to turn into a caress and pull him tightly to her. The very act of touching him in tenderness, even giving in to her feelings and desires for one moment, as if in testimonial of how it could be between them if only life were more fair, sparked a rush of warmth and desire in her body, and she arched her hips against him with a moan of need.

"Oh, Fitzhugh..." she gasped. Dropping her head back, she arched hard against him...lost to reason...lost to everything except the need to love him and to be loved by him in return.

So sweet was she, so passionate, and yet Fitzhugh knew she would fight him at every turn. She would place herself in dire jeopardy rather than submit to him in marriage. "I believe I told you once before, nothing you can do...nothing you say...can stop me from taking what I want from you," he muttered in her ear. "Fools! Wagering on something I took a year ago. Something that I claim as my possession from this day forward. Do you still say you despise me and the things I do to you?"

Eben jerked, as if struck. Even now, he would taunt her with her helplessness and ineptitude in resisting any advance he wished to make in her direction. Proving to her, again and again, that she was a slave to him. He could not and would not say words of tender feeling to her, for he did not feel anything other than triumphant at his conquest over her will. She wanted to scream at him, to rake his face with her nails to inflict on him the pain she was feeling inside, anything to turn the all-consuming love she felt for him into hate. She shoved at his rock-hard chest.

"Yes! Yes! A thousand times, yes! I despise everything you do to me. Now pray get off me," she declared, bracing herself away from him when he would have kissed her again.

"Nay, little cat. There is more pleasure to be had of this."

Eben gritted her teeth and met him eye-to-eye, letting anger burn the need for tears away. "Yes, but 'tis no more pleasure than others have given me. And I choose when and with whom I experience that pleasure. Now, get off me!"

Fitzhugh's face became still, and his eyes grew hard. Without a word, he rose to leisurely adjust his clothing. His face was set, and his eyes were narrowed at her in speculation.

Striving to rise with some dignity, Eben flipped her petticoats down and straightened her skirts. Turning her back on him, she gripped the folds tightly in her hands to still their violent trembling. When she heard him start toward her, she moved to place distance and furniture between them.

"You are deplorable, Eastmore. Leave my sight and never—do you hear me, never—come back into it again! Why can not you understand? I despise you, above all else!"

Fitzhugh stood for a moment, studying her. Water and fire together. That was what they were. Perhaps never to be compatible. And could she have spoken the truth when she would fling other lovers in his face? Her very eagerness for his touch, that freedom of responsiveness that he cherished about her, leaped to his mind and played against her favor. At odds at this moment to deal with that unbidden thought, he chose to retreat. Sketching a small bow, he abruptly spun on his heel and walked through the door. Not a word did he utter. He just departed.

Stunned, Eben stilled for an instant, listening, waiting. When he did not return to explain, to ask forgiveness or to fling angry words at her head, she swayed.

"Fitzhugh—?"

Suddenly she knew. He had left. Truly left, never to return to her. This time they had pushed each other too far. He had believed her lies! Lies she had spoken in anger and hurt, but lies nevertheless. He truly hated her now. As she should hate him, but somehow couldn't. Turning, she fell on her knees and buried her face in her arms on the striped Grecian sofa.

"Oh, God, what have I done? What have I done?"

Chapter Twenty-Two

During the following fortnight, Eben's world became a void. It was as if she had passed from this world and had no connection with it, though leaving heavy marks upon it in the matter of gossip and scandal. No one called. No one left cards. The silver salver in the entrance hall remained empty. After months of invitations and calling cards overflowing onto the table and ofttimes onto the floor, it was a sad sight to see it so neglected. The doorbell never rang. Hastings's voice did not call out announcing a young lord for Eben or a gossipy dowager for Lady Lillian or Lady Adair. Suddenly it was as if the Victors did not exist to polite society. At least not to their faces.

Outside the house, the Victor name was on everyone's lips and in everyone's minds. The lineage was discussed as far back as anyone could remember . . . the tales changing as often as there were people telling them. Scandals were dredged from old memoirs or invented. Many times a story concerning one or another of the Victors would alter six times from one end of a ballroom to the other. But no matter what gossip was dragged out for view, the talk always ended with the latest one, the match race and the maid's virtue, with wagers mounting among the young eligibles and much smacking of lips and savoring of the tale by the ton. Never had an incident so rocked a season.

Lady Lillian passed her time in her apartments, with Bess her constant companion. Long days were again filled with imaginary illnesses and complaints. Over and over, through tears from weak, reddened eyes, she beseeched Bess to tell her where she had gone wrong as a mother. Why was she so ill-fated with her children, that her sainted son should die at such an early age and her only daughter should so disgrace her? Out of concern for her mistress's health and sanity, Bess would administer drops to make her sleep. Although Lady Adair suspected the drops were more for Bess's peace of mind and sanity than Lillian's, she did nothing to dissuade her.

Lady Adair, being of a more practical mind, spent the time turning out every closet in the house. Inspecting linens, tossing the worst into the bandage bag to be sent to the local hospital, setting some aside to mend and packing the usable ones in camphor for protection against mice. Storerooms were dug into and the piles sifted for giveaway or stacked for keeping. "A busy mind is not as apt to worry," became her newest adage to live by, although she was doubting its effectiveness two days into the ordeal. While Lillian was not speaking to Eben, in fact going so far as to leave any room that her disgraced daughter entered, Lady Adair was not so cruel. What was done was done, after all, and plans should be made, whatever the outcome, and therefore Eben spent much of the time dusty and with cobwebs in her hair, sorting through closets with her aunt.

"The way I see it, Eben, if you lose, you may be marrying whomever, and most of the decisions are taken out of your hands. I actually do think society is waiting on the outcome of the race to choose sides and make its judgments. No one is willing to commit themselves to an early point of view. But I must say, I doubt very much you will ever be received in society again, so there is the slightest chance the winner will cry off the marriage. Being hampered with an outcast as a wife might not sit too well with the young man's family." Lady Adair pondered the question. "If it affects his inheritance in any way, he might be forced to cry off. That is the worst that can happen. Then we might be looking over Freddy Portsmythe again, if he would even be interested, for he does like his social life. Or maybe some elderly widower with a small fortune."

Eben shuddered, but said nothing. Keeping her head bent to whatever the task was at hand, she accepted the chastising, along with the laying out of a rather dim future. "Whatever you think is best, Aunt Addie," she murmured, time and time again.

"We will only have the dregs to choose from. That we can be sure of. But, pray, do not have children! They would never be accepted," she continued. "Effectively the Victor line is dead, as far as society is concerned. Win or lose. Except for gossip, of course. No doubt that will live on for a generation or two."

"I am so sorry," Eben said. "You see, that means so little to me that I never thought."

"That's obvious, girl. But if you win, there'll be several thousand pounds. You could pay off the debts and settle the pensioners. But that's about all. There'll be very little to live on for the remainder of your life. A small annuity, with careful investing. Altogether, a distressing choice. There must be something I've overlooked. Something . . ."

When Eben could no longer tolerate her aunt's plotting, she escaped as best she could. She sought solitude in a small, forgotten bedchamber at the back of the house. Sitting there amid dusty holland covers, she would peer out the window at the mews, watching Jamie Deal with the horses, lost in drifting thoughts. Grady was her constant companion. As if sensing her distress, he would curl into her lap and purr while her hand absently ruffled, then smoothed, his gray striped fur. The back of the house had been purposefully chosen over her own bedchamber at the front, when, on the first day following the wager, she had observed the rerouting of the promenade from Rotten Row to Grosvenor Square, for the ton would come to point and stare.

Anger, as well as guilt, had driven Eben to abandon her window seat to pace the long-unused bedchamber in the back like a caged lion. Let them look, and to bloody hell with them all! It was on this particularly fractious day that Eben discovered a pastime to make the hours fly and relieve the tension that knotted her neck and shoulders. Discovering a fencing foil in the dank depths of a closet, she now spent hours, clad in her breeches and a soft pair of kid dancing slippers, lunging, thrusting and parrying, in front of a large pier glass. Working herself to exhaustion not only eased her tension, it also honed any softness from her frame put there by society living. She now sported a true Corinthian body, if there could be considered such a thing for a lady. Lean of frame, with taut muscles, she moved with a lightness in her step and a fluid grace that any cat would have admired.

The absence of callers was not a major concern to her, but being made to feel a prisoner in her own home was unbearable. And the loss of social life for her mother affected her greatly. Lady Lillian spoke of nothing else but retiring to the country after the race, no matter its outcome. Although Lord Melton had called and sent notes several times, she had steadfastly refused to receive him. A mistake of the first order, as information from the outside was sorely needed, Lady Adair repeatedly informed her, but to no avail. Her sister merely dissolved into tears and wailed about humiliation which tried Lady Adair's and Bess's patience no end. Eben would have been most touched by Ottobon's absence, had she not known he had retired to the country to ready his entry for the race. If only he had been in town, to cheer her with his funny stories and tales of scandals far worse than this one.

As it was, her life seemed to come alive only at dawn. Just before first light, she raced the black over the park in the dense darkness, on a track carefully laid out for safety and stepped off for distance by Jamie Deal, stretching him and strengthening already rock-hard muscles. As she sat tight aboard the flying black stallion with the wind snatching her breath, Eben's blood sang and her spirits knew no bounds. It was only at these times that she had no doubts of the stallion's power and strength.

The days were long for Fitzhugh, as well. Long and filled with doubt and disbelief, then condemnation and anger, then disbelief and doubt again. Only when the thoughts became too much to bear would he burst out and seek hard, lengthy and exhausting physical activity.

"Bloody damn! Give a bit of slack, Eastmore," Lewis admonished. He stood with his back pressed hard against the gymnasium wall at his country estate. The duke of Eastmore's foil was firmly planted dead center over his rapidly beating heart, as he had just been driven the length of the room by an aggressive, indefensible attack. "If you truly have an argument with me, pray let's sit down over a pint and have it out with words, as cowardly gentlemen should do. Or rather let me beg forgiveness at this very moment for any affront I might have done you, or any affront I will ever extend you in the span of my miserable life, which at this moment appears to be depressingly short.''

Fitzhugh stepped back, releasing the lord from the wall. He pulled his screened mask from his face. ''Sorry, been in a bit of a blue-devil funk lately.''

''You will receive no denial from me on that point,'' Lewis stated, removing his mask and running a hand over his sweat-slicked face. ''Whatever it is that is eating the seat of your pants must be addressed and remedied soon, or you will be avoided by everyone of good sense, for fear of engaging the brunt of your unwanted anger at every inopportune moment.''

''Again, sorry,'' Fitzhugh said, feeling the worst kind of fool for treating his friend to such a display of temper. ''Let's retire from the contest altogether.''

''That I will do, but you must also give up the tale,'' Lewis bargained. ''What has come between you and the fair Miss Victor, to cause this black and evil side of you to make such an unwarranted and unwelcome appearance?''

Fitzhugh glanced up in surprise. ''And why do you think Miss Victor has a hand in this?''

''Because I have never been accused of being blind, deaf or addlebrained,'' Lewis stated, chuckling a bit at his friend, then shaking his head in sympathy. ''Besides, you are as transparent as most heartsick puppies at this moment.''

''Well, I will admit I am in a predicament over the lady and this unfortunate situation. She is most vexing, to take part in this asinine wager! Whatever could have possessed her to do such a thing?''

Lewis cleared his throat and covered his discomfort with the activity of turning his equipment over to his man. Not foolish enough to admit his part in setting the stage for this calamity and incur the duke's wrath in earnest, he merely shrugged his shoulders. ''Perhaps she felt she had no choice. Her circumstances were dire, to say the least. You must admit that. Give some charity to the girl.''

''No choice? What of the offers she's thrown to the winds?'' Fitzhugh gritted, thinking of the times she had shaken her head at him alone. Tossing his gear aside, he stripped the sweat-soaked clothing from his suddenly tired body and sank into the tub of hot water prepared for him in the bathing room.

Lewis followed his example and leaned back in the adjacent tub. Thankfully accepting a clipped cigar from the attendant, he held it to the extended lucifer and inhaled deeply.

"Ale, my good man. And lots of it. Fitzhugh? No? Then you *are* in a foul funk," Lewis said, motioning for the attendant to set a tankard on the duke's tub tray nevertheless. Being a man of many broken hearts, he knew the appropriate cure for such a sad affliction.

"True enough." Fitzhugh readily acknowledged his foul mood, pointedly ignoring the ale and waving away the offer of a smoke. "And I do not think to burden it with a heavy head from a load of spirits."

Lewis merely shrugged. "All I can do is offer relief, old man. Your person is entirely too large for me to force it upon you. As for me, keep the glass filled." Leaning back, he sighed a cloud of smoke in great contentment. "And as to the offers she's received? Our Miss Victor is indeed a catch. Probably the catch of the season, if one is to place weight on the unofficial polls touted by the ton. Quite above all the rest." Lewis began, tilting an eye at the duke to see if he agreed, thinking to prompt him into an admission of feelings for the lady. Then, once that was accomplished, to spur him to action to sweep the lady off her feet and out of the range of all future scandals.

"Catch of the season? I quite think she has successfully destroyed all chance of being awarded that dubious honor. And if that were true, why have you not bent the knee to the lady?"

"I have." Lewis admitted with a shake of his head, as if it were a sad, sad memory at best. "And she turned me down, very prettily, but a flat refusal at the gate all the same. Quite suited, too. Have all she needs to set her predicament to rights, plus admire her greatly. Would have suited quite well, I think. But . . ."

"Refused you? In favor of Compton?" Fitzhugh sat up and splashed water over his face. Rubbing his eyes, he grasped and drained his tankard, absently holding it out to be refilled, betraying his confusion of emotions by forgetting his earlier refusal of spirits.

"No, I do not believe in favor of Compton. I believe, and I say this with best interests for both you and my dear Miss Victor in my heart, I truly believe 'twas through love of your unworthy self that she cried nay to my most honorable proposal, as well as all the rest."

"Love of... Surely you jest!" Fitzhugh turned to stare at his friend in disbelief. "If it's love of me, then why, pray tell, has she declined my offers repeatedly throughout the season! Answer me that one, if you can!"

Lewis, too, drained his tankard and attempted to answer without betraying the amusement he was beginning to feel. "I quite suspect, though I say this with no fact or absolute knowledge, that you were declined ... Repeatedly, you say? Hmmm ... could it possibly have been from the manner in which you presented your case? Satisfy my curiousity... Was your tone then similar to your tone with me this day? If so, I do not understand why she repelled your vows of love, honor and admiration. I mean, the nerve of the wench! What more did she expect? Hearts and flowers? Tenderness? Avowals of undying devotion? Or perhaps a simple statement of love... Ah, women! Delightful they may be, with their tempting ways, but must they be so unreasonable in their demands?"

Fitzhugh suddenly became quiet. Sliding deeper in the cooling water, he thought over the times he had railed at her head for the very free-spiritedness he loved, first demanding she accept him as friend, then ravishing her, taking advantage of her sensual side. In a sense, battering her innocence with the strength of his own desire. She was beyond his experience in dealing with women. Uninformed maidens were scant among his past conquests, and he appeared at a constant loss in dealing effectively with this one, for each encounter had been bungled in the worst manner possible. He straightened in the tub and sipped from his refilled tankard. Lost in his turbulent thoughts, he did not notice the amusement Lewis fought to control as he watched the expressions play over his tortured friend's face.

Fitzhugh's thoughts rambled as he endeavored to place understanding to the manner of the relationship and plot an effective mode of action. Why was it so impossible for him to comprehend that she did not have the seasoning to parry his assaults, except with fear and outrage? That her show of bravado was just that, bravado. She was totally without weapons to fight back. Nothing in her life could have prepared her for the glut of feelings raging everywhere in her delicious body. Feelings so readily displayed in her passionate responses to his lovemaking.

There was no pretense in her, that he believed. She was pure as the driven snow and did not know the meaning of dissimulation. What she felt, she demonstrated with her own wonderful brand of honesty and frankness. And that he believed to be the truth. She had thrown the hint of other lovers at his head as a desperate grasp for some way to hurt him, and perhaps to defend herself. A hastily grasped weapon for an untutored brawler. No, he did not believe she was free with her favors, except with him, and he must admit to taking, rather than asking. Once again, he had acted the cad. The feelings of guilt flooding his heart were becoming all too familiar in connection with her.

"Damn it to bloody hell!" he expounded.

"Well put, Fitz, my sad friend, very well put, indeed."

Chapter Twenty-Three

Glendale Course was a circus. People milled around, and picnics had been set out under trees on red checked cloths, wafting the mouth-watering smells of fried chicken in the air. Children ran and whooped. Ladies chattered and preened, while waving their straw hats at friends and enemies alike. There was a carnival set up at one end of the grounds and its music could be heard with a thin, tinny sound, competing with blaring band music from the other end. Temporary stands had been erected and were already filled with people, tented over with multicolored ladies parasols. There was an excitement in the very air that people took in with every breath, then exhaled in great shouts.

Betting booths were present, and men bet their past wages and their future wages. Men bet with borrowed money, and probably stolen money, as well, for when a wagering man makes up his mind about the winner of a race, he makes it up with a vengeance. Many a fight had broken out already among the commoners as to the merits of this horse or that. And a great many of the bets were down on Black Victory. For when these men looked upon Black Victory, his beauty and his fame joined in their very souls and stirred their hands toward their pocketbooks to place their wagers. Even the least romantic of them was stirred by the aged horse fighting this battle for his mistress. They would have been even more moved if they had known the slip of a girl herself would be astride the big black horse. Then again, there would have been those to give the horse no chance at all with a female aboard.

Eben turned from the doorway to enter the stall once again. Unless one looked closely, she looked like any other jockey, if a mite more curvaceous. Once again her brother's breeches and boots had come into use. Only this time she had topped them with a man's white linen shirt, her breasts tightly bound. Never had she thought to create such a huge fiasco. The match race was said to be the hit of the season. No one spoke of anything else, and even the royals were in evidence today, in a box draped with majestic purple-and-gold bunting.

If only she had someone to stand with her, someone besides dear Jamie Deal. Her aunt's angry words and disappointment stung her, while her mother's silence caused her extreme guilt. But the emptiness she felt over Fitzhugh could not even be described. It was unbearable, when she wanted nothing more than to love him, and be loved by him in return. How foolish she had been to taunt him, to lie to him with such a terrible untruth. For now there was truly no going back. No way to step away from the pain they had inflicted upon each other. Why had she not thrown herself on his mercy and asked him to just love her? In her anger, which she had only displayed to stop the tears, she had taunted him into dire actions. The horror she had felt when he walked out of the salon without a word was indescribable. Truly, he had taken her heart with him, leaving her with a large hole in her chest that weighed no less than one thousand stone.

But again, she could not share him with a mistress, and she could not love a man who would take from her whatever he pleased and then fling accusations into her face. No, Fitzhugh was not for her, not on his terms, anyway, and as she could not have him on her terms, she must somehow stop wanting him with her heart, body and soul.

"It's almost time, old man," she whispered, stroking the black's fine head and scratching the soft spots behind his ears. The stallion pawed at the floor, then bumped her in the chest with his velvet muzzle. Jamie came back into the barn from walking the length of the track.

"'Tis fast as the devil," he said. "The old man will be likin' that." With this comment, he set about grooming the stallion. Eben pulled her cap securely down over her hair and listened to his rambling, leaning against the rough wood of the box. "Been wantin' to tell ye a thing or two, lass. Can't tell ye much about handling the old man...ye know more about him than anyone. I've taught ye all the tricks I know. Now, it's up to ye to put 'em to use. Be one or two ridin' their own horses, but most have jockeys up. Them being the slickest at this game. They don't know ye for a lass, so don't look for a break there...but most will not foul ye. Smart they be, but not dirty. Ellington be aboard his own horse. Watch out for him. He be out to win, no matter what. But then, so are we..."

"I'm frightened, Jamie." Eben moved closer to the black and her dear friend.

"I know ye be, lass. Just remember, ye've got all the horse under ye that they have. But yers be running for love. The old man will break his heart for ye. So don't ye be lettin' him down," he continued, looking at her deeply. The lass did look frightened. Her eyes were huge and solemn in her white face, and her mouth tended to tremble. But he knew her as no other did. She had a backbone of iron. She would be fine out there, if no one played her false.

"I'll do my best, Jamie. For you and for him."

"In Ireland, they be saying, once in a great while there comes a man who can lay his hand on the shoulder of a horse and touch the very heart of him. Ye have that touch, lass. Even under saddle and bridle, ye make the old man here, feel like he's runnin' free."

"Tell me about the other horses again, Jamie," she asked. Eben leaned her forehead against the black's neck, wishing to be lulled by Jamie's calm words.

"Most don't count for nothin'. There be fifteen, all told. Ottobon's horse looks a flash in the pan, don't fash yerself about him. He'll never go the distance. Got a jock up. Just be in front of him and stay there. There be a bay stallion, big man near to seventeen hands, that was built for pure speed. He'll be tough. Pity but he belongs to Ellington! Then there be a white-faced mare, long and rangy, that yer ought to watch for, although I've yet to see the mare in my life to stay up there with the studs. Especially over this distance. Don't worry about the rest. Of no account." Throwing the flap of leather Eben used as a saddle over the broad back, he crooned to the big black horse. The black stood still, as if listening to a secret language.

"Do you think he can go the whole way, Jamie? I know the distances we've galloped, but an all-out race is a different matter," she asked, more terrified of losing him than of any wager.

"He won't let ye down, as long as ye believe he can do it. If ye give up on him, he'll give up, too. Now, up with ye, wee lass." Gripping her booted ankle, he tossed her lightly into the saddle. The stallion shifted restlessly, excited by all the commotion he could hear but not see. "Another thing, they all be riding flat down in the middle of their backs, whole blasted body acting a windbreak. Ye be sitting up high over the withers. Keep yer face down to his neck, and ye can help him, not hinder him. Sit light, lass, and the old man will not fail ye." Jamie patted Eben on the toe of her boot, and the loving, familiar gesture strengthened her. "Watch for them to box ye on the rail, with a horse in front of ye, leaves ye with no place to race. There be money riding on this race. Shouldn't be surprised with some thievin'."

A hush fell upon the crowd as Black Victory was led out of the barn. Eben again pulled her cap down securely. Glancing toward the carriages drawn up to the fence, she knew her mother and aunt were there, believing her too upset to come out of her room today and trusting Jamie Deal to ride. Her mother had merely tossed her head and replied that she certainly would hope Eben would stay out of sight, after her disgraceful behavior, but her aunt had arched an eyebrow at the flimsy excuse and not bought into the lie for one second, though she had kept her own counsel.

Fitzhugh was probably there, also, cozied up to some female. Eben grimaced. At least her pride had not allowed her to open the note that had come from him only yesterday, but to send it back with seal intact, as she had done, merely left her in a muddle of indecision. What had it said? Was it an apology? Or simply another reprimand? Now, at this moment, when she was feeling so alone, would she act the same? No, possibly not. She might open the note, answer it by begging for an interview and throwing herself into his arms. Oh, she was all sixes and sevens! She just could not believe, deep inside herself, that he had no feelings for her. One could not love another as strongly as she loved Fitzhugh Eastmore and not have that love returned even in the smallest way. Again she ran her eyes over the line of carriages. Apparently he had no horse entered as she'd had Jamie Deal check and recheck all week. Now, not seeing him at the barns, she could only wonder about him. She could not imagine him missing the race and the chance to see her humiliated.

"Look! 'Tis the maid's horse!"

The call went from group to group, starting low and quickly climbing to a roar, as everyone cheered the horse that was going to win the young girl the fortune needed to save her home. Black Victory reared higher and higher, taking exception to the noise and the pushing of the crowd. Quickly guardsmen formed a line, clearing a path to the track, shoving and pushing the crowd back, away from the flashing hooves. Eben could now see the other horses milling around, waiting for the start. Bang-up bits of blood and bone, all of them! The black stallion spied the horses, as well. His nostrils quivered, and his pointed ears were so taut the tips almost met. His neck arched, and he shook his head in challenge.

"'Tis off ye be, lass." Jamie Deal released the lead line and, with a pat on the toe of her boot, sent her out onto the track.

Every vantage point in and around the outer fences on the course was jammed with excited fans. The inner fence was lined with the carriages and high-perch phaetons of the elite. Another great roar went up when the stallion pranced out to the center of the track. Again Black Victory reared, Eben easily sitting his strong back. When he finally came down, she patted his neck and spoke to him, trying to calm the both of them. Her own heart was racing as if it would leap from her chest.

"Easy, Black. Save a little for the race. Just win for me, and we'll take them home. Then you can fight them all!" she promised in a soothing tone. Thankfully, he seemed to respond to her voice and to her steady hands on the leathers, settling some with his ears flicking back to her. Glancing over to the bay—Thunderbolt, Ellington had called him—Eben's forehead creased in a frown. Hell's blood! He was fast even standing still! Shameful he belonged to the abusive Ellington! Where was the mare Jamie had told her to watch for? There, standing with her head down, totally relaxed. The mare looked as if she should be pulling a rag wagon, instead of running a stakes race. She was red, with white legs and a great white face. Long-legged, and bony, a clown in white paste makeup. Eben was able to make out the face of her jockey, but did not recognize him, though he doffed his hat to her in greeting.

The lineup was simple—find a spot wherever, and once they were in a straight line, a pistol shot would start them. The race was to be twice around the three-quarter-mile track. Jamie Deal had told her to stay toward the outside, and let the others fight for the rail. That would give her less chance to be boxed on the rail. That was where the clown-faced mare was lining up, alert now, but still not wasting energy. Eben was having trouble keeping Black Victory on the ground. He was more interested in fighting than racing, and insisted on issuing a challenge to every stallion there. She fought him to the ground once more, and circled him behind the other horses, which were lining up nicely. Seasoned racehorses all, and the routine was familiar to them. Lastly Eben started the stallion toward the spot on the very end, only to have Black Victory lunge at the horse next to the mare. Wheeling him quickly, she managed to avoid contact. But at that second, the pistol was fired and the black was left half turned, standing flat-footed.

"They're off!" A great shout went up from the crowd.

Spinning Black Victory, she got away like a wildcat, with a wailing cry of despair from her supporters ringing through the air. Eben saw the mare sweep with wonderful speed right across the face of the field, and then settle down to the best position, on the rail, where she ran easily, with no effort, and kept the rest at bay. Thunderbolt came up even to her side and kept pace. The rest of the field were already laboring well to the rear, only able to fight it out for third place, and Eben was among them. That was how they swept around the course for the first round. As they went past the crowded stands, the shouts rose up as if from a single voice, seeming to slap the riders and horses in the face with a physical force. There was the high joyous chant of the supporters of the mare and the bay stallion, and the groan of despair of those who had bet on Black Victory.

He was out and away from the pack now, but a great distance from the leaders. And yet Eben was making no effort to urge him. She crouched even lower, ignoring the throbbing in her cramped thighs, burying her face in the thousand stinging whips of Black Victory's mane. She had a strong, high grip with her knees, to keep her weight off the running muscles that came up under the saddle; but outside of position and a firm but light grip on the leathers, she was making no effort. That was why they yelled at her. That was why the excited men called her a fool and a crook, and threatened to have it out with fists after the race. But Eben knew that whatever Black Victory had in his body, his heart and his soul, he would give when she asked for it.

She knew by the ears that twitched back toward her, and the easy way he ran, that he was waiting, too, for her, ready for the supreme effort. And so Eben sat quiet. She wasn't exactly tense. It was something stronger, this pull on her heartstrings, this knowledge that she was riding for possession of everything she held dear. Little by little, as she hung quietly, in perfect balance, over the splendid racing machine beneath her, she saw they were creeping up on the leaders. She knew this test was unfair, that ten years ago the stallion could have competed on an even plane and bested the best of them, but his age, against these youngsters, was unfair. The pace was jarring. She wondered if he would have anything left to enter the backstretch with the leaders, anything but heart? That would have to be seen.

They rounded into the backstretch and Black Victory was coming closer. Eben saw Ellington turn his head, and then his bay moved faster, and the mare moved faster beside him. Like a team, the mare and Ellington's stallion were keeping together, while the crowd went mad with excitement. Not only their supporters but now the majority of people, even those who had not bet at all, were beginning to yell. For they saw the black stallion creeping up with every giant stride.

The horses approached the turn, toward the head of the stretch, and Eben set her teeth, making her call. The answer took her breath away. It was like leaping from a great height. The lurch of increased speed came as a surge of strength for Eben. And with that first rush, as they rounded the turn into the stretch, she came straight up on Thunderbolt and the mare. Then the two stallions jarred together. Thunderbolt lagged; Black Victory, thrown completely out of stride, fell well to the rear, while the mare went winging on alone. A scream of rage and disappointment went up from those at hand, along the fence, and a murmur could be heard from the stands, where they could see something amiss. Murder flashed through Eben's heart. Ellington would die for this!

And the black? Could he come again? Could he loose again that long, bounding stride that seemed to eat the distance? She called, with her heart in her voice, and Black Victory answered. He swayed a little, and Eben steadied him with her hands. Then he found his stride again and surged ahead. Thunderbolt, running with wonderful strength, was beside the mare again, but bearing well out toward the center of the track. The gap was plain and free before Eben. She chose to put Black Victory through it, instead of trying to pass on the outside. It seemed unbelievable that Ellington would attempt to foul her a second time.

The finish was not far away. The two white poles gleamed nearer and nearer. The frenzy of uproar came halfway down the track to meet the surging horses. Men were standing on the fence rails, flailing their arms, as if that would help bring their favorites home. Women, less brave, stood looking at the ground, their lips moving, white-faced and overcome.

The same rush of speed poured out of Black Victory in answer to Eben's call, the same breathtaking outburst as before. By a certain heaviness and brittleness in the great body beneath her, Eben realized it could not last for long. The great sweep of the black's stride carried him rapidly into the space between the mare and the bay. The head of the black was at the hip of the mare, then suddenly the bay stallion started to swing in again, to bump the black off stride. Everyone in the stands, everyone along the fences, could see the dirty move, and a howl of rage went up. Eben, seeing it coming, swept her cap from her head and slapped the bay's sharply on the shoulder with it on the downstroke.

Another roar went up, not for the striking of the bay stallion, but for the tangle of ebony curls that tumbled from the cap and now sailed behind the rider on the black. Ellington looked back in surprise, for when the bay stallion was struck, it veered away, spoiling his foul move. Eyes widened in great shock and instant recognition, then narrowed in an ugly mask of hatred.

"You bloody bitch!" Screaming in uncontrollable rage, Ellington brought his crop down in a stinging blow across her face.

A flood of blood and tears blinded Eben. Her cry of pain, and the sudden shrinking of her body on his back, was like a spur applied to the great black stallion's heart. His lungs shuddered with each breath, but he answered the cry. Eben felt the final, desperate effort come out of the quivering body. The stride that could not be made more rapid beat faster. The stride that could not be lengthened grew longer.

The long-legged piebald mare drew back in jerks. Those jerks were Black Victory's giant, shattering strides, one after another, closing the distance. The face of the mare's jockey seemed not in the least degree excited. His whip moved rhythmically, and there was somewhat of a smile on his face. A smile that turned to a grimace when he saw the black stallion passing with such great effort, bearing his bloodied and blinded rider to safety.

Ellington, his face contorted, screamed out curses and plied his whip viciously, drawing blood from the bay. Even with that, he steadily fell behind. And then, with two great pulses, Black Victory was beyond the mare. The two white poles flashed past, and the race was over. The black slowed carefully and turned back of his own accord toward the grandstand.

The din was of men gone wild. They came pouring over and under the rail, toward the heaving black horse, screaming Eben's name. There is only one madness that pitches the voices of men that high—the madness of victory. Movement became almost impossible as the throng pressed closer and closer. In vain, Jamie Deal was beating at them to let him through, when suddenly a pistol shot rang out, quickly parting the crowd.

"Give way now!"

As the crowd complied with the command of authority, a tall figure shoved Jamie Deal through the hole, toward the stallion, who stood his ground, exhausted though he was, determined to keep the crowd away, with hooves and teeth if necessary, from the small figure slumped on the turf beneath his hooves.

"Easy, Black. Easy there, old man." Jamie Deal approached cautiously. He feared the stallion would accidentally trample Eben in his excitement, but Black Victory willingly moved aside with Jamie, to let the tall man bend to his mistress. Wearily he hung his fine, black head for a moment, his sides heaving, as Jamie rubbed his lathered neck.

Seeing Eben sprawled on the track beneath the wild black's hooves, her ebony curls tumbled across a face so pale, so still, had frozen Fitzhugh with shock and dread. But even then he had not been so paralyzed with dread as when he knelt beside Eben, half-afraid to touch her, lest his worst imaginings prove true. He gently turned her limp body against him, tears of relief springing to his eyes as he felt a strong pulse at her throat. Pressing his lips against her silken curls, he restrained his impulse to gather her tight in his arms and smother her with kisses. Running his hands over her limbs, he could feel no obvious breaks and saw no blood, so he carefully gathered her into his strong arms and set out for the barn. The stallion crowded close, with Jamie Deal trying to attach a lead rein to the head held high in watchfulness.

"Get back! Or I'll turn him loose on ye! Can't ye see the lassie's hurt?" Jamie Deal yelled at the crowding mob. Everyone was trying to touch the lathered stallion or his unconscious mistress.

At the barn, the many guardsmen attempted to restore order, shoving the crowd and shouting. Easing Eben down into the straw, Fitzhugh called to the hovering Jamie Deal.

"Best cool that horse out, Jamie, or she'll have us both for fodder when she comes to. I'll take care of our Eben."

"Aye," Jamie answered, with a wide grin and a last look at his mistress. "Aye." Quickly throwing a robe over the steaming horse, he led him out into the noise of the crowd again, more controlled this time by the guardsmen, until they saw the black and the din rose toward hysteria again.

Fitzhugh quickly loosened the neck of her shirt, placing a light touch on the hollow of her throat he checked her pulse again. Then, with gentle hands, he pushed the heavy hair from her face. His fingers grew still at the sight of the long, bloody welt across Eben's eyes and nose. The muscles tensed along his jaw as he muttered a nasty promise. "Ellington will not live long enough to regret the hour of his birth for doing this. Someone get me water! Now!"

Grooms and stable boys jumped to do his bidding. Taking care, but using the time she was away from herself to his advantage, he bathed the angry cut to assess the damage to the white face. His teeth gritted each time his linen handkerchief came away red with her blood. Eventually the sting of the cut brought Eben to herself.

"Wh-what happened?" she murmured, trying to rise shakily. Unable to open her eyes, she attempted to determine the reason with her hand. "Oh . . . my head! Jamie Deal, did we win? What's the black?"

"Easy, Eben. All's well," Fitzhugh assured her, gently intercepting her hand. "You won going away, and the horse is with Jamie Deal." He quickly caught the hand again as it tried to touch her smarting eyes. "Just a little cut . . . You're going to be fine."

"Gonna kill that Ellington! Bloody rotter! Abuses that bay, my horse now . . ." she stated, sagging back against Fitzhugh's arm, her words fragmented. "Got me in the straw again, have you, Eastmore?"

"Do not gammon with me now," he said, sighing heavily with relief at her quick return to spirits. No head injury here.

Eben had a fleeting thought that now it wasn't important that she marry Barnaby, because Fitzhugh was here and Fitzhugh was all she ever had wanted, but consciousness slipped away before she could make him understand that she had lied about the others and he was her only true love.

"Barnaby . . ." she murmured.

Fitzhugh's smile disappeared, and a look of pain crossed his face. He gently laid her back in the straw. Granting space to the track vet rushing to kneel at the girl's side, he stood abruptly. Stepping back, he raked a hand through his hair, his thoughts a riot. How could she call for that milksop? Could it be possible that she loved him? Loved Compton, regardless of what Ottobon said? With a troubled countenance, he ran his hands roughly over his face. It perhaps was the kindest thing he could do, for both of them, to leave her life as she had repeatedly told him to do. He'd always taken her outbursts as shows of childish temper, not truth. But then, hadn't she refused his offer more than once? And told him more than once that she was going to marry Compton? Maybe he was deluding himself that he still had a chance? Hadn't she returned his note begging to explain and to tell her of his love? Perhaps he was the fool in this instance, reading the lay of the land wrong from the jump? Though he did not believe, as she seemed to want him to, that she had spread her favors indiscriminately. Her divulgence was just one more show of childishness, her attempt to stand equal from the disadvantage of little experience in the arena in which she found herself thrust.

"Stand aside, or I'll part your hair with this parasol, you blackguard! Where's my niece?" The awesome Lady Adair swept into the barn, with a guardsman dragging on each arm, followed by a distraught Lady Lillian, leaning heavily on Bess. He had to grin at the comic picture portrayed as he waved the determined guardsmen away.

He acknowledged her with a slight bow. "Lady Cromwell, your servant."

"Where's my niece, Eastmore?" she demanded. Fitzhugh quickly swept an arm toward Eben, now covered with a blanket and attended by the vet.

"She's suffered a nasty welt over the eyes, but there should be no lasting damage. The doctor is tending her. She regained consciousness for a moment. Told me to tend her horse, and kill Ellington."

"Sounds like her," she snorted, relaxing somewhat at Fitzhugh's control of the situation. "Did she say anything else— Doctor? What doctor?"

"I speak of the track veterinarian there."

"Lillian, for God's sake, and mine, please stop that caterwauling!" she demanded. "Track veterinarian, you say!"

"And she asked for Compton," he stated, with a grim face. Pausing for a second as she bent over her niece, he impatiently pulled her back to her feet and toward him, demanding of her in a rush, "What's this with Compton?"

Amazed at being so rudely handled, Lady Adair opened her mouth to deliver a rounding set-down, but jolted to a halt with one look at Fitzhugh's face. Her eyebrows lifted with a dawning expression. So at last the tale comes out. She had known something was set between these two, and now perhaps she was to understand. Taking careful note of the duke's tortured face, she was frank with him.

"She accepted his offer. But then he cried off... or rather his mama cried off... over this. But there may still be talk of a Christmas wedding. What are you going to do about it?" she asked him challengingly. For a moment, she believed he would speak honestly to her of the feelings plainly expressed on his face, and with the tender look he sent her niece, but then his face set and the moment passed.

"Nothing I can do. Not if she wants him. Right now, I have a small matter to take up with a small man. If you will excuse me, my lady. My carriage is at your disposal." With this, he stomped out, taking the just-arriving Lord Ottobon with him, leaving Eben in the care of her relatives, though what good the swooning Lady Lillian and the weeping Bess could be was not clearly indicated.

Lady Adair looked after him sadly, then down at her scarred niece. So that was the way it was. Shaking her head, she sighed deeply at the foolishness of young love.

"But it's your grace, body and soul, I think she truly wants above all else, only she can't seem to admit it as of yet."

Chapter Twenty-Four

Eben was only away from herself a short while. Shorter than she would have wished, when she tried to open her eyes and her head throbbed with a thousand native drums. But when she would have winced with the head pain, the sting in her eyes made her groan. She was unsure if the buzzing in her ears was from within or without. The air was charged with excitement, and the noise of hundreds of voices chanting came from outside the stable. Again she attempted to open her eyes. Finding the left too swollen to move and only a slit in the right through which to see, she grew frightened. A fear that was heightened by her mother's crying and moaning beside her.

"Oh, my baby!" Lady Lillian wailed, the rest thankfully muffled by a handkerchief. Her sobs were echoed by Bess, who alternated her wails with pleas to the heavens above for deliverance.

"Egads, Lillian! Bess! Both of you, out of here!" commanded a short-tempered, very worried Lady Adair. "One cannot think with so much blubbering! All of you keep back. Give the girl some air, for heaven's sake!"

"Aunt Addie?" Eben called, her voice sounding surprisingly strong for the pain in her head. Struggling to a sitting position, she held her throbbing head in one hand, carefully avoiding her eyes.

"I'm here," her aunt answered her. "Don't try to touch your eyes, dear. It's not bad, Eben truly it's not. Just a welt, but the cut is open, and your hands are not the cleanest."

"Tell me what's going on. Can't we get out of here?" she asked, aching to understand the noise and excitement of the crowd. Her aunt gently pushed her down flat again.

"I very much doubt it just yet," Lady Adair answered honestly. "You have quite set this place to a riot with your winning. Of course, that stunt with the cap, you riding and all. But we'll see to it as soon as it's safe."

"Safe? Are we in danger?" she cried, quickly sitting up, trying to see through the slit in her right eye. "Damn that Ellington. I can't see! Where are Jamie and the black?"

"Don't worry about them," Lady Adair assured her, restraining her again. "Just lie back and try not to strain your eyes. They're bringing the carriage closer, and we'll see about removing ourselves."

"Why is there so much noise? The race is over and done with." Then, unable to hide her joy, she crowed, "He won, Aunt Addie! He won!"

"You have too much of your father in you for your own good, Eben Pearl," she snorted. "And that's what all the noise is about. The crowd is unruly over your winning."

"Where's Fitzhugh? He was just here, wasn't he?" she asked, trying to follow her aunt's instructions and lie still, but wanting ever so much to join in all the hullabaloo.

"Yes, dear, he was just here. He left with Ottobon, something about killing Ellington."

"Now there's a champion idea," she declared, attempting to regain an upright position.

"Eben Pearl! Lie down this moment," Lady Adair commanded. "I shall not say one more word to you. Thank God! Here's our way out of this riot."

A troop of guardsmen came into the stable. Followed closely by Jamie, the black stallion, and a group of jockeys and Corinthians. The barn swelled with their yells and laughter, and calls the length of the barn for Eben to join in the celebration.

"Try and stand now, Eben. The carriage is right outside, and they will escort us home," her aunt said, giving room to the young gentlemen who rushed to help, only to find themselves shoved rudely aside by Jamie Deal.

"Here we be, lass," he said, taking her blindly searching hand to pull her to her feet. Quickly he steadied her when she would have swayed. "Terrible way to be actin' after such a race. 'Tis no way to enjoy yer victory, sitting in the straw!"

"Isn't that the truth, Jamie." She brightened with his teasing. "It only hurts when I try and move my eyes." She winced. "Then it fairly savages my poor head."

"Then ye shouldn't be moving yer eyes, lass," he solemnly advised, guiding her through the crush of men. "Don't fash yerself about it. A mite of lay-down and ye'll be right as rain in the morning."

"Let me touch the black before I go. He'll be worried, with me toppling like I did." Leading her to the stallion over her aunt's grunt of protest, he laid her hands on him. Eben quickly ran her hands over the neck and the massive chest, feeling the dried sweat on the now cool body. The velvet nose came around to bump her in a familiar gesture of affection. "Hey, old man. Guess we showed them what's what," she whispered in one twitching ear. Satisfied, she turned toward the door. "Bring him home as soon as you can, Jamie. I'll not rest easy until I know he's there."

"He'll be there when ye wake in the morning, lass," he promised, taking her arm and guiding her toward the door.

The guardsmen linked arms and formed a solid walkway to the carriage, holding back the screaming crowd, who seemed to go wilder at the sight of the slight girl standing in the doorway in her tight breeches and bloodied white shirt. They chanted and screamed. Eben laughed and waved both hands high over her head, which only made them scream all the louder.

"Victory! Victory! Victory!" they chanted.

"Eben Pearl, pray do not encourage them! Into the carriage with her, Jamie." Lady Adair pushed her niece forward. "The guardsmen have their hands full as it is."

A closed carriage with the Eastmore crest stood as close to the barn as possible, and a pair of burly footmen stood ready with the door open. Bess and Lady Lillian sat inside, both dabbing their eyes with handkerchiefs. Lady Adair groaned at the sight of them.

"Jamie, stay with him," Eben ordered. "Don't you be celebrating and leaving him alone. Ellington . . ."

The rest was lost in the shouts of the people, but even without seeing the nod of his head, Eben knew he would not let her down. She climbed into the carriage on wobbly legs and sank into the seat with an exhausted sigh. The thoughts of home and a hot tub were becoming increasingly welcome.

Many hours later, exhaling her own great sigh of exhaustion, Lady Adair turned over once more in her bed. Sleep was elusive, even tired to the very bone as she was. The night was very advanced, and she had only just retired to the quietness of her own room. Plumping up her pillows with another sigh, she turned onto her back and stared up into the canopy pleated tightly on the frame above her bed. The doctor had come and gone.

"Fool that he was. Men! Rather women than men should be doctors. It was born inside a woman to know what should be done with an ailing child. Men have to retire to some school for two years to learn what a woman knows by instinct," she muttered, giving another tired sigh.

After the race, the younger members of the ton, Corinthians all, had stormed the house. All bearing huge bouquets of flowers, jockey silks or banners, and more than one with a snootfull of spirits. After seeing quite a few, Lady Adair had finally stationed a footman outside the front door with a memorized statement and strict orders to turn them all away. It had been a tedious afternoon, but it was finally finished. And at last Eben was bathed, fed and tucked into her bed for the hundredth time, as she would insist on hanging out the window and encouraging the hurrahs of the boys crowding the square. Hopefully, finally abed and asleep, she would come to no more harm before morning. Turning over again, Lady Adair snorted. Such a scrapper she was! Quite like her old aunt, huh? The thought brought a smile to her face. Once again that forbidden thought came to Lady Adair's mind, and she allowed the words to be spoken aloud for the first time.

"Eben should have been mine. Mine and Ebenezer's. Her beauty comes from her father's dark looks, but with her fire and strength, she is like me. She should have been mine, Ebenezer, you wastrel, you!"

Stupid thought, after thirty years, and the man in his grave. Her mind shifted gears. But Eben, such a match with Eastmore! If only she could bring them together. He'd not let the opinion of the ton stand in his way. A delicious yawn took control of her face, and her thoughts became drowsy. Yes, an excellent match. But something more to the pair of them than anyone knew. Something happened there. Such intense feelings between the two of them. Another, final yawn, and she drifted off.

"My lady," an unwelcome voice insisted. "My lady, wake up!"

A rough shake on her shoulder finally resulted in a mumbled, unladylike oath and an eye opening to a candle flame near her face. Startled, Lady Adair attempted to shake sleep from her mind and attend to this person who was determined to disturb her rest.

"What?" She yawned again. "Is it Eben?"

Relieved to see the lady finally waking up, Bess set the candle on the night table. Shaking out the brocade gown lying on the foot of the bed, she clicked her tongue disapprovingly. "Nay, 'tis that man!" she began. "He's barged right in, and won't take no for an answer."

"Man?" Her sleep-fogged mind refused to comprehend. "What man? It's the middle of the night!"

"'Tis nigh on to dawn, my lady. And 'tis Lord Eastmore! Hastings has told him but he just keeps insisting!"

"Eastmore? Insisting on what?" she asked, rising to slip her arms into the robe Bess held out for her. Ridiculous way to behave! Waking a body out of a sound sleep, unless it was an emergency. "Is he hurt?"

"Nay, my lady. He's just insisting on seeing Miss Eben." She clicked her tongue and shook her head with strong disapproval. "Such goings-on . . ."

"All right, Bess. I'll take care of this." She stuffed her feet into slippers and smoothed her braid with one hand. "Thank you. Go on to bed now. I'll handle this."

"Sorry to wake you, but he's insisting, and Hastings didn't know what to do," she muttered. "Gave Miss Lillian a draft and couldn't wake her even if I cared to."

"Fine, Bess," she assured her, attempting to get rid of her nosiness before seeing Eastmore. "Where is Lord Eastmore?"

"Outside in the hall."

"Outside in the...what?"

Flinging open the door, she stared down the hall at a distraught Hastings, barring the way to Eben's bedchamber with outstretched arms. He was wearing a hastily donned flannel robe over his night rail and his scrawny legs gleamed white beneath the ragged tail. His straggling white hair was disarranged and standing straight up on his head, but his demeanor was every bit that of the outraged family protector.

"See?" Bess pointed. "Just as I told you!"

"Eastmore! What in the devil is going on here?" she demanded, advancing on the duke. "This is unforgivable!"

"Your servant, my lady," he said, with an elegant bow, as if they were meeting in a ballroom instead of the upper hall of her home at first light, and outside her niece's bedchamber, no less!

"Lord Eastmore! Explain yourself!"

"I came...I must see...I *will* see Eben!"

"Hastings, thank you. I will attend His Lordship," she said, placing a hand on one rigid arm in an attempt to release the man from his vigil. "It's quite all right, I assure you. Lord Eastmore means us no harm, do you, your grace?"

"Of course not!"

"Nor is His Lordship in his cups. Are you, your grace?"

"Absolutely not!"

Hastings relaxed somewhat, comfortable in the knowledge that Lady Adair was capable of handling most anything coming her way. But while he moved to one side, he remained nearby and ever watchful. Satisfied, Lady Adair turned to Fitzhugh.

"Now, Lord Eastmore, an explanation, if you please. And it had best be top-drawer!" she demanded again. Standing with her arms folded over her ample bosom and her hair braided for night, the lady was every bit as formidable as any dowager queen in full regalia.

"I would like to reassure myself that Eben is...I mean to say..." Fitzhugh stammered to a halt, feeling somewhat ridiculous, and unsure how to continue, except with honesty. "Adair, please."

"She is quite asleep, you know. The doctor gave her drops, and she will not wake before morning." Fitzhugh merely nodded, but did not remove his large frame. Lady Adair studied him for a moment. His amber eyes burned into hers with a look of... could that be pleading? Possibly. With a sigh, she decided there was no harm in his request, and it obviously was of the utmost importance to him. "Just a moment, Fitzhugh."

Stepping quietly into the rose-and-ivory room, she lit a candle on the night table. Eben lay on her back with one hand tossed over her head, sound asleep. The tabby cat was tucked next to her. Quickly straightening the covers over her shoulders and checking for modesty's sake, she opened the door to Fitzhugh, motioning to him to be quiet. To her great surprise, he handed her his beaver topper as he passed quickly to the bed. With a smile, Lady Adair laid it gently on the dressing table and moved to a chair where she could observe the man and her sleeping niece.

Carefully Fitzhugh eased himself down on the bed beside her. His face hardened when he saw the red and raw welt across her eyes. He gently smoothed her hair back from her forehead, his fingers lingering against the cool skin in a soft caress. Grady sat up with a wide yawn. He was greatly interested, as always, in any new developments... such as company in the middle of the night.

"Grady, come here," Lady Adair softly called to him. "Grady... get off the bed."

Startled for a moment, Fitzhugh jerked his eyes to those of the attentive cat. His sober mouth curved into a wry grin. "Hullo, Sir Grady," he murmured, before turning back to Eben. Taking her limp hand in his, he stroked the soft back with his thumb. Lady Adair watched him take a deep breath and release it as a long sigh. As if the entire weight of the world rested on his shoulders and he found it heavy indeed. Turning the soft hand over in his, he bent his head to place a kiss in the palm, gently folding her fingers over the kiss, as if he would save it for her until she awakened. Tucking her hand under the covers, he leaned toward her slightly, whispering. Lady Adair strained to hear.

"Goodbye, my love."

Abruptly he spun and left the room. Even as quickly as Lady Adair followed him, he was down the stairs and out the front door in a thrice, leaving a gaping footman at the front door, a disapproving Hastings midway up the stairs, a stunned Lady Adair at the top of the landing, and a soft beaver topper on Eben Pearl's dressing table.

Chapter Twenty-Five

Someone had opened the window, and sunlight, filled with dancing dust motes, streamed into the bedchamber. Birds sang in the willow tree gracing the small park at the center of Grosvenor Square, their unwelcome melodies sounding as an insufferable din to a throbbing head. Several groans of protest came from beneath the pile of white linen on the tester bed, until finally the mound rose, sliding away from Eben, who gave in to the demand of wakefulness.

"About time you decided to rejoin the world." Lady Adair's voice came from the chair beside the bed. "I thought maybe falling off your horse had addled your brain."

"I never!" Eben flared. Then, grabbing her head in both hands, she moaned. "Why does my head feel as if it's going to split apart?"

"Laudanum! Blasted doctor insisted on slipping you drops once we finally got you into bed," Lady Adair snorted. "He feared you would suffer vapors or swooning or some other nonsense ailment men believe all women fall prey to. I tried to tell him you were strong as that horse you fell off of, but he insisted. And for a brief moment, I will admit, I thought he just might know a bit more about what was good for you. There is a rather nasty..." She hesitated, then gave a snort of derision. "But now I see I was right after all! The man is a fool!"

A weak grin came from Eben as she threw the covers back, as if she were going to rise, telling her aunt, "I must go see to the black..."

"Absolutely not!" her aunt declared, literally pushing the weak girl back on the pillows and straightening the covers. "Jamie Deal is right outside. He's been wearing a path in the only good hall carpet we have for the past four hours, waiting for you to wake up. You'll just have to settle for his reassurances about that animal!" Striding to the door, Lady Adair flung it open to show a worried Jamie, standing with hat in hand and a frown creasing his brow. "Best come talk to her, Jamie. I'll never keep her in bed otherwise," she declared.

"Aye, my lady," he whispered. Jamie Deal, having never been above stairs in either house, much less in one of the ladies bedchambers, nervously wiped his feet before stepping gingerly over the threshold and into the room.

"Good Lord, man! Whatever was on your boots is already out there for all your pacing!" Lady Adair said, laughing at him. She waved him inside and closed the door behind him.

With a sheepish grin, he approached the bed, only to come to an abrupt halt at the sight of Eben's face. "Bloody damn, lass!"

Eben's hand immediately flew to her face in terror. "Hand me a mirror, Aunt Addie!"

"Time enough for that later," her aunt said, stalling.

"Then I'll get it myself," Eben declared, making a move to throw back the covers again and leave the bed.

"All right! All right! Just remember, it looks far worse than it actually is. . . ."

Eben took the silver-backed mirror and quickly surveyed the damage to her face. A stranger's battered face stared back at her. A gasp escaped her pale mouth, but no words came forth. The black hair had been drawn back with a band, baring a white face with two huge, bruised eyes colored violently black, blue and purple from eyebrows to cheekbones. Across both eyelids and the bridge of her nose was a swollen, angry welt crusted here and there with a bloody cut. The forehead, cheeks, mouth and chin, though very pale, were untouched. She drew a shaky breath and lowered the mirror to her lap.

"'Tis a grand thing that I am so blessed with blunt, for I quite fear I am losing my looks," she jested lightly. Her tone belied her shock at her appearance. "Thank heavens it doesn't feel as bad as it appears."

Gently taking the mirror from her hand, Lady Adair placed a cool hand on her forehead and reassured her. "The doctor says that once the swelling and bruises are gone, you'll never know it happened."

"Seems to me we've determined that man to be a complete fool once already this morning." She gave her aunt an impish grin and gingerly settled herself higher on the mound of goosedown pillows.

"Here, Jamie. Pull up a chair and keep her pacified," ordered Lady Adair. "I'll just nip down and see about some breakfast for her. No dinner last night, and it past noon already." Efficiently she bustled out of the room, her voice fading down the hall.

"Lass, 'twas the most exciting race I ever seen in my life. The way ye was left at the start had my heart in the mud. But then the old man took off like a scalded cat..." He demonstrated the speed with his hands. "And that mare! Never seen anything as fast! Runs as easy and just stays in front."

She reminded him of her main concern. "Jamie, the black, is he laid up this morning?"

"Nay, looks like he never left the barn!" He waved his hand at her. "He bedded right down last night, and tore me shirt this morning when I tried to be brushin' him."

"Thank God! I was so worried." She relaxed at the good news. Then a shy smile came over her face. "He was truly magnificent, wasn't he, Jamie?"

"Aye, lass. 'Twas thinkin' he was a goner, I was, when the bay fouled him and he fell so far behind. But his heart was big enough to come back for ye."

"I was afraid he couldn't do it a second time. That Ellington! To foul me in the first place, but then to try a second, where everyone could see him. He couldn't hope to get away with it. I knew he'd not play fair!" She clenched her fist, and her face became set. "I'll make him pay for that. And this." She indicated her face.

"Eastmore went after him, but he couldn't find him. He left the bay standing on the track, lathered and whip-marked..."

"That's a horrible way to treat a game animal! That stallion gave his best, only to be beaten and abandoned! Ellington doesn't deserve to own such fine cattle! I'm sorry Fitzhugh couldn't find him!''

"No more..."

"What?"

"The bay stallion is out in back ... eatin' his head off. Awful marked up, but them welts will be healin'...just as yers are doing, lass.'' A dawning slowly spread over Eben's colorful face.

"We won, didn't we, Jamie? We won the whole thing! We're safe now, aren't we?''

"Aye, lass, ye be safe. 'Twas terrible scared I was when I saw the bastard—excuse me, lass—swipe ye with the leather. Guess he be figuring he owed ye a whippin'. Then when the old man carried ye out of range, I be lost in the race. But when I couldn't get close to ye and I saw the old man with an empty saddle, my heart fairly stopped.''

"I can remember striking the bay with my cap when Ellington would have brought him over into us again,'' she reflected. "And I remember the look of such hatred on his face, just before he struck me. Then all I remember is being blinded, and feeling like my face was on fire. From then on I just hung on to the black. I could hear the noise, then nothing.''

"Ye must have just slid down the old man's leg, 'cause that's where we found ye. The mob was tryin' to get at ye, and the old man was holding them off. But he let me come right up to him, and Eastmore carried ye to the barns.''

"Yes, Fitzhugh was there. Everything was so hazy.''

"Aye, he sent me out to walk the old man. Saying ye'd be skinnin' us alive if I didn't. Saying he'd be looking out for ye, which he did till yer mam came. I reckon he'd be one to always take care of ye,'' he hinted broadly. A moment of silence passed, with Eben's face pensive and still.

"Yes, I suspect that's so.''

Hearing this, Jamie Deal went on quietly. "I be seein' his face, ye know when he left ye. And it weren't pretty. He's going after Ellington, I be telling myself. That man was hurting in his heart for ye, lass. And he's a bonny one if I must tell ye.''

"You are my friend, Jamie. Maybe my only friend, unless my mother is speaking to me again. And as my friend, you've always spoken the plain truth to me. Do you think he does care, even a little?''

His eyes strayed over the pitifully bruised face of the lass he had always considered his stand-in daughter. She wore her heart in her eyes and waited for his answer. ''Ye've been like me own, lass. I wouldn't lie to ye. Yon man had a blind fury come on him when he saw what was done to ye. He wouldn't a thought twice to kill Ellington for touching ye, but he couldn't find him. A man only does that if something that sits deep in his heart be hurt.'' Two tears seeped from the swollen, discolored flesh to trace down her cheeks. The sight stirred Jamie, just as weeping does most men. ''I talked to the jock of the piebald mare after they took ye home. The mare was put into the race by Eastmore. The chap says Eastmore put the mare in to take care of ye. He knew how fast she was, and figured if you couldn't win, he would. The jock was worried 'cause he was told to look out for ye. That ye were His Nibs's lady, and he was not to let anything happen to ye. Was frightful scared he'd be sacked for lettin' ye get hit.''

''That piebald mare belongs to Eastmore?'' Eben was stunned by what she was hearing.

''Not any more,'' Jamie grinned. ''She be having her breakfast betwixt the black and the bay. They both be trying to impress her, but she's having none of it.'' He grinned at her for a moment as she dabbed tears from her eyes. ''Ottobon be taking them others to Victor Mall for ye. There are some mighty fine cattle for yer stable there.''

Lady Adair breezed into the room, followed by Lady Lillian and Bess, the latter bearing a laden breakfast tray, drifting the smell of eggs, bacon and toast down the hall. ''That's enough stable talk. The girl needs a nourishing breakfast, and more sleep. Off with you now, Jamie, before you two cook up another harebrained scheme that lands my niece in more hot water.''

Jamie Deal left with a wink at Eben. Settling the tray on the bed, Bess clucked her tongue and moaned over the state of Eben's face, tears welling up in her old eyes. Eben tried to reassure her with a smile.

''Don't carry on so, Bess. Or you'll have me puddling up, too and that makes it sting.''

"Sorry, but you just look so..." Sobs overcame her, and without ceremony or tact Lady Adair pushed the weeping woman into the hall and closed the door on her sobs. Turning to set the cat off the bed, she pointed a finger at Eben.

"Eat!"

Grady immediately jumped back on the bed and resumed his already warmed spot next to Eben. No one paid him any mind. Lady Lillian sat beside the bed.

"Daughter, I am so sorry for the way I acted. When I saw you fall, I feared you were dead and I'd never be able to tell you how very dear you are to me." A tearful storm threatened to overwhelm her mother, also.

"Lillian, you promised!" admonished Lady Adair.

"I know...I know..." Lady Lillian said, dabbing at her eyes.

"Mama, I know you love me. And you've every right to be furious with me. I have acted unforgivably! I do not know what comes over me. I simply do not think until I'm embroiled in a scrape." Eben started to rise, but the tray and her aunt settled that idea in midaction. "I will try to be better. I swear to you both!"

Lady Lillian merely nodded, for words would only bring fresh tears.

"There's been a parade at the front door. Numerous young lords dropping by to inquire of your health," Lady Adair said, buttering a slice of Eben's toast and absently biting into it. "I had thought to tell Hastings that we were not at home to callers, but so many of them were bringing bank drafts with them that I quite changed my mind about receiving them!"

"Really? Oh..." Eben's eyebrows started upward, but came to an abrupt halt, as pain extracted a groan.

"And—" Lady Lillian leaned forward eagerly "—this came, too. By special messenger! With a huge spray of flowers. Pray open it. It has had me on pins and needles for hours, but Adair declared we must wait, to let you break the seal, as it should be."

Taking the ivory note, Eben broke the raised gold seal, her bruised eyes quickly scanning the note. Then she commenced reading aloud to her mother and aunt: "With kindest wishes for a timely recovery, your friend always, Barnaby."

"Oh, him!" Lady Lillian pooh-poohed in disappointment. "I thought it might be from— Oh, Adair! You kicked me!"

"Hush!" Lady Adair reprimanded her sister. "That note shows more backbone than the boy's displayed in his thirty years. You can bet his mother would not approve of him sending flowers to your grave. So perhaps . . . unless . . ."

"No more of that now. What's done is done. Let's make plans of another sort. You say the wagers have been paid?"

"All but Ellington's. And I doubt you'll hear from him. Although Lord Ottobon says public outrage will force the estate solicitors to honor the wager. After this morning, I quite imagine Eastmore has seen to that," Lady Adair said.

"This morning? Fitzhugh was here this morning?" Eben asked, instantly alert.

"Yes, almost at first light. I was fast asleep when Bess woke me. No reassurances that you were fine would do. Seems he was coming up to your room to see for himself, even if he had to walk over the top of poor Hastings." Both ladies watched Eben's face closely, then exchanged knowing glances when the bruised face softened into a secret smile.

"What happened then?"

"Why, I threw on a dressing gown and acted as chaperon while he came into your room. Nothing short of a bullet was going to keep him from seeing you." Lady Adair smoothed the ebony hair from the girl's forehead, then picked up her hand. "After all his storming, he came in on tiptoe, even with me telling him you were drugged, sat on the edge of the bed, and watched you sleep for a moment. Then . . ."

Eben raised her eyes to her aunt's face. "Yes?"

Her aunt turned her niece's hand palm up. "He raised your hand and pressed his lips to your palm, here." Her aunt placed a fingertip lightly to the upturned palm so that Eben could imagine the light touch was Fitzhugh's kiss. "Then he said—" here she gave a long sigh "—goodbye, my love. And he left."

"Left?" Came the faint question.

"So romantic! And I slept through the whole thing!" her mother wailed, just as she had each time she got Adair to recite the tale for her.

"Where was he going, Aunt Addie?" Eben whispered, tears rising in her voice.

"I don't know, dear. He was dressed for travel, and the footman said he had a boot filled with luggage on the brougham waiting for him." Lady Adair patted her shoulder. "Try not to fret over it right now. Time will tell the whole story. Come, Lillian, let's let her rest. I doubt all this excitement is good for her." Picking up the tray, Lady Adair shooed her sister out the door. Lady Lillian had thought to stay, but her sister's bulk pushed her toward the door.

"At least she ate a good breakfast," Lady Lillian noted, flitting out the door ahead of her bossy sister. "Adair! You don't have to shove!"

With a wan smile, Eben made one more request of her aunt. "Aunt Addie, please, would you send a note to Mr. Vandevilt, asking him to call at his earliest convenience. And tell Jamie Deal to ready the horses. As soon as I can get legal matters out of mind, I'm going home. Oh, how I long for Victor Mall."

Her aunt nodded, then closed the door. Eben wearily leaned her head back into the pillows. Home. Home to heal her hurts. The pain in her bruised eyes was minor compared to the pain in her heart. He had come to her. Damn that doctor for that foul draft. He had come, but only to say goodbye. Where could he have been going? Did he think she could marry anyone else . . . after realizing he loved her? He loved her! Jamie had said so. And then her aunt . . . He loved her! Sliding deep into the bed, she hugged Grady to her. If so, how could he leave her? Didn't he love her with the same consuming need that she felt for him? Tears of weakness rolled down onto the top of Grady's furry head. If only she felt well enough to leave this cursed bed. She would pursue him to the ends of the earth to ask just those questions. Unable to stem the tears, Eben laid her palm against her trembling lips, as if she could return her lover's kiss. Wherever he might be.

The Victor's solicitor's earliest convenience was as speedy as Eben had hoped. The next morning, promptly at eleven o'clock, Mr. Vandevilt was shown into the salon to attend both Eben and Lady Adair. Lady Lillian, not surprisingly, had gone to call upon Lady Emily Cowper, armed with the romantic tale of the kiss in the palm of the sleeping beauty. Although she had been heartily warned to confide the tale to no one, surely one's dearest friend in all the world did not count as just anyone.

"Lady Cromwell, your servant." The man bowed over the lady's hand. Turning to Eben, he quite did a double take. "My Lord! Miss Victor!"

"Pray sit down, Mr. Vandevilt." Eben laughed at his expression. "Let me assure you, thankfully it looks far worse than it feels. Actually, 'twas only the sleeping draught the doctor gave me that kept me abed all of yesterday."

"I am so relieved to hear that, for the wounds do look quite fierce," he said. And in truth he did look relieved.

"Trust me, sir. You could not have been more shocked than I, when I first glanced into a mirror." Again Eben laughed, then eagerly moved on to business at hand, passing a considerable stack of bank drafts towards him. "This is what I wanted to see you about, Mr. Vandevilt. I want to pay current on the pensions first, and then settle all papa's debts. Then let's see how we can stretch anything left as far as possible."

"I do not quite understand." The elderly gentleman leafed through the drafts. "I did hear about this, er . . . wager, as I'm sure everyone did, and expected to hear from you when the news of your, er . . . triumph reached the office. But, miss, I thought you realized, when I did not contact you further . . ."

"Egad, man! Realized what? Spit it out!" Lady Adair's patience had dissolved.

"Why, that the debts had been paid! Quite two months ago!" he exclaimed. "Everything, including the last bill from your dressmaker. And the pensioners, quite handled for the entire year."

"Paid? By whom, pray tell!" Eben demanded.

"I am not at liberty to say. The gentleman, er . . . benefactor . . . desired his name never be mentioned. I must adhere to that pledge, although I thought it strange at the time. I naturally assumed you knew of it somehow." The elderly solicitor grew pensive. While one did make allowances for nobles and their eccentricities these Victor's had never been an easy lot to deal with, and this new generation quite took the prize.

"Mr. Vandevilt, you really must tell me his name. So that I might repay him. You must see that," Eben reasoned.

"I did stress that possibility to the gentleman, but he quite convinced me that the funds were never to be thought of as a loan. It was a gift, straight out. So you see, this money here is yours to use as you will. I shall, of course, bank it for you and await further instruction. But as for the other..." He shrugged his shoulders, indicating he would do nothing toward revealing the identity of her benefactor. Honor was everything, and this man would uphold his pledge.

"I—I see." Eben stammered, dazed at this new turn of events.

"Splendid! And now, if you have no further need of me? I shall take my leave. Appointments, you understand." Receiving no answer, the solicitor bowed himself from the room, silently resolving to turn the Victors over to a junior partner immediately upon his return to his offices.

Eben's eyes met her aunt's, both pairs disbelieving. "Barnaby?" she posed.

"Naaaw!" they both drawled in unison, causing a fit of giggles to descend.

"It could be no one but Fitzhugh, Aunt Addie," she added wistfully, sighing deeply.

"I am quite taken aback by all these rapid developments. I think, my girl, you should tell me the whole tale from start to finish. I feel as if I have just slept through the first act of a murder mystery and have gotten quite lost in the plot."

"I fear I cannot. My heart is too tender to even think of it, but then, I can think of nothing else. I came so close to the most perfect love, and through my stubborn pride have thrown it away." Eben rose from the striped sofa and wandered to the window overlooking the blooming garden. "I just want to go home. Home, to heal this raw pain inside me."

"Then we shall, posthaste!" Lady Adair proclaimed, slapping her hands together.

"Aunt Addie?" She turned beseeching eyes on her wise aunt. "The kind of man who would do that, give that kind of gift without telling, without expecting gratitude? He just couldn't be the worst kind of bounder, could he?"

"Whatever do you mean? I think Fitzhugh Eastmore is a most admirable man!" Lady Adair exclaimed in surprise.

"I feel that he must be also, except..." She tapered off, fidgeting with her dressing gown ribbons.

"Eben Pearl, what has gotten into you now?"

"It's just, I have seen him with his mistress, Lady Louise Sinclair, more than once!" she cried, turning toward her aunt, tears gathering in her poor, battered eyes.

"My dear, please do not cry. Tears only make those pitiful eyes hurt all the more." Pulling her niece down on the sofa beside her, she carefully dabbed with a soft handkerchief. "Now, you listen to me. Men, especially single men the age of Lord Eastmore, have mistresses. It is a fact of nature."

"Not only single men! Look at Papa!"

"Regrettably, that is true. But do not condemn Eastmore on those grounds. He is a man, widely traveled, and considerably older than you. He would be highly suspect and prone to appear in society with red heels if he didn't have a mistress or two, don't you think?"

Such sane logic stunned Eben. Had she punished Fitzhugh for the sins of her father? "That's true. I just so want to be the only woman in a man's life. Not ignored by my husband, as my mother was. I could not bear the humiliation. And I do not want my children to find themselves destitute after my death, as I have."

"Eben Pearl, you are nothing like your mother. No man in his right mind could ignore you for very long without retribution of the most volatile sort."

"Oh, why must men be so carnal?" Eben cried, throwing her hands in the air.

"Men have needs, physical needs, that must be taken care of somehow. Don't interrupt!" This when Eben would protest. "And I have long suspected that women have these same needs, also, but control them better than men. Probably because we are forced by nature to bear the children, through great pain and suffering. Sad state of affairs, actually. Should have been set up to take turns, don't you think?"

"Dear Auntie! You are so outrageous! I fear you were born quite before your time." Eben laughed. "And I so desire to be like you!"

"Just be your own wonderful self, dear. And enjoy the sensual side of your nature, instead of condemning the lusty side of a man as fine as Fitzhugh Eastmore. Next time you see him, and do not doubt you will see him again, welcome him with open arms, instead of fears shown as hasty judgments."

"Oh, Aunt Addie, I shall. Believe me, if I ever see him again. No! *When* I see him again, I shall," she vowed, although, her behavior had been so deplorable, she greatly feared he might never wish to see her again.

Chapter Twenty-Six

It was Christmas Eve. And a white Christmas Eve. Great flakes had begun to fall from a gray sky early that morning, and now a dazzling sun was out, making the afternoon a glittering crystal palace. Victor Mall wore a new dress that transformed familiar contours and turned the drive into a magic lane, all shimmery in a clean white drape.

Having already made several excursions into the snow, Eben had never felt so young, and so free from the weight of worry. She had pelted two of the stable boys in a merciless snowball battle earlier and then turned on Jamie Deal when he tried to leave the barn, receiving a fierce trouncing for her prank, ending with snow in her mouth and stuffed down the back of her sweater. This was a wonderful snow. This you could press between your hands into missiles. You could feel the chill of it melted on your cheek, taste its cleanliness on your tongue. Great buckets of the clean snow had been carried into the cellar for its transformation into the much loved snow ice cream for the servants' party tonight.

Not tolerating confinement to the house on such a marvelous day, Eben had taken Victoire out for a gallop through the snow to quiet both their spirits. As usual, the run had ended at the mares' pens. There were so few now, but those that remained were safe. She leaned on the rail and watched the black stallion frolic in the whiteness. He was fat and sassy, having been home these long months, running loose with the brood mares and playing cock of the walk. The piebald mare was with him, too. Perhaps it had been a mistake to turn her in with Black Victory, for she did not see the mare as truly hers, not in the face of Fitzhugh's discovered generosity. And while it was possible he might have desired to race the remarkably fast mare this coming spring, he would now have to wait, for she carried Black Victory's foal in her belly. A foal that, with this dam and sire, was sure to be a streak of lightning. Eben had already christened it Victory Race, whether filly or colt.

Now, looking over the mares, she called to a once gray mare, now white with advanced age, heavy and shapeless except for her fine head and regal bearing. A suckling colt clung to her side—fuzzy black like his papa now, though he probably would turn to dapple gray as he matured. Only yesterday, Eben had carefully noted the date of his birth, and the sire and dam, in the bloodline register under the name of Victory Parade.

Black Victory gave a trumpet of challenge and came racing to the rail fence and Eben. The white mare flattened her ears and veered away, herding her foal a safe distance from the stallion, but the black's eyes and ears were not for the mare. They strained far out into the distance, toward Victor Mall. Eben shaded her eyes, but could see no one else venturing out on this crisp, snowy Christmas Eve. Black Victory screamed another challenge and reared high on his hind legs, shaking his head.

"Easy, old man, you're jumping at ghosts, you know." She laughed at the prancing stallion, guarding his small harem of mares. The black trotted up and down the fence, making no move to leave the pen, even though she knew he could have cleared the fence easily from a standstill. "Go on, you old fuzzy bear. Go back to your wives," she said.

Laughing still, she waved him away from the fence. Playfully he spun and made a mad gallop across the pasture, drawing the piebald mare into an impromptu race. The white mare watched them without interest. The foolishness of youth was past her, as one would think it should be with the twelve-year-old stallion. Eben turned once more and scanned the hills. It was unlike the black to challenge thin air, but she saw nothing.

Stretching her arms high over her head and twisting her body, she felt good. She drew a deep breath and exhaled in a long sigh. This very afternoon was just the most perfect time to be alive. Victoire, tethered to a tree just a bit away, whickered to her. Eben saw her circling restlessly.

"All right, we'll go home. Looks like the sun's going, anyway," she called to the gray filly.

Starting across to the line of trees, she kicked at the snow with her boots. Suddenly an impish look came over her face, and with a quick glance about her to make absolutely certain she was alone, she fell backward into a span of fresh, untracked snow. Lying on her back, she moved her arms and legs back and forth to make a snow angel. Laughing out loud at her own foolishness, Eben did not hear the soft crunch of footsteps behind her, or realize she was not alone, as she had suspected, until a slight shadow fell over her face. Startled, she looked up a very long pair of legs, past a rather fine wool greatcoat, to the amused face of the duke of Eastmore.

"Hell's blood, man! You near frightened me out of my wits!" she gasped, attempting to regain her feet in a dignified manner.

"You'll never fail to amaze me, Miss Victor. Whatever were you just doing?" The deep voice was just as she had dreamed it every night for the past six months. "If you would be so kind as to enlighten me to the meaning of your thrashing in the snow, it would please me greatly."

"The pleasure would be all mine, your grace," she teased, happiness welling in her chest, "for you sound as if this might be one time when you do not sound off at me in anger."

"Good Lord!" He sounded quite startled, thinking to step toward her. "Surely you are roasting me!"

"No!" Her yelp caused him to reverse his intended step hastily.

"Eben, I mean you no harm," he assured her, confused and concerned over her reaction. Could it be that she was afraid of him?

"You would trample the snow angel?" With a wide grin, Eben pointed down at their feet.

"I beg your pardon?" He looked down, not understanding the shape in the snow, and thoroughly confused at her meaning.

"Here, step around this way." She directed him around the outside of the pattern. "See? A snow angel. Didn't you make them as a child?"

"I am sad to say, there was not an abundance of snow where I spent my childhood," he retorted with a smile for her. From the proper angle, Fitzhugh readily discerned the long robe and wings of an angel, patterned in the snow by her exuberant flailing. "Ah, little cat, you shall make a wonderful mother, for there is the perpetual child inside you."

"And now you are trying to gammon me. You know perfectly well your low opinion of me, and have never refrained from expounding upon it. Except once. You were quite a different man after the race, and I was greatly in charity with you," she teased him, her heart ready to burst at the very sight of his much-loved face.

"That one time, and never before?" he asked, bending his head toward her.

"There was no other occasion," she stated positively, shaking her head.

"Then I am quite beyond redemption. I see I must apologize many times for my uncivil behavior," he conceded with a glint in his eyes. "I will make it my life's work to put you in constant charity with me."

"Pray do," she said, cordially. "I shall be happy to hear your apologies on this subject whenever you bring yourself to that point."

"Perhaps a Christmas present could be a type of peace offering, as well as an apology. I do happen to know children are overly fond of presents, and therefore I have brought you, perfect infant, one hell of a present," he said, turning toward Victoire. "But come, before Victoire winds herself permanently into the ground. Your mother sent me after you. See? It starts to snow quite heavily once again."

"You've been to the Mall?" she asked, trudging after him.

"Oh, my, yes," he threw over his shoulder. "I've quite invited myself to stay for Christmas. Not that the Park isn't a splendid place for a holiday, but I much prefer to stay here. The accommodations are exceedingly more modern."

"Nay, your grace. Not true." Eben laughed as he led the mare out into the open. "You'll bathe in a hip tub in front of your fire, and sleep with warmed bricks at your feet. Not the most efficient way to stay warm."

Fitzhugh grasped her ankle and tossed her into the saddle. Standing for a moment, leaning against her wet boot and looking into her incredible blue eyes, he was pleased to see no remaining mark from Ellington's cruel attack upon the creamy complexion. Her mouth was smiling in the most delectable way, those amazing eyes were shining, and a riot of unruly ebony curls charmingly threatened imminent escape from beneath a man's beaver topper, set jauntily upon her head. His hand slid up her leg to rest on her thigh, the warmth of his body reaching her through the wet buckskin.

"That may be true, unless one is invited to share another's bed and body heat," he parried.

"Pray, sir—would you accost the maids of my household with your lecherous behavior?" She intentionally misunderstood him, widening her eyes in mock horror.

"I have been accused of such behavior in the past, although my taste runs to stable wenches, rather than housemaids. Now, off with you, little cat. My Turk will catch you before you are three strides away." Stepping back, he slapped the mare on the hip, starting her for home.

Challenged, Eben bent over the mare's sleek neck and sent her careering across the snow. But as fast as the mare ran, Eben's heart flew faster. He had come back to her! From wherever he had been for these very long, long months past, he had come back to her. She would not make stupid mistakes this time, or play foolish games. She would make certain that he understood, once and for all, that she loved him and loved him deeply. And she would be emphatic that she expected his full attention, and nothing else would do. For this time, she fully intended that he never leave her again.

Chapter Twenty-Seven

Tradition at Victor Mall had always decreed the gifts for the servants were distributed on Christmas Eve, followed by a quiet supper for the family and a servants' feast below stairs. Then Christmas day was reserved for the family feast, served with great pomp and ceremony. This was to be the first year in ever so many that the tradition could be upheld in any sort of grand way.

And now, descending the stairs slowly behind her mother and her aunt, Eben luxuriated in the sway and swish of ruby satin billowing out around her, burning brightly in the candlelight. She buried her hands in the folds, reveling in the feel of the rich stuff. It was chilly on the staircase, but she did not hurry, nor did she throw her shawl over her bare shoulders. Somehow that would have spoiled the fantasy. Trailing her fingertips along the polished banister, she thought of the other Eben Pearl doing this same act, so long ago. As she stopped at the first newel post, her fingers found the unicorn carved into the design, smiling to herself she thought of her children searching out the myth, just as she had done as a small child. Her children, some with the ebony hair of the Victors and some with the sun-streaked hair of their father. Raising her eyes, she scanned the hallway below her, then looked high above her head, to the fire-and-ice chandelier, in all its glory.

Though cautious with funds, Eben had restaffed the Mall to something of its full complement of maids and footmen. Though she had spent most on the farms, poultries and dairies that supported the estate and, much to Lady Lillian's regret, little on redecorating the mansion, she had nevertheless ordered the place scrubbed to an amazing degree of cleanliness. With a proper army of maids and footmen, pages and grooms, every corner, every cornice, every scroll and every chandelier had been scrubbed, polished and freshened. Or, as Lady Adair was fond of saying...every cupid's bottom had been washed. A statement that quite offended her sister.

Every carpet had had years of dirt beaten from its fibers, and every floor had been washed and waxed to a gleam before the carpets were replaced. The entire summer and into the fall had been a great flurry of activity, and the Mall now rang with laughter and life for the first time in more than a decade. It was all because of this that she was proud to have Fitzhugh in her home. She was confident that she could offer him a clean, well-aired suite with fresh, unpatched linens, and accommodate quite comfortably, as well, his valet, a man of most unusual name.

With a smile, she turned to the portrait, once again hanging in its rightful place. With her attired in the ruby dress and her hair dressed almost lovingly by Bess into the same elaborate style, it was as if the portrait had stepped down from its ornate gilded frame to rule as mistress of Victor Mall, Eben Pearl Norview Victor.

"I have done it, Viscountess. Just as I promised, I saved my home for my children, and their children, as well."

"That you have, Eben Pearl. That you have." The rich, deep voice reached her from below the landing. Eben turned slowly and assumed the same posture as in the portrait. Fitzhugh stood at the bottom of the staircase, looking up at her with an appreciative expression.

"What say you, your grace?" she asked, watching him slowly ascend the stairs toward her. "The portrait lives?"

"I say I should like to give you your first Christmas present, here, on the stairs."

"It is warmer in the salon, with the fire, but it shall be as you wish." She tilted her head, just so, and glanced at him through her sooty lashes.

"Ah...Eben," he whispered. "A man so loves a compliant woman. Have you mellowed in my absence, or are you playacting?"

"That shall remain a mystery for you to unravel, your grace, through the timely telling of the tale concerning this long absence you speak of, and one which I have taken note of myself, almost daily."

Drawing her around to face the portrait, he continued, "I wonder if the first Victor Pearl was as much a rebel? You look so much like her tonight, except for the necklace."

"Yes." She sighed, tilting her face to stare up at the painting. "Lost or gambled away, long ago. But at least the portrait is home, back where it rightfully belongs."

Standing behind her, Fitzhugh whispered into her scented neck, his breath moving the wispy hairs. "Tonight, everything about Victor Mall shall be home, back where it rightfully belongs. Everything!"

Eben started as something warm touched her breasts and slid up to her throat. Gasping, her hand touched a necklace that was being clasped around her throat. Glancing quickly down and then up at the necklace around the viscountess's throat, she gasped again and spun to face him with wonder.

"Fitzhugh! It's the same!"

He slid his fingers under the necklace of fire-red rubies, cooled by the ice of diamonds, set in gleaming gold, his knuckles grazing the tops of her breasts, making her tremble.

"You were right when you said gambled away. My ancestors must have been better card cheats than your ancestors."

"Pray don't tell that to Aunt Addie," she teased. "Fitzhugh, really, you have given me . . . us . . . too much already."

"Never enough." Holding her shoulders, he dipped his head. "I can never give you enough," he murmured against her soft mouth, his lips teasing hers a moment before withdrawing.

Eben unconsciously leaned toward him, wanting more. The distant singing of Christmas carols reached them, as the servants filed through the back hallways into the main salon. She thought her heart would burst with such complete happiness.

When Eben entered the salon on Fitzhugh's arm, it caused almost as much disturbance as her entrance into the Golden Ball. Silence reigned, and heads twisted and craned to see their Eben all dressed up, but in this audience there were none that wished her ill from jealousy or envy. Lady Adair fairly beamed at her niece and the love match that had come about, as if it had been entirely her doing and no one else's.

The main salon was dominated this evening with a magnificent fir tree, decorated with candles, red bayberry ropes and white strings of popcorn. Garlands draped the mirrors over the fireplaces and bayberry-laden candles burned brightly, scenting the air with holiday smells of evergreen and spice. Eben, on the duke's arm, approached the elder ladies. Lady Lillian's mouth became a surprised circle at the sight of the exquisite jeweled necklace at her daughter's throat.

"Eben Pearl, th-that necklace . . . My word!" she gasped.

"I do hope, Viscountess, that you are not offended. . . . I took the liberty of an early Christmas present. I realize jewelry is not quite appropriate in the proper sense, but I thought it very appropriate to return this particular piece to its rightful place . . . to Victor Mall."

"It's the necklace in the portrait, Mama. The very same necklace!" Eben explained, fingering the jewelry.

"I quite discovered it by accident, a reference to it, I mean. A setting-down of the tale in the memoirs of my late greatuncle. It seems his father cheated at cards, rather well, he wrote. Won the necklace from Victor by dubious means. I searched the Eastmore family jewelry cases until I found it. It did seem an appropriate present, as it rightly belongs to the Victors, although it is not nearly as beautiful as the jewel it now graces," he gallantly explained, causing Lady Lillian to dissolve into flutters. Eben blushed and dropped her eyes, while Lady Adair merely smiled a satisfied smile.

The servants filled the room with singing and merriment. Toasts, with glasses of hot spiced cider held high, were drunk again and again to the rebirth and long-term health of Victor Mall. Lady Lillian passed out gifts, with the help of four of the youngest pages, bright red mufflers for the men and the boys and soft white shawls for the women and the girls. Bags of hams, apples and oranges, topped with sweet red-and-white striped candy canes, were set out for each to take home. It was a rowdy party, and a happy, though tearful, one for Eben.

"Here now. There's no need for tears." Fitzhugh eased her back from the group to wipe her sooty lashes with his handkerchief. "Christmas is celebration."

"I am just so very, very happy." She sniffled, her lower lip trembling. "These people are my f-family."

"Of course they are. One's estate becomes like a family, because we are responsible for them," he explained, indulgently.

"No, you don't understand." She shook her head. "Emma there, with the cane, she was like a mother. She wiped my nose, washed my face, patched my skinned knees, made me say my prayers, when my own mother had withdrawn. John, the man with the white hair and red face, yes, there. He taught me to shoot, and held me when I wept because I had k-killed a lovely deer and hadn't realized how death ends life. Cassy, with the babe in arms, taught me how babies were conceived by getting herself caught my tenth year, then telling me all the details. Well, almost all the details," she glanced at Fitzhugh's amused face. "In the loft over the stables. And Jamie Deal, dear, dear Jamie Deal. He put me on my first pony, and picked me up from my first fall, and he's still doing just that," she tried to explain. "You see, these people, by including me in their lives, weddings, birthing and dying, made me what I am today. Because I was really an orphan, alone in this dead house, getting my rearing any place I was able."

"How fortunate you were," Fitzhugh said.

"What do you mean?"

"Look around you. So many people to love you. And they do, you know. You should have seen them shield you when I was moving every stone and bush in this country to find you last year. Neither wealth nor title, nor out-and-out intimidation, could bring them to give you over."

Eben looked around the room at all the familiar faces, and a new realization came over her. He was so right. She had spent so many years yearning that she had overlooked all that she had. So many mothers willing to hug away her fears and soothe her hurts. So many fathers anxious to teach. Her childhood had been wonderful! Why had she pined for a father so caught up in his own pain that he could give her nothing, and a mother who was ill with grief, when there had been so many waiting to fill the emptiness with their love?

"Oh, I have been so selfish. I've never told them that I love them, how much they mean to me. I've never told them!"

"Ah, Eben, you ooze love from every pore of your beautiful body. Your very soul is love, and they have always known that." He wiped the last tear from her cheek. "Now go join the party and let them see you happy. That's all the thanks they require of you." Eben rewarded him for his advice with a smile, when she actually wanted to kiss him more than anything in the world.

The party, winding down above stairs, removed below stairs to resume until the wee hours of the morning. A sideboard was laid out in the dining room for the family and their guest. Plates filled and dinner commenced, the talk turned to the race and what had followed, as expected.

"From where I was sitting, it was the most exciting thing I had ever seen. I almost fainted when I realized it was Eben on that horse!" exclaimed Lady Lillian, fanning herself with her napkin at the memory. "The very same one that poor Sheldon... If dear Bess hadn't put my salts in my reticule..."

"I knew she would be racing that black herself. Knew she'd not trust anyone else, nor have I ever seen anyone do it so well. I put Ramsey in the race on my piebald mare to help her, but he didn't seem to do too well at it." Fitzhugh refilled his glass with the excellent wine.

"However did you think he was going to help me, when he was so far out front most of the time and I was lagging with the pack?" Eben said, laughing. "By the way, I hope you had no intention of racing that mare this spring."

"Race? Hadn't thought of it. Why?" He raised his eyebrows at her in question. When she just shrugged with a wicked little grin, he added, "Besides, she's yours now."

"Can't take her."

"Whyever not? She's a good mare, saved my hide more than once. I agree she's not the most handsome..."

"Not that. I'm releasing you from your wager. You only entered her to help me. You would not have risked her otherwise."

"Nonsense! I quite thought she could win. Fancied your black, you know."

"Oh," came her small answer in sudden confusion.

"I heard Ottobon didn't race his Denouncer at the last moment. Substituted a lesser colt," he continued.

"Yes. He admitted he knew the black was faster and didn't want to lose his colt. The blighter!" Eben declared. "But he was such a great help in collecting the horses and transporting them down here that I readily forgave him."

"What's been done with them? Eighteen, all told, weren't there?"

"Sold the lot of 'em. Most back to the men who wagered them. Although Ellington's bay is in Ottobon's stable, getting fit to run. The piebald mare is out to pasture with Black Victory."

Fitzhugh turned to look at Eben, raising an eyebrow again at her in question as she tilted her head to smile sweetly for him. "I see. I, too, doubt the mare will be fit to race in the spring."

Lady Adair wiggled her glass in the direction of Fitzhugh, who readily played server and refilled it for her, as she changed the subject. "Tell us honestly, did you ever find Ellington that night?"

"That night? No," Fitzhugh answered. "Sorry to say. I almost caught up with him at the docks, but he was just that far enough ahead of me. Although I did ascertain his direction. Did you collect his portion of the wager from his solicitors?"

"Yes, they messengered it over, thanks to you."

"More thanks to Ottobon. He was to see to that part," he corrected Lady Adair.

"Poor Ellington," Eben said, tracing her hand over her eyes in memory of the stinging blow he had dealt her. "Now that it's all over, I can almost feel sorry for a man who lets his outside size make him so small inside, too."

"I, for one, shall never forgive him," Lady Lillian declared, flinging her table linen into her plate. "And now, dear company, I must ask to be excused. I am quite fagged. Such a long day, and so much excitement. And another to follow on the morrow."

Gaining his feet, Fitzhugh bade her good-night with a small bow. "Viscountess."

Lady Adair had risen, also. "Eastmore, I have discovered an excellent brandy in the library, and I think a glass sounds right up the alley, do you not? I have never held with the custom of the gents having all the fun after dinner, while the ladies retire. I enjoy a glass of good spirits, as well as a lively discussion of politics. As for cigars, I vow, someday women will even smoke in public."

"Aunt Addie! Surely you jest!" Eben gasped, then giggled at the thought.

"See, I have even managed to shock my unshockable niece," she teased. "I will wager you never thought that possible."

"Nay, but I see where she gets her temperament." He laughed, offering an arm to Lady Adair. "I quite imagine you much the same in your youth, my lady."

Following the laughing pair toward the library, Eben paused for a moment in the hallway to gaze up the staircase to her ancestor and touch the lovely necklace at her throat. This was an evening that she could repeat every day for the rest of her life and be content. Turning, she hurried to the library in answer to her aunt's call.

First handing the Lady Adair into a cozy chair beside the library fire and then settling Eben across from her, Fitzhugh poured three snifters of amber brandy from the tray that Hastings had prepared in advance. One full measure, one half measure, and one with just a taste, dispensing them according to his thoughts of tolerance. Eben downed hers in one swallow, then nearly choked as the fiery liquid hit her stomach and snatched the breath from her lungs. Lady Adair merely cocked an eyebrow at her, then, without saying a word in censure, pointedly sipped hers in mute instruction.

"You have yet to tell us where you have been these past months," she told the handsome duke. Such a lusty man, she thought. Casting a sideways glance at Eben's shining eyes, she was pleased to see her niece thought so, too.

"As I said, I didn't catch up with Ellington that night. It in fact took me the better part of the next three months to track him. He moved rather rapidly, with me never more than one step behind him. Finally, I located him in Paris and, ahem..."

"Fitzhugh! You didn't... I mean..." Eben stammered, afraid to put her thoughts into words.

"No, I did not harm him, bloodthirsty though you think I am, I merely persuaded him to accompany a magistrate back to London to face charges for his part in the deeds done during the race." Fitzhugh paused to look at Eben with significant meaning. "After that, thinking my chances here were foiled, I feared I had no expedient reason to return to England myself."

Eben studied the magnificent man standing, legs braced, in front of the fireplace, very much at home. His dress clothes did not disguise his powerfully muscled frame. She sighed. So he had followed Ellington to see that he was punished, for her. That must mean he truly did love her.

Lady Adair continued to press him. "And what brought you back across the water? Must have been a rough crossing, in the dead of winter."

He smiled into his brandy for a moment, recalling the rather interesting letter he'd received from a surprisingly forceful Ottobon, demanding he return and take charge of one ebony-haired hellraiser, as she was the only woman in the world who'd ever be right for him.

"I had an unresolved problem with a fiery red-haired lady that would not leave my mind," he answered, smiling a conspiratorial smile at Lady Adair.

Eben's entire body went numb. A picture of the Titian-haired Louise Sinclair flashed suddenly and thoroughly through her mind. Her face grew hot, and spots danced before her eyes. He had not come back for her, but for Louise! He was in love with his mistress! She felt her very soul would burst into a scream of anger if she could not get away from the pressing heat of the fireplace and that...that man! How could her aunt sit and laugh with him? Carefully setting her glass on the tray, she staged what she hoped passed for a convincing yawn.

"I think I shall retire, also. If you will forgive me," she said, rising and passing to the door, forcing her body, to move casually. What she really desired was to slap his grinning face and run howling up the stairs to throw herself full-length upon her bed.

"Ah . . . good night then, dear," her aunt bade her, with a confused frown on her brow. She sensed something had gone amiss, but could not come up with a single comment that should have put her niece off. The unbidden thought of old age, senility and brain decay flitted through her mind, but was quickly dismissed by the lady. No, something was amiss!

"Miss Victor, rest well." Fitzhugh bowed over her hand, smiling into her eyes. Eben gritted her teeth to keep from lashing out at him.

Having managed the stairs with ladylike dignity, Eben now paced her bedchamber angrily, her ruby satin draperies flaring at each turn. Once again she had allowed herself to be deceived by that man. Just when she had begun to trust that he would not hurt her, he flung his mistress into her face. And in her own house no less! Chances foiled, indeed. Everyone in London had to know of the scalding set-down she had received from Lady Compton, and they would be more than pleased to tell the tale far and wide that the offer of marriage had been called off before it could even be announced. She stopped her pacing abruptly, her brow furrowing. Why was he even here? To humiliate her with tales of pining away over his red-haired lightskirt in London? If he had come back for Louise, why was he drinking her brandy on Christmas Eve? Probably because that lady was with her husband this holiday. Suddenly the memory of her vow to avoid stupid mistakes through hasty judgments fired her resolve. There must be no more misunderstandings. She would just ask him. Dare him to lie to her face. Angrily she flung open her chamber door and stormed out.

Lady Adair, having decided to retire, met her angry niece on the first landing. "Eben? Eben Pearl, attend me a moment!" Eben halted her headlong flight and turned toward her wise aunt with sparks in her eyes. "Stop and take three deep breaths before you storm in there to fling accusations at his head. Open your mind, girl, and your heart!"

Startled, Eben felt her anger abate somewhat. With a thoughtful nod, she continued more slowly down the stairs. Entering quietly, she saw Fitzhugh pouring another glass of amber brandy. "Fitzhugh..." She paused, unsure how to go on.

"Yes, Eben?" he answered. Then, seeing her indecision, he came to draw her to the warming fire.

Looking into his beloved face, lit by the fire, Eben's heart melted, and she wanted ever so much to just walk into his arms. But, pulling her hand from his, she turned her back to resist the temptation. For to touch him, or even look at him, was to lose her courage.

"Fitzhugh, do you remember the day I drove your grays? We lost the shoe and waited at the inn for the smithy?"

"Yes, very well," he answered, quietly, to give her courage. Waiting patiently for her to broach the subject that had her so visibly upset.

"And I asked you then to be my friend?"

There was a moment of silence from behind her, and then, "I have always been your friend, Eben."

Friend...and nothing more? Her heart sank, and she rushed on before courage could desert her completely. "I also asked you that day, why men do not marry their mistresses, if women of that sort draw them so strongly? You said you would tell me at another time. I think that time needs to be now, if you will."

"I wonder if I can explain it to you?" Fitzhugh frowned at her turned back and the smallness of her voice, wondering what was in her heart to question such now. "There are just differences between the women in a man's life," he stated.

Eben turned and sat in one of the chairs beside the fire, trying to read his face. He was sipping brandy and staring into the fire thoughtfully, picking his words carefully. "What differences?" she prompted him when the pause grew lengthy.

"Well, obviously the first woman of consequence in a man's life is his mother. If she is the right sort of mother, she will not only be kind, gentle and understanding, but will also guide and instruct him in the manner he is to treat the women who come into his life after her. A mother brings out the best or the worst in a man." Although he paused, she knew he did not expect her to comment and did not feel he needed encouragement to begin again. "Then, when he gets older," he continued, "there are women who come into a man's life whom he admires for their physical beauty and finds extremely pleasurable, but they are only a passing flame and he has no intention of encouraging their heat to last." She turned her head a little away from him, and because he was not talking directly to her, but rather to himself, he did not notice the flicker of feeling that crossed her face. "These women are like flowers, beautiful as they come into bloom, but when the bloom dies one throws them away, because they no longer attract."

"They may not want to be thrown away," she murmured.

"That is, of course, inevitable in some cases," he conceded. "But they are temporary, if a man's mother has taught him well. If not, sometimes he looks to these women for everything, as they remind him of his mother. Do you understand?"

"I—I am trying very hard..." she stammered, thinking of the way Ellington treated her and, she assumed, all women. Then came the unbidden thought that Fitzhugh had had no mother for most of his life. What had he said of a Muslim rearing?

"Let me finish. When a man looks for a wife and the mother of his children, again he is inspired by his mother and her teachings. Often as not, just when he thinks he has found her, he discovers some flaw and he must go on searching. When he is young and idealistic, he is quite sure he will find her in the genteel women he is introduced to, but as he ages he settles."

Now Eben heard a touch of cynicism in his voice. So, she thought, did he find her lacking as the mother of his children? Could he not imagine his babes in her arms? If not, then he must have come here to pick her as a flower, to be enjoyed until the bloom died, then discarded.

"I think I understand quite well." Rising, she started toward the door. "I thank you for explaining it to me."

His voice stopped her halfway to the door. "Eben? What is all this about?"

"I merely wished to know your intentions in coming here," she answered, anger and hurt making her voice tight. "And now I understand my intended position in your life, which I find unacceptable. I would rather die on the stem, than be plucked in my glory, to be used until my bloom fades, then discarded."

"What the bloody hell?" he exclaimed. "Make yourself clear, Eben!"

"What I am saying, as clearly as I can make it, your grace—" spinning toward him, she allowed her banked anger to rise "—is that I refuse to be tumbled and tossed! Go back to your red-haired wench, problem or no, and leave me alone!''

"Red-haired wench? What red-haired wench— Oh, for God's sake!'' Fitzhugh demanded, now thoroughly confused.

"The red-haired wench you have the nerve to fling in my face. In my own house, I might add.'' Her voice was low and throaty with fury. "The Lady Louise Sinclair, I would quite imagine.''

Fitzhugh's amber eyes narrowed thoughtfully, then, as he sorted it out, opened wide. Slamming his glass down on the table, splashing liquid over the rim onto the polished surface of the gilded table, he quickly stepped toward her. Startled at this action, she backed up, but not quickly enough. Catching her wrist, he dragged her forcefully into the hall, where he halted so suddenly she ran into his broad back. Looking around, he puzzled for a moment.

"Unhand me, you cad, or I'll—'' Unable to free her hand from his, she kicked his shin savagely, causing her satin-clad foot far more damage than his leg.

"Aha!'' he exclaimed, jerking her toward the entry dressing room. There he enveloped her in a cloak, which she immediately flung off to glare up at him. He angrily jerked her against him, and through tightly clenched teeth he said, dangerously, "Do not fight me so, Eben! Or I shall use more force to quiet your tantrum than you will like.'' Intimidating her into silence for fear he would carry out his threat, he again shrouded her, and dragged her onto the terrace. "Hell's bloody teeth! Blasted weather!'' he exclaimed at the sight of the heavy snowfall that greeted him.

A strong wind blew the fine snow into spinning columns to swirl up the steps and onto the terrace like so many wintry dancing dervishes. Quickly swinging Eben into his arms, he set out for the barn in the driving stuff. Carrying her weight easily, he cursed the wet ground roundly, but did not slow his pace except to fling the side door to the stable open.

"Fitzhugh . . .'' Eben began.

Swinging her to her feet, he pointed a finger beneath her nose and spoke to her sternly. "Move one inch, and I swear upon your life, I will beat you.'' Moving away, he fumbled with an oil lantern, his face angry in the flare of light as the wick caught his lucifer. "Now, come here."

"No! I will not be ordered about in my own barn!" she declared, crossing her arms and defying him with an obstinate stance. "You have no right..."

"Do not provoke me further, Eben Pearl!"

Moving to place the lantern high, casting a halo of light into the barn, he held out his hand to her. Something in the relentless tone of his voice warned Eben not to press her circumstances, for he did seem tried beyond all patience. Walking slowly toward him, she circled a bit to stay out of range of his long arms, lest he make to snatch her wrist again.

"What do you want of me, here, at this time of night?"

"Someday, Eben Pearl, you will learn that there are people in this world to trust," he said, facing her with a set face. "And you'll meet that person with charity in your heart, and claws sheathed. There is the red-haired wench that has given me so much trouble. Merry Christmas!" He gestured to the box stall behind her, before striding to the door and turning once more to her. "Now, with your permission, I shall retire. I am chilled to the bone, wet to the knees, and have quite ruined a splendid pair of evening slippers with your foolishness. I shall see you in the morning! And at that time, I expect a full, and contrite, apology!"

Eben jumped at the slamming of the door. Clutching the cloak even tighter around her, she shivered, but not sure if the cold or his anger was the cause. Turning to the box, she stared into a pair of bright, inquisitive eyes.

Quite fired by the excitement of unexpected company in the middle of the night, the filly reared and tossed her head, sending her mane flaring out in a blaze of red fire. Eben's eyes widened, and she gripped the brass door rim with white knuckles. The filly, prancing with a splendid grace of motion, arched her fluid neck and gave a saucy glance at Eben to see if she was being properly admired.

"Victory Flame. It is you! It is!" she whispered, throat tight with emotion.

The whisper caused the small pointed ears to perk, and her body quivered with the fire of a hundred red dawns in the lamplight. Eben quickly opened the door and stepped into the stall, her cold hands reaching for the filly as if her red coat would warm them. The filly accepted the attention with much pushing and shoving, as any spoiled, hand-reared foal is wont to do.

"Well, Flame, he said everything that belonged to Victor Mall would be returned tonight. And with you, it has. Now what am I to do?" she said, fighting tears that threatened to overtake her as they seemed to do more and more lately. "Once again, I have acted deplorable. I did just what Aunt Addie told me not to do. I accused him wrongly, and now he is livid with me."

With a final pat and scratch, Eben latched the door over the protests of the spoiled red filly. Walking slowly to the door, she doused the lantern. Maybe a good night's sleep would set her racing thoughts in an organized pattern. That, and an early-morning talk with her aunt. Swinging the door open, she confronted the cold, wet snow. The wind swirled it in the air, and it hung heavily from the trees, piling into drifts against the barn.

"Egad, and me in new slippers and yards of trailing skirts!" she exclaimed with dismay.

She had never been one to be worried overly much by convention, and it was not a problem to thwart her for long. Quickly stripping slippers and silk stockings from her feet and legs, Eben hoisted draperies, petticoats and folds of velvet cloak up to her ivory thighs and sprinted to the house on bare feet. Praying silently that no one was peering from a window on this side of the Mall, she giggled at the undignified sight she must present. Teeth chattering and feet blue, she did not slow down until she was in her own bedchamber. Struggling with the many hooks on the ruby gown, she managed to strip it and the layers of petticoats from her shivering body and slip into the night rail warming before the dying fire. Huddled by that fire, she briskly toweled her wet hair and practically thrust her feet into the warm ashes.

"Damn him!" she swore.

Her oath changed to a giggle as she pictured him carrying her out in a snowstorm and then leaving her there to make her own way back. They were indeed a match! She really should take her frozen feet and warm them against his backside.

Would serve him right! Her hands, untangling her hair, slowed, then grew still. Her head came up, and there was a dangerous glint in her azure eyes that Jamie Deal would have recognized.

What had her aunt said? Welcome him with open arms, instead of fear? She did not fear Fitzhugh, nor did she mistrust him any longer. She knew she loved him with her entire being and would spend the rest of her life proving it to him. Didn't she intend informing him of that very thing in the morning? So what difference did a few hours make? Spinning toward the door, she forced herself to stop in midstep, her body tense with longing.

"Think! For once in your life, think!" she admonished herself, aloud. Walking to the dresser, she carefully brushed the snarls from her hair and fluffed it around her face. "There's my reputation to consider. Conventions that must be upheld, servants' gossip to mind. I must do nothing to bring shame upon myself," she reasoned. Turning slowly, she looked at the neatly turned-down bed. Tapping her pursed lips with a forefinger, she carefully laid the brush down. Then, in a flurry of night rail, she jumped into the bed and mussed the sheets. "There, that will fool them!" With that, she was out the door and running lightly down the hall on tiptoe.

Lady Adair, awake and reading in bed, heard the light tread pass her door and, with a smile, sighed to herself. Her manicured hand absently ruffled the fur on the warm cat beside her.

"Well, Grady, there will be a Christmas wedding after all. To hell with posting the banns! I was about to despair that the girl had warm blood in her veins at all!" Grady stretched and rolled his gray tabby body upside down to present his belly and his soft, vibrating throat for scratches. "A duke for Eben. Lord Melton arriving tomorrow for Lillian. And me? I am not dissatisfied with my lot. I have my chocolates, my brandy, and you, greedy puss," she said, then tapped him on the nose with a forefinger. "And do not for one moment think that I misunderstand the accident of your hairy foot in that candy box, Sir Grady!"

Without knocking, Eben stepped quietly into Sheldon's old room and closed the door, leaning her back against it. The candle was still burning beside the bed, and Fitzhugh, like

Lady Adair, was propped against his pillows with an open book. The weak flame cast shafts of light across his streaked hair and lit his startled amber eyes when he glanced up.

"Eben! What the devil—?"

"I am inviting myself to share your warmth, your grace," she teased, advancing slowly towards him. "My fire has gone out, my bricks have cooled, and it is entirely your fault that my feet are quite frozen, and therefore you shall have the pleasure and responsibility of warming them again."

Fitzhugh laid his book aside without taking his eyes off her lovely face, a slight smile dancing at the corners of his sensual mouth. This was the Eben he loved and wanted in his bed and his life, the tease, the prankster, the beauty.

"Do not come any nearer, Eben Pearl," he cautioned, "and expect to leave this room, or this bed, before morning."

"Your grace—" her hands lifted to the ribbons closing her night rail "—I have no intention of leaving this room—" slowly her fingers pulled the top ribbon loose "—nor this bed, before morning."

"Eben, I am quite serious," he warned again, watching her fingers with narrowed eyes, his body responding to her implications.

"I mean to compromise your good name, destroy your credit with the ton, and render you quite unfit for the petticoat line."

"Last chance to turn tail and run, little cat."

"Please, do not be overly concerned, Lord Eastmore." With a slight shrug, the gown whispered down Eben's ivory body and lay in a pool at her feet. "For I do intend to wed you before the week is up."

Fitzhugh's eyes wandered from her slightly pink face to the perfection of her full breasts, topped with rosy nipples puckering in the cold, then across her tight, flat belly, down to the muscled thighs, and finally back up to the small triangle of black curls. Eben's body responded to his gaze as if it were his hand touching her. Rising from the bed, he scooped her into his arms and snuggled her beneath the covers, warm from his body. Flinging his own nightshirt over his head, he allowed Eben a brief glimpse of a hard-muscled body before joining her. Drawing her into his arms, he fitted her body to his. Then, with a startled jerk he exclaimed, "Hell's teeth, woman! Your feet are like ice!"

Eben laughed, drawing his head down, she whispered against his mouth. "Hush now, and just love me. Just love me."

"Always, my Eben Pearl!" he promised, taking possession of her mouth in tiny little nibbles, as if he intended never to relinquish it again.

* * * * *

MORE ROMANCE, MORE PASSION,
MORE ADVENTURE...MORE PAGES!

Bigger books from Harlequin Historicals. Pick one up today and see the difference a Harlequin Historical can make.

White Gold by Curtiss Ann Matlock—January 1995—A young widow partners up with a sheep rancher in this exciting Western.

Sweet Surrender by Julie Tetel—February 1995—An unlikely couple discover hidden treasure in the next *Northpoint* book.

All That Matters by Elizabeth Mayne—March 1995—A medieval about the magic between a young woman and her Highland rescuer.

The Heart's Wager by Gayle Wilson—April 1995—An ex-soldier and a member of the demi-monde unite to rescue an abducted duke.

Longer stories by some of your favorite authors. Watch for them in 1995 wherever Harlequin Historicals are sold.

HHBB95-1

PRESENTS
RELUCTANT BRIDEGROOMS

Two beautiful brides, two unforgettable romances...
two men running for their lives....

My Lady Love, by Paula Marshall, introduces
Charles, Viscount Halstead, who lost his memory
and found himself employed as a stableboy by the
untouchable Nell Tallboys, Countess Malplaquet.
But Nell didn't consider Charles untouchable—
not at all!

Darling Amazon, by Sylvia Andrew, is the story of
a spurious engagement between Julia Marchant
and Hugo, marquess of Rostherne—an engagement
that gets out of hand and just may lead Hugo to
the altar after all!

Enjoy two madcap Regency weddings this May,
wherever Harlequin books are sold.

REG5

Harlequin® Historical

From author Susan Paul

This spring, don't miss the first book in this exciting new series from
a newcomer to Harlequin Historicals—**Susan Paul**

THE BRIDE'S PORTION
April 1995

The unforgettable story of an honorable knight forced to wed
the daughter of his enemy in order to free himself from
her father's tyranny.

Be sure to keep an eye out for this upcoming series
filled with the splendor and pageantry of Medieval times
wherever Harlequin Historicals are sold!

Gayle Wilson

**The talented new author from
Harlequin Historicals brings you
the next title in her series set amid the
sophistication and intrigue
of Regency London**

THE HEART'S WAGER
April 1995
The compelling story of an ex-soldier and a casino dealer who must
face great dangers to rescue his best friend from certain death!

Don't miss this delightful tale!

And you can still order THE HEART'S DESIRE
from the address below.

Claire Delacroix's UNICORN TRILOGY

The series began with UNICORN BRIDE,
a story that *Romantic Times* described as
"...a fascinating blend of fantasy and romance."

Now you can follow the Pereille family's ongoing quest
in the author's April 1995 release:

PEARL BEYOND PRICE

And if you missed UNICORN BRIDE, it's not too late
to order the book from the address below.

To order your copy of the UNICORN BRIDE (HH #223), please send your name, address, zip or postal code along with a check or money order (please do not send cash) for $3.99 for each book ordered ($4.50 in Canada), plus 75¢ postage and handling ($1.00 in Canada), payable to Harlequin Books, to:

In the U.S.	In Canada
3010 Walden Avenue	P.O. Box 609
P. O. Box 1369	Fort Erie, Ontario
Buffalo, NY 14269-1369	L2A 5X3

Please specify book title(s) with your order.
Canadian residents add applicable federal and provincial taxes.

HUT-2

Harlequin invites you to the most
romantic wedding of the season.

Rope the cowboy of your dreams in
Marry Me, Cowboy!

A collection of 4 brand-new stories,
celebrating weddings, written by:

New York Times bestselling author

JANET DAILEY

and favorite authors

Margaret Way
Anne McAllister
Susan Fox

Be sure not to miss Marry Me, Cowboy!
coming this April

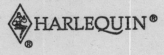

Fifty red-blooded, white-hot, true-blue hunks
from every State in the Union!

Look for MEN MADE IN AMERICA! Written by some
of our most popular authors, these stories feature some
of the strongest, sexiest men, each from a different state
in the union!

Two titles available every month at your favorite
retail outlet.

In March, look for:

UNEASY ALLIANCE by Jayne Ann Krentz (Oregon)
TOO NEAR THE FIRE by Lindsay McKenna (Ohio)

In April, look for:

FOR THE LOVE OF MIKE by Candace Schuler (Texas)
THE DEVLIN DARE by Cathy Thacker (Virginia)

You won't be able to resist MEN MADE IN AMERICA!

HARLEQUIN®

Don't miss these Harlequin favorites by some of our most
distinguished authors!
And now, you can receive a discount by ordering two or more titles!

HT#25577	WILD LIKE THE WIND by Janice Kaiser	$2.99	☐
HT#25589	THE RETURN OF CAINE O'HALLORAN by JoAnn Ross	$2.99	☐
HP#11626	THE SEDUCTION STAKES by Lindsay Armstrong	$2.99	☐
HP#11647	GIVE A MAN A BAD NAME by Roberta Leigh	$2.99	☐
HR#03293	THE MAN WHO CAME FOR CHRISTMAS by Bethany Campbell	$2.89	☐
HR#03308	RELATIVE VALUES by Jessica Steele	$2.89	☐
SR#70589	CANDY KISSES by Muriel Jensen	$3.50	☐
SR#70598	WEDDING INVITATION by Marisa Carroll	$3.50 U.S. ☐ $3.99 CAN. ☐	
HI#22230	CACHE POOR by Margaret St. George	$2.99	☐
HAR#16515	NO ROOM AT THE INN by Linda Randall Wisdom	$3.50	☐
HAR#16520	THE ADVENTURESS by M.J. Rodgers	$3.50	☐
HS#28795	PIECES OF SKY by Marianne Willman	$3.99	☐
HS#28824	A WARRIOR'S WAY by Margaret Moore	$3.99 U.S. ☐ $4.50 CAN. ☐	

(limited quantities available on certain titles)

	AMOUNT	$
DEDUCT:	**10% DISCOUNT FOR 2+ BOOKS**	$
ADD:	**POSTAGE & HANDLING**	$
	($1.00 for one book, 50¢ for each additional)	
	APPLICABLE TAXES*	$_____
	TOTAL PAYABLE	$_____
	(check or money order—please do not send cash)	

To order, complete this form and send it, along with a check or money order for the
total above, payable to Harlequin Books, to: **In the U.S.:** 3010 Walden Avenue,
P.O. Box 9047, Buffalo, NY 14269-9047; **In Canada:** P.O. Box 613, Fort Erie, Ontario,
L2A 5X3.

Name: _____

Address: _____ City: _____

State/Prov.: _____ Zip/Postal Code: _____

*New York residents remit applicable sales taxes.
Canadian residents remit applicable GST and provincial taxes.

HBACK-JM2